Heart of A Lion

Hillary Fields

St. Martin's Paperbacks

ISBN: 0-312-97917-7

Printed in the United States of America

St. Martin's Paperbacks edition / December 2001

St. Martin's Paperbacks are published by St. Martin's Press, 175 Fifth Avenue, New York, NY 10010.

10 9 8 7 6 5 4 3 2 1

For Mom, for having such an even keel,
and
For Dad, for understanding stormy seas.
I love you both.

PART I

The world is supported by four things only:
the learning of the wise,
the justice of the great,
the prayers of the righteous
and the valor of the brave.

—FAVORITE INSCRIPTION ABOVE THE PORTALS
OF LEARNING CENTERS IN MUSLIM SPAIN

CHAPTER ONE

"I'm going anyway," declared Lady Isabeau de Lyon. "And *you* cannot stop me."

It was a brave statement. Unfortunately, however, it did not come out very effectively.

Though the lady delivered her challenge with all the vehemence of one who believes devoutly in her cause, the defiance in her voice was sadly undermined by the unmistakably childish lisp that marked her piping tones. Isabeau's slight stature and the white-blond curls fairly dancing with affront atop her eight-year-old head did nothing to further her cause either. Nor did the normally wide, summer-blue eyes that now had narrowed mutinously to mere slits, or the rosebud lips that pouted stubbornly to underscore her determination.

Her companion was having none of it.

"The devil I can't. Watch me."

At sixteen, Jared de Navarre was full of self-importance, the new growth of muscle on his youthful squire's frame and the fuzzy reddish down sprouting on his upper lip far outpacing the burgeoning of tact in his otherwise astute young mind. Jared grabbed for Isabeau's skinny arm, took hold despite her howl of outrage and her sudden fierce struggles.

The boy and girl fought a battle in miniature together on the dusty, rutted dirt road that led from the castle belonging to the girl's father to the prosperous nearby town of Lyon. As they strove, kicking up puffs of ochre dust and taunting one another, lazy summer insects droned by them, unconcerned by such petty bickering. Fragrant pollens, swept airborne from the wildflowers dotting the withering pasturelands on either side of the road by the ghost of a breeze, bathed both of them with particles of pale yellow, orange, and purple powder.

The top of Isabeau's bright curly head did not even reach so far as Jared's shoulder, but she held her own with stubborn determination, though her continued wriggling made her arm slowly redden in his grip. And then abruptly Isabeau seemed to tire of her escape attempts, and to decide it might be more prudent if she took another tack with Jared.

Growing still, her eyes widened winsomely, and she allowed moisture to sheen them until they resembled the clear-scrubbed sky after a storm. "Oh, please," she lisped prettily. "I can't bear to miss it. You *must* let me go—or come along with me, if you say I may not go alone."

But her captor, having known her practically since birth, was having none of these gentler persuasions either. Jared merely snorted and shook his head, rolling his eyes at her blatant attempt to cozen him. For the next several minutes, the girl's eight-year-old voice wheedled, pleaded, whined, and then demanded shrilly, but her companion held firm.

"Nay. I'm not going with you, Isabeau, and you most certainly aren't going alone. It's far too dangerous for a little thing like you, goose," he declared, tousling her flaxen hair with one sword-callused hand before she could duck it. "You'll stay right by my side today where I can watch you, as I promised your good mother I would while she and your nursemaid are both ill with the summer ague."

The youth took his promises to both the master and mistress of the duchy extremely seriously, for they had taken him in and given him a home and a position of respect when his own indifferent parents would not. The welfare of their daughter was a responsibility the recently elevated squire did not intend to shirk. Still, he was not unsympathetic to the little girl's plight. Jared's tone softened, and he looked down upon her more kindly. "If you like, and you promise to remain out of the way, you may take a place under the oak tree by the practice field and watch my sparring with the other squires." By his tone, it was clear the youth thought he was bestowing a great honor upon his truculent charge.

Isabeau made a face, obviously not agreeing. "But Jared, you practice *every* day with the other boys in my father's household. I'm sure he wouldn't mind if you took *one* afternoon off while he's away at the councils in Paris. 'Sides, you know you can already trounce the rest of those boys with one arm in a sling." She grinned slyly, knowing her companion was not immune to flattery, his prickly adolescent pride always open to a compliment. "I think you should give the poor lads a day to rest after the last beating you gave 'em. That ol' fatty Tomas, for one, could use a week to recover after the way you thumped his brains with the flat of your sword the other morning. The lump on his head is as big as a magpie's egg!"

"Besides," she wheedled, returning to the topic that truly held her interest, "don't you want to see the boy saint? Everyone's talking about him. They say he works miracles, conjures visions, heals the sick!"

"You want to see a vision?" Jared snickered. "You'll be seeing stars from Jocasta's clouting if you don't get back home to the nursery by dinnertime. And I doubt the gentle Lady Margery—saint that she is herself—would be any too pleased with your truancy, either, should you turn up late, dirty and disheveled after gallivanting about all day gawking at charlatans and penny saints with the meanest of your father's villeins." The cynicism in Jared's newly deepened voice sat poorly with his open, handsome features and lucent amber eyes.

Isabeau's pout grew to nearly comical proportions. "I'm not worried about *Joey,*" she scoffed. "Old Jocasta never catches me out; she can hardly see anymore anyhow. I could be all the way to Jerusalem and back again before she ever missed me. And as for Mama, I'm sure *she'd* understand why I have to go see that boy preacher today. Perhaps," she added, knowing how Jared worshipped and adored her admittedly wonderful mother, "if I asked him to, the holy boy might even bless a small token to make her well." The little girl paused to turn her luminous, pleading gaze on Jared once more. "Anyway, don't you *want* to come along? There hasn't been anything this exciting in our province in years!"

"I hardly think one lunatic shepherd boy and his ragtag band of followers constitute 'excitement,' " Jared replied loftily, unmoved by her entreaties. "And as for miracles, the only real marvel will be if they don't steal the shopkeepers blind and still end up begging at your father's castle gates before sundown."

"You don't understand anything," Isabeau sniffed. "That boy is the *chosen* of *God*," she stressed with a child's sincere sense of urgency. "I tell you, he's a messenger straight from Jesus! Everyone's saying so. He's going to take children just like us to save the Holy Land." Her gaze turned dreamy. "Think of the adventure, Jared! Going all that way to the East, battling the unfiddles for the love of God!"

"Unfiddles," indeed. She couldn't even say the word right, let alone explain its meaning, the youth thought with a snort. "And what do you know of adventures and war and *infidels,* missy?" he asked archly, stressing the proper pronunciation just to point out Isabeau's ignorance.

Born in the small independent kingdom of Navarre to the southwest of Lyon, with Muslims of various sects maintaining several enclaves in nearby Spanish sovereign territory, Jared had a much clearer idea of the nature of said "unfiddles" than did his wide-eyed charge. But in her current state of mind, he didn't think Isabeau would listen if he told her that in his experience they were all disappointingly, thoroughly human, different clothing and customs notwithstanding.

"You wouldn't know a Saracen if one pinched you on the bottom," was what he settled for, not above enjoying the opportunity to lord his greater knowledge over the little girl he loved—and loved to torment—like a sister. "And prithee do tell, my brave warrior lady: Just how do you plan to fight these dreaded infidels when and if you do ever find them?" he teased, taking her arm once more and waggling it back and forth between them to show what slight strength was in the muscles. "You can't even lift a sword, you silly girl, for the sake of our Lord or anyone else. You've no idea what you're talking about, wanting to listen to that boy preach a lot of nonsense about holy vows and crusade. You've never seen true fighting."

Isabeau snatched her offended arm back. "*You've* never seen real fighting either, O noble *chevalier*," she snorted. "Practicing against the quintain scarcely counts as striking a blow for our Savior."

Jared fought the urge to tweak Isabeau's sun-freckled nose. "You've been listening to Father Jervis again," he pronounced with debate-ending finality, her newly rabid proselytizing a clear echo of the family prelate's beliefs. "He's the one who's got you in such a lather over this crusade business."

Isabeau's face fell as the truth of that statement came home to her. Perhaps she really *didn't* know as much about the ideals she was so glibly spouting as she should. After all, she'd only been introduced to the concept of holy war yesterday . . .

With her knees slowly numbing against the cold stone floor of the family chapel during matins that morning, she'd listened raptly to the good father as he sang the praises of the boy Stephen, a twelve-year-old shepherd from Cloyes-sur-Loir to whom, it was being said, God had granted a sacred vision. The boy was now traveling the countryside and speaking to all who would listen, gathering followers his own age and even younger to aid him in his quest to free Jerusalem from the unbelievers.

Before Father Jervis had brought word of the wondrous shepherd boy who'd descended with his human flock upon their peaceful little corner of France, it had never truly occurred to Isabeau to wonder about the lands that lay across the sea, or the people who inhabited them. Her world had always been bounded by the thick stone walls of the stately castle in which she'd been born, and the woodlands, vineyards, and sheep pastures of the fertile territory surrounding

it. Until yesterday, Isabeau's days had been full enough
with chasing her favorite playmate about the bailey, and
driving him to distraction as often as she could. The greater
world outside those walls, with its constant wars, political
machinations, and fervid religious movements, had never
captured her fickle attention much before.

Still, now that she knew of it, she wanted to see the boy
saint from Cloyes preach more than she'd wanted anything
since . . . She thought back—since last Christmas when her
mother had promised her a hound puppy!

Thousands upon thousands of children were rumored to
have gathered around young Stephen already, spurred on
by his promises that when they reached the coast, the seas
would miraculously dry up beneath their feet, providing a
clear path across the Mediterranean to their destination in
the Holy Land. Jerusalem itself would throw open its gates
for the self-styled "crusade of innocents" when they came
to it, or so the shepherd claimed. Stephen himself was said
to ride at the head of the throng upon a golden-canopied
cart the others had made for him, and he had vowed to
enter the sacred walls borne upon it.

Isabeau wanted to see *that* more than anything.

Images of the wondrous conveyance she'd heard about
caught fire and burned in Isabeau's fevered imagination.
After all, *she* was the daughter of a duke, and she didn't
have anything nearly so grand in which to ride about! Indeed, she thought, miffed, she was barely allowed to try
the reins on the tinker's pony cart, and that only when Jared
or one of her father's guardsmen was watching. Any boy
who had such a chariot all his own must indeed be special.
To miss that spectacle would be tantamount to . . . well, she
didn't know what could be worse than that.

Nothing ever happened around here, Isabeau thought
mulishly—nothing *she* was allowed to take part in anyway—and she was tired of waiting to grow older before
she was permitted her own adventure. Jared was allowed
far more freedom than she was. If *he'd* wanted to go, no

one would have stopped him. It wasn't fair, and she wouldn't stand for it!

After all, why should her betrothed get to do so much more than she did?

On the practice field two hours later a perspiring Jared de Navarre, firstborn son of the wealthy but distant Lord Sebastian, castellan of Navarre, aspiring young knight and promised future husband of the even younger Lady Isabeau de Lyon, paused in his latest bout with the unfortunate squire Tomas to wipe the sweat from his eyes. He'd just given the other boy a thorough pummeling, and he couldn't help but glance over to the side of the field, where his fiancée had earlier reluctantly settled herself beneath the oak tree, to see if she'd appreciated his manly prowess. But clearly, she had not.

She was no longer there.

Jared's blood ran cold, the sudden chill of dread freezing his innards.

Without a word, the terrified squire dropped his blunt-edged training blade and took off down the road toward Lyon.

Behind him, the slower, stockier Tomas wheezed painfully and lurched to his feet. "Where are you going . . ." he started to call, but the other boy was already little more than a trail of dust far away down the sun-baked road. Tomas looked on in puzzlement for another moment, watching the afternoon light glint off Jared's mail coat as he disappeared, then shrugged and decided to be thankful for the moment's reprieve. If he were wise, he told himself, he would use the time to practice for their next bout.

He couldn't know that there would be no more sparring matches between himself and the far more skilled young de Navarre.

Jared would never fight for mere practice again.

CHAPTER TWO

Maybe this wasn't such a good idea after all, Isabeau thought as she was jostled by the girl beside her for the third time in as many minutes. *Maybe I should just go home* . . . But then she thought of how Jared would tease her if she backed out now, when she'd barely reached the outskirts of the city and hadn't even caught a glimpse of the boy saint yet.

Already, Isabeau was tired, footsore (it had taken much longer to walk into town than she'd remembered the trip taking when she'd traveled this way on horseback with her family in the past), and beginning to feel rather peckish, not having thought to bring along anything to eat. Usually her parents or one of the guardsmen who always accompanied them thought of all that for her—for on all of her previous excursions outside the castle walls, she had always traveled in the company of a troop of her father's knights to deter any potential mischief-makers. This time she had no such protection, and she was beginning to feel the lack keenly.

Isabeau, who had never before known real fear, found herself very much afraid now, and she didn't like the feeling. Jared would probably tease her for being so faint-hearted, she told herself reprovingly. But the worst of it was, she knew he wouldn't. If she went home now, sheepish and shamefaced, he'd most likely only ruffle her curls, give her one of those stiff, man-boyish hugs she seemed to live for these days, and make nothing more of her foolish disobedience. Jared was too kind, in his own careless, absent way, to make her suffer for her mistakes . . .

A sharp cackle and another jolt from the urchin who'd already bumped into her three times interrupted Isabeau's thoughts just then. The filthy, ragged thing standing next to her near the edge of the crowd mumbled something she very much doubted was an apology, staring at Isabeau strangely before turning her attention back to the remnants of the fingernail she'd been chewing furiously. A moment later, the girl turned to the tumbledown handcart by her side and began to rummage inside it, seemingly at random. Bits of rotting hay and tattered, unidentifiable belongings flew every which way.

Isabeau edged away from the wild-eyed, muttering girl, who looked to be about fourteen or so, and tried not to notice the busy crawling of lice in and out of her lank, straw-colored hair. She touched her own bright curls self-consciously, backed up another step, and bumped into another child herself. The boy, no more than nine or ten, spat and scowled angrily at her.

So many children! She'd never seen such a gathering of young people before in her life, had not known there could be so many children in all the world.

Nor that they could prove so unfriendly and frightening to a girl of noble birth. Before coming out amongst the common folk, Isabeau thought anxiously, she should have thought to change into something less conspicuous than the fine linen smock and embroidered silk surcoat in which her nursemaid had dressed her this morning. Though her father was well loved in this demesne for his generosity to his vassals, and their family had been accepted, even welcomed, as overlords in the province for several generations now, her mother had taught her it was never wise to flaunt their privileged station before the townspeople. Isabeau knew as much, but she'd been so eager to escape Jared that she hadn't wanted to take the time to race back to the hall and change—and possibly risk capture in the process. Now her fine raiment, usually a source of pride, only made her feel the hard stares of the other children more keenly. Unease trickled down her spine as she looked around fearfully.

Lord, was this what crusading was really about? It was nothing like she had imagined. The crowd, thousands upon thousands strong, had been congregating outside Lyon all morning, waiting with barely concealed impatience and a palpable air of desperation for word of their next move. They were gathering now primarily upon the Croix-Rousse—the second of Lyon's two great hills—on the site of an old Roman amphitheater that nestled itself into the side of the incline near its summit, where the town walls themselves lay.

The ruined arena commanded an impressive view of the verdant sloping hills and the banks of both the Saône and Rhône rivers that gave Lyon its lush life. One segment of the old semicircular theater's crumbling Roman wall backed against the newer but still moss-edged granite walls of the modern town itself. It was a perfect place for the people of the city to look out upon the world.

Inside the boundaries of those walls, the townspeople of Lyon now packed every spare surface of the fortifications, trying to get a better view of the incredible, unique religious event taking place on their very doorstep. All eyes were on the astonishing influx of children, some of them barely old enough to toddle, overtaking the hills and valleys of their normally quiet, peaceful town. Along each rough-hewn block and crenellation, scraped knees and swinging legs showed where Lyon's own curious children had taken roost, and those who were taller, or less fortunate in their choice of vantage points, crowded close behind them to look out.

Isabeau, a latecomer and therefore standing near the edge of the crowd far down the hill from the theater itself, gasped at the sight of a small body slipping unheeded from one of the high stone ramparts, falling to land on the heads of the people below. She quickly turned away from the awful vision, glad to be safely on the outskirts of this unbelievable throng. It was chaos!

Isabeau remembered a very different view of this city, a much more comforting view. In her mind, as she shut her eyes and ears to the frightening sights surrounding her now, she saw it again as it had been when her father had taken her upon his massive shoulders one spring afternoon last year. He'd showed her the ruins of the aqueducts and temples, the Roman baths and fortifications of old Lyon that had long since been outgrown by the burgeoning expansion of the prosperous city built on its foundations. She recalled him explaining to her in his wonderful low rumble of a voice how the soldiers of the ancient empire had once ruled nearly all of Europe (and the rest of the known world) with an iron fist and the strictest of laws. Under the guise of that bloody rule of law, they had even martyred several Christians right in that very amphitheater back in the early days, or so Lord William had averred, deepening his tone for effect and making her squeal and bury her face in his thick beard with thrilling fear at the tale.

The Romans, he'd concluded, stroking his daughter's springy curls, had tolerated no challenge to their reign. But things were very different these days, it seemed. Looking around now, having cautiously opened her eyes again to the vastly changed environs of her hometown, Isabeau could see no rule, no one at all in charge of the milling crowds. Even the city guardsmen, she saw, identified by the distinctive insignia they sported upon their tunic fronts—a silver lion on a red field—did nothing to stop the occasional scuffles that broke out, overwhelmed by the sheer number of children and adults roaming about. Craning her neck to see toward the front, closer to the walls, she caught sight of some merchants who had come with food and water for the hungry children who'd already traveled so far just to get here.

At first Isabeau thought they had come to succor the needy younglings with charitable offerings, as she knew her mother surely would have ordered had she been there to witness it, but then she realized that the opportunistic traders were only giving their wares to those that still had money to pay for them. It was a pathetic few who did, she saw, watching a food riot break out several dozen meters ahead of her and once again fingering the rich embroidery of her own garment guiltily.

This was Stephen's vaunted army? These were the people chosen by Jesus to regain his earthly kingdom? How could these . . . these poor, starving wretches hope to retake Jerusalem from the hands of the Saracens? Isabeau's unease grew. Maybe Jared had been right to scoff at this whole crusading business. Maybe this wasn't God's work, after all, but the devil's!

Hot, tired, and worn from their travels already, nearly all the children were straining to hear what their leader, rumored to be standing somewhere upon those very walls with his entourage right now, would say. Perhaps, Isabeau thought, he was waiting for the right moment of divine inspiration to step forth upon the theater's stage. Yet what could he possibly say to comfort his ragged followers? The children who had followed Stephen for so many months on the strength of his promises were obviously restless now, hungry and desperate and beginning to lose faith. It would not take much to spark their anger; loose their frustrations upon whatever source was handiest. Even the sheltered Isabeau could sense it.

This definitely hadn't been a good idea, she thought nervously. Maybe she should slip away quietly now, while there was still time, and pray that she made it home before anyone noticed her absence.

But she had yet to see the boy preach—or, Isabeau thought wistfully, to catch sight of his golden-canopied chariot. If she went home without seeing even that much, all her hardships this day would be for naught. Most likely, her disobedience would be discovered (Isabeau *always* seemed to get caught when she defied orders!) and she would be punished for her dangerous escapade when she got back to the castle. What galled her most, however, was not that she would be punished, but that she would have to suffer her punishment without even having accomplished her original goal, without having appeased her burning curiosity. And she *was* curious.

Even through her fear at the overwhelming situation she'd stumbled into, Isabeau's wonder at the awesome gathering remained. What could have caused such a vast, disparate crowd of children to come together, and stay together, despite so much adversity? What force could have made them trek all the way across France in the blazing heat, with barely any food and no adults to guide or protect them from harm?

She must at least see the shepherd Stephen once! she decided. Isabeau stretched up on her toes, hoping for a glimpse, only to feel a sharp pain in her left instep.

"Ow! Prithee watch where you place your feet, sir," she cried, startled as the boy into whom she'd earlier bumped now stepped on her foot seemingly deliberately.

"Ooh, Florie," the louse-ridden girl with the wild eyes suddenly crowed, coming up close to Isabeau again. "Did that nasty boy hurt ye? Come to your big sister now, dearest, and let me soothe it for ye." She reached with one grimy hand for the younger girl's shoulder, but Isabeau shrugged away in growing fright.

"I'm afraid you've mistaken me, miss. I'm not your sister Florie."

"Not—not Florie?" the girl said in a quavering voice. "Ah, but you look so like her! Surely 'tis you, my own sweet Florie. I knew it could not be true, what they said happen'd to ye. Ye were al'uys such a good swimmer . . ." She faltered.

As the straw-haired girl's brows drew up in a knot of simpleminded confusion, Isabeau began to feel sorry for her. Clearly, the girl had suffered a loss, and it had touched her fragile mind deeply. "Perhaps your eyes are only tired, miss," she tried, reaching out to pat the girl's arm as tears formed in the older girl's watery, infected eyes.

It was a mistake. Gold flashed off the signet ring she wore on the smallest finger of her right hand as she touched the other's ragged garment. Isabeau heard the boy next to her suck in his breath. A second later he had called for his friends.

"Hey, boys, would ye look at that!" he exclaimed. "By the rood, I'll swear that's pure gold and no mistake." Several other boys elbowed their way into the circle that was rapidly forming about Isabeau. "What do ye think we could get fer that?"

"A week's provisions, I'd say," a runty lad with one squinty eye and several already blackened teeth piped up.

"Ale fer all of us!" another, rather burly boy of about eleven declared.

"Wine, even!"

"Aye," the first one said with relish. "All that and more, boys, maybe enough t' get us off this stinkin' crusade t' hell, and back t' Paris where we belong." He turned to Isabeau, pressing up close to her menacingly so she could smell the sour scent of his tunic and the even worse odor of the long-unwashed flesh beneath. "That's a might-fine ring ye got there. I'll have it off ye, mademoiselle," he threatened. "Along wit' any other gems an' valuables ye might have wit' ye t'day."

The boy spoke such crude Parisian-accented *langue d'oïl* that Isabeau, who spoke the southern *langue d'oc* herself, had trouble understanding his dialect. Still, there was no mistaking the menace in his tone. Isabeau's heart sank and she stepped back, inadvertently coming closer to the lunatic girl who was beginning to seem like her only protection. The girl looped one skinny arm around her back, and Isabeau leaned against it, not above accepting the offered shelter now. Things were beginning to turn ugly. After hearing Father Jervis preach the crusade so enthusiastically yesterday, this was not the spirit of pious inspiration she'd thought to find among the children led by the shepherd Stephen. This was more like a peasant revolt! Oh, why had she ever disobeyed Jared?

"Stay away from my Florie, ye dreadful boys," the girl hissed, shaking her fist at the youths. "If ye don't, there'll be no more free rides fer ye in my cart, I promise ye that!"

"Now, now, Crazy Lucille," said the runty one, doing his best to smile winningly through the gaps in his crooked teeth. "Ye know that ain't yer baby sister, now don't ye? This be just some sweet highborn lass what's got lost and now wants t' donate her jewels t' the poor—an' that's us!"

He lunged for Isabeau, grabbed her away from the other girl's grip. He yanked her into the circle of his friends and before she knew it, Isabeau felt grasping hands all over her, feeling her for pockets and purse, ripping away anything of value they could reach.

She screeched for help, she fought and kicked, but it was useless. No one came to her aid, and out of the corners of her eyes she could see a crowd of disinterested spectators, children like herself, watching the boys stripping her to her undersmock and yanking even her embroidered slippers from her feet. The ringleader, the one who'd noticed her ring first, now went for it and Isabeau clenched her fist rebelliously around the small gold circlet.

She had never been treated so shabbily in her entire life! Isabeau thought, outrage beginning to supplant her earlier terror. Where were her father's guardsmen? Where was Jared? Surely someone would come to help her soon—it was unthinkable to the cosseted duke's daughter that they would not!—but until they did, she was not going to give over to these brutes easily. Isabeau de Lyon was no fainthearted coward.

"Nay," she shouted, angry and fearful both, but defiant above all. "You'll not take my ring from me, you cur! My father gave me that." But the boy had her fist in his strong, wiry grasp, and he had not one ounce of mercy as he wrenched at her fingers to open them.

"Aye, and now yer givin' it t' me, ye stuck-up bitch," he growled, and applied his teeth to her tiny digit.

Time stopped.

Everything went still. Then after a single, sickening lurch, the world began to move again, but this time only very, very slowly. Her ears heard sound in a strangely hushed fashion as Isabeau watched the sluggish welling of blood begin to flow from the second knuckle of what had been her little finger. Equally slowly, she took in the sight of the crimson liquid staining the teeth of the victorious bully who now yelped with triumph, spitting something small and pink upon the ground and ripping the golden signet ring from around the stump of her pinky. She let him do it, in her shock not even feeling the tug upon her lacerated flesh as the disputed jewelry came away in his fist. She watched the crowd revolve around her once, then twice. She saw the straw-haired girl peer anxiously into her eyes, then saw the girl's face recede toward the sky.

"Oh, my poor Florie! Lookit what ye done to her!"

Those were the last words Isabeau heard before her head struck the rocky ground behind her and the world rushed away into black oblivion. Her last thought came a moment later, in the vacuum.

Why is Jared not here to help? Doesn't he know I need him?

CHAPTER THREE

Despite every effort he made to control his body's tremors, Jared still found himself trembling helplessly, exhausted both mentally and physically after a day of frantic, fruitless searching and anxiety. Night had fallen nearly an hour earlier, but even before the sun's last purple rays had faded into darkness, dragging with them his hopes of finding Isabeau quickly, Jared had known he'd taken a careless mistake and made it immeasurably worse with his foolish pride. He had done wrong today—terribly, egregiously wrong. Now he must confess his sin before the one person he most wished would absolve him of it—and the one least likely to do so.

Lady Margery wasn't likely to forgive him for losing her daughter.

Nor, when she learned of it, would she appreciate how long it had taken him to sound the general alarm that had summoned dozens of guardsmen and castle folk to seek little Isabeau. The castle's garrison had begun their sweeping, wholesale search for the eight-year-old girl just half an hour ago, but they couldn't be blamed for the delay in finding Isabeau. Indeed, seasoned warriors all, they had mobilized to meet the challenge with admirable swiftness—as soon as they'd been informed of the situation. No. Jared must take all the blame for this ever-worsening disaster squarely on his own shoulders.

Teams of the duke's men were scouring the countryside even now, on horseback and afoot, with torches and their master's prized bloodhounds to aid them. Knowing that time was of the essence, they'd recruited every available man, woman, and child on the castle grounds to help with the search, stopping all other activity in the bailey in order to seek the duke's young daughter. The whole countryside was coming alive with the news that their darling Isabeau had gone missing.

Now it was time to inform Isabeau's mother.

In the dimly lit antechamber to her apartment suite, Jared waited for his audience with the duchess alongside the captain of the castle guards—a hulking, battle-scarred veteran who, except for Lord William de Lyon himself, had been the man Jared most idolized in the duchy since his fosterage. Now Sir Guy, usually ready with a pat on the shoulder or a gravelly word of praise for the squire he'd always claimed raised the standards of knightly valor for the rest of the castle's fosterlings, refused even to look at his protégé. Instead the captain stood silently next to Jared in the shadows, his dark-brown eyes averted. The expression in them was impenetrable.

What would I not do for one of those reassuring gestures now? Jared asked himself longingly. But he knew he'd not receive one. He didn't deserve it. He had failed to watch over his dear, rambunctious little Isabeau—such a small task, but such a big responsibility! he now thought mournfully—and in doing so, he had failed the gentle Lady Margery who'd entrusted him with that grave duty. How he had abused the trust of her far more formidable husband, Lord William, Jared could hardly bear to consider.

Had it been just a month ago, on the very day of his elevation to squire, that he'd so solemnly taken an oath before his liege to protect the de Lyon family in Duke William's absence? It had been such a proud day for Jared. He'd felt honored beyond belief to receive this symbol of the duke's trust in him, knowing the man would not have raised him up so soon before departing for the north had he not believed Jared would uphold his faith while he was gone. But by God's wounds, he berated himself miserably, instead of proving his worth, he'd failed the duke utterly!

For the first time in a very long while, Jared found himself recalling the cruel, vituperative denigrations his own father had so often rained down upon him from his infancy. The budding self-respect he'd gained since his fosterage began to crumble under the weight of his terrible failure today, and Jared felt the lash of his father's derision again as keenly as if the man himself were standing before him right now, blasting his son with the full heat of his contempt. He imagined how Lord Sebastian would look at him in this moment, his eyes full of cold triumph, as if his firstborn son's delinquency were some sort of victory for him—almost as if he took some twisted pleasure in having predicted Jared's worthlessness.

Despite all that had occurred in the years since he'd last been forced to endure his father's vicious, gloating diatribes, and despite his growing prowess in the knightly arts of late, Jared was unable to replace the man's jabs in his mind anymore with the salve of his foster family's confidence in him. In spite of what he would have liked to believe, what Lord William and Lady Margery had always encouraged him to believe, Jared knew the real truth now.

He was no better than what Lord Sebastian had always claimed he was—a disgraceful, good-for-nothing knave who would never bring aught but shame upon his family's good name. At the very first opportunity, the young squire thought dismally, he had betrayed those who'd placed their trust in him, just as his father had predicted he would. The curse of his mother's blood indeed must run true in him, just as the unforgiving castellan had prophesied.

When he'd discovered the truth of his much younger wife's outrageous and ongoing betrayals—betrayals that had had her sharing a bed with everyone from the castellan's most trusted guardsmen to his lowliest stableboys—Lord Sebastian had quickly and efficiently destroyed all hope of their ever being a family again. At least Joscelin, Jared's brother, had resembled the castellan too closely for Lord Sebastian to consider denying the fair-haired younger boy, the squire thought miserably. Thank God Jos had been spared the contempt and cruelty the castellan had heaped upon his eldest progeny—all for resembling his auburn-haired, amber-eyed harlot of a mother.

If he could have, Jared had often thought bitterly, Lord

Sebastian would probably have sent his older son off to rot
in a convent cell too, as he had done to his wife, and not
merely dispatched him to distant Lyon for fostering. Yet
Jared couldn't regret his sire's callous decision, regardless
of the man's motives—not when it had landed him among
people he'd grown to treasure so dearly. The duke and
duchess of Lyon had given him the loving family his own
parents could not provide, and he had cherished the gift
above even his own life.

If only he could give that life now to restore little Isabeau to the arms of her parents!

Somehow, he must make this situation right. That much
Jared knew. But *how*? How was he going to bring Isabeau
back safe and sound—especially after the awful clue he'd
found just an hour ago? All evidence pointed to the worst
possible conclusion, Jared knew—that Lord William's only
daughter had fallen victim to foul play.

The door swung open then, interrupting the squire's agitated musings and bathing him and the loyal guardsman in
the soft glow of jasmine-scented candlelight. Lady Margery
awaited them, or so said the concerned, round-cheeked
maid who admitted the two men to the chamber. Jared took
a deep breath and entered, followed closely by Sir Guy.
Blinking a little in the sudden light, it took Jared a moment
to locate his liege lady, but when he did, finding her seated
on a padded stool by the fire, he dropped immediately to
his knees before her. The duchess, he noted as he knelt,
was swaddled in a warm quilted robe and pressing a hand-
kerchief to her reddened nose. Sir Guy took his stance by
the door meanwhile, tall and solid and watchful.

"Forgive me, Your Grace . . ." Jared choked out, anguished.

As always, the sight of the lady struck him—even puffy-
eyed and flushed from her cold, she was stunningly lovely
to him, the very chivalric image of pure, untainted womanhood. Lady Margery's long blond curls, still every bit as
bright as her daughter's, were held back from her perfect
oval face only by a silver circlet that anchored a short

lavender gauze veil at her brow. So lightly confined, the tresses streamed like a river of moonlight down her back and arms as she perched gracefully atop the stool, making it appear more akin to a throne than any ordinary seat. She looked like a fairy queen out of legend to the awed young squire, and Jared could not speak for a moment. He was agonized to cause this kind lady even an instant of pain. After what he had done, would she now turn away from him as had his own father? She seemed far too angelic a creature ever to do that.

Lady Margery's deep indigo eyes, the lids admittedly a little red, widened in concern at her fosterling's dramatic gesture of abasement. She reached one slender hand out as if to stroke Jared's flushed cheek, then stopped short and let her fingers drift back down to rest in her lap. "Jared," the exquisite duchess began in bewilderment. "Whatever is the matter? My maid Cécile just woke me with word that you had urgent news for me . . ." She glanced anxiously over to where Sir Guy stood silently, asking her next question equally of both men. "It isn't William . . . pray, say it is not William!"

"Nay, my lady," Jared managed. "To the best of my knowledge, your lord husband bides well yet in Paris." He paused, not knowing how to say what he must, but knowing he could delay no longer. After a glance of his own toward the guards' captain, who nodded back severely, clearly determined that the squire own up to this catastrophe himself, he finally breathed the words. "It is Isabeau, Your Grace . . ."

One slim hand flew to Lady Margery's throat and she swallowed hard. Her face went absolutely ashen. "I think you'd better tell me everything," she said hoarsely. "And I do mean *everything*." Her deep blue eyes, filled with worry and determination, focused hard on Jared. Now the full strength beneath the fragile exterior was revealed, showing the duchess of Lyon to be every bit the warrior her husband was in defense of their only child.

Jared did as he was told, leaving out nothing of his own culpability.

"I thought—nay, I hoped I could find her on my own," he concluded miserably, "but when I arrived in Lyon, the crowd was so large, so spread out . . . I swear I could not have picked out my own brother amid such a sea of people. At that point, Your Grace," he confessed, "I should have realized the enormity of my task and returned immediately to summon the guard to help me search. Yet I was anxious to bring Isabeau back home without troubling anyone, and so I persisted alone for some hours longer." Jared hung his head as he continued, his voice barely above a whisper. "Though I searched until darkness approached, I could find no one who would admit having seen your daughter, and at last, with no trace of her and little light left to guide my way, I knew I needed the aid of wiser men." What Jared could not admit to his lady, even now, was just how much he had secretly hoped to conclude the business of finding Isabeau with no one the wiser about her absence.

At first, seeing that his betrothed had sneaked away from the practice field, he had not thought about his actions. He had simply taken off in search of her. But halfway down the road Jared's head had begun to clear, and he'd thought to wonder if it might not be wiser to run back to the garrison and recruit others to help him locate her. In the end, he'd gone on alone simply because he had not wanted to bear the laughter and taunts of the other boys or the knights of the castle guard when he was forced to ask their assistance in playing nursemaid to his betrothed. Even confronted with the shock of the enormous crowds outside Lyon and the sullen, uninformative behavior of the children he'd questioned, he had persisted on his own, wasting hours with fruitless searching. It was only later, when he'd made the awful discovery he had yet to report to his liege lady, that he'd realized this behavior was pride, pure and simple—and that in a situation this dire, pride was utterly irrelevant.

But he would not burden the duchess with his guilt.

Lady Margery needed facts more than she needed confessions just now.

"The worst remains to tell, Your Grace. I did not find your daughter in Lyon, but I did find this." Reluctantly, Jared forced his fist to uncurl from around the small object he held clutched in his palm. He could not bring himself to tell Lady Margery about the flecks of blood he had cleaned off it with shaking fingers along the long road home, nor of the shifty, wretched varlets who had given it up only under the threat of his naked blade. "A young ruffian led me to it after some questioning on my part, but he could not give the whereabouts or fate of its rightful owner." He spared the duchess the description of the rather rough tactics with which he had reacquired the ring after spying the suspicious-looking group of boys trying to exchange it for bread and ale. With no leads to go on, and a growing fear that Isabeau might become swallowed up forever among the throng that was already beginning to break camp and move along southward, Jared had turned for home as soon as he'd seen the bloody token. If he were to find his betrothed, he'd finally admitted, it would take more than he was capable of alone. But was it already too late?

Jared now somberly proffered Isabeau's ring to Lady Margery. "I fear some ruffian has robbed Isabeau of her belongings, Your Grace, and that she may be in grave danger even now." His throat closed upon the words, but the determined squire forced himself to go on. "Yet regardless of any peril, I swear to you on all that is holy, I *will* find your daughter and bring her back safely into your arms—if it is my very last act on this earth."

Until now, Lady Margery had remained curiously motionless, waiting with her breath held in check while Jared told the story, silently gathering the facts. One would have thought she was carved from stone, so still was she. But upon seeing the tiny ring resting on the squire's trembling palm—a ring her husband had had crafted for their daughter last year by one of the finest goldsmiths in Paris—a small, strangled exclamation escaped her cherry-red lips. Her slender fingers quivering, she reached out to touch the band hesitantly, then withdrew them without taking it. Inside, she knew, were inscribed the words *"Pour mon petit coeur d'lion."* For my little lion-heart.

"Lion-heart" had always been Lord William's pet name for his adored only child. Their daughter, the duchess knew, would need every bit of that courage now.

"I charge you to keep this ring, squire," she said at last, her voice a mere whisper of sound. "Keep it until you find the one to whom it belongs, and bring her back safely to me as you have sworn."

Jared swallowed painfully and nodded his head, closing his fingers once more about the fragile golden circle as he accepted the onus she had laid upon him.

"One thing more, Jared de Navarre," Lady Margery continued softly, and for the first time the young squire was sure he saw a trace of anger, of blame in her gaze. "For your sake, it may be best you do not return to my presence until your promise is fulfilled." And the duchess of Lyon turned away from her fosterling, the boy who was to have married her precious daughter, clearly dismissing him from her mind as well as her chambers as she turned to rap out orders to Sir Guy.

Jared barely heard her words to the captain of the guards. Paralyzed with guilt and with the knowledge that his liege lady clearly—and rightfully—blamed him for her daughter's disappearance, the distraught squire could not leave immediately following her dismissal. Indeed, he was not even able to rise from his supplicating position at Lady Margery's knees for several moments, though she seemed not to take notice of his continued presence. He was too bowed and racked with silent sobs to move right away. But hearing the two discuss their plans for the expanded search, Jared gathered his wits and gazed up at the hauntingly beautiful duchess once more, ignoring the errant strand of russet hair that had plastered itself to his damp cheek.

"On all that I hold dear," he whispered, not sure that

either adult heard him, "I never shall return to this place without Isabeau. I *will* find her, or die in the attempt." Gathering himself, Jared bowed and strode resolutely from the chamber.

He did not turn back, and therefore did not witness Lady Margery's compassionate gaze as it followed him out the door.

PART II

The Worldly Hope men set their Hearts upon
Turns Ashes—or it prospers; and anon,
Like Snow upon the Desert's dusty Face
Lighting a little Hour or two—is gone.

—THE RUBAIYAT OF OMAR KAYYAM, VERSE 14

CHAPTER FOUR

Sayyad al-Zul did not issue invitations lightly.

*Unfortunately, that may be all I can say I know for sure
about the man who paid me so well to be here today,*
thought the Frankish mercenary called the Black Lion. Rumor and speculation surrounded the one who'd summoned
him like a cloak of deception, revealing nothing but what
al-Zul wanted those whispering the tales to repeat. Yet this
much he had gathered: For the legendary renegade to have
summoned him, the man must need his services very badly.

The Black Lion wanted to know why.

He was awaiting the arrival of his enigmatic host, and
had been doing so for some time now. Shifting minutely to
ease the pressure on his knees, he knelt straight-backed
upon one of the embroidered satin cushions strewn about
the floor of the luxuriously appointed little anteroom into
which a silent, bowing servant had earlier shown him. After
that one adjustment the Black Lion moved no more, though
he allowed his gaze to roam about the chamber freely. Silently impressed, he noted the jewel-bright mosaic work of
the tiled floors and walls, the exquisite craftsmanship of the
few pieces of mother-of-pearl-inlaid ebony-and-cypress
wood furniture that adorned the room. And of course, he
did not fail to notice the elaborate latticework of the harem
screen that took up most of the upper portion of one wall.

Though he couldn't actually see them staring out at him,
he would not have been surprised to discover that there
were eyes beyond that barrier watching him, judging his
smallest movements. Indeed, he would have been surprised
if there were *not*. The warrior knew such covert observation
was to be expected of a man as paranoid as the one who'd

invited him here, and thus he was careful to show no signs
of irritation or impatience at being made to bide here so
long.

A slight breeze was the Black Lion's only refreshment
as he silently passed the time; it brought with it the scent
of the carefully tended roses in the garden beyond the
chamber's open archway to the west, and the trickling
sound of water splashing in the fountain in that garden's
center. Thirst began to tickle his throat, but he ignored it.
The smell of the evening meal being prepared—tenderest
lamb and rice cooked in savory spices, from the smell of
it—drifted in from somewhere beyond the garden to tease
his nostrils, reminding the warrior of how long it had been
since his last full meal.

Sayyad was a cunning one indeed, the Black Lion
thought, to so tempt and tantalize a man he knew was just
in from short rations traversing the mountain wastes below
his isolated fortress. But he would not fail such a simple
test as this. Instead, ignoring the clamoring of his senses
that urged him to seek out sustenance, the mercenary focused his attention inward and used the time to go over
what he knew about his host.

Sayyad al-Zul.

He turned the name over in his mind, mentally translat-
ing it. *Shadow Hunter.* It was the perfect title for a killer
rumored to be able to blend seamlessly with the darkness
of the blackest night, and to strike down his enemies with
no more warning than a cloud passing over the surface of
the moon. But more intimidating yet than his name was the
fact that the man had once been an Assassin.

Just knowing he'd belonged to such a radical organiza-
tion was enough to tell the mercenary something of al-Zul's
nature. The adherents of this politico-religious movement,
headed by a man known only as the Old Man of the Mountain (a reference, the Black Lion had been told, to his command over the nearby mountaintop fortress called Alamut,
or Eagle's Nest, also located in the Elburz Mountains),
were feared by sultans and sheiks alike. Even Saladin him-

self had been rumored to have been targeted by the leader of the Assassins at one time.

Simply put, no man was safe if the Old Man wanted him dead.

But this Shadow Hunter, al-Zul, was known to be a renegade, a separatist who had broken with the cult leader to pursue an agenda of his own, the Black Lion reflected. And strangely enough, the Old Man had so far tolerated this apostate's unauthorized activities taking place virtually on his very doorstep. The mercenary could only surmise that al-Zul's intentions, whatever they were, pleased the master of Alamut enough to let him live. But outside of Alamut, no one knew quite *what* Sayyad al-Zul was after.

He'd raided countless caravans and villages with the aid of his loyal band of *fidai'in*, the suicidally devoted Shiite heretics whose name was whispered only with utmost terror by ordinary folk. Sayyad himself was rumored to be utterly fearless, a true dervish in battle.

The ex-Assassin was said to possess a sorcerer's powers, and could appear and disappear at will amid the most heavily guarded encampments. He could cut a man's throat with a mere flick of the wrist, people said, and do it so skillfully the victim himself would not notice until his head tumbled down into his sherbet an hour later. Yet the strangest tale of all, the one so odd the mercenary had no doubt but that it was true, was that al-Zul had a very special calling card— one that pierced the hearts of his foes with superstitious fear. Each time he struck, he was known to leave this token by the victim's side as a sign of his "visit," though he cleverly left no trail for vengeful relatives or clansmen to follow.

A perfect white rose, all the more chilling for its pure, delicate beauty, never failed to grace the scene of his attack.

None could claim to understand the meaning behind this strange emblem, but even the proud Bedouin, who trembled before no man, feared Sayyad al-Zul's wrath. No one, from emirs and petty pashas to the fiercest tribal warrior, wanted him for a foe. Yet the man's true name and his origins

remained as shadowy as the sobriquet the notorious renegade had taken upon himself. Until he had taken up resi-
dence here in his own fastness within the barren,
inaccessible mountain range bordering the Caspian Sea after breaking with the Assassins, no one seemed to have
heard anything about the "Shadow Hunter"—or from
whence he'd come. His purpose was even more concealed
from public knowledge than his past—but no less dark, the
Black Lion was sure.

*This Sayyad fellow may well prove a man after my own
heart,* the mercenary reflected wryly. It was pure common
sense not to reveal too much of one's past. His own carefully guarded vulnerabilities and the motivations that had
driven him over the past sixteen years were a tale the Black
Lion told to no one. And from all he'd heard about the
man, Sayyad al-Zul was not the type to willingly hand over
such intimate ammunition to anyone either, friend or foe.
The cunning renegade would not be such a fool as to give
up the advantage of anonymity. He might be insane, a rabid
cult fanatic as most members of the Assassins (a word de-
rived from *hashishin,* or "smokers of hashish") were rumored to be, but he was most definitely *not* a fool. The
Black Lion had seen as much in the precautions the man
and his followers took to keep their mountain lair secure.

The mercenary had to admit, it had made even him, a
hardened soldier of fortune, rather nervous to journey so
deeply into the heart of territory held by the Assassins. The
Elburz Mountains were no place to travel lightly. But
money was money, and Sayyad had paid him plenty to
show up at this secluded, well-fortified mountain hideaway—and to bring with him his troop of battle-forged
mercenaries, who even now awaited word of the outcome
of this meeting in a camp of their own outside Sayyad's
formidable gates. There would be much more in the way
of remuneration to come for all of them, or so Sayyad's
emissary had averred, if the Black Lion cared to claim it
from his master in person.

The Black Lion did, indeed, care to claim such ready

pay—if the Assassin would only come forth and explain
what he must do to earn it.

Weary of waiting, the mercenary allowed his thoughts
to drift, though his taut-muscled body, honed through years
of constant warfare into a nearly perfect fighting machine,
remained prepared for instant action. Inevitably, however,
once freed his mind began to mull again over the disturbing
news he'd received from home. He'd gotten the letter
nearly a month earlier, much handled and weather-stained
from its long journey, and the information it contained was
far older than that. Yet he still had not completely digested
it in his mind. The mercenary told himself he couldn't afford to dwell now on the contents of the missive he carried
next to his heart—nor on the letter's source—though it felt
as if it were slowly burning a hole in his breast right
through his tunic. Still, he couldn't help brooding upon its
distressing tidings.

His father, ill for some years already, had finally died;
and now his younger brother, besieged by rapacious enemies who sought to steal their lands, begged for his assistance—or so said the lady whose faithful letters over the
years had been the Black Lion's only link to the world he'd
left behind. The short, bleak missive had ended with the
same appeal as had all the rest. The one that never failed
to tug at his gut, no matter how he braced himself against
it.

Come home. All is forgiven.

If only he could forgive himself.

But the exiled warrior knew it was an impossibility. He
had sworn a sacred oath, and he had not fulfilled his vow.
Unless he found a way to do so—though for years now,
he had not held out even the faintest hope of that possibility—he could never return home. Not even to bury his father or ride beside his brother in defense of their ancestral
lands. He must forget about the green hills of his youth in
the West, and forget as well the role of landed lord he had
been brought up to play in that life. He was no longer the
naïve boy who believed the code of honor and justice al-

ways prevailed. He lived by a different code now; a very simple code.

Kill for coin.

It was the way of all mercenaries. The best the Black Lion could do for those he'd left behind—other than to stay away so he did not spread his taint upon their innocent souls—was to send aid in the form of money to his beleaguered sibling. And for that, he must suffer the indignity of waiting upon such as Sayyad al-Zul, who seemed to think nothing of keeping him hanging on his pleasure all afternoon. He must take the slights of those who offered him employment, must live with the ignominy of prostituting himself for gold. What did such indignities really matter in the face of the utter fruitlessness of his entire existence? He would go on, the warrior thought grimly, just as he had for half his life, offering his strong right arm as his bargain. After all, with no honor left to speak of, it was all he had to sell.

It was the same with each of the warriors who followed him, the mercenary knew. Thus he and his men had made the long journey north and east into these desolate, wind-scoured mountains from the more populous regions to the southwest, surviving both the hardships of the road and the hostile glares of Sayyad's people, who had met them partway along the narrow, treacherous Safid Pass that was the only viable entrance to this place. Those taciturn warriors, bristling with arms and sporting ferocious attitudes that fairly begged for a fight, claimed to have come to guide the mercenaries to the well-hidden fortress of their master, but it was clear to all that their main purpose had been to make sure the Black Lion and his men did not get "lost" and accidentally witness something Sayyad wanted kept secret along the way. Assassins, after all, were famous for guarding their privacy.

This particular mercenary, however, had no interest in his prospective employer's secrets. *No,* he told himself, *the only thing I want from this paranoid, unpredictable lunatic is his coin.* Having lost all else of importance long ago—

including his hope, his faith, and his naïve youthful belief in the inherent decency of humanity—good solid coin was the stuff for which the Black Lion lived these days. Fortunately, Sayyad had promised him and the warriors who followed his banner plenty of that. He would hear out what the Assassin had to say, and bring the news of it back to his men.

Always assuming, of course, that the elusive renegade finally did choose to reveal himself at some point today.

Does he ever *plan to show his face?* the mercenary wondered.

* * *

I must go down there, the Shadow Hunter thought starkly, staring down from behind the harem screen overlooking the audience chamber at the warrior waiting below. *There is no choice. I need him. But, oh, sweet merciful Allah, if it was anything less than the life of my heart's dear sister hanging in the balance, wild horses could not make me face that Frankish mercenary!*

The Shadow Hunter had been staring down at the Black Lion for some time now from this hidden vantage point, not moving, breathing only shallowly. *At least I do not hold this uneasy vigil alone,* the legendary Assassin thought with craven cowardice. The one person in the world al-Zul called friend shared the tiny spy-space, a comforting presence, indeed, compared to the Frankish warrior below. *I only hope he does not guess the truth.* But the Assassin's comrade was cursedly perceptive.

"So that is the great Black Lion," the eunuch Jamal ad-Din murmured to the shadowy figure at his elbow. Jamal stood side by side with Sayyad in the semidarkness of the chamber behind the harem screen, watching their guest. As his companion gazed broodingly upon the reception room the mercenary occupied below, Jamal noted a slight stiffness marring the loose-limbed ease of al-Zul's stance, and a definite sharpness characterizing the renegade's breathing as well. He wondered what could have caused such tension in his usually calm, confident friend.

"Mm," Sayyad grunted noncommittally, as if realizing only belatedly that some response was required to meet the eunuch's offhand comment. "So it is." The Assassin's raspy whisper strained to keep all inflection from this uninformative utterance. It would be better if Jamal never guessed how difficult Sayyad was finding the prospect of meeting with the mercenary.

Even with those they trusted, as al-Zul trusted the eunuch who had been such an unfailing teacher, friend, and ally over the years, the game of pretense was one they practiced habitually. Caution was a trait both conspirators had learned too early on in life to let go easily. Yet the Assassin relied on Jamal ad-Din's judgment as on no one else's. Whenever the eunuch visited this mountaintop fortress, whether on Sayyad's business or his own, the renegade invariably sought out his wisdom and counsel—and more often than not, that entailed asking Jamal to keep a watchful eye on unwary guests from behind the harem screen while the Assassin met with them below. Since the eunuch had made a life's work of such secret observations, it never occurred to him to be offended that al-Zul chose to keep his contributions secret. After the surreptitiously surveyed meeting, the pair would meet again to exchange observations and trade insights, knowing that two minds were always more perceptive than one. It was a longstanding strategy with which both were comfortable.

Today, however, the Assassin had a queasy feeling that Jamal's covert scrutiny would reveal more about the host than the guest to the eunuch's keen eyes. The shock Sayyad had received upon seeing the mercenary would be hard to hide.

"He has the patience of a cat on the hunt, I'll grant him that." Thinking it odd his companion was taking so much time before confronting the Frankish warrior, Jamal went on when the preoccupied Assassin ventured no further opinion on the mercenary, and made no move to go down and join the man either. "For some time I have been watching this not-so-tame beast you've summoned, *ra'is*." Jamal used the Arabic term of respect for one who is a leader in his own domain. "He has waited in that chamber for you nigh on two hours with barely the shift of a muscle," the eunuch continued with a hint of reproof for Sayyad's bad manners. "Yet somehow, I sense he will be ready to pounce in an instant should he find the prey he desires. The only question that troubles my mind is: What does such a man seek?"

What, indeed? wondered Jamal's cautious ally. That question was just one of the many racing through the Assassin's fevered thoughts. Yet the most troubling conundrum of all, the one that most begged an answer, was not what a mercenary such as the Black Lion sought, but rather how fate had arranged for the particular mercenary sitting below them to *be* the fabled Black Lion in the first place. This was the mystery that disturbed Sayyad. But when the veiled figure finally spoke, little of that inward disquiet was in evidence. Instead, the soft, whispery tone was calm, dismissive.

"What does any mercenary ever seek? He wants money, of course. And he will get what he desires—I intend to tender him quite a princely sum for his services," the Assassin admitted. Sayyad's tone became a shade defensive then, though no one but Jamal would probably have noticed the change. "What difference if I let him prove his patience first with a short delay? It will do the man no harm to await my pleasure."

"True," the eunuch admitted carefully, still sensing that something had caused his friend's uneasiness. Despite the careful posturing designed to throw him off, to the acutely sensitive Jamal, Sayyad appeared more agitated than usual, even for the tightly wound Assassin. "Yet it seems unlike you, *ra'is,* to behave with such unaccustomed, ah . . ." The eunuch searched for an inoffensive term.

"Rudeness?" the renegade finished for him, unfazed by the suggestion of incivility. "Perhaps it is a trifle discourteous to keep him waiting," Sayyad acknowledged. "It's of no consequence, however. The Black Lion will not perish over so slight a wound, I think." Again, that strange, angry-sounding derision was present in the Assassin's voice, and Jamal took note of it. But his friend's thoughts had already turned elsewhere.

Al-Zul had indeed always intended to keep the mercenary waiting for a short time—it was not an unusual or unreasonable way to gauge a man's mettle—but that plan had gone awry the very instant the Assassin caught sight of the Frankish knight. Instead of discomfiting the Black Lion, Sayyad found that the test of nerves meant for the guest had turned itself back upon the host! The Shadow Hunter had taken one glance at the man—and had nearly fallen from hiding amid the shadows in amazement. It was the shock of that first glimpse, not some fiendish test of patience, that was making the renegade delay so long before granting the mercenary audience.

The Assassin had expected hiring the private military troop they required would be a simple matter—the very least of the problems sure to occur on the dangerous mission they were about to undertake. To succeed in their goal, they'd needed a warrior of fearsome reputation to head their forces; a merciless, conscienceless fighter whose experience and commitment could be trusted to help foil a dangerous enemy and win from him a treasure more precious than gold. Going over their few options and the overwhelming odds against them, Sayyad had believed their only hope lay in hiring the man known to the world as the Black Lion.

Some had said he was a Saracen of unknown but perhaps princely lineage, others a renegade Frankish crusader who'd long since forsworn his faith. Others still had claimed he had no faith at all and would sell his sword to the highest bidder, Muslim or Christian—but hastened to add that, once sold, that sword never failed the buyer. Though his true name and his past were shrouded in mystery, the Black Lion's list of triumphs in battle had been convincing. Several weeks ago, Sayyad had sent an emissary to find the man and issue him both a bribe and an invitation to meet in this mountain lair, hoping to strike a deal for his services and for those of his mercenary companions—battle-hardened soldiers of fortune all. At the time, it had seemed a simple, elegant solution to the challenges that faced Say-yad.

Now that assumption of ease was being entirely over-turned, for the man who'd arrived in response to the Assassin's summons was no stranger, no anonymous hired sword. Indeed, he was the farthest thing from it.

The Shadow Hunter *knew* the Black Lion, and knew him well.

Sixteen years might have passed, and a lifetime of heartache besides, but Isabeau de Lyon could hardly fail to recognize her betrothed.

It can't be! It can't be! Isabeau still chanted these words frantically over and over again in her mind as she stood beside Jamal in the dark, using them like a mantra to protect her from the truth. Her pulse was pounding wildly, the blood rushing in her ears as she tried to remember how to breathe. *It's impossible!* she told herself. And yet there was no denying it. Oh, *why* had she not taken more pains to discover the mercenary's true name before she'd so blithely sent for him? Such a simple question it was to ask; yet the answer was so shocking it rocked her to the core. Isabeau tried to blink away the evidence of her own eyes, but to no avail. There was no disclaiming the vision before her.

Below her knelt the husband she should have had, in the long-ago life of privilege and ease that had once been Isabeau's birthright—a birthright long since stolen.

A birthright she'd tried desperately to forget.

A welter of wild emotions were unleashed to rush through the heavily veiled renegade—she who had once been the cherished only daughter of the duc de Lyon, but now was known simply by her trade—Shadow Hunter. Seeing Jared, recognizing him despite the years that had passed and the changes wrought in him by time, came as a shock so great she could hardly breathe.

He had grown up well—better than any young boy had a right to—Isabeau thought to herself with a shiver as goose-bumps ran up and down her anxious flesh. This "Black Lion" she'd summoned was not so dark after all, it seemed. Rather, his hair, as she had remembered Jared's being, was a deep, rich auburn. Yet now, unlike the close-cropped, usually messy locks he had sported as a young squire, he wore it long, the front pulled back from his face with a simple leather thong, the rest reaching partway down his wide shoulders to lie atop his mail hauberk in gleaming waves like dark, heady wine.

And those shoulders of his! They were utterly extraordinary. Why, the way they moved beneath the chain mail, it was just like poetry, she thought. Supple, strong, the muscles flowed like the smoothest verse across bone and sinew, shifting with effortless grace and power as he shrugged the tension from his rangy frame and sent flares of light forth from the polished armor links to dazzle the eye. The warrior in her, trained through years of harsh necessity, admired his undeniable prowess. The womanly side of Isabeau, seldom indulged, yearned with a strange new urge to test that power in a completely different manner . . .

It took an effort of will to return her gaze to his face, telling herself that she'd stared purely to size the man up and gauge his skill. But Jared's harsh, weathered countenance only threw Isabeau further off kilter as she tried to superimpose it over the memories in her mind of his stripling's features and downy beard. His face, once pale, was bronzed now, hard, clean-shaven, and with planes that seemed to have seen many distant horizons and to have conquered them all. No trace of boyish softness remained.

His lips, she saw, were full and shapely, expressive even when thinned with annoyance, as they became as the wait dragged on longer and longer with no sign of his host. But she saw that that generous mouth of his no longer held even the promise of a smile now, as it always had when they'd been children together. Jared, like her, seemed to have lost the capacity for mirth with his youth.

Continuing to stare, she noticed that his nose was quite striking, molded with a sort of severe nobility under his slashing dark brows. She remembered that it had seemed rather too large for his features all those years ago, but no longer. Now it fit his arrestingly handsome face perfectly. Yet it was his eyes that captured her far more than all else together, even from this distance.

She'd remembered them being brown. What Isabeau had not recalled, however, was that they were so much *more* than that. Amber, luminous, and glowing with banked fire, they were the eyes of a lion indeed. And Isabeau, despite her Assassin's training, still felt like prey caught beneath their gaze when those orbs shifted upward momentarily to sweep the inner defenses of her fortress home and paused briefly to scan the latticework behind which she hid.

His was not the first well-muscled specimen of manhood the Assassin had ever seen—though possibly it was the comeliest. Just looking at him, comparing him mentally with the image of the boy she had once known, sent strange waves of heated sensation slithering under her skin. The feelings that came over her were completely foreign to the Assassin, and she found them extremely disorienting. Debilitating, even.

Isabeau had never thought to catch sight of this man again; not this side of Paradise. But there he was, bold as day, waiting for his audience with the infamous renegade who had invited him to this lonely place on the edge of nowhere. Waiting, had he only known it, for the little girl he'd let slip through his cursedly careless fingers on that fateful summer day.

Emotion overwhelmed the Assassin.

In truth, it took all her strength not to call upon her guard in that moment—whether to fall upon Jared in anger and smite him down, to spirit him away from this place and out of her sight as fast as they could, or throw him in chains into the depths of the darkest oubliette in the fortress she'd fought so hard and so long to secure, Isabeau wasn't sure. All of her senses were screaming one word: *danger*. Yet strangely enough, if she was honest with herself, Isabeau had to admit that the first feeling she recognized in her heart was not fear or hatred, bitterness or grief. No. This feeling might be incredibly intense and wholly inexplicable, but it was unmistakably *joy*.

Jared was here!

After this first giddy thrill of recognition, however, the renegade forced herself to dismiss the feeling, for it made no sense to her. *Why, after the way he abandoned me then, should I be happy to see him here now—so obviously,* damnably *healthy and vital?* Why, she wasn't happy at all.

She was merely thrown by the coincidence, that was all, Isabeau told herself, and certainly that was true enough. *How* can *it be he?* she asked herself yet again. Jared had never so much as left the south of France in his life, as far as she knew, unless it was to return home to nearby Navarre. Because he had never come to find her when she'd disappeared all those years ago, she'd just assumed de Navarre had remained safely in the West and had eventually taken up his place among the ranks of the nobility.

When she'd allowed herself to think of him at all (which was not often), Isabeau had always imagined her erstwhile betrothed growing up as his destiny dictated; winning his spurs, jousting at tourney with the other young knights to gain reputation and fortune; eventually becoming a lord in his own right. There was no reason for her ever to have imagined otherwise; no reason she could think of for Jared to venture so far from the world he knew. So how was it possible that the famous mercenary she'd heard so much about in recent years and her lost betrothed could be one and the same man? The Assassin had no answer for this perplexing question.

And after this first bout of confusion came an intense, bone-deep wariness. *What* does *he here?* she wondered suspiciously. *What can de Navarre want from me?* As the Assassin Sayyad al-Zul, Isabeau had made many enemies over the years, and none of them, she knew, would hesitate to use an old friend against her if they thought she might let down her guard in his presence. But of course, that was ridiculous! she told herself bracingly. She was just being paranoid. Jared could not know the identity of his potential employer, she reminded herself, so she had no reason to fear him. Yet. After all, *she* had contacted *him,* not the other way around. This was all simply a bizarre coincidence. She still held the upper hand.

As far as de Navarre knew, his betrothed was long dead, another sacrifice to the all-consuming Christian ideal of crusade. Probably, he had forgotten all about the girl he'd been promised to in the days of their innocent youth. Perhaps he had even married someone else long since and raised a family of his own back in his faraway homeland. But no, she thought. The legend of the Black Lion had been years in the making. Jared had to have come to the East several years ago at least in order to have won such renown. *Yet,* Isabeau reminded herself bitterly, *that doesn't mean the man couldn't have wed and begotten himself some squalling russet-haired brats before he turned his hand to crusading these last few years. And I'll bet in all that time he never once wondered about the fate of the girl he was sworn to protect.*

Anger came upon Isabeau then, swift and sudden as a blazing wildfire, searing away all other emotions. Curse him to the blackest hell! Why had Jared come to her now, when it was so incredibly, heart-wrenchingly *too damned late*?

Of course, it had been she who had summoned him here today. Isabeau had to remember that. She had to get a hold of herself before emotion carried her away! She had to force reason to stem this tide of feeling or it could very possibly destroy not only herself, but everything she held dear. *Now is not the time to fall apart,* the Assassin told herself sharply. Too much was riding on her ability to function logically, even in the face of so great a shock. She must pull herself together! She had to look at the situation objectively.

In her hour of need, she had called upon the Black Lion, purely on the strength of his fierce reputation. She had not

known more at the time than that the man was a deadly
fighter, a warrior of the greatest valor. And she had to admit, it did seem she might have gotten what she'd asked
for with the arrival of Jared de Navarre. The mercenary
before her, even now taking over her audience chamber
with the sheer force of his magnetic presence, was everything the Black Lion was reputed to be. *And,* she mused
involuntarily, *so much more than I ever guessed my long-
lost betrothed would become* . . . But she must not entertain
such idle thoughts! She must think what was to be done!

   Think, Isabeau told herself sharply. *Make a decision.* But
in the end there was really only one choice to make.

CHAPTER FIVE

"As salaam aleikum," said the slight, wiry man who'd suddenly appeared at the Black Lion's elbow.

It took every bit of his will not to start violently in alarm. Surreptitiously, Jared forced the hand that had reached instinctively for the dagger concealed at his wrist to relax, hoping his conditioned reflex had gone unnoticed. Under the terms of their arrangement, they had both agreed to come unarmed to this meeting, though in truth he doubted his tardy host was any less prepared to meet the eventuality of hostility than he was himself.

"Aleikum salaam," Jared replied smoothly enough. His pause had been almost infinitesimal, and in his tone he allowed nothing that would betray his momentary surprise. Though of Frankish origin, the Black Lion had no difficulty responding to the traditional Arab greeting with flawless Arabic of his own, having mastered the tongue years earlier along with many of the customs of those who were nominally his enemies. Yet immediately, though he strove to appear at ease before his host and to project nothing more dangerous than bland civility, he sensed that peace would never be upon the man to whom he had just wished it.

The Assassin fairly oozed aggression. Short, as many men of Eastern origin tended to be, built with something of an acrobat's taut, explosive energy, the man was a bundle of nerves, his high-strung nature clear even through the dark, enveloping ascetic's robes and the thick swaddling of veils he wore. This man was no jovial, smiling dignitary, content to let the usual greeting ceremonies take on their natural leisurely pace. No, this man did nothing slowly, and the mercenary was willing to bet he never, *ever* relaxed.

"Do not move," the renegade called Sayyad ordered sharply when the mercenary made to rise and bow before his host as custom demanded. His voice emerged as no more than a gravelly growl of sound, and one of his lean, sinewy hands motioned sharply at the mercenary in the universal gesture to halt. "Stay just as you are." Belatedly, the hand relaxed its posture, the gesture becoming a modicum more graceful as he modulated it to a wave. "Please. Do not trouble yourself."

Jared raised a mental brow at this overly harsh reaction as he checked his motion and knelt back upon the cushions, though outwardly his forehead remained smooth, his expression unrevealing. Unthreatening, just as he had been taught. Muslim courtesy, and the flowery expression of it, was one of the skills this once-impatient warrior had found hardest to learn when he had first come to the Holy Land, but once achieved, he had taken his education to heart. Often over the years this studied diplomacy had served him well, for in the course of negotiating for the use of his sword, he had had occasion to exchange elaborate pleasantries with some of the most eloquent philosophers, clever merchants, and persuasive religious leaders in all the Abbasid-controlled lands of Arabia and beyond.

Sayyad, with one flowing, graceful motion, seated himself cross-legged upon a cushion facing his guest, but seemed prepared to say nothing more as he tucked his hands up into the voluminous sleeves of his dark robe. For a long moment, the Assassin merely studied the other man, seeming to weigh him. He did not offer his visitor any of the usual refreshments, or inquire about his journey. Instead, his shadowed eyes simply bored challengingly into the mercenary's own.

Jared met this challenge easily, however, staring back with a faintly sardonic, inquiring gaze of his own. Neither seemed willing to look away first. The silence grew heavy upon them both, only the tinkling of the garden fountain somewhere beyond al-Zul's right shoulder breaking the oppressive atmosphere.

Well, if Sayyad chose not to proceed in the traditional manner, it seemed *he* would have to take on the burden of carrying the discourse between them, Jared decided finally.

A twinge of impatience he couldn't squelch arose in his breast. He hadn't traveled hundreds of miles, dragging a troop of the best-trained, sharpest mercenaries this side of Christendom along behind him, merely to engage this odd little fellow in a contest of stares! He felt a spurt of annoyance—the first he'd allowed himself since arriving in this place—and decided to introduce himself to get the conversation started.

"I am Jared de Navarre—" he began.

"I know who you are, mercenary," came the derisive rasp of his host's hoarse voice, interrupting him. "Who has not heard of the mighty Black Lion—the warrior known as the scourge of Tyre, the Lion of Antioch, the savior of Damietta?" There was a strong hint of irony in the question, though it was not completely clear whether the renegade was directing it toward himself or his guest.

Ah, Jared thought with satisfaction. So the Assassin *did* intend to parlay, as his invitation had suggested. And with his first verbal sally in these negotiations, he'd just told his guest he knew all about the exploits that had, over the past decade and a half, made Jared de Navarre one of the most sought-after fighters in this war-torn, so-called Holy Land among Saracens and crusaders alike. Al-Zul had also told him, in so many words, that he wasn't overly impressed by de Navarre's nearly legendary reputation.

It was a good opening salvo, Jared acknowledged. The mercenary could almost hear the sardonic smile in the Assassin's tone, for the man's disguise had made him focus closely on the subtle, dangerous nuances of the husky whisper coming from behind it.

Veils were unusual in a man, he knew, but not unheard of. Mystics and astrologers had been known to wear them for centuries, and the Bedouin regularly covered their faces to protect their skin against the harsh winds and blowing sands of their native land. But few, if any, could claim to keep their faces covered as religiously as this man was said to. Jared had heard more than one tale that tried to explain this odd practice of al-Zul's, yet until today, faced with the man himself, he'd been inclined to believe the simplest explanation—that Sayyad's vanity kept him from baring the scars he'd gained in some early battle. Now Jared changed his mind.

There was no vanity in this man, that much he knew instantly, warrior to warrior. But instinct told him there was definitely *something* other than a simple scar hidden behind the barrier Sayyad held up before the world. He found himself curious, though it was not his practice to involve himself in the peculiarities of his potential employers' habits. Too much curiosity was not healthy for a man in his profession, the warrior reminded himself. He was here to do a job, naught more. He must remember that.

"I see my reputation precedes me," Jared said mildly, though he wasn't fool enough to believe the Assassin had flattered him with his words. As the man lounged with studied ease upon the cushion opposite Jared, the mercenary sensed a tension in the air between them for which he could discern no reasonable explanation, at least under the circumstances. *He,* de Navarre, was the one who ought to feel nervous, arriving unarmed (well, mostly unarmed) and alone as he had reluctantly agreed to do at this meeting. So why was *al-Zul* so jumpy, here on his own ground, surrounded by his own forces? Though he tried to hide it, there was a definite stiffness in Sayyad's posture and the intent way the man regarded Jared across the small space between them.

Fanaticism, devotion, perhaps even madness—all these were there for his inspection, and expected, considering Sayyad's deadly reputation. But that was not all that was present in the man who faced him now. No. Somehow, though he knew they had never met before, Jared felt there was some personal antagonism here. How had he made this man his enemy? It was as though the very fact of his existence or his identity had displeased his host in some way. But if that were true, why had he been summoned today?

The Assassin didn't leave him guessing long. "That reputation is the reason you are here," he said with a bluntness uncharacteristic of an Arab—indeed, nearly unheard of up until now in the warrior's experience with Saracen employers.

Jared reluctantly decided to put aside the oddness and unspoken tension of this encounter for now—after all, he reminded himself, he'd never had dealings with a member of the Assassins' cult before. Perhaps the *only* thing they could be counted upon to do was not follow other people's rules. Quite possibly, Jared thought sourly, Sayyad treated all his guests with equal incivility. He decided to relax and go along with the brusque tone of the audience. Indeed, it was a bit of a relief for once to be able to come to the point succinctly, instead of spending hours talking around the subject at hand over endless tiny cups of coffee or sherbet. Still, Jared couldn't resist throwing in a small, honey-coated jab of his own, to see if he might bring his host to be a bit more forthcoming.

"Go on, please. I am curious to discover how my puny, insignificant renown in battle has brought you to request my services at this juncture. For years, I have been intrigued by your own much greater reputation as a warrior and have longed to meet the man who has struck such fear into the hearts of so many."

Sayyad appeared completely unmoved by Jared's sally, and by his sardonic flattery as well. If anything, he seemed to grow more abrupt, more contemptuous. The man spent a long moment studying the mercenary, staring him up and down as if measuring every detail of his physique and prowess. He gave no indication what he thought of them, however, his stiff posture not relaxing one iota.

"Well," the Assassin said at last. "Now you have satisfied your urge. We have met. We have agreed that we are both warriors of some repute in our respective arenas. Need we waste more precious time lauding one another's virtues, or has your ego been served a sufficient helping of praise?"

Jared told himself to let the insult pass. Even so, he felt a flare of righteous anger at the insolence of this renegade Assassin. Sayyad was not the only one with a deadly reputation here, and the mercenary did *not* like being toyed with! He had come a long distance on the strength of this man's promises, and so far, al-Zul had shown him nothing but discourtesy and disregard.

But if there was anything the Black Lion knew how to do, it was hold his temper, and it would do no good to lose it now. "I think my self-regard remains in good standing, thank you," he replied with just a tinge of sarcasm. "By all means, let us get down to business if that is your desire. You paid me to be here today for a reason, I presume— other than to insult me and waste the valuable time of myself and the men at my command?" Through the heavy veils, Jared couldn't tell if the thrust struck home. Certainly, Sayyad did not visibly flinch at the pointed barb.

"There is an emir," the renegade said calmly. "A man by the name of Malik al-Fayed. Perhaps you have heard of him?" The Assassin's disgusted voice showed his low regard for the man—or was it for the mercenary he'd summoned? It was impossible to be sure through all the wrappings he wore.

Jared nodded carefully, giving up any further attempt at drawing out his host. "He has been making something of a name for himself in Baghdad these days, from what I hear." What he did *not* say was that he had also heard of the man's propensity for vice of every sort, from swilling palm wine and other spirits forbidden to Muslims to indulging with astonishing frequency in the pleasures of the harem. Other, whispered tales spoke of the emir pursuing far darker delights as well, whenever and wherever he found them.

Malik al-Fayed was widely known to be a debauched, dissolute sadist, but a powerful one, whose star was on the rise with those in power in Syria. "I also hear tales that he intends to consolidate his influence with the new ruler in Damascus, while still currying favor with Sultan al-Kamil in Cairo and the caliph in Baghdad," the mercenary added.

"Those rumors are true. You must have excellent sources," Sayyad complimented, though his tone, muffled behind the thick veil, was just barely courteous.

"I try to keep abreast of shifts in the currents of power," Jared admitted easily. "Such alliances and struggles are what keep me in business, after all. But what, if I may ask, have this petty tyrant's machinations to do with your own affairs? The man's no danger to you that I can see."

"That is not for you to know!" Sayyad spoke sharply. "That son of a swine may be no danger to me—may God damn his black soul—but I surely intend to be one to *him*!" The anger in al-Zul seemed to rise unchecked for a moment, tensing the small man's body to one tight knot of fury, but at last he managed to collect himself with a deep breath that was audible even to Jared. More calmly, the renegade Assassin continued, rasping, "It is not his machinations but his belongings with which I am concerned."

At the mercenary's polite, puzzled expression, al-Zul sighed, the sound more a growl of frustration than an exhalation of breath. "The reason you are here is simple. I want you and your men to help me steal al-Fayed's most prized possession—a treasure so precious, he keeps it hidden from all eyes but his own, and from whose loss I hope he shall never recover. I intend to ruin the man," he admitted baldly, "to shake him right down to his foundations by pulling the cornerstone of his pride right out from under him when he least expects to be vulnerable. And I want *you* to help me accomplish this theft."

Well. *That* was an unusual request. Certainly, Jared could not remember ever having a similar mission proposed to him in all his nearly sixteen years as a professional sword-for-hire. If it had not been so preposterous, it would have been insulting. "I beg your indulgence, *ra'is*," the mercenary said, diplomatically using the title of respect so as not to offend his temperamental host. "But perhaps you have the wrong idea about just whose services you are trying to buy. I am not a thief. Nor are my men mere bandits or outlaws for hire."

"Of course not," Sayyad rasped derisively. "If you were petty thieves, you'd be no good to me. Have no fear, warrior; I know *exactly* whom I have summoned." There seemed to be a great weight of significance to these words, though Jared could not puzzle out what it might be. It seemed, too, that the Assassin was also suggesting that, given a choice, he would not have wanted to hire Jared or his men. The man's next words confirmed it.

"Expediency has required me to call upon you." Unspoken in the sentence was the word *anyway*. "But I am well aware," the Assassin continued, "of your small team's reputation for accomplishing what larger, less well-trained bands could not, using your years of training together and your own strong skills as a leader to conquer impressive odds. I have also"—he paused, and this time Jared thought he heard a sort of reluctant satisfaction in the man's voice—"heard of your troop's propensity for using subtle tricks and sabotage when necessary to achieve your goals. Trust in me when I assure you there will be plenty of call for your particular 'skills' in the days to come. We are after much more than simple spoils of war, mercenary," the renegade assured him grimly. "If we do this right, we will be undermining the entire base of Malik's power, and ensuring he never does harm to another human being so long as his damnable soul continues to walk this earth. With the aid of your devious warriors, we shall hit al-Fayed where he is weakest, and pray he never recovers from the blow!"

Jared noticed the Assassin's disdain toward him even as he accepted the renegade's backhanded praise. Strangely enough for a man whose very profession was steeped in stealth and deceit, Sayyad actually seemed disapproving of the Black Lion's unorthodox methods in battle. Or was it the man himself of whom he disapproved? Why then, if that were so, Jared wondered once more, would the ex-Assassin want to hire him and his band? The man must truly be desperate for their help.

Good, he thought. *That will ensure us a hefty wage.*

Feeling slightly mollified, but still mystified, Jared asked, "In that case, may I be permitted to hear more about this mysterious thieving mission you wish us to engage upon on your behalf?" The mercenary was beginning to grow tired of his host's uninformative banter. He wanted details!

"You may not. When the time is right, you will be informed of your duties. Suffice it for now that I am assured you and your men have the requisite expertise to complete the job."

The mercenary had to laugh. "You wish me to agree to send my troops into battle for you without even knowing where we are going or what we are to do when we get there? Al-Zul, you must be as daft as your reputation claims."

Though the Assassin bristled visibly beneath the taunt, Jared noticed he did not rise to the bait. "You will not be going into battle *for* me, de Navarre; you'll be going *with* me," he said calmly. "And my men. Under *my* command. There will be no questions asked or answered, and your strict obedience will be required at all times. Do you understand? *My* word will be law, not yours." Sayyad paused as if to let this sink in, and the Assassin would've had to have been blind not to read the displeasure in de Navarre's thunderous scowl when the mercenary heard that.

"My men respond to no one's orders but my own," Jared replied flatly. "They will have it no other way."

"Agreed." The Assassin conceded after only a moment's seeming consideration, almost as if he'd expected the mercenary's caveat. "That will pose no problem—so long as *you* respond to *mine*." The man could clearly see Jared's reluctance to accept this edict without further information. "It is your choice, of course; to stay and accept this assignment, or return to your men now with no further remuneration for your troubles—though, of course, with the full protection of my guards to ensure that you and your knights return to the foot of the mountains safely," he added silkily. "So. Which will it be?"

Jared didn't miss the threat implicit in this offer to escort them "safely" home. But he didn't fear it either. Sayyad might be lacking in some of the niceties of the usual customs, but even he, surely, would not be monster enough to try and slaughter his own guests on their way home from his territory. Not even a reputed heretic like this one would dare shatter the sacred Muslim law of hospitality. Nor, in truth, did the mercenary fear the odds against him—*fidai'in* or not, he'd pit his score of soldiers against Sayyad's rebels any day. After all, there couldn't be *that* many of the bandits, or al-Zul would not have needed to hire mercenaries to supplement them in the first place! No, he didn't believe they would come to harm at this man's hands. But Sayyad's reminder that they might go home essentially empty-handed after following the promise of such a handsome profit was a pointed one. Jared did not like to waste his time or squander the uniquely well-honed skills of his warriors.

"One question I must ask for the sake of my men, and I will have it answered honestly, or this discussion ends right here, right now."

The Assassin nodded solemnly. "Ask it, and I will answer if I can."

"What are the chances of my men's survival on this mission? I will not blindly send them out on a suicide run."

The ex-Assassin's eyes locked with Jared's own for a long, considering moment. "It is a difficult endeavor we undertake. Some of them," he admitted frankly, "may not come back alive."

Jared stared back equally frankly. Sayyad al-Zul, he noticed with mild surprise, had blue eyes. However, he had no intention of commenting on that interesting but irrelevant fact during such a pivotal point in their negotiations.

"It's going to cost you," was what he said instead. And he meant it.

*   *   *

"You almost seemed as if you knew this mercenary, this Black Lion," noted the tall eunuch with the curiously flaccid muscles and wasp-waisted figure unique to his kind. He glanced sharply at Isabeau, his liquid brown eyes almost black with concern. The Assassin had rejoined him in the hidden room above the audience chamber once her parlay with the mercenary was over, and Jamal could see she was even more tense than before. He'd sensed the storm brewing beneath the calm exterior of his friend, noticed the long, abstracted silences both before and after her meeting with the mercenary, and his deeply creased ebony features betrayed his anxiety for the renegade Assassin. In all the years he had known this extraordinary woman, kept her secrets and served her cause with every drop of devotion in his body, he had never felt such agitation emanating from within her as he did now.

There was a long pause as he waited for the Shadow Hunter's response.

"No, my old friend, I'm afraid you are mistaken," she denied at last. "I do not know the man at all." Isabeau hesitated for another moment before dropping her revealing next words upon this, her only ally in the world. "You see, Jamal, once we two were to have married—and yet now I fear there are no more perfect strangers between heaven and earth."

For Jamal's own safety, and to ensure the continuing secrecy of his affiliation with the Assassins' cult, of which he had long been a member, the eunuch needed to be aware of all the facts. Even so, it was a struggle for Isabeau to let the words hang in the air between them. Gathering up the trailing edge of the scarf that veiled her face, she wrapped it more securely about her head. Only a pair of sky-colored eyes remained visible, and they were blank as heaven as she turned away from her trusted comrade.

"What!" Jamal blurted, unable to think of anything more coherent to say. "Wait, *ra'is,* how can this be . . . ?"

"I do not wish to discuss this matter in depth, old friend," the renegade warned tautly, turning back reluctantly to face him.

Jamal searched for a way to change her mind, floored by Isabeau's astonishing revelation. A thousand questions swirled in his mind, not least of which was how this new wrinkle would affect their long-planned scheme. "I think at the very least you must tell me some of it, *ra'is,*" he urged in his light tenor voice. "Your history with this man may have a profound effect upon our future plans."

"It will have no effect at all!" she denied strongly. Isabeau could see she had not convinced her friend, however, and so she continued unwillingly. "Was it not you, Jamal, who advised me to forget my previous life when you paid my purchase price on the slave blocks of Alexandria those many years ago?"

"Yes, it was," he admitted, startled that she would bring up a piece of their shared history the two rarely discussed. "But surely this is an exception!"

"It is no exception, Jamal," she cut in harshly. "There are only a few relevant facts, and these I will share with you. The rest will remain buried where it belongs—safely in the past. Will you agree to abide by my wishes in this?"

Jamal nodded, knowing he would get no answers at all unless he did.

Isabeau sighed, her fists knotting as she prepared to speak. "You know that I am of France originally—that, at least is no secret, since I spoke only Latin, Greek, and the tongue of that land when you bought me."

Jamal remembered that day well. The eunuch, a slave himself, had thanked Allah many times that he'd been forced to study Latin and Greek along with the Sanskrit, Arabic, and Persian his own true master, the Assassins' leader, had required him to learn. Otherwise, he could not have communicated with the scared, confused little girl who had grown up to alter his own destiny so greatly. It came to him sharply now that if he, Jamal ad-Din, known before the world as chief slave-procurer and harem master for the powerful emir Malik al-Fayed, had not chosen the young Frankish girl for the emir's harem that day, neither of them would have been standing here today.

Nor would they be on the brink of mounting a dangerous rescue operation that would unmask and destroy them both if they failed. But fate had decreed this moment long before either of them had been born, Jamal knew. Perhaps this new development with the mercenary was merely a reflection of the strange way kismet had of bringing together people who were meant to share one another's lives. He must learn to accept these odd twists of fate, Jamal reminded himself, calming his fears with fatalism as he had done countless times over the course of his life. With that in mind, the eunuch again nodded mutely at his protégée, content to wait to hear the rest of her explanation.

"Well," she said calmly, "this 'Black Lion' comes of a region close by my own home in France, and it happens that we knew each other there. Our families were allied, and de Navarre was fostered in our household. Our fathers arranged the betrothal shortly after my birth, I believe—I cannot remember the exact date of the agreement, but I know I don't recall a time before Jared and I were promised to each other. It was simply a given, and we never questioned it." For a moment, there was perhaps a note of nostalgia in the Assassin's voice, but she soon overcame it, continuing dispassionately.

"However, around the time I had reached eight years of age, I was lured away from my home and eventually sold into slavery—that much you know as well, since 'twas you who finally bought me to serve in al-Fayed's household." Now her tone had become wry. "In any case, I never heard another word about Jared or anyone else from home again after that. In time, I ceased to wonder about them. It was another life," the renegade concluded fatalistically. "There is really naught more to it." Isabeau shrugged as if this explanation should say it all.

"Naught more!" At least the Assassin's strange tension during her interview with the mercenary made sense now, but Jamal could not believe his friend had been able to go through with it at all. He knew more about her than she liked, having shared her destiny for the better part of two decades, and he could only imagine the stress such a confrontation with the past would have caused this scarred young warrior. Again, he marveled at the strength of the woman he had once trained, and whom he now willingly served. "You and I both know better than that, *ra'is*," he chided. No one could be sanguine at such a time, not even a cold-blooded Assassin.

"I admit it is coincidental that Jared should have come back into my life at this juncture," she conceded, ignoring Jamal's meaning. "But is it really so odd? Many young men of Europe have come to the East over the last hundred or so years, seeking glory and fortune. Perhaps he was no different in his purposes."

"But do you not wish to reveal—"

"No!" Isabeau practically shouted. "No, I do not!" More calmly, she continued, hoping she sounded reasonable. "What good would it do now anyway? What possible benefit would there be in churning up old memories best forgotten—especially when we both know nothing can come of the revelation?"

"But if you told the man—"

"Aye, what then?" The ex-Assassin laughed mirthlessly. "Jared would never understand what I have had to do, what I have had to *become* in order to survive. Nor what still remains to be accomplished. How could he, Jamal? Despite his impressive reputation, the man can know nothing of the struggles I have had to face. Besides," Isabeau argued passionately, "you, who have had so much cause to witness how women are mistreated in this world, must surely see that I could never share the secrets of my gender and identity with this or any other man—it would be suicide! No, old friend." The Assassin shook her head firmly. "I intend to let it lie. I will say nothing—and neither," she warned darkly, "will you."

Implicit in the command was a threat Jamal recognized. His former student in the arts of execution had long since surpassed the master—indeed, that was part of the reason he served her so devotedly now. He bowed deeply, displaying his understanding and compliance with her decision. "It shall be as you command, *ra'is.*"

Isabeau could see the eunuch was still worried. By Allah, so was she! It hadn't been an easy decision to swallow. She'd agonized, but at last she'd been forced to acknowledge the truth. There'd been only one important question at hand, and that question had been: Did it really *matter* that the Black Lion was Jared de Navarre? In other words, did it change the *facts*? And the answer had been *no*. Isabeau felt grimly sure she'd done the right thing in hiring her erstwhile betrothed. But that didn't mean she had to like it. "I never would have taken the Black Lion on, knowing what I know, had not necessity commanded it," she admitted candidly. "Were our need not so great, and his forces not so perfectly compatible with the plan I have devised, I would have sent him on his way hours ago, when I first recognized him. But as things stand, I believe we shall have need of the more subtle talents of de Navarre's soldiers before this mission is complete."

Upon receiving word of her enemy's movements from Jamal's spies in al-Fayed's household several weeks ago, she'd been forced to act quickly. She had not had time to discuss the full details of the scheme with the eunuch earlier, since he had only arrived at her home base in these mountains this morning himself, practically blazing the trail for the Black Lion's mercenaries. Now, Isabeau put her strong, slender right hand on the eunuch's shoulder, drawing him close and more fully explaining the plan she had devised. Long used to the sight of the scarred digit that had been both curse and blessing to Isabeau over the years, neither of them paid heed to the artificially foreshortened little finger of that hand. They were both intent upon more important matters of strategy.

As she finished talking, Isabeau saw Jamal nodding in enlightened understanding. "So you see, my friend, the timing and the particulars of the ambush require just their sort of skills. Besides, it's too late now to hire anyone else, and you know it. You yourself sent the news of Malik's imminent move to me not a month ago, and it stands to reason he will not wait much longer with autumn on its way and the traveling season soon to end."

Jamal could not disagree with Isabeau's summation, and he was impressed with the scheme she'd devised. But he could not help voicing some continuing reservations.

"*Ra'is* . . . I must tell you, I have a terrible feeling something may go wrong with the raid you plan. I have not wanted to burden you with this, but I fear there may be a spy among the members of al-Fayed's harem—one who may have caught wind of the coming ambush despite our many precautions."

Isabeau sucked in her breath. "That is bad news indeed, old friend. Can you be sure of it?" But she knew the answer before she'd even finished the question. If Jamal had known for certain their plans were no longer secret, he would not have brought word that it was time to strike. And if he'd been sure of their betrayer's identity, that traitor would already be dead.

"Not yet." He confirmed her suspicions. "But I suspect Ullayah."

"*Ullayah.*" Isabeau spat the name like a curse. "Of course." Malik's neglected first wife was a bitter, distrustful woman, one who lived for others' misfortune. As was common among the competing members of any large harem, she eavesdropped religiously, gathering bits of gossip and innuendo with her web of loyal servants and informants as a spider catches flies. Such news in her hands could prove deadly indeed.

"Never fear, *ra'is*. Should I discover even the slightest proof that she is aware of our plans, the witch will meet with a most unpleasant fate." Jamal smiled nastily. "You recall those honeyed dates she favors, do you not?"

Isabeau nodded.

"Perhaps a bad batch will come her way, should I learn she has been spying too closely upon my activities."

The Assassin could not feel sorry for the woman, having suffered from her cruelty many times in the past. "Indeed, Ullayah's greed for sweets was ever her downfall," she agreed facetiously. Then the renegade grew solemn again. "How serious is this threat, do you think?"

"Not serious enough to change our plans, I believe," the

eunuch said decisively. "This opportunity is too rare to waste, *ra'is*."

Indeed it was. Malik's household would not be vulnerable like this again for many seasons—perhaps not ever. It had to be now, or never. There would always be risks in life, Isabeau told herself bracingly, but only the bold would seize its rewards. "I agree, Jamal. We must proceed as planned—unless you can think of another reason to hold off?"

"No, I admit that I cannot. Yet still, this former association you have with the mercenary worries me greatly," Jamal confessed, coming back to the subject of the Black Lion. "What if he should discover the truth despite all your precautions, and seek revenge for your deceit? Your very life could depend upon hiding your identity from him."

"Don't fret, old friend. I intend to make sure de Navarre *never* knows who I used to be." The tone in the Assassin's voice was dark with finality. But then she squeezed Jamal's shoulder again in reassurance. "Come," she said in a lighter tone. "I know you must return soon to Malik's palace before your 'slave-buying' trip begins to seem suspiciously lengthy, and there are still many things we must discuss before you leave. Most importantly, now that the mercenaries have been engaged to help our cause, we must make our final arrangements for the attack that is to come.

"With the help of the Black Lion and his men," she concluded, "I will want to ride upon our old enemy's position within the very week—or as soon as your little 'friends' have passed me the message that it is time to make our move. You do have them at your service still, do you not?"

"I do. Word will reach you in plenty of time to set the ambush."

"Excellent." The Assassin sighed in relief. "If fate is on our side, we will snatch our precious jewel right from the hand of that wretched, misbegotten son of a devil, and finally put his reign of cruelty and terror to an end."

"Insh'allah." Jamal replied solemnly. If Allah wills it.

Aye, and if my betrothed does not figure out who I am in time to stop me! Isabeau thought apprehensively.

She would just have to make sure he didn't.

CHAPTER SIX

Sayyad al-Zul, the Black Lion reflected, had possibly the bluest eyes he'd ever beheld in his life. Even a week after his first sight of the Assassin's singularly striking gaze, he *still* couldn't get it out of his mind!

Though curiosity about the men who paid for the use of his sword wasn't generally one of his besetting sins, it simply would not let Jared go lately—not when it came to the enigmatic renegade who'd hired him this time around. Indeed, his thoughts seemed filled with nothing else.

The mercenary kicked a clod of dirt with one booted toe and watched it explode into a puff of pale dust, scowling angrily as he stared into the fierce morning sunlight. His own sharp amber gaze, already weary of the view about him, didn't bother taking in the mercenaries' campsite with more than cursory interest. Wedged uncomfortably in along the side of the treacherous, winding road leading up to Sayyad's mountain retreat, there wasn't much of it to see anyhow. Just a few battered tents and cold, charred fire pits were tucked in amid the dry scrub and boulders, along with a line of pickets where their horses foraged for fodder among the withered grasses.

The vista before him was a wasteland of ochre and brown and gray. But all Jared could see was blue—two blue eyes burning in a black-veiled face.

Damn it! Why the hell did he keep thinking about them? For some unknown reason, he couldn't help picturing their extraordinary indigo hue, the endless deep mystery of them hidden behind stubby, close-cropped lashes. But eyes bluer than the depths of the Caspian Sea were not the only thing puzzling the mercenary about his new employer. After all, al-Zul wasn't the first Arab of Jared's acquaintance to claim the strange inheritance of light-colored eyes in a darkly tanned face.

Kurds, Afghanis, Circassians, Armenians, even some of the nearby mountain tribes all had been known to have blue-eyed children, for these groups had for centuries made it a practice to capture both wives and concubines from the Caucasus and other regions north and west of the Arabian Peninsula. Such racial intermingling had given many a proud Arab prince lighter skin and hair than even Jared's own. No, the mystery wasn't in the color of Sayyad's jewel-hard eyes. It was in what went on behind them.

Not for the first time, Jared wondered: Who *was* Sayyad al-Zul? What did he really want of the mercenaries he'd hired? Why did he need them when he'd forces of his own to call upon—and when he'd so clearly been contemptuous of Jared and his knights from the first? But the warrior was no closer to having answers than he'd ever been. A week after their frustrating first meeting, Jared still hadn't figured the man out.

Of course, that might have had something to do with the fact that, for the last seven days, he had not encountered the Assassin even once!

The Black Lion had waited, as ordered, with his band of warriors in their makeshift camp not far outside Sayyad's gates. For an entire week, they'd been anticipating the news that the Assassin and his men were ready to move out and begin this mysterious "mission" of theirs. But so far not a single word had come. In fact, there had been no activity whatsoever going on outside al-Zul's iron-bound gates (nor, as far as they could discern, *inside* them) since a lone traveler, a eunuch by the look of him, had left the citadel shortly after Jared had returned to his men to inform them they'd been hired. For all the mercenaries could tell, everyone within the fortress could have died of some strange plague while they waited. Christ knew the men had come up with more outlandish theories than that to pass the long hours while they'd remained camped by Sayyad's doorstep.

During the balance of these seven days, he and his men had spent the time polishing their weapons, mending their equipment, resting their horses, and practicing their arms until the already well-trained men were, in their leader's opinion, almost too sharp. Certainly, they were impatient with the unexplained delay, bored of idle speculation and eager for action. Jared looked out over the camp once again, this time focusing his attention on the men occupying it.

He had to admit, they were an odd bunch.

Tall or short, young or old, even Muslim or Christian; there was no single way to categorize them as a group. Some wore full metal links of armor and long tunics in the crusader style; some the pointed helmets and quilted, leather-reinforced cuirasses of the Muslim soldier. Others still wore no protective gear at all. Some carried battle-axes and maces; others scimitars or pikes or even light hunting bows. Some of the men were large and muscle-bound, obviously intimidating even to the untrained eye; others were smaller, less overtly menacing—but were, as Jared knew, far more murderous when cornered.

Thieves, deserters, disgraced knights, and killers-for-hire, his crack military troop was made up of the unwanted men other commanders had tossed aside—to their detriment and his own good fortune, de Navarre thought with a wolfish grin of satisfaction as he observed them. Poets, princes, and pilgrims had also joined their number over the years, attracted by the Black Lion's legend. As long as they could fight, and as long as they were willing to swear their allegiance to Jared's banner, they were all welcome to join.

The bond of outcasts everywhere was the tie that united them, for they were all in one way or another exiles from their own communities. Jared had taken them in and had trained them relentlessly according to his own personal philosophy—which was to use the strengths of each man's individual specialty in war, instead of trying to beat them all into one formless mass of brute soldiers.

A poacher, for instance, expert with the bow, would not be asked to swing a cudgel or ride down upon an enemy in the open when his skill at shooting could avail the company more from a distance. Similarly, a knight whose expertise lay in jousting and unseating his opponents from the saddle at full gallop would never be selected to sneak up on an enemy scout on foot in the dark of night—not when another could do it with more stealth and safety. To look at them, one would never guess that this motley assortment of scruffy, scarred veterans were among the best-trained, most tightly knit, deadliest group of warriors the Eastern world had ever seen. But looks, of course, were deceiving—and that was exactly as Jared liked it.

In the Black Lion's Pride (as his men liked to call their company), Bedouin fought alongside Norman, Saxon beside Spaniard, and even a former Mamluk bodyguard—one of an elite corps of Egyptian slaves trained from earliest youth to defend their masters to the death—was counted among the odd assemblage of men. This man's master had perished young, leaving the much sought-after guard free to offer his services anywhere, but despite many more lucrative offers, he had joined the Black Lion's Pride in the first act of volunteerism of his life. Jared knew that true loyalty observed no national boundaries—and above all, his men *were* loyal.

Time after time, this score of soldiers had guarded his own and each other's backs, and at his slightest word willingly would perform feats of heroism that no other commander could have dared ask of them. They might be odd-looking, they might be the so-called dregs of society, but Jared knew he could count on them to come to his aid no matter how great the risks. This they did cheerfully, for in one way or another, their leader had already done as much for each man among them. He would lay down his life for the least of them, Jared admitted privately; for the men of his "Pride" were the only family the exiled knight dared claim anymore.

Even so, nerves were stretched taut among the mercenaries, and growing more so by the day. Jared's own patience was waning just as much as his men's, and yet there had been no word from their newfound employer. If Sayyad had not paid them so handsomely in advance (the large chest of treasure that was the mercenaries' agreed-upon fee having returned with Jared to their camp the very first day, along with a store of fresh supplies to supplement their own thinning rations), the mercenary knew his men would have been on the verge of revolt. They were not used to dealing with such cryptic clients.

As it was, he'd heard more than a few joking comments from the mercenaries about taking their money and departing under cover of darkness while the getting was still good. Though he had to admit the idea was tempting, Jared had no doubt it would be a much smaller band of warriors that emerged from the base of the Safid Pass to reach the foot of the Elburz mountain range should they opt for that alternative.

Even in his short visit inside Sayyad's fortress, the defensibility of that place—as much as the strength of its occupants—had impressed him. Built partially into the rock of the mountain itself, in addition to the airy courtyards, spacious inner chambers, and meticulously tended gardens Jared had visited, the unnamed fortress had two tall, graceful minarets, one on either side of the gates, for viewing the pass below as well as for disseminating the traditional muezzin's call to prayer. They would be seen if they tried to leave, he knew. And anyone who had a reputation as deadly as al-Zul's, anyone who had mastered a stronghold such as this one, would not take kindly to having his money stolen and his bargains broken.

Even had it not been a matter of honor to uphold their agreement, the Black Lion wouldn't have thought it wise to sneak away now. Thus, while his soldiers spent their time carping and complaining about their boredom, Jared spent *his* thinking about the man who'd hired them—blue eyes and all. After all, it wasn't as though he had much else to do.

Frustrated, he sat himself down on a convenient boulder and gazed up at the silent gates of the citadel once more, staring as though he could force those walls to divulge their secrets simply with the power of his will. Soon, the dazzling brightness of the morning sunlight and the thin air of the mountains had him drifting off into daydreams—daydreams of cursedly vivid blue eyes. Only moments later, however, Jared felt a sudden sharp jab at his kneecap, forcing him reluctantly back to full alertness. He didn't bother to look down at the source of the annoyance, merely sighing wearily.

"Be off with you, Big Pierre, before I boot your ugly rump right off the edge of this cliff." Though he'd chosen to ignore it, he'd heard his second-in-command's soft approach well before the other had been in range to touch him.

But "Big Pierre," barely a meter tall, didn't intend to be ignored. And clearly, the irritable dwarf didn't seem too worried by his commander's threat. "Come on, de Navarre. Let's get out of here, why don't we?" He waved angrily at the sealed gates of the fortress up the hill. "That lunatic Assassin is never coming out of there. Maybe you scared him off with that ferocious roar of yours, eh, Black Lion?" Pierre snorted in disgust. " 'Shadow Hunter' indeed. I bet *I'm* as good an Assassin as al-Zul is," he bragged. A sharp, wickedly pointed stiletto suddenly appeared in the dwarf's pudgy hand to underscore the point.

Jared had seen what Pierre could do with a blade, and he didn't dispute the claim. For nearly fifteen years, the Black Lion had trusted his deceptively diminutive friend to guard his back more than any other warrior he'd fought beside. Ever since the day when, in a filthy back alley in the crusader city of Antioch, Pierre had saved a seventeen-year-old Jared from a gang of street thugs who were doing their best to rob and murder him, de Navarre had known there was far more to this fierce little fellow than anyone guessed.

Not only was the dwarf a skilled acrobat, a cunning lock-pick, and a clever thief, he had a mind twice as sharp as the many daggers he kept secreted about his person. Older than Jared by only a few years but far advanced of his protégé in experience, the inappropriately named Big Pierre had made his living as everything from a carnival performer to a sultan's spy—or so he claimed. Certainly, the dwarf had no scruples about doing whatever was necessary to keep those he loved alive—and when he'd taken Jared under his wing, the number of those he loved, including himself, had been raised to exactly two.

Pierre was also the only person Jared had ever trusted with the secret of his true quest here in the Holy Land. The cynical dwarf might not approve of his friend's long, almost certainly futile search, often claiming he'd do as well to seek the Holy Grail, but he had kept de Navarre's confidence faithfully. There were few who would do as much, he knew. Even Jared himself had long ago been forced to admit his self-imposed task was ludicrously unlikely to meet with success. At least Pierre had not mocked him for trying.

And so, when others dared laugh at the idea of making the child-sized soldier his next-in-command, Jared only smiled and said, "Big Pierre may be no taller than my waist, but he's twice the man I am." Perhaps not in battle, for few could claim to match Jared's skill in that arena, but in strategy, the dwarf was a brilliant tactician, and Jared nearly always listened to his counsel. Today, however, was an exception. It might not trouble Pierre's limited conscience to take the Assassin's gold and run, but Jared had staked his word on the deal, and he didn't intend to go back on it.

He plucked the stiletto from the dwarf's hand and pretended to examine it for a minute. "We're not going anywhere yet, Pierre, so get that idea out of your mind for now," he said at last. The mercenary flipped the knife end-over-end between his agile fingers, then abruptly tossed it back to his lieutenant, who had to scramble to catch it hilt-first. Ignoring Pierre's good-natured curses, he cautioned, "Good as you are, my friend, I wouldn't bet against al-Zul in a wager. The man's as cold as Damascus steel and twice as deadly."

Pierre made a rude sound of disparagement, but the look in his eyes said he'd taken the information to heart. "Well, invisible as he is, it's no wonder he's got a reputation for sneaking about," he temporized. "Let him come out and face me man-to-man and then see how he fares, eh? I could use a challenge after all this lazing about!"

"Why don't you take Alaric or Baudoin or one of the others and see if you can't scare us up some meat, if you're so restless?" Jared suggested unsympathetically. "Come to think of it, take Ali. He hasn't had his bow out in so long the string's probably dried out. Tell him we need fresh game."

"Game?" the dwarf sneered. "What game? There's nothing bigger than a lizard to be found on this entire godforsaken heap of rock these buggers like to call a mountain—and anyway, you'd have to fight the vultures for it even if you were lucky enough to find such a prize."

"Well, then, why don't you go do that?" Jared replied distractedly. "They're about your size anyway."

This time it was his shin that was the target of the dwarf's wrath. Luckily, the metal greaves that encased his lower legs protected Jared's flesh from the not-so-friendly blow. "Watch it, Pierre," he warned. "You aren't the only one out of patience today."

"Aye, don't I know it." Growing serious, the little man confessed, "I don't think the men will hold much longer like this. Tempers are short."

Jared sighed again, knowing it was true. The Assassin was obviously waiting for some kind of word to arrive before embarking upon whatever operation he planned for their joint forces. But Jared, from his vantage point parked by the only entrance to the Assassin's fortress, had seen no one arriving or leaving over the last several days. Whatever signal Sayyad was anticipating, it had yet to come. For now, all was disturbingly quiet, and a false sense of calm seemed to have descended on the lonely mountainside.

As if to mock him, a gray-dappled dove cooed softly as it flapped its way across the cloudless sky overhead. Both men paused to watch it.

"We'll bide here a while longer yet," the Black Lion pronounced.

* * *

High atop the tallest tower of her lonely citadel, Isabeau stroked the soft breast feathers of the carrier pigeon thoughtfully, then carefully tucked the tired little creature safely into the dovecote with its mates. It had done its work well, she thought, clutching the tiny scrap of vellum that had been attached to its leg. In her excitement, the Assassin could almost feel the message written on it burning through to her palm.

Jamal's little "friends" had come through for them once again, and now that the signal had been delivered, the long wait could finally end. After years of plotting and scheming behind the scenes, it was finally time to act!

The Assassin savored the sweetness of the long-awaited moment as thoroughly as she could; yet soon enough the sweet taste of triumph soured in her mouth as an uncomfortable thought crowded its way forward into her consciousness—a thought that had her fists whitening into tight knots of anxiety at her sides just when they should have been raised above her head in jubilation. The dread that had turned her joy to worry simply would not be allayed, no matter how she tried to brush it aside.

For despite the adrenaline rush she felt at knowing her long struggle was about to bear fruit, Isabeau could not help recalling that by her side in this all-important engagement would ride the one man in the world she could least count upon—the one man who, sixteen years ago, had so devastatingly proven to her that childhood idols were no more than wishful dreams that vanished with the harsh light of day.

No matter how much time had passed in the interim, and no matter what events should occur in the future, Isabeau knew she must never dare forget Jared de Navarre's true inconstancy. Much more than her own life depended on it this time.

* * *

"What in the name of all holy hell is *that*?"

That same afternoon, Jared found himself blinking in disbelief as he asked the question impartially of anyone within reach of his voice.

The fully equipped caravan that had materialized at the gates of al-Zul's fortress—camels, baggage mules, drivers, and all—was a sight right out of one of Scheherazade's tall tales. In truth, a djinn with all his demon's powers could not have conjured up a more unexpected vision in this desolate spot, though how any other force might account for the outlandish apparition moving steadily toward them, Jared couldn't imagine. What such a caravan was doing here, jangling and clanging its way down the mountain path toward the mercenaries' camp, would take a great deal of explaining.

But unfortunately for the Black Lion, the head of this bizarre convoy, though no genie, still wasn't keen on long explanations.

The Assassin, walking alone at the front of the long line of pack beasts, took it upon herself to clear up the mystery to a certain extent. Not being deaf, Isabeau had heard the outraged mercenary's question quite clearly, but she didn't intend to satisfy his curiosity much if she could help it. There were many things he and the other hired swords didn't need to know yet—and some they never need learn. The Black Lion and his men, she reminded herself unnecessarily, were not to be trusted, only used.

"*This,* commander, is the expedition you'll be leading," she said shortly as she reached Jared's side and halted.

Nervous despite herself at the sight of her erstwhile betrothed, Isabeau took even more care than usual to keep her voice low, though she was long used to modulating its contralto pitch to match a man's deeper range. She felt grateful for the thick gray cotton *kaffiyeh* she wore wrapped about her head and face in the Bedouin fashion, for it hid her unaccustomed agitation from the mercenary as well as her own men. Outwardly, she appeared as calm and impassive as usual, though her belly was in knots standing face to face with the tall, commanding warrior who had once been her favorite playmate.

Never had she felt quite so close to being unmasked, though of course it was a danger Isabeau had faced on a daily basis for several years now. Only a thin barrier of fragile cloth stood between herself and utter ruin, and today more than ever she felt her lack of safety keenly. *What would Jared say if he could see my face this instant?* the Assassin wondered, feeling a surge of highly inappropriate adrenaline. *How would he react if I simply ripped aside this cursed shroud and declared myself before the world as the girl he once knew?*

Without volition, Isabeau's fingers had already begun to curl themselves into the dark fabric of her veil before she was able to overcome this strange and surely suicidal impulse. Jared would not care to celebrate the coincidence of their strange reunion any more than she did, she told herself harshly. Looking up into his cynical eyes, the Assassin could see nothing of the boy he'd once been remaining in those molten-gold orbs now. No, all innocence had been burned out of that cold amber fire long ago. Clearly, de Navarre was no better than his profession indicated. He was mercenary to the core.

As she clenched her suddenly cold hands into fists, the notorious Assassin could feel her usually skillful digits trembling with some sort of suppressed emotion she wasn't sure she cared to identify. Isabeau rubbed the abbreviated tip of the little finger of her right hand absently with the pad of her thumb, a nervous gesture that was as habitual for her as it was unconscious. Was it fear she was experiencing, or some other emotion? she wondered.

Whatever it was, Isabeau couldn't deny that something about this man made her feel less sure of herself than usual, less in control. Perhaps it was only that de Navarre had known her when she was still in swaddling clothes, but in his presence Isabeau felt like anything but the cold-blooded killer she was known to be. Nor did it help that the mer-

cenary refused to treat her with the respect due such a
murderous ally.

"You must be joking." Jared laughed in the veiled Assassin's face, noting the angry darkening of his employer's
deep blue eyes as he did so. "A caravan? You want me to
lead a *caravan*?" He swept his gaze over the line of beasts
and bundles, noting the scowling faces of al-Zul's bandits
standing stiffly at the reins of the baggage animals. They
looked as uncomfortable as fish asked to swim upstream
through desert sands.

Instead of their usual high-domed, turban-wrapped steel
helmets and armor chest plates strapped round with deadly
weaponry, they were decked out now in a range of civilian
attire from the plain, undyed goat or camel-hair garb of
mountain tribesmen to the soft cotton kaftan and trousers
worn by Persian camel drivers beneath the thicker, striped
woolen overrobes called *abba*. Some of the bandits—the
ones Jared noticed were most clearly out of sorts in their
rich new outfits—even wore finely dyed *cabai* along with
their turbans of silk or close-woven cotton. The traditional
embroidered silk robes with their diagonal front opening
crossing from left to right across the chest and their series
of intricately knotted silken ties used to fasten them would
mark these men as wealthy merchants if one did not know
better.

Sayyad himself, garbed in his usual plain gray-and-black
Bedouin robes and headgear, did not appear out of place
among the group, and might have passed for a camel driver
as well. Whatever weapons he carried—and Jared was willing to bet his life there was no lack of these—were well
hidden from the casual observer today.

With this simple change of garments, Jared reflected, the
bandits and their leader had managed neatly to give the
illusion of being harmless traders, instead of the merciless
desert raiders they really were. Yet though the master of
these wolves in sheep's clothing seemed confident despite
his unthreatening guise, the *fidai'in* did not look as pleased
at their own change of attire. Indeed, the mercenary ob-

served more than one among them putting a surreptitious hand out in search of the scimitar he was not carrying, clearly itching to ward off any hint of ridicule from the foreign band of warriors their master had hired. But he saw, too, that they remained stoic, loyal to their leader despite the indignity of being forced to act as mere caravan guards. And that leader was quick to defend them in return.

"This is no jest, Black Lion," Isabeau gritted out. She did not appreciate being laughed at, especially in front of the warriors she led. Her fierce desert wolves were already grumbling at being stripped of their usual defenses and asked to play the part of the merchant-sheep who were normally their prey. "Your men are to act as guards and scouts at the helm of this convoy," she declared firmly. "And *you* will assume the role of its leader."

Turning her head, she growled an order to one of the men ranged behind her, and the bandit came running up with an armload of cloth, bowing deeply before handing it over. She took the bulky bundle, shaking it out to reveal a brocade-trimmed silk *cabai* and trousers in jewel-toned blue, an undertunic of soft creamy-white cotton, and a striped *abba* with threads of purple, white, green, and rust woven through it. There were even soft doeskin *khuff* boots included in the parcel, of a size that looked to match his feet.

It was the garb of a caravan master, clearly richer and more elaborately decorated than that of anyone else in their party. The robes indicated the role Isabeau wanted Jared to play as much as her words had. "You will wear this to hide your Frankish armor, and your soldiers will all be provided with matching garments to make them seem more like regular hired guardsmen than the motley assortment of oddities you look now—though I doubt," she said sardonically, "that we will have anything suitable for *that* one." She nodded to indicate the dwarf, who had come to stand at his leader's side.

Big Pierre bristled, sensing insult, but Jared stopped him with a hand at his small shoulder. *Patience,* he reminded

himself, even as he tried to infuse the same into his friend.
Stay calm. "I believe I told you several days ago that my
men are not thieves, Sayyad. Well, neither are they simple
shepherds to drive this ridiculous herd of yours across the
desert. Besides," he said with silky contempt, "if it's herd
dogs you want, you seem well enough supplied with mutts
of your own."

The Black Lion's Pride, all twenty of them listening
closely to their leader's words, snickered openly at this insult. There was no love lost between the two roughly equal
groups of fighters, Jared's men having developed a healthy
dislike for the bandits who had so sullenly and suspiciously
dogged their every move along the journey to the Assassin's fortress. The mercenaries were watching the exchange
avidly now, enjoying their commander's mocking witti-
cisms and spoiling for a fight.

The bandits, naturally, raised their hackles like the dogs
to whom Jared had just compared them when they heard
his words. Men stepped forward angrily, scowls turning to
outright growls of dislike. For a moment it seemed that an
all-out brawl would develop between the *fidai'in* and the
mercenaries. But the usually excitable Assassin chose to
defuse the tension this time, rather than encourage a fight.

"Fear not for the sake of your precious pride, de Navarre, for this is no ordinary caravan," Isabeau assured him.
She forced herself to speak calmly, though animosity was
rising in her at the Black Lion's unwarranted provocation.
She wanted to spit at him, to curse him for his scorn and
challenge him to a duel that would leave this oversized cat
mewling like a kitten. But she could do none of those things
at the moment, for the Assassin still needed this infuriating
man she'd hired, though she wished his wretched soul
damned to perdition and beyond.

Remember, she told herself silently, *he is nothing but a
hired sword. It is beneath me to exchange insults with a
faithless jackal like this, whose loyalty can be bought for
a few dinars.* Aloud, Isabeau continued evenly. "Though it
is meant to *look* so in the eyes of our enemy, this caravan

is anything but innocent. Come, see for yourself," she invited, lifting the canvas covering of one of the myriad bundles strapped to the side of the camel kneeling nearest her.

Intrigued, the mercenary strolled over, his muscular form setting the Assassin's smaller, slighter figure in shadow as he came close. He noted that al-Zul shied away noticeably as he joined the lithe renegade at the well-laden camel's side, but made little of it as he peered beneath the tarp and into the shadowed recesses of the large basket strapped to the beast's back. Sayyad, it seemed, was a jumpy one indeed. It took Jared a moment to understand what he was seeing. "You're selling swords?" he asked in disbelief, beginning to suspect but still not truly getting Sayyad's drift.

"The blades are not for sale, you fool," Isabeau said impatiently. Had the years made her betrothed thick-witted as well as untrustworthy? "They are for our own use—at the proper time, of course." She could see the suspicion turning to comprehension in Jared's sun-bronzed features as she explained. Up close, the Assassin could not help noticing the extraordinary length of his eyelashes, and the gloriously rich texture of his skin beneath just a few days' growth of stubble. She so seldom got to see a grown male face without the obscuring presence of a beard, Isabeau reflected. That must be why she could not help staring so. It was strange to see Jared's this way; forbidden, somehow almost . . . naughty. He smelled faintly of sandalwood, Isabeau thought, apropos of nothing, and then forced herself to remember what she had been talking about.

What difference if he smelled like goat dung or attar of roses? The only thing that mattered was whether he could wield a sword! "The caravan is merely a ruse," she continued once she'd gathered her wits, "a cover for our real activities. The swords, spears, and shields we bear will be our arms when the time comes for battle. The rest of the bundles are either empty, or simply contain provisions for the journey ahead." Isabeau paused to let that sink in, aware that she had not yet shared their destination with Jared, and that he would soon realize as much, if he had not already. She went on hurriedly.

"Now, if that answers your questions, it is time we were on our way." Turning her back on the mercenary captain, Isabeau tossed her last words tauntingly back over her shoulder. "You have exactly two minutes, de Navarre, to get your men together and follow. Dare I hope you can accomplish *that* much at least without a long-winded explanation?"

Gesturing brusquely to the *fidai'in* to move out, she brushed past the annoyed mercenary and mounted Zephyr, the beautiful white Arabian mare being held for her by one of her men. She spurred her horse onward to merge with the line of bellowing camels and braying pack mules being urged into motion by her men, well aware that the mercenaries would have to scramble to come after them. Left to bring up the rear like this, Isabeau knew they'd be forced to eat her dust all the way down to the foothills below, and she took a certain grim pleasure in the knowledge. She'd have little else to cheer her up with de Navarre breathing down her neck!

Isabeau turned her back on the Black Lion, determined not to look at him again for the rest of the day—perhaps not even for the rest of the journey, if she could avoid it. Somehow, she doubted she would be so lucky.

Fuming with outrage at the Assassin's less-than-subtle insinuation that his mercenaries were dallying, when it was al-Zul who had—not once but twice!—forced him to wait upon his pleasure, Jared ground his teeth and swallowed the urge to throw the bundled cloth he held in his fist at the retreating head of his cursedly closemouthed employer. Though his questions were by no means answered, the mercenary found he had little choice but to collect his men, hurriedly break camp, and obey the Assassin's orders. But he did *not* have to like it—and his hot amber glare, burning into al-Zul's back, made it *quite* clear that he didn't.

All the way down the mountainside.

CHAPTER SEVEN

By Allah and all his blessed prophets, Isabeau thought irritably, *will that cursed mercenary* never *stop staring at me?*

She didn't need to look back at the warrior she'd hired to confirm what she already knew. Every step of every mile they'd traveled in the past five days, Jared de Navarre had followed her with his gaze, just as she instinctively knew he was still doing at this moment. He'd tracked her every move, stalking her with his eyes—almost, the Assassin thought uneasily, as if this fierce hunting lion sought to make her his prey!

They were more than halfway to Baghdad now, despite the difficulty of dragging their counterfeit caravan down through the rocky Elburz Mountain foothills and across the many miles that lay between them and that city. And yet still the mercenary would not cease his brooding observation of her. They'd passed silently through the rough, seamed and broken ground beyond the mountains where only the most desperate would attempt to eke out a living, and thence into more hospitable territory, all without cessation of the mercenary's darkling regard. They'd skirted small mud-brick villages and journeyed across a series of hilly, green-grassed goat pastures where the fodder for their beasts was plentiful; trekked past crystalline salt flats where the sun reflected stingingly off the crunchy ground and the wind covered them all with a fine coating of salty grit that seared the moisture from their lips and made their eyes water painfully. Still that sore, burning gaze had kept up its scrutiny.

They had then passed through the last of the arable lands between the Assassin's retreat and the invisible, ever-changing border of Sultan al-Kamil's dominion, and continued over a barren stretch of true Arabian desert, with

nothing but sand dunes and shimmering mirages to look at.
But Jared was not distracted by such chimeras, and his eyes
had remained fixed unwaveringly upon her, where the Assassin had mingled with the camel drivers in an effort to
make her presence as unobtrusive as possible—to her enemies, of course, she'd told herself, not to her faithless
former betrothed!

The caravan had for several days been following the
Great Silk Road used for centuries by traders to bring their
goods west from Persia, the savage lands of the Turks and
the Mongol hordes beyond it, and even far-off India and
China. These days, however—and fortunately to Isabeau's
mind—they were virtually alone in traveling the Silk Road,
since recent unrest between the power-hungry Mongols and
the Turks had made the easternmost peoples of the sultan's
empire leery of bringing their valuable goods to market
along this vulnerable route. Soon, she knew, they would be
arriving at more fertile lands again, and before they reached
their destination, they would come upon lush ground indeed, the most fruitful in all the sultan's domain. As the
poets said, Baghdad, fortuitously situated between the life-
giving Tigris and Euphrates rivers, was truly at the navel
of the world.

And once there, once they had flushed out Isabeau's enemy, perforce the mercenary de Navarre would no longer
dog her every footstep with that brooding glare of his. He'd
be too busy fighting for his life along with the rest of them,
the Assassin thought; for she knew full well that when they
reached their journey's end a most perilous battle awaited
them. Isabeau would welcome the challenge, as long as it
kept her from the Black Lion's glare!

Used to being invisible, to operating anonymously and
with utmost stealth, it was an unpleasant novelty for the
Shadow Hunter to ride out in the open and suffer the scrutiny of curious, suspicious men not sworn to her cause—
allies though these mercenaries and their leader nominally
were. Even the presence of the loyal *fidai'in* at her back
somehow failed to create a comfortingly substantial barrier

between the veiled Assassin and the warrior captain who so unnerved her.

By her orders, the Black Lion's men were positioned to guard the rear of their procession, and were situated well behind her own bandits, who posed as drivers and scouts at the front of the convoy. Jared, playing master of the caravan, rode at the back surrounded by a protective circle of his knights—but this positioning served as much to let the mercenary keep his eye on her, Isabeau suspected, as to obey her command that they keep up the illusion of being an ordinary trading expedition. Even when they camped for the night, the two rather antagonistic groups maintained a healthy distance from one another, and Isabeau always chose to put herself at the extreme limit of that span. Still, the renegade could feel Jared's presence all the time, day and night, as closely as if he were breathing his hot, angry breath upon the very nape of her neck.

They'd paused this evening, as they did five times daily without fail, for the faithful among them to worship, though they had no imam to guide their religious observance nor muezzin to lead the chant. Facing southeast, toward the holy city of Mecca, the faithful among them knelt and made obeisance. Even the mercenary's men, many of whom were Christian, respected the ritual; those who did not wish to pray simply took the opportunity to rest from the heat of the late-summer sun, eat of their rations, or quietly make repairs to their gear. Viscerally aware of him every bit as much as he seemed to be of her, the Assassin knew Jared himself was kneeling now at the back of the caravan among those of his men who observed the call, though Isabeau doubted he was worshipping any more than she was—not with the intensity of the glare he continued to direct at her back.

Despite the fact that she'd been forced to accept Islam while still in childhood and had rarely questioned the outward trappings of the faith since, Isabeau herself found it impossible today to think pious thoughts with that never-ending scrutiny always upon her. By the Prophet's holy thumb, it was enough to drive her mad! Her new pet lion hadn't taken well to her ultimatum that he ask no questions and follow docilely behind her disguised bandits without so much as knowing their destination for a certainty.

Though the Assassin was fairly confident he'd guessed they were heading for Baghdad from the hints she'd let drop during their initial meeting and from the direction of their travels so far, her impudent hireling seemed to think he was entitled to a much more thorough debriefing. He'd repeatedly tried to seek her out along the way and demand information, though she had refused to oblige him on all such occasions. *And he won't get anything out of me by intimidation either, glare though he may,* the Assassin thought angrily. *It's just too bad if that great cowardly cat fears to enter battle without the comfort of foreknowledge to soothe his nerves.*

Isabeau tried to ignore the tiny, niggling voice in her head that suggested de Navarre's request for further information was only prudent, the sign of a smart commander who took all the facts into consideration before he acted. She dismissed the annoying thought from her mind as curtly as she had dismissed and disregarded the Black Lion himself over the last five days, refusing to answer any of his questions except with the words, "All will become clear when the time is right. And the time, mercenary, **is** not yet right."

She'd known, though she'd tried to ignore the pricking of her conscience, that she was being infuriatingly cryptic. Yet, if anyone deserved to suffer a little discomfort and uncertainty, Isabeau consoled herself, surely it was de Navarre. After all, hadn't *she* spent far too long waiting and wondering in vain for *him,* never knowing . . . ?

The Assassin cut that perilous thought short with ruthless finality, turning her gaze toward the blood-red sun hanging low upon the horizon. Only a few hours remained before darkness fell, and the worst heat had already perished from the day. She stared blindly into the western sun until its crimson color filled her heart and mind as well as her vision with more suitable subjects for her to brood upon. *Vengeance,* she thought starkly. *Justice. Those are the only considerations I can afford.* If there was a prayer in her heart as she knelt among the others upon their woolen mats, it was that she would not forget this. But Isabeau found to her great dismay that it was only the Black Lion she could not put out of her mind.

What did he see, she wondered helplessly, watching her as closely as he did?

For some foolish reason, she simply couldn't stop picturing what might happen if she lifted the veil she'd hidden behind for so long and revealed herself to him. The impulse she'd felt that first day of their journey had not dissipated as she'd hoped it would, but rather had grown more and more pressing as the days went on. Bizarre as the desire was, Isabeau couldn't help wondering what Jared might do if she presented him with the truth of her identity. Thinking about it had become almost an obsession.

Would he be astonished at the sight? she wondered. Happy? Appalled, or even angry? Or would he perhaps be disappointed with the woman she had become?

In all likelihood, the man would not even recognize me, Isabeau told herself bluntly. After all, she bore little resemblance now to the little girl he'd lost these sixteen years past. And even if he did somehow know her for who she had been, it was ridiculous to think Jared might still want anything to do with her now. They had both changed so much . . .

What would I look like to Jared now, after so many years? Isabeau wondered a little wistfully. But the fact was, she herself was not even sure! The Assassin so seldom dared remove her disguise, even in the privacy of her own chambers deep within her mountain fortress, that she did not truly *know* how she appeared. As Sayyad al-Zul, she had developed so many reflexive methods for keeping her face and form hidden from others that she had effectively hidden them from herself as well.

Blond, she knew—hiding her cursedly bright hair had

always been one of the hardest things for her to do, until she had discovered how to braid its length into the folds of her turban or *kaffiyeh*. This was a practice that had proven even better than keeping it short, for it held her head coverings in place admirably well, and no Muslim man or woman would ever dream of pulling the turban from another when the *Qur'an* abjured all to keep their heads modestly covered.

Slender, too, and willowy, she knew. Her physique, though athletically well developed from years of exercise, was also unfortunately rather curvy. Neither the rigorous series of dance and acrobatic practices she'd endured as a pleasure slave in Malik's harem nor the grueling training regimen in the martial arts she'd adopted during her time with the Assassins' cult had managed to change that! Growing up, Isabeau had often prayed for small breasts or boyishly slender hips to detract attention from herself, but Allah had a funny way of ignoring certain prayers. Having grown reluctantly into her womanly shape, she had been forced to live day in and day out under a veil of secrecy, with tightly bound breasts and rounded hips and buttocks that could only be concealed by padding out her middle and wearing several enveloping layers of robes over all. She could barely imagine how she might look standing naked in her entirety, for she had rarely had the leisure or safety to take a good long look.

Even her face, Isabeau mused to herself, was really just a collection of foreign-seeming features she only glimpsed occasionally, reflected in a polished piece of armor or in the surface of the lonely, isolated pond in the mountains near her fortress home where she went to bathe and meditate. And she had done her best to disguise those rarely seen features from the world as well.

She knew her eyes were an unfortunately noticeable shade of blue, like those of the Norman knights who so presumptuously came East to carve out pieces of the Holy Land for themselves. She'd often wished in vain for normal, serviceable brown eyes that would draw no comment or curiosity. The best Isabeau could do was to alter their long, curly lashes and sandy, winged brows, and to that end, she'd taken to cropping the lashes short and darkening her eyebrows with a dye made of walnut juice, which she hoped would camouflage their too-fair and too-feminine appearance. Unfortunately, though, the stain only lasted a few weeks, and she was often forced to go without it on long missions when carrying the cosmetic was impractical. At such times, she merely tugged her *kaffiyeh* farther down upon her head until it nearly met her veil, leaving a bare inch of space between her nose and brow out of which to see. Though uncomfortable, it was better than the alternative of going unmasked, which was really no alternative at all. Her features were just too pale and foreign—and too obviously female—to bare before the world. Yet how did those features add up to a whole? Of that, the renegade was unsure.

Isabeau knew her nose was slim and straight, and that though it was without particular flaw, it did not conform to the strong, aquiline outline that was fashionable in the East. She knew that her lips were infuriatingly, girlishly pink, her skin tellingly fair, and her cheeks still maiden-soft, though somehow it always surprised her to see any of these inconveniently delicate features and realize they were her own. Even her hands and feet were too damned small to pass easily for a man's—though thankfully her hands at least were saved from being called dainty by their rough calluses and the scarred missing portion of the smallest digit on her right hand.

She knew what these pieces of her collective whole looked like, strewn out like a tinker's goods all tumbled together in her mind. But what Isabeau's critical self-inventory didn't tell her, and what she wanted to know now for the very first time in her life, was whether or not she was *pretty*.

The question, so steeped in feminine insecurity, terrified the ruthless Assassin.

*   *   *

Why can't al-Zul lead his own blasted caravan? Jared wondered angrily as he watched the distant Assassin kneeling in prayer near the front of the long cortege. The reputedly cold-blooded killer showed every evidence of serenity as he worshipped a God the mercenary himself had long ago ceased to believe in. Jared, however, felt anything but serene as he observed his aggravating employer's devotions.

The renegade was clearly a competent leader, he thought, if his men's tight-knit cooperation and obvious loyalty during the journey so far were anything to go by. So why had he chosen to hire another man to head up this ostensible "trading" mission of his, instead of taking on the role of commander himself? It made no sense to Jared. Why would Sayyad choose to hide among his men, a mere anonymous member of the crowd? He'd even permitted—*ordered* was more like it—Jared to give all the instructions concerning the day-to-day running of the caravan to both groups of fighters, effectively turning control of his own bandits as well as Jared's mercenaries over to the Black Lion.

Sayyad was keeping only their destination and true purpose as his own province. But those were no small things to hold back, the irate mercenary thought. Why would he not at least confide *where* they were going, if not what they sought to accomplish once they'd arrived? As a hired sword, de Navarre preferred to deal with certainties, things he could see and touch and understand. Cold steel, hard facts—that was what had kept him alive all these years. None of this bloody mysticism and equivocation al-Zul was forever throwing his way.

By Christ's blessed wounds, I feel like a fool in this getup, Jared thought, flapping the wide sleeves of his voluminous silk robe irritably out of his way as he knelt upon a woolen mat spread out in the sand. There was no one to see them anyway, so why not prance about naked if they bloody well felt like it? They'd passed no one but goatherds and simple farmers since they'd left the mountains days ago. For whom were they maintaining this absurd pretense?

The unanswered questions continuously hounded the Black Lion, even as he'd hounded his mysterious employer these last five days with his baleful glare, hoping to drive the infuriatingly uninformative Assassin into speech. It hadn't worked so far, Jared had to admit. Sayyad had ignored all of Jared's inquiries, had dismissed his concerns, and indeed, had evaded nearly all contact with the mercenary altogether to date on this journey. So Jared was still acting as ringmaster of this bizarre desert circus, and he still had no idea why. With so little information at hand, there was no way for Jared or the other mercenaries to anticipate what dangers might lie ahead, and thus no way for them to prepare for what they would face when they arrived.

This, his men grumbled—and Jared privately agreed— was no way to conduct a civilized war.

Only for their captain would these jaded warriors go against their better judgment and commit themselves blindly to a battle not their own. And Jared would never ask them for such a commitment unless he believed the benefits outweighed the risks. He might play fast and loose with his own safety, recklessly throwing himself into the hellish fields of war time and time again to drive away the demons of regret and remorse that plagued his soul, but he would never be so careless with the men under his command.

Looking into Sayyad al-Zul's fervid eyes during that first confrontation, he'd seen something that had made him believe he should accept the Assassin's coin and take on his mysterious mission despite the unanswered questions that remained. That afternoon he'd sensed that, like himself, al-Zul played the game of war only to win. But over the past several days, Jared had begun to wonder if he had not committed himself and his men too hastily to this callous killer's cause.

How many lives, he wondered, would the Assassin willingly sacrifice in order to succeed? Without knowing the man's plans, he couldn't be sure just how recklessly al-Zul

played with all of their fates. Though he'd expected Sayyad
to distrust them—for what sane man would trust a band of
warriors who sold their loyalty along with their swords to
earn their daily bread?—he had not anticipated the extent
of the man's secretiveness. The Assassin had effectively
blindfolded and disarmed them, and Jared's men did not
like it any more than their leader did. By refusing to even
acknowledge the validity of their leader's questions, al-Zul
had effectively treated the men of the mercenary troop like
. . . like lackeys, Jared thought heatedly; mere pawns to use
and dispose of as he chose. Well, hired help he might be,
the Black Lion decided, but he was not going to blindly
follow this enigmatic maniac's orders another minute. To
hell with this ridiculous secrecy and furtiveness of Sayyad's. He'd had enough!

As the Muslim ritual ended and the men began to roll
up their prayer rugs, Jared made up his mind to confront
his mystery-loving employer and force the truth out of him.
He got up from his knees and started toward Sayyad purposefully.

"Al-Zul," he challenged gruffly as he passed through the
last of the renegade's men and reached his quarry's side.
He saw the slight Assassin's back go rigid. So swiftly he
could barely follow the fluid motion, Sayyad al-Zul rose to
his feet and faced him. The very speed of his conditioned
reaction reminded Jared of how deadly this man was known
to be, even as, above the ever-present veil, hard blue eyes
colder than winter ice bored into his own. Jared forced himself to stand his ground.

"De Navarre." The Shadow Hunter responded evenly
enough, though sarcasm was evident to Jared in the way
Sayyad returned the disrespectful tone of the address. "Is
there something you require?" The tiny sigh that followed
the Assassin's slightly whispery intonation gave the im-
pression of a man put-upon by some tiresome menial who
could not perform even the simplest chore without constant
oversight.

Jared was having none of it. "Hell, yes, there's something I require!" he growled furiously. "I require answers, damn it, and I won't be put off any longer. My men are beginning to chafe at all this secrecy. They want to know why you've got them decked out like a pasha's pet body-guards when you've plainly got muscle enough of your own with those rabid bandits you've disguised to look like helpless desert traders. The *fidai'in* follow you like dogs panting constantly at your heels, eager as pups to defend their master. Why not let them? And while you're at it, you'd do well to explain why you've passed yourself off as a mere camel driver while you've got *me* all tarted up for the world to admire like some damn fool of a merchant with more style than common sense." Jared gestured angrily to indicate his ornate robes. "If there were anyone but the buzzards around to see us, I'd think you were hiding beneath that disguise, afraid to be seen," he taunted.

The mercenary waited to see what sort of reaction that would get from the touchy Shadow Hunter. But though the renegade's blue eyes glowed with sapphire fire, the veiled Assassin did not rise to the bait. "Sometimes," the gravelly voice said softly, "it is better not to be observed, even by the birds in the skies. Buzzards have keen eyes indeed, mercenary, but there are other desert scavengers yet more eager to pass the news of our coming to my enemies. Better one mercenary think me a coward in disguise," the renegade said contemptuously, "than that I herald our proud approach before the world like the veriest of fools."

The man's paranoia was unbelievable, Jared thought incredulously. He was seeing spies behind every dune! But did al-Zul have cause to suspect such close surveillance, or was he merely the madman some claimed? He wasn't sure yet, but for now he decided to humor the man. Jared continued more calmly, hoping he sounded reasonable to Sayyad. "My warriors want to know what's going on, al-Zul, and so do I."

"Well, then, you'd better set a good example for them and learn to curb your curiosity, de Navarre." Al-Zul's tone was one of utmost reasonability, but the renegade's furious glare belied the cool statement. "If you can't exert control over your men, mercenary, then you're of no use to me at all. I assumed I was hiring professionals when I took your troop into my employ. Was I wrong in that assumption?" the Assassin asked acidly.

"Nay." Jared denied the accusation. "But it is not unprofessional to want to know what we're up against, and who, and *where* we'll be up against it!" He fought the urge to reach down and grab the front of the slight Assassin's robe, shaking him until the truth was jarred loose. Seeing Sayyad's eyes narrow at the slight, instinctive movement he made before he could check the impulse, he knew he'd risk pulling back a bloody stump if he dared such aggressive action. The renegade's small, oddly delicate-looking hand had reached defensively for the dagger at his belt almost before Jared finished the thought of laying hands on him. But though he would have relished the candor of a fair fight to settle matters between them, the Black Lion didn't think it wise to engage in open warfare with his employer quite yet, and so he made no further move to test the Assassin's quick reflexes. Not that he wasn't tempted, damn it. Sayyad al-Zul had to be the most frustrating, infuriating person he'd ever met!

"You will learn all you need know when the time is right. And the time, mercenary, is not yet right." Sayyad reiterated the tiresome refrain stubbornly, and Jared nearly changed his mind about laying hands upon the aggravating Assassin. Instead, however, he simply gritted his teeth and took a calming breath.

"You realize you are compromising my ability to mount an effective defense by handicapping me in this manner, do you not? And any offensive action you intend to take would be far more likely to succeed if we worked together on our strategy." He tried to use reason to reach the stubborn renegade.

"I agree," Sayyad said mildly.

"Then why will you not explain—" he began.

"I intend to, Black Lion," the Assassin interrupted, still

speaking as though surprised at an annoying employee who was being unreasonable.

"Well, what are you waiting for, then? When do you plan to reveal this mysterious mission of yours?" But Jared knew he'd set himself up for the answer before the other man smugly gave it.

"When the time is right." Al-Zul turned away and reached for the reins of the magnificent white Arabian one of the *fidai'in* had brought up as they spoke. The Assassin put one foot in the stirrup and leapt lithely into the saddle.

If the others hadn't also ridden beautiful beasts similar to it (a gift given to the bandits by the local Bedouin breeders in lieu of tribute, Jared had learned), the valuable mare would have set Sayyad apart. As it was, only the Assassin's commanding seat upon the horse made him stand out among the other superbly mounted desert outlaws. He looked to have been born in the saddle.

"When the time is right," the renegade assured him once more, "I will reveal all you need know. Until then, mercenary, cease plaguing me with these incessant queries of yours. If you do not," al-Zul finished warningly, "you may soon find cause to regret your wagging tongue."

And before Jared could challenge this threat, Sayyad had touched soft-booted heels to the mare's flanks and sent her into a gallop that threw sand out in a wide arc behind her, leaving Jared spitting grit and cursing the Assassin's name to the darkest realms of the netherworld.

Not for the first time, and not for the last time, he feared.

CHAPTER EIGHT

By the Prophet's very beard, I cannot believe I ran from him! Isabeau thought incredulously as she leaned forward over her saddlebow a half hour later, panting from the hard gallop she and Zephyr had just finished. *I abandoned my own campsite—in front of all my men, no less,* she marveled, *just to avoid confronting a man who was once the most adored companion of my childhood!* The knowledge made her feel nauseous. Isabeau patted the mare's sweaty neck, not sure who needed the reassurance more, herself or her horse. Beneath her veil, she scowled blackly.

Grown men had been known to faint at the mere rumor of her approach, and yet Isabeau de Lyon, known before all the world as the dreaded Shadow Hunter, an Assassin out of legend, bane of the mighty, and darkest nightmare of her enemies, had fled like the veriest peasant half-wit at the first sign of trouble, just to get away from a man supposedly in her own employ!

As she soothed her already calm horse with hands that still trembled slightly, Isabeau told herself she'd turned and ridden away solely because she still needed de Navarre, and the men who followed him, alive. She told herself she'd left because the Black Lion didn't deserve that strong masculine throat of his slit and his cursedly handsome head handed to him on a platter, simply for expressing his frustration. But in her heart, the Assassin knew expediency had had nothing to do with her impulsive action. The sad truth was, she'd run because the idea of engaging in hand-to-hand combat with Jared had brought images to mind that had precious little to do with blood and death.

Taking her hands to his flesh would have been disturbing, yes, but it hadn't been squeamishness that had troubled the Assassin enough to make her turn tail and ride away less than an hour ago. Nay. Her true aversion to the mercenary's proximity had had an altogether different quality to it—a quality Isabeau wasn't comfortable naming even in the privacy of her mind. All she was willing to admit, even to herself, was that she felt safer with the Black Lion at a healthy distance. Still, although Isabeau wished it was purely a matter of disgust, though she longed simply to hate Jared, she had already found she could not.

She'd wanted to despise him for a coward—a craven, base-hearted knave—and it would have been so much easier if she could have. But Isabeau had eyes to see, and she had not been able to deny the evidence put before them these last several days. Jared was no crass soldier of fortune, but a shrewd, adaptable leader who cared for the well-being of his men even beyond his own. Despite herself, she'd been impressed. She'd seen the loyalty of his troops—odd lot though they were—and could recognize as well the excellent condition they were in. No doubt Jared's compulsory daily training bouts had been the cause of that, she thought with grudging respect. Those men would follow him to hell and beyond if he asked it of them. One had only to watch them drill with their commander to see it.

Each evening, when most would be eager only to rest and eat, the men of the Black Lion's Pride—a name she found appropriate though she pretended outwardly to sneer at it—stopped only long enough to make camp before beginning a series of sparring matches designed to keep them in fine form for battle. After a few days of observing this, even her own initially derisive bandits had asked if they might adopt the practice, not wanting to seem lazy or undisciplined by comparison to the mercenaries.

Jared de Navarre, she admitted grudgingly now as she stared sightlessly at the windswept dunes before her, was everything she had hoped the Black Lion would be. He was bold, strong, and true. He had the respect of his own men, and was fast gaining that of hers as well. She knew the mercenary would speed them all to victory when the time came, if only fate was on their side.

Nay. His suitability for the mission ahead was not the problem. It was her own foolish reactions to that eminently masculine competence he exuded that had led Isabeau to this present turn of events. Much as she'd wanted to dismiss her once-betrothed as a man without honor or valor, a worthless cur, Isabeau could not do so, and it was that, more than anything else, which frightened her. She could not afford to like the Black Lion, or—dear God!—to find herself drawn to the man. Such folly could prove fatal, not only to herself but to those whose lives she held in trust.

Especially Zahra, the Assassin thought with a surge of guilt. *If my dear jewel is to be rescued, she'll need a savior who won't lose her head like a fanciful maiden over the mere preening and flexing of some handsome cavalier—no matter what connection she shared with him in the past.*

She must think only of Jared's usefulness as a warrior, Isabeau told herself firmly now. Not his intimidating masculinity or the bright light of intelligence in his golden eyes. There must be no more of the maudlin imaginings or feminine vapors that seemed to overcome her lately every time she came within ten feet of the man. And lest she risk losing the respect of her own men, the authority she had worked so hard to wield over those ferociously independent outlaws, she must start proving herself every bit as strong as her mercenary hireling immediately. She must not fear to challenge him in future, nor quail before his innate aura of command. After all, Isabeau reminded herself, Jared had shown no qualms about confronting *her.* Indeed, the maddening mercenary seemed almost to relish their confrontations!

Still, she knew that if Jared plagued her for answers about their mission, it was only because he felt obliged to for the sake of his warriors. It was for their well-being that he took so many precautions, not his own. There was a bleak sort of recklessness about him, familiar to the renegade Assassin only because she shared it herself. Recognizing it, Isabeau instinctively sensed that if it had been only himself at stake, the Black Lion would have ridden without fear or hesitation into the very maw of perdition if it stood between him and what he sought.

Once again Jamal's question rang in her mind. *What does such a man seek?* But the Assassin felt almost afraid to discover the answer.

As she turned her horse back to the camp she knew the men would have pitched in her absence, Isabeau reflected that since her betrothed's unexpected reentry into her life, none of her thoughts had been comfortable ones. She suspected she would never feel at peace again until Jared de Navarre was out of her life for good.

* * *

And certainly I won't if the man keeps going around without a shirt on! she thought a few moments later. A decidedly uneasy flutter crept into Isabeau's stomach as she took in the tableau playing itself out before her.

Having reached the perimeter of the camp her warriors had set up with the aid of their hired brethren, Isabeau pulled Zephyr up sharply at the sight that greeted her eyes. The sun was at the very edge of the horizon now, and its reddish rays seemed to bathe everything with an infernal glow, including the two men within the sandy circle that had been drawn to mark the perimeter of tonight's practice field.

Both men gleamed with perspiration from their efforts, but Isabeau barely noticed the blond Nordic giant who faced the Black Lion in the ring. Nor did she take more than a cursory interest in the men who gathered about Jared de Navarre and the other knight—a man called Harald, if memory served aright—although part of her brain remained alert enough to acknowledge the avid interest her bandits paid to the contest. Sitting stock-still atop her mare, riveted by the scene in front of her, the Assassin could do little more than watch alongside the rest.

Bared to the waist, Jared de Navarre was a striking sight indeed.

His longsword balanced horizontally above his head, the exquisitely defined muscles of his arms and shoulders bulg-

ing as he held it perfectly still, poised to strike, his stance
was both confident and careful. His strong, muscular legs
were braced wide apart in their loose silk trousers, which,
sweat-dampened, clung indecently to the lines of his hard
thighs and buttocks. The balls of his feet took his weight
evenly as he shifted with catlike grace, and each sinew and
muscle group seemed to beg for his slightest command,
eager to oblige. Clearly in his element, a naturally feral
smile of enjoyment split the mercenary's darkly tanned face
as Jared circled his opponent.

The Black Lion, Isabeau thought involuntarily, was the
perfect image of a warrior. His reflexes were instantaneous.
His instincts were dead-on. And his strength was more than
impressive. Watching him circle his opponent, the Assassin
doubted even she could have bested him with that sword.

The Norseman had best make peace with his gods, she
decided, watching the burly blond knight brace his own
blade hopefully against his commander's inevitable attack.
But as she'd suspected, it was no use. With a dazzlingly
swift maneuver that sent flares of dying sunlight down the
length of his sword, Jared spun about, catching Harald's
blade and binding it with his own. Faster than the eye could
follow, the polished steel was stripped from the Norseman's
hands, arcing over his head to land quivering outside the
circle, almost at Zephyr's feet.

The mare, trained for battle, shied only a step or two
and calmed quickly under the Assassin's hand. Isabeau,
however, was not as quick to relax. Her heartbeat pounded
in her ears, her throat dried to dust, and her palms grew
clammy on the reins. He was brilliant indeed with that
blade, she acknowledged reluctantly, moving as though his
whole body were liquid steel, and the sword but an extension of his will. The mercenaries—and no few of the bandits as well, Isabeau noticed, had begun to clap and cheer
in appreciation of Jared's masterful move. To hide the nervous tremors of her own fingers, she applauded along with
the others, though she stayed well out of the circle of ap-
preciative men ringing the two combatants. Even the de-

feated Harald was grinning, she saw, theatrically shaking out his hand as if to reduce the shock of the blow. "Gets me every time," he grumbled good-naturedly into his long, plaited mustaches as the applause began to die down.

But the renegade's tough, slender hands continued to clap.

Slowly.

Deliberately.

Mockingly.

A hush fell upon the two groups of warriors at the sound, and all turned their eyes toward the returned Assassin as she threw one leg over Zephyr's saddle and slid smoothly to the ground. Jared, she saw, grew still inside the circle, his back stiffening for a brief moment before he turned to face the scornful sounds she made. Still the renegade continued her sarcastic ovation. She'd show the mercenary just how little his exhibition had impressed her. It was the only way to prove herself his match after the embarrassment of their earlier confrontation!

Jared bowed with equal irony in response, then straightened and slid his long steel blade home in the sheath that was strapped across one magnificently bared shoulder. "The show was not quite to your taste, al-Zul?" he inquired politely. "Perhaps you'd like to give us a better one?"

Of course, the ever-irritable Assassin *would* come and ruin the one simple pleasure he'd enjoyed this day, Jared thought with a tinge of annoyance. Sayyad always seemed ready with a goad or a taunt to cut him down to size just when he was in a pleasant mood. If he didn't know better, he'd think al-Zul pushed him to the limits of his patience purposely! *First he keeps information from me, then he leaves me standing in a cloud of his dust—which he's done not once but twice now!* Jared reminded himself angrily. *And now he returns with this obnoxious attitude to crown the day off just perfectly. That little robed runt is really asking for a fight,* he seethed. Exasperation was fast replacing his earlier cheer.

"Ah, I would be pleased to demonstrate how a real warrior fights, if only there were a worthy opponent at hand," the Assassin quipped in return.

Isabeau kept her voice at its usual low pitch, though she found herself feeling strangely breathless. She saw that Jared was hardly winded from his bout with his Nordic comrade, breathing slowly and evenly in contrast to her own rapid respiration. Watching the rise and fall of that broad, lightly furred chest was doing strange things to her pulse rate as well as her breathing, Isabeau noticed. She felt the sudden urge to flee again.

Don't back off this time! she ordered herself harshly. *Remember your vow. You must treat this man like any other; for the Shadow Hunter would never run from such a challenge. De Navarre must be made to see I do not fear him. Indeed,* he *must be taught to fear me.*

She stiffened her spine and stared the mercenary straight in the eye.

And nearly quailed at the knowing stare he returned.

Laughter was ripe in those golden eyes—and then briefly, as the merriment faded, she felt the presence of something else in them as well. She didn't know quite how to qualify it—Isabeau could identify the feeling only as an animal awareness so deep and instinctual it made her tremble with sudden fear. But no; fear didn't exactly describe the sensation, Isabeau thought dizzily. Perhaps *anticipation* was a better word for how she felt, or even some nameless state in between the two. He just seemed so . . . so *attuned* to her all of a sudden. It was as if Jared had seen right through her disguise and discovered the woman beneath. It was impossible, and yet despite the years the mercenary seemed almost to recognize his betrothed beneath the careful façade Isabeau had erected to protect her identity. She had to blink and look away for a moment even though she'd resolved not to shrink from the Black Lion.

Suddenly, inexplicably disconcerted, Jared forced himself to break eye contact with the Assassin, so unnerved he did not notice that the other looked away at the same time. For a moment there, he'd had the strangest sensation. Almost as if he had *known* al-Zul; as if he could see beneath the veils and recognize some hidden facet of the Assassin's nature that was beyond his own conscious awareness, some incredible secret lurking behind the fierce blue eyes and quick temper. Jared felt disoriented, and to cover it he spoke more flippantly than he'd intended.

"Well, normally I'd offer to find you an opponent more your own size, al-Zul, but it looks like Big Pierre is occupied at the moment."

Always quick to sense insult, Pierre looked up from the bag of rations he'd been rummaging in at the sound of his name, a large pomegranate forgotten in one hand as he scowled at his commander. He offered Jared an amazingly inventive rude gesture involving both arms, one leg, and his tongue, but did not deign to offer a verbal rejoinder. De Navarre merely smiled a bland, tolerant smile at his lieutenant in return and offered back a simpler gesture that mutely told the little man where he could dispose of his crudity.

Neither man seemed to find anything unusual about the byplay, but Isabeau sneered behind her veil at the sight of such blatant insubordination. In truth, the Assassin was glad to have something to focus on besides the Black Lion's disturbing scrutiny, even for a moment. How could anyone maintain order with such an insolent court jester always at his heels? she wondered derisively. Though she'd reserved judgment on the mercenary's diminutive second-in-command in the past, in her current state of agitation it seemed natural to take the little man's liberties as a sign of Jared's poor leadership and generally lax discipline. There would be no room for such clowning about when the time came for them to engage the enemy, she thought hotly. He'd best remember that. It was time to wipe that silly smirk from the warrior's well-sculpted lips.

"Though I'm sure your pet dwarf would prove the more worthy opponent, mercenary," she snapped back, "I'll settle for you." The blood began to race through the Assassin's veins in anticipation of a fight. Oh, how she would relish cutting this insolent jackanapes down to size!

"All right, then," Jared said mildly. Rather than fearing the renegade's challenge, the mercenary welcomed the chance to test his mettle, curious to see this "legend" in action. "I'm happy to oblige, of course. But what say we make the match a bit more interesting for me, Sayyad? It hardly seems worth the effort of getting my hands dirty with your scrawny self otherwise."

"How do you suggest we do that, O noble Lion's Breath?" the Shadow Hunter queried with silken contempt. Then, unable to contain her ire, she added, "Somehow it doesn't surprise me that you would not deign to raise a paw over so trifling a matter as defending your honor if it threatens to disturb your lazy catnapping." Isabeau was getting angrier by the minute, though she tried to hold her temper at bay. The plan was to defeat the mercenary, she reminded herself, not play right into his hands! "But of course, for gain it is another matter," she continued tauntingly. "For gain, a man like you is always ready to raise his banner and roar like the king of beasts. So tell me, hired sword, what reward do you have in mind this time?"

If al-Zul was looking to get a rise out of the Black Lion, the Assassin had failed with these pointed barbs. Jared had long ago accepted that men would assume his honor could be as cheaply bought as his weapons. It was the way of mercenaries, after all. And in truth, Jared could not dispute the charge applied to him as well as it did to any other hired soldier. Any claim to righteousness he'd had, had been lost in a moment of carelessness more than a decade and a half ago, and he had become resigned to the bleak fact that it stood precious little chance of ever being regained. What had been lost to him was lost forever, he thought grimly, well before he'd ever met Sayyad al-Zul. Yet it irked the Black Lion that this cold-blooded Assassin should so boldly throw about a word like *honor* when the man himself shamelessly pursued the only occupation more ignoble than Jared's own.

At least when Jared fought, it was face to face, man to

man, with equal odds for each combatant. Could this "Shadow Hunter" who sought his prey slinking through the darkness with a garrote or a blade up his sleeve claim as much? Jared didn't think so. But he would not point this out to Sayyad, a man for whom reason clearly took second place to umbrage. Instead he decided to take out his satisfaction for the man's insult not on the Assassin's purse, as the man clearly presumed he would, but in his embarrassment before the bandits he led.

"It's no great matter I propose, O stunted Shadow Stalker," Jared smiled nastily. "I merely suggest that if you want to fight me, you'll agree to a small wager to raise the stakes. No money need change hands this time—I believe I'm already walking away with enough of your fine gold to satisfy even the most avaricious of mercenaries. Instead, al-Zul, I propose an exchange of promises, hazarded upon the outcome of our duel. I shall want you to reveal a certain secret if I win. If I lose, on the other hand, I will swear to leave your privacy intact and seek no further answers to those questions with which you claim I so incessantly plague you."

The Assassin forced herself to ignore the Black Lion's taunts, much as they pricked her already mounting ire. The man was tricky, damn him, and if she lost her temper, she might fail to sense whatever trap the cunning warrior was surely building for her. Yet to have him cease his constant staring and nagging queries—to have him leave her *alone* for even a few days—it might be worth it! She needed the time to focus on the endgame that was so vitally important now.

"What is this secret you wish to know?" Isabeau asked the question harshly, expecting that the mercenary would demand to know her plans for the battle ahead. But his reply stunned her with its utter, unapologetic presumptuousness.

"If I win, al-Zul, I want to see your face."

Behind her, an audible gasp was heard from the *fidai'in* at the Black Lion's audacity. Not even they had seen the

Shadow Hunter without the veil that protected the infamous
killer's countenance from the view of ordinary men! Indeed, it had become part of Sayyad's legend that the Assassin's own men held him in such fearful reverence that
none had ever dared to gaze upon his visage. For this hired
mercenary to suggest such terms in a wager was impudence
indeed!

The bandits in their civilian disguises milled about the
practice circle uncomfortably, fingering hidden weapons,
even as de Navarre's men crowded closer in anticipation
of the fight sure to come. Once again the two bands seemed
clearly on the brink of outright brawling. Only the prospect
of seeing their commanders settle the matter between them
kept the men from crossing the line into open warfare now,
and both of their leaders knew it. There could be no backing down at this stage.

"You won't win," Isabeau managed to say through gritted teeth. Fear and fury warred within her. She could do
no more than seethe at the Black Lion's arrogance, even as
she felt the terror of possible exposure coming over her
again as it had so repeatedly since Jared de Navarre had
found his cursed way back into her life.

"Then there's no harm in agreeing to the bet, is there?"
Jared asked. He posed the question quite reasonably,
though he knew his actions amounted to no better than
baiting the Assassin. Though admittedly fed up with Sayyad's arrogance and his mysterious ways, the mercenary
found himself rather surprised by the terms of his own proposed wager. What had made him say he wanted to see the
Assassin's face? It would have been much more sensible
to ask the man to reveal their destination or their mission.
Yet suddenly he'd found himself consumed with the need
to know what lay behind Sayyad al-Zul's many layers of
disguise, and the words had fairly left his mouth of their
own accord before he could call them back and request
something more practical.

Well, it was too late to take it back now, Jared thought
with a mental shrug. "Do you agree, or are you too vain—

or cowardly—to risk showing your face to me?" It was the second time he'd taunted the renegade with cowardice, and this time he got the reaction he was looking for.

"Curse you, mercenary. No one may hope to live who questions the Shadow Hunter's courage twice in a single day!"

All of a sudden, Isabeau found she had lost every last bit of her restraint. One moment she was under control, her usual icy self-discipline in place despite the anger boiling in her gut. The next, her temper was completely and utterly gone; vanquished like a shadow before the sun.

She wanted to do damage, and she wanted to do it *now*.

Isabeau's highly trained reflexes went on full alert, her senses screamed with sudden acuteness, adrenaline rushing through her veins until reason was drowned out beneath the deluge. Like a cornered animal, she went on the attack. *Kill or be discovered,* her brain advised her. *Bring the mercenary down before he can reveal your secret to the world.* She went into a reflexive crouch, the tiny, deadly-sharp knife she carried tucked inside one sleeve drawn before either group of warriors standing on the sidelines could react.

The men began to mutter among themselves, shifting nervously, not sure whether to back their respective masters or stay out of the fight. Knowing her men would prevent any treachery on the part of the hired fighters, Isabeau ignored them, focusing only on the mercenary captain who was her target. Sizing him up, she thought only of the fastest way to bring the agile warrior down to the ground. Down where he could be destroyed.

Despite his surprise at the Assassin's sudden attack stance, Jared instantly met Sayyad's defensive posture with one of his own. *What does the fool think he's doing?* he thought incredulously. *I can't believe he's really taking me up on this—and with only that puny knife for a weapon? It's ridiculous. Al-Zul may be an Assassin by trade, but I'm twice his size and I've got half again his reach—not to mention twenty years of combat under my belt. The man's a lunatic!* He shrugged his longsword in its scabbard off over his shoulder, tossing it down outside the ring and drawing his own short-range dagger in preparation for close assault. Yet, as he'd anticipated, the fight was over almost before it began.

He hadn't, however, anticipated the outcome.

I've only one chance. That much Isabeau knew deep in her bones. *I must strike hard, strike fast. And by the Prophet, touch that sleek golden flesh of his as little as possible!*

The renegade drew upon the years of relentless training that had made her such a successful protégée of the Assassins' cult master. As he had taught her, she marshaled her body's raging energies, drawing them into the center of her being, forming herself into a living lightning rod of raw power. And then she let loose the lightning in a move so swift and pitilessly accurate that the vision of the spectators blurred trying to follow it. Between one heartbeat and the next she had gone from poised crouch to completed maneuver.

The Assassin was there one minute, gone the next. But gone *where?* Jared had only a split second to register the fact that the black-robed figure had left the ground, flipped high in the air *right over his head* and landed lightly in the sand behind him. Before he could so much as yell out his surprise, the Black Lion had found himself pounced upon, his throat caught in the unbreakable grip of one ruthless arm, his legs kicked out from beneath him with one powerful sweep of his opponent's leg, and himself beginning to go over backward—hard. Though the veteran of innumerable street fights and close-range combat encounters, Jared found he had no defense against what he was up against now. It was as if some supernatural force had taken over the slight Assassin he had until now believed to be thoroughly human.

While he was still reeling with shock at the swiftness of the attack, the world revolved itself ninety degrees, flinging him at great speed from vertical to horizontal, flat on his back. The air whooshed out of Jared's lungs as he hit the sand with a dull thud, and he found he could barely swallow through the sudden obstruction pressing at his throat.

Al-Zul's foot, he realized. The surprisingly diminutive boot compressing his windpipe seemed to have small respect for his need to breathe. Nor did the wickedly sharp little knife that pressed itself beneath his ear seem much more considerate. Indeed, it appeared ghoulishly eager to find its way across his neck and make acquaintance with his other ear.

"Gah," said Jared, expressing his feelings adequately if not eloquently. It would have to do, the mercenary decided, as he didn't think he was capable of much greater articulation at the moment. He was too busy trying not to die.

What had happened was undeniable. He'd been bested—as he had not since the days of his youthful training as a squire—and lay now at the uncertain mercy of his volatile opponent. Unbelievable as it seemed to the Black Lion, he had lost both the wager and the fight, without ever landing a blow. He looked up at the furious Assassin silhouetted against the dying sun, sensing the man sought to master himself, to rein in the blood lust that had overtaken him.

And at last, Jared took in the full measure of his employer's capabilities. For the first time, he truly believed al-Zul could kill at a whim, without pity or remorse. Looking into the coldly furious blue eyes that burned above the ever-present veil, Jared was forced to admit that his best hope for survival lay in the renegade's ability to check himself, and not in anything he himself could do in defense of his hide. With the knife pressed so close to his jugular, he was all out of options.

Isabeau stared down at the man she held at her mercy. Emotion, never her ally, felt ready to overcome her utterly now. Rage, battle fever, and a sudden, wholly unanticipated jolt of pure anguish mingled in her breast as the fury of blame and recrimination she had thought long dead in her surged to the surface all at once. Swamped with too many

emotions to bear, she glared at Jared but saw only her own
pain.

You deserve to die! she screamed soundlessly; her heart
aching from old wounds that had festered far too long. As
she held her blade against his vulnerable, pulsing artery,
the accusations swirled through Isabeau's mind in a mael-
strom of reproach and condemnation. *You failed me. You
betrayed me.*

You abandoned *me.*

The unexpected emergence of that mindless, childish re-
monstration froze Isabeau in place. Where had *that* come
from? the renegade asked herself in shock. For one long,
breathless moment, she found herself wanting nothing more
than to finish the job she had begun, watering the dunes
with the blood of her once-betrothed. Yet in the next, she
felt the even stronger urge to toss her blade away into the
sandy wastes, fling herself upon Jared's wide, manly chest,
and beg for consolation in his arms.

Confusion made a muddle of her thoughts as she stared
into his rugged features, strained from the effort of evading
the knife she held at his throat. Logically, Isabeau knew
the mercenary was no more to blame for her misfortune
than she had been herself, but to the little girl who'd idolized and trusted Jared de Navarre, logic had played little
part in the resentment she had harbored for him over the
years. It had been either hate him, or hate herself! Now,
she did not know which to do.

Though she held the blade, Isabeau became aware in that
moment that Jared was the victor in this contest between
them, and she the one at his command. Yet she must not
let him sense it. *Get a hold of yourself, damn it,* Isabeau
ordered herself harshly. *Get your mind out of the past and
focus on the present! You need this man, remember?
Zahra's fate depends upon his aid, whether you like it or
not. You cannot risk her safety on the whims of your hot
temper!* Expelling a deep breath, the Assassin slowly regained a grasp on her passions.

"Hardly worth the effort," Isabeau said at last, mocking

Jared's earlier words though she felt anything but triumphant. Drained was more like it. Contemptuously, she removed her boot from the mercenary's Adam's apple and turned away from him in disgust. Sighting on the dark, purplish-red fruit still held suspended in the shocked dwarf's palm, she flung the tiny dagger at the pomegranate.

Big Pierre yelled in surprise and shook his hand, dropping the fruit. He looked at his offended appendage, then at the sandy pomegranate at his feet, and finally up at the Assassin in confusion, for both he *and* the treat he'd meant to have for his dessert seemed unscathed, yet he had felt the shock of impact.

Jared had risen to his feet meanwhile, ruefully rubbing his bruised throat. "Looks like you missed, Sayyad," he said, infusing smugness into his tone to cover his complete consternation. He still couldn't believe how easily the man had thrown him! The mercenary had never seen a move like the one al-Zul had used on him, and he was torn between being furious and wanting to ask the Assassin to show him how it had been done.

"Did I?" Isabeau asked disinterestedly. She'd gotten a lock on her emotions at last, and she merely felt weary now. She'd accomplished what she'd set out to prove. In the eyes of the men she led, she still reigned supreme. Her legend, instead of being diminished by the mercenary's challenge, would only grow after this seemingly effortless victory. But the Shadow Hunter knew the true toll of their latest encounter had only begun to be counted. She had a feeling that the repercussions of this evening's events would continue to haunt her for a long time to come. "Well, perhaps I did miss, mercenary," she conceded, sounding as if she didn't give a damn. "But all the same, were I you, I'd advise my diminutive friend to be careful how he eats his supper tonight."

And with that she turned her back and pushed her way through the silent, gaping mercenaries and the jubilant *fidai'in*, who offered congratulatory slaps on the back to their leader as she passed. The renegade forced herself to maintain an insouciant pace as she strolled away toward the other side of camp, though inwardly she felt like running once again, as far and as fast as her feet would take her. With Jared, even winning felt like losing, and Isabeau would not soon forget the lesson.

Jared, meanwhile, exchanged bemused glances with Pierre, who had approached carrying the contested fruit in one hand. Silently, he held the item up for his commander's inspection. A small incision marred the hard rind of the pomegranate, dark purple liquid oozing from it like blood from a wound. The dwarf pushed his thumbs into the hole and broke it open. Inside lay Sayyad's tiny knife, nestling ominously among the tangy seeds in the center. Neither man said a word, but the muted gasps and mutters of the men still gathered about the practice circle spoke for them.

It was impossible to throw a knife with that much accuracy. Unlikely as it was that the Assassin should have hit the small target at the distance Sayyad had done it, it would have taken an almost supernatural hand to gauge the force and torque of the blade's flight to such a degree that it would pierce the outside of the fruit without exploding out the other end. Yet al-Zul had performed the feat quite casually.

"Suddenly," Pierre said, "I'm not quite so hungry."

"Neither am I, old friend," Jared said softly, staring after the small veiled figure. "Neither am I."

CHAPTER NINE

"At last, The Time Is Right," Jared announced.

The mercenary's deep baritone was rich with irony at his own grandiose declaration. "Or at least so says this note from our enigmatic friend Sayyad," he amended as Pierre, catching his sarcasm, lifted a bushy eyebrow in inquiry.

Reaching across the campfire that separated them, the dwarf took the creased slip of parchment his commander handed him. The letter, however—a brusque missive that began with the cryptic words Jared had quoted and ended with an invitation for the mercenary to dine at his host's tent this evening—yielded nothing further in the way of information to either of them.

It was four days after Sayyad's unexpectedly violent confrontation with the Black Lion in the desert, and the Assassin's camouflaged convoy had now reached the lush farmlands and orchards that lay just outside the city of Baghdad. Watered by the Tigris and Euphrates rivers between which it sat like a great, round jewel, the triple-walled capital of the Abbasid caliphate was a wondrous sight to behold—though Jared reflected that it didn't seem to be Sayyad's intention that they behold it at close range.

The false caravan had taken shelter along the river wharves just outside the city's walls on the western bank of the Tigris. It was a place reserved for watering the beasts and marshaling together the pack trains of the many traders who would set off at dawn's first blush with their goods for Damascus and other points west. Arriving in the early morning, Sayyad's caravan had made haste to merge with the busy stream of merchants, pilgrims, fishmongers, and ferrymen who swarmed the banks intent on the day's business, but had soon claimed a place all their own upriver at the most remote edge of the settled banks, where it was quieter and a convenient bend in the river shaded their ac-

tivities from the eyes of all casual observers. Only one other
caravan was parked near them now—transporting some
rich man's goods, by the look of it—but the disorganized
nobleman's household, busy with its own concerns, seemed
to take no notice of the edgy "merchants" who'd quietly
camped by their side.

Date palms, lime, banana, and fig trees grew in profusion
along the bank where they'd pitched their tents and bedded
their animals. This early in autumn, the sweet, sticky fruit
of the dates was just barely ripe enough for the men of the
fake trading mission to pluck and eat as they reclined beside
the wide, slow-flowing river and enjoyed the respite from
their hard journey. Though the Assassin had given orders
upon their arrival this morning that no one was to venture
inside the city without Sayyad's own express orders, the
mercenary himself was not sorry to be stuck outside. The
Black Lion's long years of wandering had taken him to
Baghdad several times, and he knew the caliph's capital
city to be a hotbed of political intrigue and casual cruelty
as well as a legendary utopia of heady luxury and learning
institutions for those fortunate enough to be able to afford
them.

Jared thought it just as well that Sayyad's target, whatever it was, did not appear to reside within the city. It would
have been tricky, indeed, to strike inside those walls and
then hope to escape capture on the way out. Even disre-
garding the scores of seasoned Mamluk troops who protected the caliph's palace—an awe-inspiring pleasure dome
that took up fully a third of the city—Baghdad, like any
other Eastern stronghold, was rife with dangers for the unwary or the unprepared.

And at the moment, Jared was feeling uncomfortably ill-
prepared for whatever might lie before them. At least out
here, their escape route was elementary—if they needed to
run on short notice, they could just retrace their steps, skirting the crowds on the banks this time as they fled. Had
they tried anything inside the labyrinthine streets and alley-
ways of the city, more than likely they would have found

themselves hunted and cut down like dogs to die in the gutters. Thus, the shady little oasis of calm they occupied outside the walls suited the mercenary very nicely.

It would have been a peaceful scene, indeed, if Jared had not sensed this pause in the caravan's journey had more of a siege mentality to it than a feeling of respite. The aura Sayyad's bandits projected was one of heightened tension, to say the least, and his own men had begun to pick it up as well. He hadn't needed to wait for al-Zul's order to position sentries in a ring around the perimeter of their encampment, though he *had* raised an eyebrow at the command to be discreet about it. Unable to assess their peril with the scant information at hand, their patrols at the verge of the caravan's enclosure had more the air of a garrison preparing to defend themselves than of a strike force gearing up for attack.

If the Assassin's men knew any more than did those of the Black Lion's Pride, they weren't sharing the information. They merely hunkered down beside their animals in their trader's guise, saying little but scowling illustratively. Whatever was going to happen, Jared suspected it would happen soon, and the invitation from al-Zul tonight merely confirmed his suspicions. If the closemouthed Shadow Hunter finally meant to share his intentions, the assault he planned could not be far off.

Jared sighed and shrugged at Pierre across the space that separated them. The two had been sitting before the Black Lion's tent, feeding a small fire over which they'd spitted a rather stringy-looking hare one of the others had bartered for that day. "Guess this feast is all yours, my friend," he said. "It seems I'm wanted at the master's table this night."

"Be careful what you say and do there, as well as what you eat," Pierre advised with less than his usual level of humor.

Both men had seen the messenger the Assassin had sent off into the city this morning as they halted outside, and both had watched the young bandit return in haste to report to his master that afternoon. No information had been forth-

coming until now, however, and the mercenary and his lieutenant had been discussing the possible reasons for the
scout to have ventured into the city while the rest of the
caravan remained without. They'd agreed that Sayyad must
have a contact within the walls and that the Assassin had
probably received word from his man inside. But what the
news had been, neither of them could fathom, nor what it
would mean for them.

"God knows what al-Zul is up to now," the dwarf concluded, scowling. "I wouldn't put it past that demon's
spawn to drug your sherbet or put poison in your pilaf."

"At this point, I wouldn't be surprised at anything that
lunatic Assassin does," the Black Lion returned as he stood
to obey the summons and brushed absently at the wrinkles
on his silken merchant's robes.

As it turned out, he was wrong.

The interior of the tent Sayyad occupied was dim, and as
Jared ducked beneath the flap to come in after hearing a
muted call to enter, it took a moment for him to make out
the outline of the Assassin seated so still upon the pile of
cushions on the floor.

It took somewhat longer for Jared to register what the
man was doing.

The slight, cross-legged figure who faced Jared still had
a few unexpected moves in his repertoire, it seemed. For
even in the faint light of this canvas-and-wool audience
chamber, he could quite plainly see that the Assassin was
smoking a hookah. And from the smell of it, the fragrant
substance smoldering in the silver-chased glass pipe was
not the usual blend.

So the rumors are true, the Black Lion thought.

"Yes, the rumors are true." Isabeau answered the unspoken question in Jared's eyes, her voice as smoky as the
substance in the tall hookah that stood before her on the
carpeted floor. She raised the pipe's long, flexible stem to
her lips right through the folds of her cotton veil and inhaled a shallow breath's worth. A moment later, sighing,

the Assassin exhaled an aromatic cloud that coiled up in snakelike spirals from beneath her veil to obscure the blue of her eyes from the mercenary's sight.

Which was exactly as she wanted it, the renegade mused darkly. The more barriers between them, the better. The smoke turned a reddish-gold in the slight illumination provided by the single lamp glowing in the billowing, fabric-walled chamber, making the Black Lion's tall form waver and blur before her eyes. Outlined as he was in shimmering silhouette by the early evening light from beyond the tent flaps, Jared's was an imposing presence indeed. Her stomach tightened, twisting with unbidden anxiety at the sight of his lean yet powerful frame in her doorway. The mere sight of this beautiful, deadly warrior set her pulse racing and her thoughts scattering to the four winds each time they came together.

Was she truly ready to face this man again? Isabeau asked herself silently. Ready to trust him with her secrets? Seeing him now, so familiar and yet so foreign, the Assassin honestly didn't know if she could take the leap of faith required in order to bestow upon the Black Lion the explanations for which he'd so mercilessly hounded her during the first part of their journey. Granted, she'd no plans to reveal more than the barest minimum of information necessary for the mercenary to perform his part in tomorrow's decisive play. It was unlikely that he'd be able to ruin her scheme with what she would share tonight, and that, at least, was comforting. But Isabeau doubted Jared would be satisfied with so little. As surely as the sun would rise with tomorrow's dawn, she knew he'd press her for more details, and the pressure of de Navarre's insistence was something the Assassin was unprepared to handle right now. Her nerves were stretched taut enough as it was.

She'd endured years of untold sacrifice and struggle steering events toward the showdown with her enemy that would decide so many fates tomorrow. Dealing with Jared de Navarre was only one factor—albeit an unexpectedly difficult one—in the multidimensional strategy she'd masterminded to make this day come to pass. Allah knew, it wasn't even the most important. Yet somehow, after all that had gone between them—all the bitterness, betrayal, and mistrust that still welled up in her heart at the very sight of him—inviting her erstwhile betrothed into her confidence felt like the hardest thing Isabeau had ever had to do.

She could afford no surprises now. The renegade must be sure she could count upon the Black Lion's full cooperation! And to guarantee that cooperation came easily, to be sure she had the mercenary completely under her control, late this afternoon she'd hit upon an ingenious idea. Tonight, she'd decided, she would invite him to partake of the Assassins' Ritual.

Isabeau waved Jared inside at last, after keeping him standing for what must have seemed an uncomfortably long time in the entranceway—long enough to subtly indicate who was in charge, she thought, while also courteously allowing the mercenary's vision time to adjust to the dimness of the chamber. She wanted him to take in the atmosphere of solemn mystery she'd been at pains to create within the small pavilion. She wanted him to realize this was no day like any other. Silently she offered the Black Lion a seat among the cushions and carpets she'd arranged opposite hers.

"There is a custom among my brethren, the *hashishin*." Isabeau used the traditional term for those of the Assassins' cult. "No doubt you have heard of it." She gestured languidly with one lean hand to indicate the ornate pipe at her knees.

Jared noticed suddenly that the tip of the smallest of the man's fine-boned fingers was missing, abbreviated after the second joint. He was vaguely surprised that he'd never noticed before, even as he told himself that such minute details were foolish to dwell upon in a situation like this.

"Yes," he replied belatedly, as he seated himself. "I have heard of it. But until today I did not know whether the tales were true. Now . . ." Jared trailed off. "It has to do with what's in the pipe you're smoking, if I am not mistaken?"

"Indeed," the Assassin confirmed. "It is part of the ritual we go through before entering into battle. And although the stories about our simple custom may be exaggerated by legend or twisted to reflect the political agendas of our detractors, the basic facts are true."

This much, Isabeau admitted easily. She was revealing no great mystery of her former master's secret society by telling this to Jared. The Assassins themselves had promulgated the tale long ago in order to frighten their enemies with the lengths to which they would go to make themselves fearless before battle. Thus, she was only confirming what he already knew. The reminder of this ancient custom, however, the part not promoted in their sect's propaganda, she intended to keep to herself.

"The night before any major clash at arms, in order to prepare oneself, to, shall we say, acquire the proper frame of mind, the warrior smokes this special preparation." In truth, during her own tenure at Alamut, Isabeau had heard a rumor among the acolytes that the real reason the Old Man of the Mountain encouraged his "blades" to smoke before accepting a mission was that the chosen apprentice would believe himself already accepted into Paradise once he inhaled the substance, and thus be unafraid to die in the service of his holy master. Her own dealings with the cunning cult leader had not led the renegade to believe him incapable of such manipulation. She had learned much about the art of conniving from emulating him.

"You will partake with me tonight," the Shadow Hunter concluded simply. "And then we will talk of what is to come."

It wasn't a request, and Jared wasn't fool enough to take it as such. He knew what the substance in the hookah's brimming bowl was supposed to be able to do, though he had never yet sampled it himself.

Hashish.

CHAPTER TEN

Hashish.

The Assassins were, indeed, known to dose themselves with its mind-altering fumes. It was part of what made them so awe-inspiring to their enemies. It was said that a man possessed by the potent dreams it brought about, lifted from ordinary fear or caution on clouds of its smoke, would not fear to die in battle, for he would think himself invincible.

Tonight, it was the price of admission to al-Zul's secrets.

Pierre had been right, Jared thought wryly as he leaned back upon the soft cushions to take in this new twist his uneasy relationship with the Shadow Hunter was about to undergo. The Assassin did, indeed, intend to drug him—and it only slightly mitigated the mercenary's trepidation knowing that Sayyad would be dosing himself as well. Yet the mercenary found himself not unwilling to take this journey of the mind alongside the mysterious man who had hired him. Perhaps he might gain some perspective about the enigmatic Shadow Hunter tonight by sharing the man's private rites. With only the barest hesitation, he reached out to accept the pipe Sayyad offered him.

If she'd hoped to render the mercenary malleable or unquestioning, Isabeau suddenly had the feeling that she would fail in her objective tonight. If, however, she wanted him attentive, focused only upon her, she might have succeeded more thoroughly than she wished. He was already watching her intently, curiosity shining in those gold-coin eyes of his. Those piercing, leonine eyes that seemed to see right through her. The Assassin suppressed a shiver and silently thanked Allah once again for the veil that concealed her face from the man to whom she had formerly been betrothed. The sooner the Black Lion experienced the pacifying effects of the hashish, the better!

After she'd passed the pipe stem to Jared, averting her

gaze from the sight of those full, manly lips encompassing the silver-cased reed exactly where her own had done, Isabeau sat back on her heels and watched to make sure he'd held the smoke sufficiently long in his lungs. She herself was careful to take no more within her body than she could easily metabolize, for after several years' experience with the ritual of Assassins' Courage, as it was known among her brethren, the renegade could monitor the drug's effects upon her to the finest degree. To make it seem as if she ingested more than she actually did tonight, Isabeau would pretend to inhale several times more often than she really planned to, knowing the veil would disguise any sign of her deception. After all, the intent tonight was to render Jared unguarded, compliant, and hopefully unsuspicious; not to leave herself open to the same failings. Soon, Isabeau hoped, he would begin feeling the effects. Until she was sure he did, however, she would wait to speak of the serious matters that had brought them together tonight.

Still, she ought to say something. The Shadow Hunter, unused to idle conversation, searched her mind for something appropriate. "We have reached the journey's end," she observed finally, lamely.

"Have we?" Jared asked, leaning back casually. "I was not entirely sure, since you gave me nothing upon which to base such a conjecture."

"Mm. Well, I was confident you'd figure it out, mercenary," Isabeau replied noncommittally. She didn't think she appreciated his censorious tone. And that predatory look in his lion-gold eyes . . . It was positively alarming! The Assassin suppressed a shiver.

"My thanks, al-Zul. You'll find I'm not *quite* as thick-witted as I look," Jared shot back, grinning ferally.

Isabeau didn't think she liked the way this was heading. She knew only too well Jared wasn't stupid—he didn't look it, and he sure as hell didn't act it! Indeed, the mercenary was too perceptive by far.

At that moment, as if anticipating her need for a distraction, one of the Assassin's men entered the pavilion silently, bearing several steaming dishes atop a small, ivory-inlaid tray. The man set the tray between them, arranging plates and eating utensils and whisking the covers off heated dishes of what smelled like spiced rice mixed with lamb and dates. The scent of well-prepared food filled the tent.

Jared was suddenly ravenous.

He'd never felt so hungry in his life, he thought, though oddly enough he'd filled his belly not all that long before, and hadn't felt even the slightest pangs when he'd entered the tent a few minutes ago.

"Please help yourself," the Assassin urged graciously.

At his host's encouraging indication, Jared set to with a will, barely noticing that Sayyad ate only sparingly of his own portion. It must be the difficulty of maneuvering those morsels of lamb and rice beneath his heavy veiling, he reflected a bit giddily. Did the man *sleep* beneath those ridiculous shrouds? It was a wonder he didn't smother.

Intent upon filling his plate with delicacies, the mercenary almost missed the rather sardonic question his host posed next.

"I trust you are recovering well from your . . . ah . . . fall of the other evening?" the Shadow Hunter asked mildly, speaking with what Jared presumed was a perfectly straight face. At least, the Assassin maintained a perfectly straight *voice,* the mercenary thought to himself drolly, finding his own musings unusually amusing. Putting down his plate with a certain amount of reluctance, Jared rubbed his throat ruefully where the other man's boot print had left a bruise that had yet to fade completely.

"Yes, I am quite well now, thank you," he replied. "Although my pride may take a little more time yet to heal." A little flattery couldn't hurt at this point, could it? Jared thought. Suddenly, though he couldn't have said where the idea came from, he found himself determined to try to warm this cold-blooded killer up, just to see what results he'd have. His curiosity, normally well suppressed behind a wall of cynicism and cold practicality, seemed rather close to the surface just now—and the secretive Assassin, eerily illuminated in the flickering lamplight, was the most fascinating object he could imagine for it to focus on.

"I was impressed with that move of yours, al-Zul," he admitted candidly. Jared paused to take another puff from the hookah, then let the harsh, fragrant smoke plume out from his nose and mouth contemplatively. Sayyad did the same after a moment, he saw, again sucking the smoke in and blowing it out right through his veils. "I've never seen anything like it in all my years of combat," he confessed. "The way you leapt straight into the air like that—'twas magnificent! Someday I would like you to show it to me again."

Demonstrate her skills for him like some trained monkey in a bazaar? Ha! Isabeau thought. As if she would so easily give away the secrets it had taken her so long—and cost her so much—to learn. "Well, naturally I would be happy to do what I did to you again, mercenary—that is, if you think your pride can bear another such fall," Isabeau said blandly.

She had not failed to notice Jared's increased appetite, though nerves had suppressed her own hunger almost to the point of nausea. The Assassins' special herbal preparation was beginning to do its job, Isabeau thought with satisfaction, but it would take more than this to really render the Black Lion at her mercy. She reached for the pipe again and saw that it had gone out. Leaning down to reignite the hookah, she lit a long, narrow strip of dried palm-frond in the little brazier whose ruddy coals warmed the slight autumn chill out of the space, holding the flame against the pipe's bowl. To get the oily hashish smoldering again, she had to draw a long breath of the smoke into her mouth.

Just when she would have exhaled, Jared suddenly started to laugh.

The surprise of hearing those deep, masculine sounds of mirth made the Assassin suck in her breath again, and she had to struggle not to choke audibly on the smoke trapped by her cursedly obstructive veil. Instantly, part of her knew she'd just inhaled a lot more of the drug than she should have, but that cautious, alert portion of Isabeau's mind didn't seem to be working overly well with the Black Lion laughing at her across the small space of the tent. She wished she could blame her warm, tingling reaction on the hashish, but knew she could not. She had the same unfortunate response to the man with or without the aid of mood-altering potions.

For some reason Jared had found the Assassin's dry comment enormously funny. He couldn't stop himself from laughing! "Ha, ha, ha—'be happy to'—ha, ha—'do it to me'—ha, ha, ha—'again'!" He broke into guffaws. "That's clever, al-Zul. Very clever indeed!" How bizarre, the mercenary thought numbly, to find anything the humorless renegade said amusing. Yet this seemed like the funniest jest he'd heard in years.

The drug was definitely beginning to work, Isabeau thought, but *which* drug—the one in the pipe or the one sitting across from her? Troubled, the masked Assassin wasn't sure which was proving the more potent opiate. Isabeau sternly fought the effects of those rich, manly chuckles on her body, straining to erase the answering smile from her own face until she realized she had no need to do so. The veil she always wore would hide her pleasure from Jared. *This damned veil conceals everything,* the renegade thought with a surge of annoyance for the barrier that stood at all times between her and the rest of the world. *Strange, then, that I keep wanting to discard such a useful convenience . . .*

It was only the effects of the hashish, she knew. Just as Jared's hearty laughter was the result of its bewitchment, not of anything witty she'd said. She must fight its influence over her, even as she encouraged it in him. Knowing the Black Lion had nearly reached the proper altered state, she decided to get back on topic—and as always, speaking of her enemy sobered Isabeau instantly.

"You know why you are here tonight," she began again

in her low, husky voice, cutting into the mercenary's mirth with her dark tones.

"Yes." Jared exhaled slowly, relaxing back into the cushions. Now *this* was the Sayyad he recognized. Harsh. Grim. Direct. He should pay attention to what the Assassin said, he knew. Yet his body's subtle reactions to the storied substance he'd ingested kept distracting him. His throat burned with a raw, tearing sensation each time he breathed it in, and his eyes stung slightly from the oily smoke. Still, he could feel nothing truly extraordinary as yet, the mercenary thought with a tinge of disappointment, though his cheeks and lips seemed to have developed perhaps a slight tingle. Well, all right, he amended inwardly, it was rather a pronounced tingle, but that was *all* he felt; certainly no great infusion of courage or outlandish hallucinations, as he'd half expected. Maybe the mystical effects of hashish had been exaggerated in the legends.

Sayyad seemed to have suffered no severe consequences from smoking the hookah either, he noticed, despite the funny way the Assassin had of inhaling copious amounts of it through his many wrappings. Jared stifled another sudden, inappropriate urge to laugh at the sight of the cold-blooded killer blowing smoke out through his scarves and sternly forced himself to focus on what his host was saying.

"What you do not know, mercenary, is what will be required of you on the morrow," Isabeau said slowly. "That is what I shall explain now." He was ready to listen, she judged.

"Good," Jared said feelingly. "It's high time you shared this information, Sayyad, if you ask me. I was beginning to think you planned to drop me and my men blindfolded into the middle of an ambush and expect us to bluff our way out!"

If only she could have, Isabeau thought wistfully. That would have solved a lot of her problems! Instead of responding to the mercenary's sarcasm, however, she decided to continue as though she hadn't heard his biting comment.

"My spies have returned with the news I was anticipat-

ing. And as I had hoped, the household of Emir Malik al-
Fayed is at this moment preparing itself for a move to
Damascus," she continued briskly, ignoring the sudden cot-
tony awkwardness of her tongue inside her mouth. Best to
get this all out quickly if she could. "It is as you have heard;
the emir wishes to be closer to the sultan's sphere of power
in Damascus, in order to court the man's nephew who has
newly been named ruler there. To this end Malik has pur-
chased a major property in that city, and, now that it has
been prepared for his arrival, he plans to transport his possessions overland starting tomorrow. Much of his luggage,
personal property, and portable wealth are already outside
the walls, packed and ready to load upon the beasts who
will carry it to his new home," she informed Jared, then
continued determinedly to the point of her narrative.

"This morning I ascertained the location of the caravan
carrying Malik's household retainers and possessions. It is
situated right here by the riverbanks, and accordingly, I
have taken pains to establish our own encampment close to
their position. In fact, though they know it not, those unsuspecting fools lie right under our noses at this very moment!" Isabeau's raspy whisper was rife with satisfaction
she couldn't hide. "As my spies advise me, only the man
himself and the members of his harem have yet to be up-
rooted, remaining inside the walls of Baghdad tonight with
the balance of his servants, guards, and household slaves.
But with tomorrow's sunrise, they will leave the city as
well." Jamal had been thorough as usual, she thought.
Through the go-between they'd set up for her scout to meet
in the city this morning, he had made sure Isabeau knew
every detail of Malik's plans, down to the location of the
least of his slaves.

"Ah," replied the Black Lion with what he hoped was
an air of enlightened intelligence. "I see." *So that's why we
camped next to that other caravan,* Jared thought hazily,
after avoiding contact with so many others all day. He
found himself capable of little more than merely listening
as the renegade went on—listening and watching the slight,

veil-swathed Assassin across the stuffy chamber as though he were the most fascinating creature ever to cross the mercenary's path. The Shadow Hunter, so small of stature and yet so utterly commanding, never failed to intrigue him.

Uncomfortable beneath the scrutiny, Isabeau paused briefly to raise the hookah's stem to her lips and puff a little cloud of smoke in between lips that seemed to have grown curiously numb. The smoke-filled room danced before her eyes. It must be a trick of the light, the Shadow Hunter thought, distracted momentarily by the flickering of the single lamp at her side. It took her a minute to drag her gaze away from the golden flame, which seemed to mirror hauntingly the fire glowing in Jared's eyes. She must be hallucinating, to think such ridiculous thoughts! the Assassin chided herself in annoyance. She hadn't ingested all that much of the powerful drug yet, had she?

Isabeau let her breath sigh out again without inhaling deeply, then passed the pipe stem back to Jared, who obligingly matched her puff for puff. Words seemed strangely unnecessary at this moment, and she wanted nothing more than to lie back in silence and bask in the oddly comforting presence of her hired comrade-at-arms. She wanted to forget about everything but him, if only for a little while. Yet she knew she could not afford such a senseless indulgence.

After making sure the mercenary had gotten a decent draw inside his lungs, the Assassin continued doggedly. "Once they leave the gates, the wives, concubines, and the other slaves will travel under guard down to the banks of the Tigris to join up with the rest of the 'baggage' "—here Isabeau spoke with unintentional bitterness—"while the emir himself goes to take his place at the front. Malik's caravan master will undoubtedly pause briefly to water the animals one final time and form up their convoy upon the riverbanks. And that is when we will fall upon them," she concluded simply. "When the confusion is greatest."

She wondered if Jared could possibly guess how much it had cost her to trust him with this much when Zahra's very safety rested on his discretion. Probably not, the ren-

egade decided with a snort. A man like him, to whom
promises obviously meant little or nothing, could never understand the importance of the vow she had made to her
dear Zahra so many years—too many years!—ago. No, he
would never understand the love and loyalty that motivated
her, she thought bitterly. This jaded warrior-for-hire loved
no one save himself, the Assassin mused, breathing shallowly of the fume-rich air in the tent.

Brooding on her own dark concerns, she was unaware
that the smoke was beginning to permeate her lungs despite
her lack of intentional inhalation. In truth, the Assassin was
too busy sizing up the warrior who shared her tent to notice
much else. Isabeau studied the mercenary closely, finding
herself angry at him again though she wanted simply to
feel detached. It was impossible to be anywhere near this
man and have no response to him, however. By the
Prophet's very bones, he might be fickle and untrustworthy,
but he was also beautiful! she thought grudgingly.

Her proud lion lounged upon the cushions like a great
russet-and-gold cat, relaxed and at ease with his molten-
gold eyes lidded at half-mast. Jared de Navarre seemed the
very essence of manhood, stretched out like that on one
elbow with his glorious warrior's musculature outlined all
in soft blue silk. His deep auburn hair, hanging in glossy
waves to his shoulders, gleamed with health and uncommon
color, even in the scant light of her tent. And his face! It
was so handsome it nearly hurt to look at the mercenary's
rugged, masculine countenance in repose.

If she'd had a harem of her own, Isabeau thought inadvertently, Jared would be the crowning glory of it.

Oh, wicked, wicked thought! How could she waste time
like this, conjuring up such unlikely fantasies now, when
she had so much of greater importance to consider? Isabeau
grew furious with herself as well as with the magnificent
male opposite her, and cursed the heady decoction she'd
allowed to cloud her thoughts. How would the mercenary
react if he knew that the mere sight of his physique was
driving her to distraction? Oh, the humiliation! It was an

unbearable concept, and one she was devoutly glad would never become reality. Glancing over once more, she noticed that Jared was still smiling slightly as he reclined upon her fine brocaded cushions. For one frightening instant she imagined that he had read her thoughts, but then, sighing with relief, she realized he was only smiling politely in response to her last words.

But what had she said? she wondered foggily. Oh, yes. The ambush. Jared certainly looked remarkably undisturbed by the news that they would waylay al-Fayed's caravan in the morning. He seemed to have digested her words without dispute, and was merely nodding to indicate that she should continue.

Apparently it didn't faze this seasoned mercenary captain that the caravan they would attack was a large one, though he must have seen the size of Malik's convoy and the many watchmen already milling around it as they'd passed them on the riverbanks today. Including guides, guards, and handlers, at least sixty men comprised the heavily laden pack-train—not counting the women, household slaves, and other dependents—but Jared didn't seem worried about the odds. The drug must, indeed, have mellowed his usually edgy demeanor, to leave him so relaxed in the face of this news. It was a good thing that hashish did not tend to make one forgetful, only complacent, the Assassin thought wryly. Otherwise she'd be explaining herself all over again in the morning to her stupefied hireling.

"With the dawn will come our ambush," she went on at last, mustering her scattered thoughts with an effort. By the Prophet, she'd smoked far more than she'd planned! "Camped beside them in the guise of innocent merchant sheep, our wolves will fall upon them while their forces are still in disarray, attacking with such sudden fury as cannot be denied. Now listen well, mercenary," she commanded thickly. "In the midst of this attack I intend to break off from the rest with a few chosen men—you need not be concerned with this part if you do your job right—and bear down upon the prize I seek, reclaiming this treasure and speeding it out of the devil's clutches while Malik and his men are still too disorganized to stop me." Breathless, beginning to be caught up with the excitement of her own plan, Isabeau ignored Jared when he opened his mouth as if to protest. She pushed on.

"Once you see me give the signal that this object has been attained, you are to call your men back, break off the attack, and retreat before reinforcements can arrive from the city. I will leave it up to you to decide the location where you choose to fall back, for unless aught goes awry, that will be the last you ever need see of me or my bandits. We shall all scatter—I and my *fidai'in* back the way we came—you and your Pride in any direction you choose, so long as it is not mine.

"Do I make myself clear?" she demanded.

The drug had slowed his faculties more than he liked to admit, Jared thought to himself. It made him unsure which of the Assassin's ridiculously presumptuous statements to address first! After a moment, he decided to tackle the most obvious consideration right up front. From a practical standpoint, this flaw in the Assassin's plan seemed singularly telling.

"First of all," he said, though for some reason his tongue wasn't working quite properly and he seemed to be able to hear an echo of his own voice. "Before I even address the question of what you're sending us after, which you still haven't confessed—and don't think I haven't noticed that little fact, Sayyad!—" he said as he waved one elegantly boned, sword-callused finger at the Assassin in exaggerated rebuke, "will you kindly tell me why are we waiting until tomorrow to attack? If, as you say, this Malik's belongings are all outside the walls tonight, and his personal guard remain inside the city to protect him, wouldn't it make more sense to strike before they arrive? Tomorrow there will only be more of them to fight," he pointed out, hoping his logic made more sense to the renegade than it did to himself all of a sudden. "Also, the Mamluks, his personal bodyguard, are sure to be far fiercer in defense of their master than any hired warriors he's likely to have guarding the baggage. Why not surprise them in the hours just before dawn and steal this mysterious treasure of yours then, before the emir and his reinforcements arrive?"

There, that made sense, didn't it? Jared hoped he'd be able to remember some of the other objections he'd intended to make by the time Sayyad finished explaining this one to his satisfaction. For some reason he was having a hard time focusing on anything for long, even his anger at the presumptuous man who'd spent so much gold to purchase the services of the Black Lion's Pride—a man who now, it seemed, intended to dispose of those services in an extremely foolhardy manner. Indeed, despite his indignant words, at this moment Jared found himself feeling inexplicably expansive and at peace with the world at large. His whole body was possessed of a glowing lassitude that was utterly unfamiliar to the warrior whose reflexes were always stretched taut on the alert. Though his eyes were having trouble focusing, he watched the Assassin inhale another deep lungful of smoke, sure that al-Zul would provide an explanation to satisfy his concerns.

But the Assassin had no intention of explaining why the treasure she sought would not be among the luggage left outside the walls with the pack animals and furniture tonight, nor that it resided within Malik al-Fayed's harem and could not be wrested from inside the great walled city with a force ten times the size of theirs. "The treasure I am after will be traveling with Malik," she said shortly, exhaling another fragrant cloud of smoke. It was a great concession even to share this much. "He keeps al-Zahra by his side always, jealously guarding his jewel from the sight of all others."

Isabeau used the term *al-Zahra* for the first time with Jared, knowing that he would most likely translate it as *the jewel,* though it could also mean *she of the bright face* when referring to a person. It was too dangerous to risk telling the mercenary that the treasure she sought was human, but she wouldn't stoop so low as to lie about her target either.

Isabeau despised falsehood. Instead she reached for the pipe between them, hoping to stall his inevitable questions. If she was lucky, he would be so addle-witted by now that he'd react complacently to the plans she'd unveiled.

Unfortunately for the renegade, Jared had never been complacent in his life. "A *jewel*?" he echoed in disbelief. "You want me and my troop of veteran knights to fling ourselves like the greenest foot soldiers into the midst of a full-fledged caravan, not to mention the company of hand-picked Mamluks guarding it, just so you can reclaim some sort of *jewel*?" Jared's voice was disbelieving.

"Yes," she replied stonily, once again not liking his tone. "That is exactly what I wish you to do."

"Malik's men outnumber us nearly twice over," Jared felt it necessary to point out. Was it his imagination, or was Sayyad utterly insane? The hashish had made him question which of them was the more demented. After all, *he* was the one who'd accepted this lunatic's coin. Perhaps he, too, had lost his mind somewhere along the line.

Tonight, hunkered down in this dark, stuffy tent beside a legendary killer, sharing his rites and his grudging hospitality, Jared felt out of his depth in a way he had not for many years. Perhaps it was because, since he had realized the futility of his personal quest more than a decade ago, he hadn't cared about anything, hadn't *felt* anything as strongly as he did in the presence of Sayyad al-Zul. If nothing else, the man certainly had a knack for goading his temper like no other!

"That is why the element of surprise is so important," the Assassin replied reasonably enough, "—that, and your Pride's reputation for sabotage, are the reasons I picked you. I felt sure you would find a way to even out the odds before we enter the engagement. Why, mercenary? Do you feel yourself incapable of succeeding? Tell me now if that is so!" Isabeau made a dare out of these words, almost challenging him to back out now.

Jared ignored the implication of cowardice. "No," he replied slowly, thinking through the ramifications. If they started acting soon, his warriors could set up some nasty little surprises for their enemy come morning's light. Unsuspecting, asleep by the riverbanks, their foes could be put at a disadvantage by many means before they met in combat. Pierre would relish such a challenge, he knew. Without so much as creating a minor disturbance, he could have al-Fayed's camels cut free from their harnesses and the baggage mysteriously scattered in the night within an hour of his commander's order, creating confusion and disorder when the emir's caravan master was forced to deal with the delay upon waking. No doubt the cunning dwarf would have a slew of other ingenious ideas as well. "It's not impossible," he admitted, "not if we plan everything just right. But that isn't the point, Sayyad. The *point* is that you've deceived us!"

"I most certainly did not," the Shadow Hunter countered.

The argument was taking on a rather surreal edge for both participants. It seemed like one in a dream, where the sleeper struggles bitterly, emotions churning at the fore, but upon wakening, cannot recall the actual subject under such violent dispute. Both knew far more was being argued between them than the facts of their original agreement. Beneath the surface resentment brewed, tension mounted. Isabeau had some faint idea of why she was angry, of course, but Jared knew only that the Assassin rankled on his nerves more than any other person he'd ever encountered. He was both fascinated and furious each time they came together, and the mystique of this surly Shadow Hunter was one he dearly wanted to resolve with a simple tug upon the infuriating veil behind which he hid. The frustration of not daring to give in to this impulse had been simmering inside the Black Lion's heart for days now, and it fueled his anger still.

"From the way you spoke of it, al-Zul, I thought the treasure you described was something Malik could not live without! You insinuated that your mission was to steal something that would leave him bereft or powerless if he were to lose it, and help to bring him down!" he protested hotly. "Indeed, I daresay you purposely led me to believe as much. That, I could have understood, and I'll wager you knew it. But now you tell me this treasure you're hunting is no more than some bauble, a plaything to fill a rich man's idle hours! How typical," he snorted in disgust. "For all your fine words and mysterious ways, Shadow Hunter, you're really just a petty thief at heart, aren't you?"

That stung. "And what are you, pray tell?" Isabeau choked out, barely managing to remember to disguise her voice in her anger. Then she answered her own accusation. "You are naught but a hired thug. For money, you sell yourself each and every day of your life, Black Lion. How dare you preach to me about greed? Money is the only thing you respect!"

He could never comprehend the true reasons compelling her to take the dangerous course she had chosen, Isabeau thought. After all, had he not abandoned her at the first sign of difficulty? So fickle a man as he had shown himself to be would never see the necessity of risking all their lives as recklessly as Isabeau intended to do on the morrow for Zahra's sake. No one who had not experienced the horror and degradation of life as a slave in Malik al-Fayed's harem could ever understand.

As long as there was the slightest hope of achieving her objective, Isabeau would not alter her decision now, though her own death be an absolute certainty. *She* would die unquestioningly for the one she loved and had been forced to abandon, though Jared, by contrast, seemed never to have given even a moment's thought for the fate of the one he'd left drowning in his wake. "That's what I should have expected when I hired you," she finished bitterly. "You are mercenary to the core, and I was a fool if I ever hoped otherwise."

"At least I do not pretend differently," Jared growled. The euphoric glow he'd felt earlier had left him entirely by now. Now he was angry. No, he wasn't angry—he was furious! How dare the man call *him* mercenary after admitting what he was after was no more than a highly priced trinket? How dare al-Zul presume to pass judgment upon *him*? The Assassin knew nothing of Jared's true purpose, of his desperate search and the interminable exile that had left him with no home, no family, and no hope whatsoever for either in the future. He knew nothing of Jared's struggles or his inner longings, nothing of his motives.

"When I hire myself out to men like you, Sayyad," he snarled, "I do it honestly. I promise only to fight your battles and to win them for you—I don't presume to claim God has granted me the victory because of my righteousness, or that my honor has anything whatsoever to do with the strength of my arms. It's only Assassins like you who pretend to have ideals, morals, some kind of mandate from on high. But when it comes down to it, you're no better than a mean, lowly brigand out for plunder, aren't you? You would risk all our lives for the sake of one single jewel!" he sneered in outrage.

"There are *some* jewels," she hissed back, "that are beyond price. But I'd never expect a mercenary like you to understand—for you, everything has a value in gold, doesn't it? Even human life!" *Even the life of his betrothed,* she finished silently. She hadn't been worth the cost, though, had she? Isabeau thought stormily. Hadn't been worth coming after. Clearly, she hadn't been worthy of his precious concern. Was anything? Or did Jared de Navarre believe gold was the only motivation that made rising from his pallet each morning worthwhile?

"Does it?" Jared sneered in return. "Well, I suppose you should know the cost of human life, dealing in it as you do, *Assassin*." Fury overtook him as he stared at that superior, smug bastard who dared to sit there hidden beneath his veils and call *him* a profiteer. Sayyad al-Zul could have no idea what he said when he accused Jared of such ignominy. Hadn't he spent the past sixteen years seeking something that could never bring him profit? On the contrary, his only payment had been in heartache and bitter futility. "And I guess you've named *our* price, haven't you; buying my men to help you pull off this inglorious mission you're planning? Damn you, al-Zul, and damn your precious jewel! At least I fight to defend life, not take it. If I am paid for that, it's no more than a soldier's due. There is no shame in what I do. But *you*, Sayyad. Even I would not stoop so low as to risk the lives of my men in order to recover a single bauble. Have you not riches enough? Why, what you paid for the services of my troop ought to be enough to deck yourself out in all the jewels of Arabia."

"Aye, and you took that money willingly, did you not?" The drug was making her head spin, and Isabeau could not keep a hold of her tongue, or her temper either. More and more this conversation was driving her into fits of fury. The drug they'd ingested only seemed to heighten her resentment as well as Jared's combative behavior, though her whole intention had been to cool both off. Still, now that they had begun to travel down this road, it seemed too late to turn back. "I told you at the beginning that we would seek one of Malik's treasures," she reminded him, taking a deep breath of the still smoke-rich air. "I never played you false or claimed some high ideal. If you inferred one, it was your mistake."

"You led me to believe it."

"Perhaps. And perhaps not. But I'm sure this is not the first time an employer has had designs that differed from your own. What do you do in the face of disillusionment— pack up your armor and go home? Please," she scoffed. "Don't tell me you've come this far just to lose your nerve. Are you telling me you want to return my gold and have me release you from our deal?"

"No," the mercenary growled indignantly, knowing he might sound as if he were more worried about Sayyad reclaiming his money than he was for his honor, but not caring. He was beyond worrying about what this hypocrite thought of him! "I didn't say I wouldn't respect the agreement between us. But do not expect me to respect the man who made it. Not when I hear you've hired my Pride merely to pilfer the coffers of an enemy. That you intend to use us as lowly pawns in a chess game for this purpose, risk our lives so intemperately. Though it sickens me to stay on and aid you in this degenerate mission, I *will* stay on. We struck a bargain."

"What's the matter, Black Lion?" she taunted. "Haven't you made enough money by now to run home with your tail between your legs if you don't like your clients' commands?"

"Many times over," he snapped.

"What, then? Have you no reason to go home?" she mocked. "No eager wife and children back in Navarre to miss your charming company and cry for your return?"

Jared suddenly remembered the letter he still carried next to his breast. The Assassin could have no idea how close to home he struck with his unthinking taunts.

"On the contrary," he said, and the words came out more softly than he'd intended. It was almost as though he were speaking to himself, for suddenly the mercenary was caught up in melancholy reverie. "I learned recently that I am needed urgently in Navarre. With my father dead and my brother besieged by enemies on all sides, struggling to defend a castle that should be *my* responsibility, I have never been needed more. If I could journey back to the West, I know I would likely be coming home to a burned-out ruin of a castle and a field full of the new-dug graves of my kin. Should I not leave soon, I will have no home at all to return to. Yet I cannot go to its defense nonetheless."

"And why is that?" the renegade asked, trying to keep her tone contemptuous, though the reminder of Jared's roots brought her own long-neglected family to mind. Somehow, hearing about people she had known but not thought of in so many years was disorienting—disarming even. It reminded Isabeau of the ties that had once bound them together.

Jared laughed mirthlessly. "Because of this." He reached inside his silken tunic and drew forth a small golden object hanging from a slender chain.

"A necklace?"

"A symbol."

Even before Jared turned the tiny circlet to face the light, Isabeau suddenly knew what it was, and her breathing suspended itself sharply inside her breast. She had blocked the memory of it from her mind many years since, but now, as a sharp phantom ache suddenly shot through her foreshortened little finger, she knew she had seen that ring before. Had worn it! The Assassin's heart turned over in her chest and she felt suddenly nauseous. Her eyes stung painfully, grew wet with unfamiliar moisture. It was the drug. Surely it was the drug. She wasn't going to cry!

"It belonged to a woman?" she forced herself to ask nonchalantly, as the Shadow Hunter might.

"A girl, yes."

"And what has it to do with your inability to return to the West?" Isabeau held her breath, waiting for the answer. Dreading it and longing for it all at once.

Why was he even telling the Assassin all of this? The Black Lion couldn't have explained if his life depended upon it. Maybe it was the effect of the drug he'd ingested, but suddenly he couldn't help talking about himself, when for over a decade he'd shared these private thoughts and memories with no man on this earth besides Pierre. Sayyad must be a devil or a sorcerer of some sort, he thought. He'd made it so Jared could not keep the words from tumbling out. But now memory had overtaken him, and he could not stop the tide.

"I made a vow long ago—an impossible vow," he began slowly. "But unless I fulfill it, I have sworn never to return to my home. Thus I am in exile, and always shall be." Jared spoke bitterly, brokenly, and suddenly felt as if Sayyad were his confessor. The man sat in judgment upon him like some inscrutable wise man, after all, hiding behind his veils and listening, just listening with those blue eyes burning zealously. Perhaps if he confessed all, Jared thought dizzily, he might finally find forgiveness.

The drug having done its work, her once-betrothed was ready to confess—but was Isabeau ready to listen? Did she truly want to hear Jared's secrets? Or would the truth destroy all her own carefully erected defenses? Isabeau told herself it was good to know one's enemies—even if they were also your allies. She told herself the things she learned might help her defend against him in the future, ignoring the plain fact that according to her own design, after tomorrow they were never supposed to see one another again. But the simple truth was, Isabeau was driven mainly by her need to understand Jared, to know what had made him the man he was now.

To know, if she were honest with herself, whether he ever still thought of her.

"What vow was this?" she demanded shortly.

Unwillingly, Jared dredged up the memory, compelled to tell his masked confessor everything. "I promised a lady, many years ago, that I would watch over her daughter. When I failed in that promise,"—the mercenary's throat closed painfully on the word *failed*—"I made her another, and swore this time it would mean my life to break it. I swore that I would seek her little girl with all my capacity, and never return from searching until my vow was fulfilled." He laughed bitterly.

"Well, the damsel I sought is surely long dead. She followed the Children's Crusade." The mercenary spoke as though that should be enough explanation, though not many in the East were familiar with the doomed religious movement that had so swept France and Germany. "My last fair lead was not long after her disappearance, and it was the one that brought me to the East. Since then, however, I have heard next to nothing that would give me any reason to hope. If my poor charge even survived the crossing, she would have been sold into slavery as so many of her fellows were. Most likely she perished then or soon after, for that brave sweet girl was never meant to be a slave.

" 'S'truth." He shook his head sorrowfully. "There was never really any doubt about what had happened to Isabeau—but it makes little difference. My promise remains binding nonetheless. I seek this lost child everywhere I sojourn, making inquiries in each village and hamlet. Of course, it is at best utterly futile, and at worst dangerous to pry into the origin of fair-haired slaves or concubines in a man's harem. I cannot imagine she still survives, yet I must continue to hunt for her in vain. I swore that I would." Jared shook his head in self-disgust. "Isabeau de Lyon died as a result of my neglect, and for my penance, I shall never see the land of my birth again."

Isabeau rocked back in shock, feeling sick, exhilarated, and uncertain all at once. *I'm not dead!* she wanted to blurt. *Jared, I am right here! Look at me, see me, I am Isabeau!* The words strangled to death in her throat, however, choking her more surely than a dozen hookahs full of hashish. Her hand went toward her veil to snatch it off before she could begin to question what she was doing. All she could think was: *By heaven's bright messengers, he never did abandon me!*

After all these years of resenting her betrothed, blaming him, making his very name synonymous with distrust, it turned out that Jared had never broken faith with her after all. Not as she had done by not believing in him. The knowledge hit the Assassin like a crossbow bolt. If what the Black Lion said was true—and what reason would he have to lie to the Assassin Sayyad?—everything she'd believed for the last sixteen years was wrong. In that case, every bit of hatred and revilement she'd piled upon this man's head would have been a terrible misjudgment of his motives—but was it truly the case? Had Jared really been looking for her so diligently all these years? She had to know for sure. The Assassin's hand fell away from the veil.

"When did you first come to the East?" Isabeau demanded abruptly. But she was afraid she knew the answer already.

Why should the renegade care about that? the mercenary wondered curiously. Still, Jared could see no harm in answering. "It is nigh on half my life ago now. I was but ten and six when I set sail from the docks of Marseilles."

Oh, sweet heaven, Isabeau anguished. *It is true then.* He had come here for her. *Stayed* here for her, suffering untold deprivations and hardships when he could have taken up the far more generous role fate had promised him back in Europe. Instead of being the callous, thoughtless mercenary she'd believed him all these years, Jared had remained faithful all along. He had not forsaken her. He had not forgotten her!

But if Jared had come here in search of her, instead of a quick fortune or a life of adventure, as Isabeau had supposed, that meant something even worse than if he'd abandoned her, as she'd believed these last sixteen years.

He had not ruined *her* life. She had ruined *his*.

There was only one thing Isabeau could do. She laughed in his face.

CHAPTER ELEVEN

Stupid, romantic fool!

Alone now in the dark, breathing hard, Jared's reddened ears echoed again with the sound of the Assassin's incredulous ridicule.

Idiot! Sayyad had sneered. *Dreamer! How do you call yourself a man, mercenary, when you've wasted your whole life on a woman? And a dead one at that.* Jared could still picture the veiled figure shaking his head with mock surprise. *The great Black Lion turns out to be a mewling pussycat underneath his fearsome roar . . . Unbelievable!*

He'd fled the awful sound of the Assassin's mocking laughter, plain and simple. He—a warrior who feared nothing and no one in this world—had turned tail and run! Oh, he'd done it a bit more gracefully than simply picking up and dashing away, but Jared had to admit it had been flight nonetheless. How else to describe how he'd risen, stiff with affront, barely capable of bidding the Assassin good night before stomping out of the tent? He'd scarcely even acknowledged the taunting reminder to regroup with his men for the attack before dawn by the southern edge of camp, directly across the river from where al-Fayed's caravan had picketed their animals.

Outside now in the cool night air, Jared struggled to clear his head. Everything was spinning; his thoughts, his perceptions, his emotions had all gone wild. Humiliation welled up inside the mercenary, burning like bile at the back of his throat until he was fairly choking on it. It was as if he'd sucked up all of Sayyad's mockery along with the smoke of the hookah, and now it stuck with him no matter how he tried to breathe it out. The renegade clung in his mind with vicious talons of ridicule and derision until Jared felt ready to tear his own hair out or attack the sick feeling in his gut with a dagger just to get rid of him. Yet that excoriating laughter lingered on.

Even when the mercenary strode across the darkened camp and shook a sleeping Pierre to wake him and order the dwarf to assemble the men quietly before dawn, he could not get rid of its echo. Ignoring his drowsy lieutenant's questions, he simply outlined the Assassin's objective and told Pierre to prepare for their ambush however he saw fit. Jared gave the devious lieutenant license to employ any nasty little acts of sabotage he might devise; he himself was presently in no condition for strategy. By morning, he hoped, he would have charge of his faculties again in time to assume command.

Yet instead of to his bedroll, where he might have hoped to steady the world lurching and spinning around him and get a few hours' rest before going into battle, Jared's footsteps took him from the camp on a meandering path toward the river. Picking his way on leaden feet between the mostly sleeping warriors, he passed silently beyond the single unbanked fire of the *fidai'in,* where a group of the bandits sat and played a lilting tune on homemade instruments they'd carried with them.

As they did most nights, the men played to keep connected with their desert ancestry, but tonight, instead of enjoying the entrancing music they made, hearing them only made Jared feel like an alien in this world. Even after so many years in the East, he was still a foreigner at heart, and the ways of these Easterners would always remain oblique to him. Especially Sayyad's. That was one man he would never understand!

As he walked, the mercenary had the vague idea of splashing cool water on his face to sober up, and perhaps to quench the fires of chagrin burning in his gut. But when he arrived at the quiet, palm-lined pool created by an ebbing current of the Tigris, he found himself not alone by the water's edge. Instantly, all his anger was forgotten.

By all that's holy, the intoxicated mercenary marveled. *The stories about hashish* are *true!*

*   *   *

There was a second, less well-known tradition among the Old Man of the Mountain's disciples. Before the cult leader's "blades" went into action on his behalf, they were required to prepare themselves in body as well as mind. They must be ready to face any eventuality, even to die in the pursuit of their objective. Known for being capable of supreme acts of will—suicide missions among them—that much was a given for those trained at Alamut. It was no easy life the Assassins led, and the movement attracted strange followers—zealots, desperados, and madmen among them. Over the years, to focus the mind and body, a peculiar custom had developed among these marked men, to be practiced only when they embarked upon a mission they could not expect to survive.

The renegade, who had eschewed many of the ways of her former brethren, still intended to uphold this one religiously, for she knew she must be resigned to sacrificing her own life tomorrow if she even hoped to succeed in her goal. At Alamut, they taught that there was only one way to accept the possibility of one's own death—and that was to confront one's mortality dead-on. Thus, before engaging her enemy in battle tomorrow, she would practice fighting tonight.

In the nude.

Dizzy despite her efforts to limit the amount of hashish she'd smoked, distressed from her unexpectedly revealing confrontation with the mercenary, Isabeau had gone down to the river's edge to complete this second portion of the Assassins' Ritual, searching for several minutes before she found a private spot—for if she must remove her clothing, perforce she must also be alone. Along the way she'd passed stealthily around the campfires of her brethren, where the *fidai'in,* still wakeful, had gathered for their own nomads' ceremonies. A group of them had begun to improvise a haunting desert tune upon flute, hand drums, and the traditional Arab lute called an *oud.* Discreetly skirting her own men as well as the mercenaries who camped nearby until she could no longer see them and only faintly hear their music, she had carefully scouted out this place.

Isabeau knew it was vital to ensure her privacy before she began to shed the many layers of her disguise, and despite her spiraling, dizzy thoughts, she warned herself to be cautious tonight, for to be discovered would surely mean to be executed. The outraged sensibilities of Islamic men— even of her own bandits, probably, should they discover her deception—could never have borne a female who dared to decide her own destiny the way she had done, and she was well aware of it. Countless generations of misogynistic tradition could not be so easily flouted. Even with her keen skills as a warrior, there was no way Isabeau could fight off the world.

Highly trained she might be, deadly both with her body and with weapons of steel, Isabeau was also a woman, and vulnerable. Disguised ninety-nine percent of the time, she tended to forget how at risk she really was, and she knew that could be deadly. It was so seldom that she was ever forced to confront her femininity that she often did not even think of it until something—or some*one,* like Jared—re-minded her. If she ever did forget completely, if she grew overconfident, she knew it would take just one small step to go from confidence to carelessness. And in her profession, Isabeau could not afford even a tiny misstep.

This practice would remind her.

Naked, weaponless, she would be forced to confront her body's vulnerability, and then to overcome it. With careful exercises in the arts of war, she would remind each limb and sinew of its purpose, of its power as a killing machine. But it was a process, just like anything else in life. One did not just throw off one's clothes and jump right in like a child wading in the river. Gradually, slowly, one confronted the layers of the truth as one warmed up the body with slowly escalating exercise.

Even as she peeled back the layers of her desert robes, Isabeau began her practice. Off went the overrobe, as she stretched to rid her body of the kinks and soreness of the day. Off went the soft doeskin boots as she dug her toes into the sandy earth and balanced in combat stance. One by one in this same way she would release herself level by level from her hampering camouflage in search of her inner strength. And of course, hated but necessary, the veil would come off last.

Isabeau had hoped the drug would induce the required meditative trance that should accompany these drills—but the whirling she felt in her head seemed more like a state of shock than of contemplation as she reeled still from the aftereffects of the Black Lion's stunning confessions. His revelations had rocked her to the core, thrown her completely off center, and she knew she needed to find that center again if she was to have a hope of rescuing Zahra tomorrow. She must concern herself only with her own problems, ruthlessly driving out from her mind any pity or compassion she might feel for the mercenary. Yet though she knew it had been necessary to alienate Jared with her scorn, it surely hadn't been enjoyable. In fact, it had felt truly awful. After all, the man had devoted his whole life to her!

She'd done the only thing she could, Isabeau consoled herself, hoping to forestall the remorse that was ruining her concentration. One by one the Assassin forced herself to continue unwinding the wrappings that hid her identity from the world, peeling off layers and dropping them to the sandy bank even as she winced to recall her own vicious, mean-spirited words. But it felt as if she were yanking bandages off a half-healed wound, not releasing her true self from bondage. It shamed her to remember how she'd taunted Jared for his dedication, told him he was a dreamer and a deluded fool, ridiculous to spend his time in such a futile manner.

Yet, barring the full truth, it was the most honest thing the renegade could have said. She'd told Jared the girl he sought was no more—and she hadn't lied. The person he had known as Lady Isabeau de Lyon had perished long ago, leaving only the Shadow Hunter to rise from her ashes.

She'd been *forced* to laugh at Jared, damn it, forced to mock his solemn quest! How else could she possibly hope to convince him to drop it without endangering her own precarious position and Zahra's one hope for rescue? Still, Isabeau didn't think she'd ever forget the stricken look upon the Black Lion's face when her cruel derision had hit him like a lance to the helm.

Isabeau wished she could have given him the release he sought, but she simply dared not chance it. It wasn't only her own life she risked, after all, but Zahra's as well, and possibly Jamal's. Had they not been counting upon her to remain steadfast, perhaps she would have exposed her long masquerade despite the horrible risks—despite the shame of seeing Jared's disgust for what she'd become, the look of horror that would surely cross his face were he to confront her and learn all she'd seen and done since she'd been the innocent child of his acquaintance.

But Zahra *was* counting upon her. If Isabeau failed to rescue her tomorrow, the sister of her heart might die enslaved to the monster who had tormented them both so unbearably for so many years. The Assassin wasn't ready to risk it, even for the sake of the man who had devoted his life to her cause. Even if she wanted more than anything to appear before him in her own guise and finally be revealed.

The renegade stood naked at last, unveiled and unbound upon the riverbank, but also painfully alone. By rote her body took up combat stance, yet even as she began the ritual of martial drills that conditioned her body and mind for war, she felt a change in the familiar patterns taking her over. Stretching and punching, kicking and leaping lithely in the air, she ran through the accustomed routines that kept her sharp as a knife. Tonight, however, even as she simulated one-on-one combat with her usual ferocity, Isabeau felt more like the carrier of life than the harbinger of death. Her body, of its own accord, celebrated its power, but not in the manner the Old Man had intended. No matter how she tried to make her limbs conform to the proper forms she'd been taught during her time in Alamut, an older, deeper conditioning kept taking over.

Before Isabeau had ever stood among the ranks of Assassins' apprentices to be taught the secret martial arts many generations of "Old Men" had imported from the Shaolin monasteries of far-off China and the wandering mystics of India, she'd been accustomed to endless hours of similarly rigorous practices. Indeed, such training had once made her the most prized pleasure slave in Malik al-Fayed's harem.

Dance had come naturally to the graceful young girl from Lyon. The arts of seduction, however, had required many more exhaustive hours of teaching to become a part of her repertoire. Yet she had learned, through enforced practices of up to ten hours a day, how to make it look as if she had been born to the Dance of the Seven Veils, to behave as if blatant eroticism were as natural to her as breathing. She'd had no choice, for if she'd refused to conform, Malik had decreed that sweet, blameless Zahra would pay the price.

Since the day she'd escaped that life, Isabeau had sworn she would never demean herself again in this way. Yet now, alone and under no coercion, her body began to take up the long-forsworn postures and poses all by itself. Attempting to perform a fast blocking maneuver with her forearms, those arms instead raised themselves slowly and sinuously into the air above her head. Instead of stiffening to jab at an opponent, her fingers crooked gracefully as though they held castanets between them, her wrists and hands beckoning as they rotated in slow circles. When she went to plant her feet, straightening her legs, those legs shifted restlessly instead and her hips swiveled and rocked in a shimmy of pure, unconscious salaciousness. Her belly, sleek and pale in its nudity, rippled in a long, slow roll designed to draw the eye downward toward the mound of her femininity, bereft of fleece after the Arab custom and touchingly vulnerable.

Isabeau could still hear the music of her *fidai'in* coming

to her softly through the cool night air, and now they were singing to accompany it. The *oud* led the rise and fall of the men's plaintive chant, and the haunting strains of the traditional Arab lute egged her on to keep up her impromptu dance. Her mood had gone out of control, though she tried desperately to tame it and return to sanity. One moment she'd been angry, the next unutterably sorrowful, and now, it seemed, she was possessed of a wildness of spirit that drove her nigh to madness.

Jared drove her nigh to madness.

Without conscious intent, Isabeau rubbed one cheek against the silky skin of her own inner arm, reaching out and up into the dark night sky as if to call upon heaven for fulfillment. Even as her hips caught the beat of the faraway drummer, her whole body joined the rebellion, and it took the renegade gliding and swirling across the sandy bank, subtle dips and sways shaking her long, rarely unbound hair into waves that lay like teasing silver and gold scarves about her body. Helplessly Isabeau felt her last hope of completing the Assassins' ritual combat practice slide away. Instead there was only this compulsion to dance the dance of seduction, and the searing image in her mind of the mercenary standing before her to watch it.

For the first time, imagining his gaze upon her, Isabeau actually believed herself attractive, truly felt desirable. If only he were here . . .

And then he *was* there.

*   *   *

Jared de Navarre had just died and gone to Paradise.

Exile, oath-breaker, and mercenary by trade, he had never expected to attain it. Yet heaven lay as plain as day before him now, more magnificent than even he had dreamed. For there, beside the moonlit Tigris, stood a goddess without question.

A naked goddess.

She could have been Athena, warrior divinity of the Greeks, with her Hellenic blond tresses and militant stance. Yet a moment later he thought she could just as well have been Salome, earthly dancer and enchantress of men, for the rhythms with which she moved seemed to flow and blend into one another, first combative, then seductive.

Her wrist, twisting, was the single most erotic sight Jared had ever seen. Just that, and no more, was enough to send the mercenary into an inferno of blazing desire that stole his very breath away. Though she hadn't caught sight of him yet, this naked apparition, with her blond curls cascading wildly about her slender, moon-bathed figure, had hooked him already with just this slightest of gestures. The most blatant of erotic posturing could not have touched him more. It was not the phantom woman's nudity—though that was undeniably stunning—but the subtle, almost feline way she used it that made Jared lose his breath and stumble suddenly to his knees to worship this unlikely vision.

He was hallucinating after all, Jared knew, for this impossible dancer by the water looked like his own lost Isabeau.

Can it be she? his whirling brain wondered, even as his body responded with painful urgency. His body did not need a name to recognize its perfect mate. He must be dreaming, or dead indeed, Jared reasoned, using the tiny portion of his brain that still had room for logic. The woman before him, swaying gently to the far-off music and unaware of him kneeling there, looked like something spun out of memory and wishful fantasy combined. She could not be real. No. Jared was definitely hallucinating.

Still, as he watched the illusory beauty whirling to and fro before him, a strange sense of *knowing* jolted the mercenary, similar to the disorienting sensation he'd felt staring into the Assassin's eyes on the day of their impromptu sparring match. If Isabeau had lived, might she have looked like this today? Jared wondered. But this . . . this glorious apparition was the product of his drug-crazed imagination, wasn't it? She had none of the earthiness or imperfections he associated with mortal women. Watching the sleek creature of moonlight twirl unselfconsciously upon the sandy bank, he nonetheless thought she had something of the youthful, pixielike spirit of his lost betrothed. The features had the same delicacy, the same porcelain purity and rare coloring. Was it his fevered imagination that had conjured up this amalgam of dusty memory and conjecture before Jared's eyes? Talking of her tonight with the Assassin must have brought this strange episode to pass.

She couldn't be real, but that didn't stop the moonlit sylph from being the most profoundly stirring vision ever to come before the Black Lion's gaze. Mouth dry, eyes burning, he knelt amid the sandy brush and simply watched. One question occupied his thoughts.

Did she dance for him?

One false turn, and Isabeau came face-to-face with the object of her fantasies. She froze indecisively, peering across the darkened space of riverbank and up the shallow hill to where this longed-for intruder had appeared. Everything in her soul screeched to a halt for a single endless second, and yet strangely enough, it wasn't panic or fear that caused her sudden pause. The Assassin felt neither as she confronted Jared's kneeling figure upon the bank and realized he'd been watching her.

Somehow, the drug just made it all right. She wasn't afraid. This was a dream, a wish fulfilled for her by the generous properties of the Assassins' heady herbal blend. The Black Lion wasn't really here watching her naked any more than she was really here herself, dancing in the buff like a moonstruck idiot when she should be preparing for war. It was inconceivable, and therefore it couldn't be real, she reasoned muzzily. Somehow, without her noticing it, she must have completed her exercises and gone to sleep back in her tent. This was all a dream she was having—a beautiful, once-in-a-lifetime dream—praise be to Allah! Whether it was wrong or right, Isabeau didn't want to wake up. Bare meters away, Jared knelt before her like a supplicant, but even as her steps faltered and she stood still before him, Isabeau felt no shame in her nudity, experiencing instead a rush of triumph that suffused her entire being unlike anything she'd ever felt before. It was triumph, yes; but something more as well.

Power.

The untapped source of strength the Old Man had always urged her to seek deep in the core of her being finally surged through Isabeau in full force. But when it did, it did so in a way the crafty ancient warlord had never led her to anticipate, for this was *feminine* power.

Always until now, she had believed her female form was the curse that had doomed her to slavery and powerlessness in the first place. She'd always believed that if she wanted power, she must think and act like a man. She'd trained herself like a man, never making allowances for her feminine figure, forcing her body to become as strong as a man's, learning tricks to overcome her slighter stature and slender limbs. She'd substituted sheer grit for muscle mass, determination for raw power, and that formula had never let her down. She'd learned to depend upon her body's training in the masculine arts of war, and it had kept her alive in return. But never, until now, had she seen the power of the feminine side of her being.

As a dancer, her body had always been a tool for others' pleasure. As a warrior, it had become a tool for vengeance. Now, suddenly, Isabeau understood it could be so much more than either one of those things. The potential was there for great mysteries to be unraveled. It was all there in the eyes of the man who watched her.

Somehow, some way, all of the answers to those mysteries lay within Jared de Navarre, staring back at her now with his lion-gold eyes afire. Amazed, panting, the Assassin realized that she did not want to run from what she saw there. She wanted to run *toward* it. The moment grew pregnant between the Assassin and the mercenary, caught together in the moonlight. And then, betwixt two heartbeats, her decision was made—or perhaps the hashish made it for her. As the music of the *fidai'in* swelled and grew to a new crescendo off behind them, Isabeau took up its challenge, tossing her head in a defiant shower of silver-kissed strands and arching her back in a sultry gesture of invitation. She spun and leapt, twined and turned, arched and writhed sinuously once again as she had before the interruption—but this time, all in the light of Jared's lucent amber gaze. All for the pleasure she read in her Black Lion's heart.

And in offering him this gift, the entranced Shadow Hunter felt a strange renewal in herself, as though the true gift had been given her instead. The gift of rapture. The gift of herself. She wanted somehow to share this welling fullness, and in the cool of the early autumn night, the scarred Assassin, survivor of so many trials and terrors, made bold to pass it on to the man who had sparked this wondrous new sentiment in her heart. Simultaneously, her heart and mind rang with the joyful refrain: *He never forgot me!*

She danced the way she never had upon compulsion, the way her teachers had assured her she could, the way her potential had promised and she had never delivered. And then she danced her way, slowly, over to where he knelt. Unashamed of her nudity, the renegade sank slowly to her own knees before him. As Isabeau lowered herself gracefully to the sandy bank with a soft fall of glorious flaxen hair tumbling all about her body, she draped her strong, slender arms around the rapt warrior's neck. Hearing his quick, gasping inhalation at the contact, as if he could not believe she was real, Isabeau made bold to assure him she was. She kissed him.

The kiss landed sweet and warm and joyous, trembling upon his sculpted lips. And it transformed the mercenary into a lightning rod, conducting pure electricity through every pore in his being. This chimera, this glorious mirage, was *kissing* him! Jared felt as though he had exploded in a shattering burst of ecstasy, as though he had tried to embrace the sun and been consumed instead.

If he had known the Assassin's drug would have such an astonishing effect, Jared thought headily, by damn, he'd have sought it out long before now! Indeed, the mercenary thought with the last rational scrap of his brain, he would have demanded it of the man—and if Sayyad had refused, he'd have fought the Assassin to the death for just one moment of such indescribable pleasure.

But the Assassin was, presumably, asleep by now in his tent, while he, Jared, had succumbed to these strange and rapturous dreams down here by the riverbanks. Al-Zul would not appreciate being woken, he assumed, even if it was to receive the mercenary's slobbering, incoherent thanks. So instead, Jared would remain here as long as it lasted, enveloped in euphoric, impossible dreams. Dreams of a river sylph with Isabeau's features grown to woman-hood, and a body of such silky perfection even his fantasies could never have conceived of it. He gathered this phantom lover closer in his arms, stroking her cool flesh all over, determined to hold on to her as long as he could.

"Isabeau," he groaned hoarsely.

The sound of her name jerked the Assassin out of her rapturous haze like a soap bubble bursting under a torrent of cold water. Hideous, gut-clenching fear shot through her where rapturous pleasure had been.

Suddenly, she felt very, very naked, despite the powerful warrior wrapped around her. Great Allah, was it a dream produced by the hashish, or was this real? Was Jared truly here with her, holding her in his strong, sweet arms? Had she really kissed him? It must be a hallucination. But, oh— what if he *was* real, and this was actually happening?

By the Prophet's very blood, it would mean Jared knew she was alive! And from thence, it would be just a short leap of the imagination for him to figure out who she was— the Assassin who had hired him! A million thoughts, ques-tions, and feelings swamped the renegade all at once, even as she still thrilled to the feel of his strong, warm hands upon her flesh. The hashish paralyzed her momentarily, freezing her with indecision. Should she flee, or attack?

Her fingers rested against Jared's strong, corded neck, holding him breathlessly close as he strewed fiery kisses up and down her own shivering throat. Cold logic told Isabeau she should kill him now for discovering her here like this.

All she would have to do was twist, and her skilled hands would abruptly cut short his life. Yet the thought sickened the Assassin in ways she couldn't begin to analyze, and she knew she could never bring herself to do it. But wait, she thought desperately—mayhap she would not have to resort to such a drastic measure. After all, what did he really see right now? Wasn't he as deep in the clutches of the drug that had made her believe the circumstances were surreal as she had been? If so, the situation could perhaps still be salvaged.

Did Jared see a stranger in the woman he now held, or had he connected her with her daytime persona? *By the desert's forty winds,* she agonized, *does he know I'm the Assassin who hired his services, lied, and kept him in the dark?* Isabeau looked down at the beautiful man cradling her naked form upon his lap. His face was bathed in the light of the moon, his eyes closed against the tide of passion as he buried his lips against the curve of her shoulder. The grimness normally writ upon his warrior's features was gone for once, as though he had regained a gift lost in childhood, never thought to be recovered. His heart knew the truth. It was too late to stop that. But his mind had not made the connection yet, and she must prevent that at all costs.

Once again Isabeau did something to Jared that night she found abhorrent. She peeled herself loose from her dream lover's embrace, feeling as if she had just rent out her heart and left it behind in his grasp. And then, drawing upon her Assassin's training, she simply disappeared.

Jared was left alone with the night, clutching empty air.

CHAPTER TWELVE

"Gulbayez."

The venomous whisper came from the foliage framing the far end of the little offshoot of the river. A soft hand, conspicuously free of calluses, pushed aside a broad palm frond, careful not to let it rustle. But its possessor needn't have worried. By the time she dared stick her head out from concealment, both parties the woman had been spying on were gone.

By the veil of Fatima herself, that was the White Rose! I should have known the bitch wasn't dead! Ullayah thought viciously. *And now it seems she's seduced some Frankish warrior into fighting for her cause, the slut. It's a good thing I made Abu take me all the way out here tonight to answer nature's call. Why,* she thought giddily, *if I hadn't convinced that prissy little eunuch I needed more privacy than the latrines around Malik's caravan could provide, I'd have missed this altogether!*

The annoyingly persistent eunuch assigned to guard her night and day tugged anxiously upon her sleeve now. "Mistress," he whispered in his thin, high voice. "Please, we must be gone from here. I am sure Jamal would not approve of this business of venturing abroad at night. We must return to camp before we are seen. Your reputation—"

"That blasted Jamal wasn't so worried about my reputation earlier when he sent me and my entourage outside the city a day earlier than the rest of the women, now was he?" she hissed furiously at the meek little slave. "He was eager enough then to throw us out among the rabble, though he claimed it was in deference to my status as first wife." Then a thought occurred to Ullayah. *Ah-hah! Now the rumors I've been hearing about Jamal's suspicious activities begin to make sense. That black bastard always had a soft spot for Gulbayez. He must be helping her now! And he must have sent me and my faction of the harem out here early in hopes of hiding his treachery.* Only sheer luck and a small bladder had gifted her with this early warning.

It gratified Ullayah to know she'd been right setting her spies on the harem master, though until tonight she'd found nothing substantive with which to hang the chief eunuch she'd always hated so. Now Jamal, along with his miraculously rejuvenated little favorite, would pay for all the slights she'd suffered! He'd learn to regret his insolent manner, and Ullayah would be there to relish every minute of his downfall. But she must be smart. Jamal was no mean enemy to take on, despite his deceptively fragile outward appearance. She needed to figure out exactly what sort of plot her old rival Gulbayez and the eunuch were hatching together before she could make a move against them. And what it had to do with the touching little scene she'd just witnessed between the White Rose and the tall, handsome Frank by the river.

If her husband's former favorite slave was still alive, shadowing the emir's convoy with the aid of that fine-looking foreign warrior she'd been wrapped around tonight, what kind of action might they be planning together? she wondered, but the explanation was already plain enough to Ullayah. Of course, there was only one answer that made sense. The bitch was after Zahra!

That blond slut had always had a thing about protecting the fragile younger girl who so resembled her, and who had suffered so much torment for the chance resemblance they shared. The two of them had been the talk of the harem at one time, and all Malik could think about, causing him to neglect his other concubines. Gulbayez had been a woman apart to Malik, she thought wrathfully, her gaze burning a hole in the spot where the other woman had stood. He'd been so obsessed with that white *ferenghi* whore, Malik would have let the rest of his harem languish in lonely neglect while he amused himself solely with her.

He hadn't seen his own peril in becoming so wrapped up in the foreign bitch. He hadn't seen how dangerous that skinny, pale-skinned upstart had been, how she had thrown the well-ordered hierarchy of the women's quarters into dissent and mutiny. Men never could comprehend how much damage a single rebellious female could do in the confined little world of a harem. No, they just locked the doors and left it up to the other women to take care of the problem. That was exactly why Ullayah had had the bitch killed the first time!

She'd thought she'd gotten the job done right as well as gotten away with it, but now it appeared that the cunning Gulbayez must have had a friend in the harem to save her from the poison Ullayah's minions had administered to her rival's food. It'd been Jamal, of course. It didn't take a genius to guess that much. That ball-less bastard had been undermining her authority in the harem from the day she first arrived! She wouldn't have put it past him to have orchestrated the whole escape, though she still couldn't quite figure out how he'd done it. *No wonder,* she thought now, *he was so helpful in covering up what I'd done to his little favorite. I thought he was trying to curry favor with me, but now I see he was just ensuring the girl's getaway. Damn him to the forty hells. And every day since then he's worked to discredit me with my husband!*

Though none of them actually *liked* their master—indeed, one would have to be crazy to appreciate that brutal sadist—that didn't change the fact that the women of Malik's harem fought tooth and nail to gain his attention. Becoming a "favorite" was the only way to earn status or wield power in the women's quarters, unless one was lucky enough to bear the master a son. Many, including Ullayah, had resented the two fair-haired girls who stole all their master's time, though they had not envied the actual attentions he'd inflicted upon them. If Gulbayez was back, it could only be because she wanted to rescue Malik's little jewel from the fate she'd once shared with her. For nothing less would any sane woman venture so close to the twisted emir after successfully escaping him!

Well, the White Rose would not prise Zahra free this

time; not if Ullayah had anything to say about it. The emir's neglected wife began to smile as she made this determination. Her shapely, red-painted lips stretched wider and wider across pearly teeth beneath her gauzy veil, and then a little chuckle of pleasure escaped her. It was followed by more laughter, louder and louder, until the little wadi outside Baghdad was fairly ringing with the sound of it. She didn't even care that Abu was frowning at her worriedly, still timidly trying to get her to return with him to the camp. For now, at last, she saw a way to pay back both her enemies together. Ullayah would finally have her revenge!

Then the dark-eyed beauty sobered abruptly. Of course Malik, damn his blind pride, would never believe a word of it if she told him what she'd seen tonight. They'd both stood over Gulbayez's supposedly dead body years ago, after all—or so they'd believed. She wasn't stupid enough to run to the emir with a tale as incredible as this and no proof to back it up. Ullayah was already out of favor enough with her lord and master as it was, despite the strong sons she had given him and the dark, voluptuous beauty that any sane, *normal* man would have praised to the heavens, instead of treasuring only those sickly white girls he so bizarrely preferred. No, Malik had never listened to her. He barely paid her more attention than he did the rugs upon which he lay, and she knew it well.

Al-Fayed wouldn't believe her tonight if she walked right up to him and swore before a whole mosque full of holy men that she'd seen Gulbayez alive. Jamal, that fiendish schemer, had poisoned her husband against her too completely, and would ensure she came off sounding like a hysterical shrew—if she wasn't refused admittance to her master's presence altogether. Though technically freed since she'd borne her master's sons, and thus of higher status than the slave Jamal, both of them knew who held the real power. Until today she'd trodden warily around him, allowed the eunuch his petty triumphs. But now he threatened to keep Ullayah from her just revenge, and she couldn't allow that to happen! She must think up a plausible story that would grant her an audience with her husband before it was too late.

If he won't believe I saw her tonight, he might still believe I overheard a troop of foreign mercenaries suspiciously near our caravan, talking about stealing Malik's coveted jewel. At least, he'll believe me if I can get this stupid Abu to confirm it—which he'll do if he knows what's good for him.

She dug her nails mercilessly into the eunuch's hand where he'd foolishly dared to place it upon her arm, imploring her with urgent tugs to return to the camp. She heard him gasp and whisper, "Mistress," again pleadingly as her sharp, talonlike nails drew blood. *I know the only thing Abu fears more than Jamal is me. He's not entirely stupid, though he's too timid to make a truly useful tool. If he adds his voice to mine, then the emir will* have *to take precautions—Malik won't dare risk his precious al-Zahra for anything. Since Gulbayez's unlamented demise, he holds her tighter to him than ever.*

Her husband would surely defend against the threat she'd reported by sending out his Mamluk bodyguards to stop the kidnappers in their tracks. *And this time, I'll make sure they finish the job I started . . . Zahra won't escape her fate any more than the rest of us. I don't care what her dear "sister" promised her. If I have my way, they'll both suffer as they deserve!*

Ullayah laughed again, wrapping her plump arms about her softly rounded belly as she gave in to mirth. She hadn't been this happy in years.

CHAPTER THIRTEEN

The morning star had yet to fade from the pinkening sky when the warriors gathered by the bank of the Tigris the next morning. But though they were already beginning to prepare for the ambush they planned to launch in mere minutes, no one observing their actions would have been able to guess as much. To the rest of the world, they seemed like ordinary traders eager to get an early start, saddling their horses and watering their pack beasts by the riverbanks even as they loaded the bawling camels and stiff-kneed, protesting mules once more with their various burdens.

Still decked out in their civilian disguises, the men of the false caravan pretended to be adjusting the baggage piled atop the newly wakened animals for the benefit of anyone watching, but in truth they were unwrapping their stowed weapons from the bundles that had concealed them inside the animals' packs. That the men continued to wear long desert outer robes that could easily hide weapons and kept their faces covered went unnoticed as well—for no one outside their camp was awake yet to notice them.

Across the river, the warriors could just make out Malik's enormous caravan through the morning mist, sprawled out like a child in innocent slumber, and just as unwary of imminent attack. Its members slept on through the pre-dawn chill, not so much as a stray dog barking to disrupt the rest of the emir's many stewards and servants. They could hardly have been *more* vulnerable to ambush than the way they had situated themselves, all scattered about the banks with no perimeter sentries to sound the alert—but to those waiting to attack them, such good fortune seemed overdue.

Tensions were high among the men of the Assassin's strike force, but so were spirits. After so many days of

travel and of uncertainty, at least on the part of the mercenaries, they were eager to be about work they knew how
to do. And warfare was something with which every man
among them was intimately familiar. Clutching blades surreptitiously beneath flowing *abbas* and murmuring soothingly to their high-strung horses, the men were more than
ready to go—especially Pierre's little group, who had already been up for hours about their own nefarious business.
All they awaited now was the order to attack.

At the head of the tightly bunched group, Jared and the
Assassin stood next to one another, overseeing the prepa-
rations. Pretending to be busy adjusting their saddle girths,
neither one looked at the other, though for very different
reasons.

Jared was remembering Sayyad's mocking words to him
in the tent last night. Seeing him again, standing there so
aloof and so damned *smug* behind his enveloping robes, the
mercenary burned with resentment and the urge to tell the
renegade where Sayyad could stick his unwanted opinions
about Jared's romantic ideals. Yet at the same time, he
couldn't deny that he also wanted to question the man about
the nature of the potion he'd given Jared, which had apparently so rekindled his desire to find Isabeau that he'd
thought for a moment he'd actually conjured her up.

For indeed, having no other explanation for what had
happened after their confrontation in Sayyad's tent, the
mercenary had been forced to ascribe the strangely potent,
utterly baffling dream he'd had by the water's edge to the
hashish. He'd been so caught in its grip, truth to tell, that
he hadn't even been able to say how he'd found his own
tent again after the hallucination had ended, leaving him
achingly alone and forlorn, with his arms clasped around
nothing but the wind. Chagrined, Jared realized he was *still*
trying to recapture those fleeting instants of unsought-for
ecstasy now, when he should be preparing his mind for
combat.

Isabeau, on the other hand, was not trying to recapture
anything at the moment. Indeed, she'd been trying to *forget*

the exquisite flavor of Jared's lips upon her own for the whole of the sleepless night she'd just spent, and had been having no success whatsoever. It was even worse at present than when she'd tossed and turned on her lonely pallet, for now this dangerous source of distraction was standing right next to her, tall and solid and so *real* she could almost taste him again. It was agonizing!

Thanks be to Allah, he had not guessed that the fantasy maiden who'd so suddenly appeared and even more abruptly disappeared last night was the Assassin Sayyad al-Zul who took such pains to keep his face hidden from Jared. And if all went well this morning, she told herself comfortingly, she'd never have to worry about discovery from that quarter again. With no maudlin goodbyes to prolong their ill-fated reacquaintance, she and Jared would part ways today in the heat of battle, and they would never speak again. He would go his way, the heavier by a weight of her hard-won gold, and she would go hers, the richer by her own heart's desire—Zahra. It was best to end it thus, Isabeau told herself firmly, swallowing down the strange, uncomfortable lump of regret that had formed in her throat at the thought. Such foolish sentiment could do naught but get her killed.

"Your men have accomplished their tampering within the emir's camp?" she asked tightly, still not looking at the mercenary. She stroked Zephyr's neck and breathed her familiar scent into the mare's nostrils comfortingly, waiting for Jared's affirmation.

"Yes. Any minute now al-Fayed's men will be waking to find their gear scattered and their animals grazing free, their pickets pulled up in the night. That is, if you still plan to wait until they awaken before falling upon them?" Jared asked this in a censorious tone, making it very clear that he disapproved of this plan.

"We must allow time for Malik and his entourage to arrive before we begin the offensive. Then, mercenary, be assured we will strike down upon them with all the fury you could desire. Until then, we wait." The Shadow Hunter's tone was final. She kept her attention upon her mare instead of her ally, checking the weapons strapped to her saddle, the fit of her tasseled leather bridle, the short stirrups she'd adjusted twice already. Anything to avoid looking at Jared. And at last, as she leaned against the mare's sturdy withers and scanned the slowly waking enemy camp across the shallow river ford, Isabeau saw a sight that helped her forget about the mercenary in truth.

"Ah!" she hissed. "There he is, that bastard son of forty devils! Surrounded by his harem and the damnable Mamluk bodyguard, just as I thought."

Indeed he was. The emir, riding tall upon a handsome bay stallion, was encircled by the women he'd enslaved, making him look like a puffin surrounded by a murder of crows. Their black-clad figures were demurely veiled from head to heels and protected on all sides by a dozen well-armed eunuch guards above and beyond Malik's own personal guard, who marched as outriders along the outer edges and rear of the procession. They came across the misty fields from the direction of the city like sleepwalkers, looking sluggish and half-awake as they headed for the riverside, banners rippling and armor clanking.

The camp itself was beginning to stir now, a few cooks kicking up their fires and some opportunistic scavenger dogs beginning to bark to greet the day. One or two men arose, scratching their heads as they took note of the camp's sloppy state of disarray, nudging their brothers to help them clean up as they saw the emir arriving in the distance. Apparently Pierre's compatriots had been subtle with their sabotage, for no suspicions had been aroused as yet, as far as the covertly watching warriors could see. The emir's followers could not have looked less menacing or more vulnerable to the outlaws who observed them.

"*Now,* mercenary," Isabeau hissed. "Gather your men and ride upon them *now*! Scatter those devils in the camp as best you can, and keep them from riding to the emir's defense when I and my men make our charge for him.

Remember: no matter what happens, stick to the plan. Don't get in my way!"

Mounting, the Shadow Hunter tossed her last words to the mercenary over her shoulder. "Farewell, Black Lion, and may we never meet again! *Hi-yaah!*" And then the Assassin was gone, a streak of black on white as she and her mare splashed first across the bend in the shallow river, followed closely by the mounts of her *fidai'in* as they charged.

The mercenary was only paces behind, his men grinning with the fever of battle as they rode to his side. Their astonished pack beasts stayed where they were at the water's edge, staring after the suddenly galvanized men who'd just abandoned them. But this was no time to worry about the fate of camels or pack mules. Now was for the madness of battle! Shouting and screaming like men demented to put the fear of hell upon their foe, the mercenaries rode breakneck into the teeth of the fray.

Jared's orders were to make sure chaos reigned. That was easy enough. He had only to let nature take its course as the astonished caravan guards began to come alive to the fact that they were under attack. As Sayyad peeled off to the right in the direction of the wealthy emir, accompanied by most of the bandits, Jared and his own men crashed on into the dismayed camp with the rest, where guards, guides, and camel drovers were already beginning to scatter in their wake like frightened children running before a storm. Running, he saw, toward the far edge of camp, where a huge pile of household goods had been stacked up in preparation for loading; rugs and furniture and fine kitchenware all tumbled together in a mountain of doubtlessly priceless belongings.

They would be trapped once they reached that convenient barricade, Jared saw, his heart thumping with savage joy in his chest. Indeed, they'd be caged just like sheep in a pen, herded there helpless by the pursuing mercenaries. This was going to be easy! Jared thought. He didn't know why Sayyad had been so worried. Still, it was strange. Al-

Fayed hadn't half the men Jared had been led to believe
he'd find protecting the caravan. Then, as they came closer,
he understood just why the Assassin had cautioned him
about the dangers of this assignment. But as he took in the
disheartening sight that met his gaze, Jared guessed even
the ever-reckless Sayyad would be dismayed when he saw
what was awaiting them.

There weren't half as many opponents as Jared had expected in the emir's camp. There were *twice* as many.
These unexpected reinforcements must have arrived during
the night, sometime after Pierre and his cohorts had completed their surreptitious mission of sabotage.

When those running to escape the hooves of the Black
Lion's Pride thundering down upon them had reached the
makeshift wall of furnishings, they'd divided themselves in
two, running to either side as though that might save them
from the score of determined mercenaries chasing after
them. This was just as Jared wanted, and exactly as his
men had hoped the attack would go. But even as the mercenaries made to split and herd the fugitives back to where
they could be taken prisoner and disarmed, an absolute *wall*
of heavily armed men came swarming out from behind the
gigantic stack of dry goods to engage them.

Their careful ambush, it seemed, was no surprise to the
emir despite all the precautions they'd taken. Malik was
ready for them!

Screaming, brandishing weapons of cold iron and sharp
steel, there were so many of these newcomers that the mercenaries were nearly swept away in that first instant by the
very tide of their numbers. Seeming to startle their own
brethren as much as the mercenaries who attacked them,
the new troop of soldiers—by their costume and insignia
presumably the rest of Malik's rabidly loyal Mamluk slaves
whose ranks had seemed oddly thin to Jared earlier—
poured down among the mercenaries, creating chaos indeed.

Howling and snapping like great dogs of war, these reinforcements turned the mercenaries' triumph to ashes as

the two forces engaged with a crash of contact so loud Jared's ears rang from it. Instinctively, he raised his great steel blade to ward off the scimitar of the snarling, foul-breathed man who came at him first. The Mamluk went down, his snarl fading to surprise as he was slashed horribly across the chest and shoulder. He was dead before Jared's horse trampled him.

"*À moi!*" the Black Lion cried, rallying his men as he saw them falter beneath the onslaught. "To me, Lion's Pride!"

Jared could hear Pierre shouting as well, his strangely deep bass rolling out from his short barrel chest as he wheeled his stout pony about and caught his commander's eye. His teeth gleamed white in his dark beard as he ordered the men to turn upon their attackers, form ranks and hack their way clear. The Black Lion himself encouraged each to use his weapon of choice, yelling to Ali to draw his bow and sight on the Mamluk captain at one end of the field, and to Harald to bring forth his heavy staff and crush a few skulls even as he himself smote two more of the enemy with his flashing sword. Taking a numbing blow to his shield, the mercenary simultaneously kicked at a man who was grabbing at his heel to unseat him, his metal-shod foot knocking a few teeth loose and disabling the attacker neatly. But even then he knew it was a hopeless fight.

Someone must have tipped off al-Fayed. The ambush they'd planned, difficult at best, had been turned back upon them quite easily now that the element of surprise—their only real advantage—was lost. The situation was hopeless for Sayyad and his men; absolutely un-winnable from a tactical standpoint. Any good commander could see it. If the bandits and their hired cousins wanted to even stay alive, their only option was to flee back the way they'd come and hope they could run faster than their wrathful enemy—thankfully afoot for the moment—could follow. Yet when Jared looked around to confirm that Sayyad agreed, as surely he must, he was shocked at what he saw.

What was al-Zul *doing*? Jared paused to blink the sweat

from his eyes and impatiently flung back the strands of muddy auburn hair that had come loose from his topknot to interfere with his vision. But what he saw didn't change despite his disbelief. The Shadow Hunter had attacked, of all things, the *harem*!

The Assassin didn't want Malik, Jared realized, or any treasure he carried—he wanted one of his women!

Outrage filled the mercenary as last night's words rang in his head. *Romantic fool. How do you call yourself a man, mercenary, when you've wasted your whole life on a woman?* Sayyad had taunted. But now, as the word *al-Zahra* took on a new meaning to him, Jared cursed as he realized that the Assassin was risking *all* of their lives on just such a prize. Al-Zahra, the jewel, was a woman!

He saw the Assassin across the battlefield, fighting with the fury of a dervish, two great curved swords flashing in his hands and the horse between his legs pivoting and wheeling like an extension of the man himself. Foes went down around him left and right, Mamluks and harem guards alike unable to withstand his wrathful blows. Most of the frightened women were being herded away to safety by those with the wit to take them in charge, while yet more Mamluks had joined the emir's side as Jared fought on the other end of the field, swelling the numbers of their enemies to at least four-to-one. Still the Assassin fought on undeterred—and it seemed Sayyad had actually attained his goal. A slender, black-clad figure, veiled from head to toe, clung to the back of his saddle neatly, culled from the flock of other women.

For a moment, it looked to Jared as though the Shadow Hunter would succeed in getting away with the girl against the odds. But he lost track of the Assassin when an angry Mamluk, scimitar swinging, charged up between them and Jared was forced to stave him off. Urging his steed over the crumpled corpse a moment later, the mercenary craned his neck to see if he could spot the Assassin again, and feared for a moment the man had gone down in the interval. But no, there he was again, surrounded by a dozen enraged men with weapons bristling. Somehow, he'd gotten cut off from his own men and was fighting alone while the *fidai'in* sought in vain to come to his aid, their numbers insufficient to break through the circle of foes that had gathered.

Jared told himself it was not his concern, even as he spurred his horse across the field in that direction, wading hock-deep in churned-up mud and fallen foes. Sayyad himself had ordered Jared and his men to stay out of this part of the fight—effectively, to mind their own business—but the seasoned mercenary knew that even the legendary renegade could not hope to triumph against so many. Calling to his men to break off their engagement with the ambushing Mamluks and back him up instead, he started across the chaos toward the Assassin. They'd be forced to retreat soon enough in any case, Jared knew, if they were not to let themselves be killed in some futile attempt to fight to the death. If they were going to fail so ignominiously, he thought, the least he could do was save his company's reputation by aiding their ungrateful employer on the way out of this fiasco.

For it was, indeed, a complete and utter rout. Obviously, they'd been betrayed by someone, somewhere along the line. Malik had not only been ready for them; if the number of his rabid slave soldiers were any indicator of his wrath, the emir was out for blood. But Sayyad didn't seem to care what happened to the rest of them as long as he got his chance at this mysterious jewel of a woman he'd snatched. As far as Jared could tell when he approached the scene, all that mattered to the Assassin was the girl who hugged his waist for dear life. Was the secretive Shadow Hunter as much a lover as a fighter? Had he dragged forty warriors to their doom for the sake of some tawdry love affair? Christ's wounds, Jared swore wrathfully, if they survived, the man certainly would have some explaining to do!

A harem guard made a pass with his saber at Sayyad just then, missed, and caught the edge of the girl's trailing veil instead, very nearly wounding her in the process. As it was, the veil was torn loose from around her head, and suddenly the mercenary caught a glimpse of blond hair swinging free beneath.

Jared's heart stopped. His mind froze with leaping hope as it always did, even now, at the sight of any fair-haired female. And then the garment came free entirely, and even at this distance he could see the great beauty that had been hidden underneath.

Sayyad and I have the same taste in women, at least, the mercenary thought crazily. They both seemed to be after rare blond women. Yet he could not tell at this distance if this was she for whom he had sought so endlessly, or just another false lead doomed to disappoint his hopes. *I must know for sure,* he thought, spurring his horse forward. Then several things happened at once.

First, Jared nearly died.

The pike whizzing at him from just behind his ear went unnoticed for a precious second because of his distraction. At his side as always, Big Pierre, his craggy face puckered with a curious mixture of protectiveness and disgust, deflected the blow with his own shield and called over to Jared. "Wake up, you great sleeping slug! Or next time I'll let the bastard pierce your ear for you!" But Jared barely heard him for what happened next.

Just as he was turning to acknowledge Pierre's admonishment, there came a cry that froze him in his tracks.

"Isabeau!"

The harsh, distorted scream rang out eerily across the battlefield. Jared's attention became riveted once more on the Assassin and his precious burden. But though he saw it coming, there was nothing the mercenary could do in time to stop what happened next.

The blonde was ripped from Sayyad's saddle by a great, burly hulk of a soldier who swept her up on his own horse, even as the Assassin took a ferocious blow to the side from another of the encroaching Mamluks. The slight, black-robed figure curled up around the wound for a second as if he would collapse, and Jared thought surely he'd been dealt a mortal blow. The force behind it, and the angle—

surely there was no way he could survive . . . But then, amazingly, the Assassin straightened up determinedly and drove his mare after the man who'd ripped the prize from his grasp.

Isabeau? Jared thought dizzily, only half his mind focusing on the task of hewing his way through the circle of opponents who surrounded Sayyad. Had the Assassin just cried out the name of Jared's sworn betrothed? He couldn't pinpoint the source of the cry, and in truth, wasn't even sure it hadn't been his imagination that had taken the incoherent screams and shouts of battle and turned them into the one name he so longed to hear. But it was vital that he find out.

Jared wondered crazily if the strange dream he'd had last night had been some sort of premonition. Could his Isabeau truly be alive? Only Sayyad al-Zul seemed to hold the answer, the deceitful little wretch. Had the Assassin purposely concealed his knowledge of their shared desire to find her after Jared had confessed it so unwarily last night? Perhaps that was why he'd mocked the mercenary so viciously—to throw him off the scent!

But Jared realized the facts didn't matter now. The reasons didn't matter. The only thing that *did* matter was that, for the first time in over a decade, he had real reason to believe Isabeau might be alive. He must go to her!

Agony streaked through Isabeau as the blade slipped past her guard and sliced through the layers of padding she wore about her chest and midsection. It cut white-hot into her flesh with a cruel savagery more vicious than any wound she'd ever yet received. But even worse was feeling Zahra being torn from her protective grasp after holding her close for those few precious seconds. She heard Zahra scream her name in panic, and snarling, turned like a wolf at bay to attack those who had dared steal her heart's sister from her grasp. But by the Prophet, there were so many of them! Isabeau couldn't even see Zahra. Couldn't see anything but a red haze of pain and unbearable failure.

And then into that haze, Jared de Navarre, riding like
the very devil to her rescue. Men fell beneath his sword as
he approached like flowers mown down by a deranged
reaper; one man cut nigh in half, another going down with
his face cleaved in, yet others screaming and cursing vilely
as they were trampled beneath the dark stallion's hooves.

She had never been so glad to see anyone in her life,
Isabeau thought faintly. Her whole right side was wet with
the blood flowing warmly down her leg and filling up the
cuff of her boot. The world around her was beginning to
whirl nauseatingly. She felt tears of exhaustion stinging at
her eyes and blinked them away as she drew in an unsteady
breath. She was thankful beyond words for the moment's
reprieve he'd created with his timely arrival—so much so
that she could scarcely gather her wits as he thundered up.

"Where's Isabeau?" Jared growled as he reached her
side with several of his men mere paces behind.

"What . . . ?" The Assassin was confused, frightened
suddenly. Why was he asking for her, when here she stood,
right before him? Had she misheard? It was possible; her
ears were ringing rather loudly at the moment. Terror and
bewilderment made her thick-witted, and she could not
catch her breath.

The mercenary must have sensed her bemusement. "Isabeau," he insisted, speaking more slowly. "Did you see
which way they took her? I lost sight of her in the mêlée."
He looked around sharply, assessing the situation. "Ah,
never mind, man. There's no time for that now. We'll have
to fall back and regroup or be cut to pieces. Come on!"

"What . . . ?" Isabeau repeated stupidly. It seemed to be
all she could think to say. Still stunned, wounded, and in
shock from the reversals their sure-to-win forces had suffered, she couldn't seem to process what was going on.
After all their careful planning, she found herself reeling
from how close she'd come to spiriting away Zahra safely
in her arms, only to fail at the last instant. Isabeau couldn't
shift thoughts quickly enough to keep up with Jared's orders.

"I said, come *on*—or stay and be killed if that's your choice. I care not, you suicidal bastard. I ought to let you rot, for what you've got us into today!" he snapped, grabbing the Assassin's arm and shaking it ferociously. "I would, too, if you didn't have some damn good explaining to do once we're safely out of here." Jared spurred his mount around, and his men fell into step behind him as they splashed back across the river as fast as their horses would carry them.

She should have killed him for talking to her that way. For daring to lay hands upon her. For ordering her about like some disgraced lackey in front of all their men. Instead, Isabeau followed numbly.

Later, she would wish she'd stayed behind to die.

CHAPTER FOURTEEN

The Shadow Hunter's fine caravan, so proud and bold as it set out little more than a sennight ago, was sadly bedraggled and harried now. The warriors who composed it could afford pretense no longer, no airs or stately pace as they recrossed the wastelands now in desperate haste. They were running for their lives!

They'd been doing so for days on end already, riding with no respite except to rest their horses and the sun blazing down on them unrelentingly all the while. Autumn's cool breezes had retreated behind the scorching temperatures of a false summer heat wave, as if purely to mock the assault team's already grave situation. They carried little water and even less food with them, but the fugitives could not afford to stop for either. The camels that might have borne their extra provisions were mostly gone, scattered during the battle except for a couple the warriors had caught as they retreated, and were using for the armor and spare gear they could not afford to jettison.

There were fewer men too. Jared had lost two during the battle, and another, a stoic hulk named Baudoin, had been wounded and was failing fast under the merciless pace of their retreat. Isabeau's men had faired marginally worse, her twenty reduced by five casualties and two slowed down by injuries that might yet prove fatal, especially if the enraged Mamluks caught them up. They'd no time to grieve for fallen comrades, however, lest they join their brethren prematurely in Paradise themselves. All of the warriors knew it. There was no panic, no dissension, but among the bandits and their hired comrades a truce had formed, a sense of teamwork and of grudges put aside that only shared ill fortune could have brought about. Were any to survive, all would have to act as a unit, and rally under a single commander.

Unspoken but nonetheless acknowledged, the Black Lion had become that commander.

The Assassin had made no protest when he'd taken over at the outset, and she simply *could* not do so now. Saying nothing of her injury, Isabeau had been growing steadily weaker in the saddle as the hours passed and lengthened into hazy, pain-wracked days. Though she wanted nothing more than to let go of Zephyr's reins and allow herself to drop to the ground in defeat, she had gritted her teeth and kept up with the others as best she could. She tried to hold on to hope despite the crushing despondency of knowing she'd failed to rescue Zahra, though the pain of it was almost worse than the searing ache of her untreated wound. She was vaguely aware that Jared was leading them back in the direction of her own fortress, which was what she, too, wanted, but she knew she was just fortunate they agreed on this—she couldn't have made him change his course even if she'd wanted to. Isabeau simply wasn't capable of taking command anymore, and there was no use trying to pretend otherwise.

As it was, the Assassin was having enough trouble just hanging on to her saddle and not succumbing to the ever-present oblivion that threatened under their bruising pace. Fortunately, after the first two days of riding, a comforting numbness had begun to settle in on her body and mind, which made it marginally easier for Isabeau to go on. But at last, even that comfort was stripped from her.

On the third day after the aborted attack, the mercenary determined that they'd gained enough breathing room to halt for more than the few moments needed to rest their winded animals. They'd reached a rocky outcropping sheltering a hidden spring from the sand and wind of the desert, lined with scrubby trees and grasses that surrounded its life-giving waters. While the beasts dipped their heads in the tiny desert spring and drank gratefully, the men drew up beside Jared in the little oasis, obviously expecting to hold council about what their next move should be.

But Jared had other ideas. Kicking one leg over the stallion's neck to slide down from the saddle, he stormed up to the still-mounted renegade the instant his own horse had stopped moving, and the light of retribution glowed fierce in his eyes.

To Isabeau, blinking rapidly against the cold sweat that had formed on her brow, he looked like an avenging angel come to claim her soul. Had she died already, she wondered dully, without noticing it? If so, it was strange to see Jared here in hell with her—unless he had come as her personal tormentor. She swayed dizzily atop Zephyr, scarcely aware her mount had stopped moving.

"Why didn't you tell me we were after the same thing?" Jared demanded roughly, glaring up at her.

She wasn't dead after all, the Assassin realized. She was just paying for her sins here on earth. Jared was her inquisitor, and would torture her with incomprehensible questions until she confessed whatever it was he wanted to hear. Not understanding what he meant, Isabeau merely raised a weary brow at the mercenary, feeling the tight heat of sunburn on her forehead where her veils had slipped back on her head as she did. It only added to the dehydration caused by blood loss and continuous exertion, putting the renegade in bad condition indeed. Her parched mouth couldn't form words to reply to the Black Lion's furious query, even had her brain been working well enough to think of any.

Impatient, Jared growled, "Don't try to deny it! Isabeau! I heard you shout the name across the field three days ago. Damn you, you must have known we spoke of the same girl the night before the battle—or should I say, before the *rescue mission*? And yet you said nothing. You meant to keep her for yourself, didn't you!" It was more accusation than question.

At first, Isabeau only heard the initial part of Jared's statement, and for a moment she thought the mercenary had said, "Don't try to deny it, Isabeau." But if Jared was reproaching her with her true name, it meant he knew who she was! By Allah, she had not wanted to deny him anything, except that one truth. Yet perhaps it was time he knew, Isabeau thought bleakly—they'd *all* find out soon enough, if she died along the trail. For a morbid instant, she entertained the image of her bandits' surprise as they stripped her body to wash it in preparation for burial. It would be fortunate she was already dead in that case, for despite their current loyalty, the devoutly religious *fidai'in* would surely have slain the renegade for her profoundly heretical deception.

Not even Jared would be able to stop their outraged retribution, the exhausted Assassin knew, in the unlikely event that he should even wish to defend her after all the lies she'd told. Probably, he would hand the men his own weapons to do the job. So what was he waiting for? she wondered. If Jared knew, why did he only seem concerned with her pretense about Zahra, and not the far greater deception regarding her own true identity? But then her foggy brain belatedly snapped out of its grim reverie and finally processed the rest of what the mercenary had said, and Isabeau realized her secret was yet safe. She also realized the significance of Jared's continued misapprehension.

He had mistaken Zahra for his lost Isabeau. He believed the jewel she sought was his own betrothed! She and the mercenary were fighting over a woman—and the woman was her! *How absurd,* Isabeau thought faintly. Helplessly, hysterically, the Assassin began to laugh.

The harsh, croaking sounds filled the little oasis like the caws of a dying raven. The Assassin's side felt as if it would split right open and spill her innards out onto the thirsty ground, and yet she could not stop! Out of the corner of her eye, Isabeau could see that the rest of the men had backed off, taking their leaders' preoccupation as a good opportunity to water their horses and fill their canteens, tend wounds and rest weary muscles, leaving the two to their fight and its resolution. Dimly, she understood that there was really nothing funny about their situation. Still, exhaustion and despair had her in their grip, and Isabeau could not stop laughing even when she was fairly choking with it.

Jared's face grew darker and darker as al-Zul dared once more to mock him, and his fist went back threateningly as if to strike the slight Assassin. But at last Sayyad held his narrow hands up to the Black Lion in a weary, placating gesture.

"That wasn't your Isabeau we left behind on the field, mercenary. I can guarantee you that much with absolute certainty."

Jared didn't know whether or not to believe that raspy, fatigued whisper, though it seemed to hold the ring of truth. He felt certain he'd heard the name of his betrothed called that day, and he sure as hell knew he hadn't dreamt up the blond-haired woman who had been dragged from Sayyad's horse! The Assassin was clearly deranged, he decided. He might say anything to protect his secrets.

"Oh? And just how do you think to guarantee it? What proof can you possibly offer me now to counteract the evidence of my own eyes and ears three days ago?" Jared challenged. But though he thought nothing the man could say could shock him anymore, he hadn't expected the irrefutable evidence al-Zul offered then.

"I can very easily prove we didn't leave your precious fiancée behind," the wounded, weary Assassin assured her betrothed. "Because she is right here, right now, talking to you."

At Jared's yet uncomprehending look, she sighed softly. "You see, de Navarre, *I* am Isabeau de Lyon."

And with that, Isabeau collapsed in a dead faint.

Jared handled the news fairly well, considering.

PART III

There was a Door to which I found no Key:
There was a Veil past which I could not see:
Some little Talk awhile of ME and THEE
There seemed—and then no more of THEE and ME.

—THE RUBAIYAT OF OMAR KAYYAM, VERSE 32

CHAPTER FIFTEEN

Isabeau lay without waking, barely breathing, for four long days.

Four days while Jared rejoiced over the miracle of her continued existence, and while he wrestled with the truth of all she seemed to have become in the interval since he had last seen this once-innocent, smiling child. Four days while he struggled to understand her deception, and while he ruminated endlessly about the untold atrocities she must have been forced to suffer without his close protection all this time.

Four days while he watched her slender body shudder and tremble with fever, grow drawn and wracked with chills. Four days while the nightmares passing through her mind played themselves out in anguish upon a delicate, womanly face that was at once familiar and totally unexpected to him. Four days while he feared that she was dying, and while he tried desperately to prevent it.

Several things had become clear to the mercenary during the interminably long, anxious period of her unconsciousness.

The first was that he had not been dreaming the night this exquisite woman—half stranger, half native to his soul—had kissed him so intimately upon the banks of the Tigris. *Ah, Isabeau,* his heart anguished, *how could you kiss me so, and then just disappear?*

His second, unpalatable realization was that she must have known who he was from the very first moment of their association. Perhaps she'd known even before he'd arrived in response to the mysterious Shadow Hunter's summons. Yet Jared tended to doubt that much—his given name was not widely known, which led him to believe her hostility on the day of their first encounter had most likely been a reaction to the shock of recognition. *Why then did*

*you say nothing when you first learned who I was? Nothing,
even later when I told you how desperately I had searched
for you these many years gone by?*

The third truth the mercenary forced himself to acknowledge was that his betrothed had probably never had any
intention of revealing herself to him. If she'd not been
wounded, if their ambush had not gone so terribly wrong,
Isabeau—no, he corrected himself, the *Shadow Hunter*—
would have ridden out of his life without even a backward
glance. Jared could not forget her cavalier words that day.
"Farewell, Black Lion, and may we never meet again!"

Ah, Isabeau, he wondered sorrowfully, *why couldn't you
trust me with the truth?*

His last, clearest, and possibly most troubling realization
was that Isabeau de Lyon was still no stranger to his heart,
though her actions since their unheralded reunion had rendered her thoughts and motives completely oblique to him.
What have you become, my little Beau? he questioned silently as he stared down upon her desperately wounded
form. *And how does my soul know you still, when you are
such a stranger to my eyes?*

Indeed, Jared's heart was filled with the knowledge of
Isabeau, filled to rejoicing, and he wanted to savor the miraculous rejuvenation of his faith that came with simply
knowing she was alive. Just when he'd been ready to give
up, when he had least believed, God had brought Isabeau
back into his arms, and he wanted to cherish the gift of her
discovery as long as he could. Yes, there was much that
remained to be explained, Jared acknowledged. This certainly hadn't been the joyous reunion he'd dreamt about!
There'd been no exclamations of surprise, no tears of sweet
reconciliation, and no jubilation to celebrate that heaven
had seen fit to reunite them after such a long separation.
But all that could wait until Isabeau was better—if she did
get better, he mused worriedly.

No. He wouldn't think that way. God would not be so
cruel as to take this woman from him again now, Jared told
himself stoutly, so soon after he'd rediscovered her! And

when she did recover, he was sure Isabeau would be able to satisfy all his questions, make him understand the mystery of her seemingly unfathomable behavior. Until then, Jared would have to wait, as patiently as possible, and simply tend her with all the devotion due his sworn betrothed. It was his duty.

He'd done what he could so far. When the Assassin had fallen from her saddle and into his arms, her revelation thudding into his consciousness with even greater force than her body hitting his own, he'd been jolted with such astonishment that he'd almost fallen himself. The mercenary hadn't even truly begun to digest the meaning of the Assassin's words, let alone believe them, until he'd shifted the feather-light weight of the robed figure in his grasp, and his palms had come in contact with the blood-soaked binding that wrapped about her hips, waist, and chest. Beneath the tight wrappings, he had felt the softness of feminine curves disguised—and the explanation for the renegade's survival had made itself clear as well. The bindings had helped absorb some of the force of the enemy's sweeping scimitar blow during the battle, and had since provided a crude but effective bandage to hold the wound closed.

Still, the blood loss had been severe, to judge by the rusty stiffness of the dark robes the Assassin—Isabeau!—wore. *My God,* he'd thought, *this is Isabeau in my arms, wounded and needing my help!* Everything had clicked into place in that moment.

Jared had gathered his stunned wits hastily, knowing this was no time to fall apart. All he could think about was getting Isabeau out of this place. The Mamluks, he feared, had not lost their taste for their attackers' blood, and had not yet given up the chase. From what the men who'd scouted behind their trail had told the mercenary, they'd gained but little lead on the emir's forces in the past three days of forced retreat, and Jared knew he could not afford to stand there poleaxed indefinitely. And so the Black Lion, galvanized, had roared into action.

He'd called sharply to Pierre, and when the dwarf stood

waiting beside him, having accepted his commander's curt order to take command of their company, he shouted over to one of the Assassin's bandits as well.

"You—what's your name?" He'd gestured brusquely, signaling the nomad to come over.

The man reluctantly obeyed, his eyes fixed upon his fallen leader, who lay limply against the mercenary's side, still swathed beyond recognition in his accustomed veils. "Rashid is what I am called, *ferenghi*," the bearded young man had said gruffly, clearly not liking to obey a foreigner but not ready to revolt yet, either, without word from his own leader. "What have you done to my master?" he challenged.

"Naught but catch him where he fell, young pup. Your master is wounded, very gravely. I need you to be smart now, Rashid. You know our situation." Jared paused expectantly.

"Aye," the man admitted.

"Then you must realize there is little time left to us, and cooperation between our two bands is essential if either is to survive." Another pause while his gaze bored into the young man's. He had sensed this man was among the smartest, the most loyal of Sayyad's troop, and had picked him out as a sort of leader, though the renegade had not seemed to trust any one above the others enough to invite him into his close counsel. Into *her* counsel, Jared had reminded himself, feeling light-headed as he hefted the limp Assassin carefully against his body. *Her* counsel. This was Isabeau he was thinking about! God, he had to get her away! Spiriting her off to safety was the only thing Jared could concentrate on, and the need was driving him wild.

The young man nodded at last. "What do you propose, mercenary?"

Jared sighed with relief. The bandit was willing to be reasonable, thank God. "If you agree to abide by my suggestion faithfully, my men will lead the enemy away from your band now, allowing you to retreat to the fortress in safety. But in return, I will ask a favor as well."

"What favor, *ferenghi*?" He did not look as if he believed the mercenary's generous offer—and why should he? It was not sensible for the Frankish warrior to offer to shoulder all the weight of their enemy's pursuit, while the bandits escaped in relative safety. It was not the act of a profit-driven mercenary, certainly. "What do you ask in return?"

"Only that you allow my men entrance to your fortress when they have returned from drawing off Malik's bloodhounds, and that you care for those among them who are wounded as you would your own. Nothing more."

The bandit had looked as if he would balk for a moment—clearly it was unheard of for strangers to be allowed access to al-Zul's bolt-hole in the absence of his specific invitation, but it was equally obvious that the master could not give such permission at present. Still, he'd known a decision must be made for all of them.

"All right, *ferenghi*. All right! We have a bargain. You draw off our pursuers, and we will allow you to take shelter among us when you return. Now, hand the Shadow Hunter over to me, and we will part ways." He stretched out his arms for the drooping figure of the Assassin, but Jared drew his precious burden away abruptly.

"No!" Then, as if realizing how defensive he'd sounded, Jared went on in a softer voice. "Sayyad would only slow you down," he temporized. "We need you to make a straight shot for the mountains, riding fast and taking the less badly wounded with you. Meanwhile, I and the remainder of my men will take a more circuitous route through the wastelands to try and lose the emir's men among the gullies and ravines of the foothills. The other wounded all look to be able to make the ride, but al-Zul would never survive your brutal pace." That much was true, he feared. Ah, God, how could they stand here dickering like a couple of hagglers while Isabeau bled her life's blood out upon the dusty ground? "I will make sure we see your leader safely taken care of in one of the village crofts hereabouts before we go on ahead," he promised.

The bandit began to protest, though he seemed to agree about their pace being too much for the Assassin. "No—that is unacceptable! We should care for him ourselves—"

"Do you want to kill your master?" the mercenary demanded harshly, cutting the man off. "That's what you'll be doing if you force him to go on like this. But fear not to leave al-Zul in my care," Jared promised. "I will allow no harm to befall your master, I assure you. I will see to him personally." When that did not seem to placate the anxious Rashid, he went further. "You have my word on it, pup. I will bring your master home to you alive."

Rashid looked over his shoulder uncertainly to where the rest of his brethren waited by the water hole expectantly, seeming to have agreed upon his election as decision-maker. "I . . . I do not know . . ."

"Come on, man!" Jared pressed. "You know there's no choice. Part ways with your master now for a few short days, or part with him forever."

"Yes. All right! But if harm should come to him, mercenary . . . Be assured, you would not enjoy the repercussions we would visit upon you. All of Alamut will fall upon you in revenge should we learn you have betrayed our trust!"

"I wouldn't dream of hurting your master," Jared had assured him with perfect honesty. *Never, for all the world, would I hurt this woman.*

When the *fidai'in* had gone, thundering off on their weary mounts with the remaining camels in tow, Big Pierre had looked up at his commander skeptically. "Why did you do that, de Navarre?" He'd nodded meaningfully at the unconscious renegade in Jared's arms. "You know that bastard Sayyad's only going to slow us down. Better to let the vultures have him and go ourselves while the getting's still good."

"Sayyad won't slow you down," Jared had assured his lieutenant absently, already shifting the unconscious Assassin so that he could mount up and brace her carefully in front of him on the saddle, where she would be least jarred by the ride. As he'd grasped Zephyr's reins to pull the mare in tow behind his own horse, he'd tossed his words distractedly back over his shoulder to his second-in-command. "*I'm* the only one he's going to inconvenience. I'm afraid we're not going with you, old friend. So do just as I told our young friend Rashid you would—draw the Mamluks off the hunt, buy us some time, and then await me at al-Zul's fortress. We may be a while, but we'll catch up."

"What's this all about, de Navarre?" Pierre had asked quizzically, clearly not understanding his commander's illogical behavior.

"The Holy Grail, Pierre. I think I may finally have found it!"

And without a backward glance, Jared had spurred his stallion and taken off with his betrothed in his arms, leaving his lieutenant behind to scratch his head and stare speculatively into the cloud of dust the horse had kicked up.

Now, Jared studied the woman lying before him again, still finding it hard to believe she was truly here with him. He couldn't have been more surprised if he *had* found the cup of Christ that day, for it felt just as much a miracle having Isabeau here with him again after all his years of searching. He looked around, his lips curving up with self-mockery. Such as "here" was.

With little notice and few supplies, the mercenary's options had been limited when looking for a safe haven in which to hide while he nursed his injured betrothed. He'd settled on this isolated little cave near the mountain foothills after a few minutes' reconnoitering of the broken desert ground had reminded him of where it was. Having spotted it on their outbound trip and scouted the location out of sheer habit—a lifetime of fighting had taught Jared to always have an escape route to cover all exigencies—he had known he'd not do better in the short time he had left before either the Mamluks caught them, or Isabeau began to fail in earnest.

The cave they'd sheltered in wasn't much, he had to admit, but it was big enough to hide them, it lay at the base of a little blind canyon in which he could corral their horses, and there was a stream adjoining it that provided fresh, cool water. Best of all, the floor of the canyon, more like the bottom of a tiny valley than a rocky crevasse, had held both grazing for the horses and enough medicinal herbs growing hereabouts to give the mercenary some small hope of Isabeau's survival.

Hope—and prayer—were really all he had left to rely on at this point. He'd tried everything he knew of to help her heal, to bring her back to him, and still Isabeau would not wake. Jared had begun to fear she never would. Perhaps, he thought sadly, she did not even wish to. Whatever demons drove her, the mercenary had seen that they did not leave the struggling renegade even in slumber. He frowned with concern down at her dear form now, still shivering and muttering incoherently upon the furs he'd taken from their bedrolls and tenderly spread out to cushion her body from the hard limestone floor of the cave.

He'd been forced to remove all of her bloodied robes and wrappings when he'd first tended her wounds. What a revelation that had been! Jared had tried to keep his touch as fraternal as it had been when they'd been children together. But Isabeau was no little girl these days—nay, she was all woman now, from her lush bosom to the curves of her hips and the slender white thighs that lay before his gaze like a banquet before a starving man. His hands had trembled like those of a stripling as he'd carefully disrobed his betrothed.

It was her wound, an ugly red gash that curved around her right side from her lower ribs all the way to her pelvis, that had finally proved sufficient to cool the heat of Jared's guilty ardor. Thankfully, it had not seemed to cut into any major organs or fracture any bones. He'd known blood loss and infection would be his greatest enemies in those first days, and that Isabeau's own strength and will to live would determine whether she lived or died. All he could do was help her win the fight. With shaking hands the mercenary had bathed and treated the wound as best he could, bandaging her with strips torn from her own bindings, which he had rinsed and boiled in a tincture of several wild herbs gathered earlier from the canyon floor.

Afterward, Jared had dressed her again in his own undertunic, ludicrously oversized on her delicate frame but softer and more comfortable than anything he'd been able to find in her saddlebags. It remained her only garment now, and Jared had begun to fear it would serve as her shroud if she did not wake from her fevered slumber soon. Isabeau looked so small and frail there upon the skins, he marveled, though experience had taught the mercenary to beware that her fragile outward appearance could be more than deceptive. This woman was also a notorious renegade, an Assassin by trade, and Jared knew he'd best not forget it.

Strangely enough, though his confusion and wariness remained, he'd felt no anger at Isabeau since she'd made her dramatic revelation; not even for a minute. Questions he had aplenty, certainly, but there were simply no recriminations harbored in his breast. He could not seem to hold negative emotions in his heart in the presence of this miraculous human being he tended. Whatever she might reveal to him about her past, however bad, however shocking, he swore he would not hold it against her. He would not forget that God had answered his prayers, and would not be so ungrateful a wretch as to look askance at His miracle. For so many years he hadn't believed it was possible, had given up belief in a just God. Now all of that had changed.

The Lord must have meant for the two of them to come together again in this fashion, the mercenary decided, and for Jared to bring his lost betrothed back at last, home to the bosom of her family. He could envision the surprise and delight of the duke and duchess of Lyon, their tender reunion with the daughter they'd never thought to see again. He could picture his own return to his homeland, the struggles he would face in Navarre to regain what his family had lost due to his long neglect. He pictured, too, his eventual wedding with Isabeau, the beautiful children they would have . . .

Once again Jared stretched out a hesitant finger to stroke her flushed cheek, marveling at her solidity, her palpable reality. No. God would not be so cruel as to take her from him again. And if He tried, Jared was damn well prepared to challenge the Almighty for her life!

It might have been wishful thinking, but he thought she seemed better today. He'd been lucky enough to catch a rabbit this morning in a snare he'd fashioned the night before, and he had cubed the meat and worked up a stew with that and the few strengthening roots and herbs he'd been able to find in the canyon. It wasn't much, but he had patiently spooned the broth into Isabeau's unprotesting mouth and worked her throat gently with his fingers until she'd swallowed some.

Aside from infection, the biggest danger in any healing process was dehydration, he knew. Jared had plenty of experience with the care of wounds, and, as leader of his mercenary troop, had made it his business to know how to handle almost any injury that might arise. It was no more than his responsibility. While he was no Hospitallar, trained to the care of all Christian souls, he knew enough to keep her wound clean, sponge her brow with cool water, and make sure her body did not consume itself from the inside out while it fought the deadly fever. The rest was up to the Lord, he thought, and only prayer would stand a chance of earning that aid. Well, he'd been doing enough praying these last four days to heal a church full of lepers . . .

Jared looked down.

Did she stir at last? His heart leapt. He thought he'd seen a hint of the deep blue irises of Isabeau's eyes shifting beneath the purplish lids. Then her throat worked for a moment; that surely was not his imagination. Jared hastened to moisten Isabeau's chapped lips with water, letting her sip a little and swallow laboriously even as his heart sang with relief. She was waking! At length that rasping, hoarse voice he'd grown to associate with the Assassin emerged from Isabeau's slender throat.

"Damn . . . you . . . mercenary," she croaked. "What . . ." she coughed, "have you . . . done?"

CHAPTER SIXTEEN

Those weren't quite the words the mercenary had hoped to hear. But then, perhaps Jared didn't know the Assassin as well as he thought he did. While she slept, it had been easy to remember her as a smiling child, the winsome girl to whom he'd been promised—or even to think of her as the sultry enchantress he'd so briefly encountered upon the riverbank the night before the battle. But now he was dealing with the renegade; a very different woman indeed.

"Isabeau." Jared tried to speak soothingly, but she was having none of it.

"Where are my men?" she demanded. "Where are my *clothes*? Son of a dog! I swear you'll pay for this, de Navarre . . ."

Isabeau was terrified, confused, and still feverish; and as always when she was afraid, she went on the attack. All she could think was that her secret was no longer her own—Jared *knew*. That meant she was vulnerable. He'd stripped her down while she was unconscious, had seen everything she'd worked so hard to hide from him and from the rest of the world. Now he knew her sex, and he knew her name. What would he do with the knowledge? What would he do with *her*?

"Isabeau—"

The Assassin tried to rise. "Where have you brought me?" She gasped in agony at the injudicious movement, then fell back upon the pallet, groaning and squeezing her eyes closed against the pain. Surely he must be furious at her deception. What punishment might he seek to inflict upon her while she lay here helpless and undressed? Or had he already . . . ? No, she thought. Not Jared. He might despise her, but he would never sink so low. That much she knew of him. Her fright eased fractionally. This wasn't Malik, or any of his sadistic minions. This was no stranger.

This was the man to whom she had been betrothed. Could she dare to trust him, even a little?

"Isabeau!" he tried again. "Don't try to move, sweetheart. You've been injured; you could tear your wound open again."

Sweetheart? "I don't need you to tell me I've been wounded, mercenary," she snarled, glaring up at him. "I was there when it happened." But even to her own ears her tone sounded halfhearted, and she knew he would guess she was backing down from her initial anger. For the first time Isabeau took in Jared's condition as well as her own, examining his face in the fitful firelight. He looked terrible! From his haggard, unshaven appearance and the bruised circles beneath his hollow amber eyes, it was clear the mercenary had not fared so well himself since she'd passed out.

"How long have I been unconscious?" she demanded, wanting to know how far the Mamluks could be behind them. Surely in the hours since she'd fallen from her horse they'd have come within miles of catching them up. Though she didn't recognize this place as being along the route they'd taken, she thought dizzily. In fact, she wasn't sure just where they were at all. "What benighted little rat's lair have you dragged me to, you wretched mercenary?"

"You've been here four days, Isabeau," Jared began cautiously. Obviously, she was still delirious. She didn't know what she said. Her insults must be part of the fever that had overtaken her. "You are safe, in a cave not far from the Elburz foothills, where I brought you when you passed out. Your men have gone on before you, and mine have drawn the task of leading off Malik's pursuit. I have seen no sign of the Mamluks in my daily reconnaissance, but I cannot be sure without scouting farther afield. I did not want to leave you for that long while you were unconscious."

Four days. It was hard to assimilate the news. By Allah, she'd no idea it had been so long! So much could have happened in that time, without her to control the fallout of their aborted mission. But there was one fear greater than the rest. "Did you tell them?" Isabeau asked sharply. "Curse you, de Navarre—did you tell my men the truth?" Even if Malik's forces failed to pick up their trail, the *fidai'in* would know how to find her. By Allah, if they knew, then neither of them had a hope of safety—she was as good as dead, and they'd kill Jared as well if they suspected him of harboring her. In their eyes, she would have committed an unforgivable sin by deceiving them so, and not all of their shared victories would be enough to cool the bandits' righteous anger at being duped by a woman.

"Please, you need to rest. Don't strain yourself so." But Jared could see Isabeau was too anxious to listen properly, her fever-glazed eyes burning with the need to know. "No," he sighed, knowing what she meant. "I didn't tell them you're a woman. No one knows but you and I, little Beau."

"Don't call me that!" Isabeau cried sharply, wincing at her own vehemence and then putting a trembling hand over her eyes. They were stinging with sudden tears at the sound of her childhood nickname on his lips. "Damn it, Jared." A moment later, she found she was crying in earnest.

Isabeau tried to hold it back; she tried to stifle the sobs, but she was simply overwhelmed. She was finally, finally unveiled; released at last from the constant, leaden burden of pretense. Only three people in the world had known of her deception before this—Zahra, Jamal, and the master of Alamut, and yet none of them knew as much of her as this man did. Not even Jamal had been privy to the close-guarded memories of her childhood, for once Isabeau had become a slave, she had closed the door on that chapter of her life completely. She'd isolated her memories of innocence and joy deep inside, where no one could ever touch them or take them away. Only to Zahra had she ever even mentioned the tender relationship she'd shared with the boy who'd once been her betrothed; and even then Isabeau had related those fond memories solely to cheer the frightened younger girl, whispering recollections to her late at night in the darkness of their shared dormitory room in the women's quarters of Malik's household.

But Jared knew all of it already. He had *been* there with her. And to him, part of her was still that little girl, who could laugh and love—and trust. Just as he was in some way still her childhood idol, the dear companion she had believed could do no wrong. It was as if the weight of the Dome of the Rock had been lifted from her shoulders. For better or for worse, Jared *knew*. She could pretend with him no longer. The release was just too powerful, and in her weakened, confused state, the Assassin began to weep.

Jared was there instantly to hold her, and he continued to hold her for many minutes as she snuffled and sobbed, her breath hitching and catching as she wept. Worn out, in pain and still feverish, she felt helpless as a babe in those strong arms.

"Shh, little Beau. It's all right. I'm here. I'm here. You are safe," Jared comforted. But it only made Isabeau weep the harder.

Safe. She didn't even know what that meant! And when he caressed the tangled locks of flaxen hair from off her salty cheeks, when he stroked her heaving back, she felt that she would drown in her tears. But Jared wouldn't let her sink beneath the deluge of her feelings, seeing her safely through the storm instead with his strong solidity, his patience, his very presence. He held her as if he understood everything. As if he would make up for all the times she had been forced to cry alone for lack of those strong arms. As if he did not hate her for what she'd become, just as though they were still children together. And when he murmured her childhood name like an incantation against her ears, she truly felt charmed by his potent magic. Waiting patiently with her through the tempest of her tears, the mercenary at last gave Isabeau solace.

"Great Allah," she croaked finally when the tears had wound down a little. "How humiliating." Her voice was muffled by the comforting solidity of Jared's rock-hard pectoral muscles, her senses redolent with the warm, heady male scent of him. Her side ached terribly, she was thirsty, and her head was throbbing unmercifully. Isabeau could not remember ever feeling so worn out at any time in her life. She felt as though she could drift into sleep at any moment, though she had only been awake a little while. Yet she was afraid to sleep without knowing the truth first. Her wet sapphire eyes looked up into his, searching for the cold condemnation she was sure to find in them. But those amber orbs were warm with understanding, not contempt.

"You have no cause to feel ashamed, sweet Isabeau," he assured.

Her memory of what had happened just prior to her blacking out was foggy at best. What exactly had she said to him before falling off the horse? "When did you first know?" she asked dully.

"You told me yourself, Isabeau, do you not recall? But in any case, I could hardly have failed to guess at some point. You have been speaking in *langue d'oc* ever since the fever came on you. You still speak it now," he pointed out. "As do I."

Shocked, Isabeau realized that what he said was true, and even as he spoke, their words began to sound oddly foreign to her ears. Yet even after all these years of disuse, it seemed proper to speak the language of her birth with Jared. How right it seemed just being with him! She leaned back against the soft skins of her pallet, dismayed though she pretended to be indifferent when he shifted to allow her to lie back down, removing the support of his broad shoulder.

"Then you know all." The Assassin spoke flatly, as if the worst had come to pass and she must brace for the consequences.

"Not everything." The mercenary reached down and tenderly brushed one callused thumb across her flushed ivory cheek, ignoring the tiny flinch she couldn't suppress at the unaccustomed intimacy. "But I hope you will soon feel up to sharing the rest. Isabeau," he began, then took a deep breath and started again. "Isabeau, you have no idea how long I've sought you. Or how wondrous it is to have found you alive."

"But I'm not alive, Black Lion," she demurred, her voice choking up once more as she turned her head away from the too-clear amber of his eyes. Sleep was overcoming Isabeau again in the wake of her emotional storm, and she could not keep awake even to argue with her erstwhile betrothed. Her voice slurred as she murmured desolately, "I died sixteen long years ago. Best you bury all thoughts of Isabeau, and forget you ever saw her again."

*   *   *

Jared took Isabeau's right hand in his, gently tracing the shape of her artificially shortened little finger with careful fingers of his own. Though she wore no veil now, revealing a face of stunning but strangely delicate beauty, the Assassin remained as mysterious to him as ever. It had been three days now since his betrothed had first awoken, and a very frustrating time for the mercenary indeed, for Isabeau had refused to talk to him. Oh, she hadn't been completely silent all this time, of course, though she did sleep prodigiously, which he knew was important to her healing. But when Isabeau *was* awake, she avoided his attempts to engage her in conversation as adroitly as she'd ever done in the guise of Sayyad al-Zul. Nor would she answer his questions, claiming fatigue or fever whenever he began to pry.

Jared hadn't wanted to press, knowing she was fragile still, and remembering just how close he'd come to losing her only a week ago. Still, she must face him eventually, for they could not hide from the past forever. They couldn't pretend the world outside their little haven didn't exist either, for they'd have to leave once she was well. And the renegade was healing now with amazing speed. She'd even been able to take a few tottering steps about the limestone cave with his help earlier today. Jared was well pleased with Isabeau's progress, if not with her silence.

He knew his troubled charge was awake again now, though she didn't open her eyes. She lay as usual on her pallet by the low-burning fire, seeming to close in on her-

self more each day, until the testy, easily inflamed Assassin
was but a memory in the mercenary's mind. That person
had been replaced by a silent ghost of a woman, who hardly
seemed to acknowledge her companion at all. She'd erected
an emotional barrier between them these last few days that
was more effective than the many layers of her veils had
ever been. The Black Lion, sitting cross-legged in his accustomed place by her side, marveled that his little Isabeau,
who'd remained eight years old in his memory all this time,
should have grown up into such a magnificent stranger. A
stranger with so many secrets.

Jared wanted—nay, he *needed*—to unravel those secrets. He needed to know everything Isabeau had been
through to bring her to this strange estate. And he would
be satisfied with nothing less than the full truth of her
story—if for no other reason than because he needed to
know the full extent of his own guilt!

All of her obvious suffering and her struggles were his
fault, he knew, for he'd never been there to protect her. The
mercenary must shoulder the responsibility for everything
that had been done to her, everything that had made his
sweet "little Beau" so cold and untrusting as a woman. He
wanted desperately to know what he must atone for in Isabeau's eyes, so that he could begin to make reparations in
whatever fashion he could. But she still didn't look eager
to talk, he judged. Indeed, if she could have, he believed
she'd have gone on pretending to sleep forever. Once more
he stroked her fingers thoughtfully, but the gesture seemed
to upset his sleep-feigning patient.

"Don't!" she hissed.

"When did that happen, Isabeau?" Jared asked softly. He
let her go reluctantly when she pulled her hand away, noting how she tried to hide the scarred appendage beneath
the furs of her bedding.

"As well to ask when *this* happened, or this," she said
bitterly, pointing to scars on her hip and shoulder respec-
tively, where the rumpled shirt she wore had ridden up to
reveal her flesh. "What does it matter when any of it hap-

pened?" she asked cynically. "What's done is done, and in the past. There's no sense crying over it now."

Now that the Black Lion knew her greatest secret, what sense did it make to hide the rest anymore? It was too late to deny who and what she was. Yet a greater fear had been growing upon her for the past few days while she recuperated and slowly regained her lost strength—how to answer all the questions Jared was sure to have without revealing the sordid details that would make him turn from her in disgust.

Isabeau was bitterly sure it would only be a matter of time before she saw that look of revulsion in his eyes, if it wasn't there already. What man could look upon her, freakish aberration that she was, and not be horrified? Perhaps, she thought, it would be better to get it over with now, and accept the pain sure to come. If she did, perhaps she might eventually hope to heal from that wound as well.

Jared could see that one of the scars was clearly the result of an arrow, while the other could have been made by either sword or dagger. His heart lurched at this further evidence of his failure to protect Isabeau, though both scars were long healed. If only he had been there to take those wounds in her stead! "I'm sorry," he said softly, but she misunderstood his meaning.

"Don't be," she said shortly. Isabeau toyed with a ragged thread on the shirt she wore, avoiding Jared's gaze studiously. By Allah, she would rather face a thousand angry Mamluks than have this conversation! There was no help for it now though. She'd avoided it long enough. "I'm sure you can't help being sickened," she mumbled thickly, staring fixedly at the seam she was slowly unraveling. "I know I'm not anyone's ideal of womanhood."

This magnificent, absolutely incredible siren thought she wasn't *womanly*? Jared took her chin between two long, elegant fingers, turning her face to meet his gaze. "Isabeau, have you looked at your reflection lately?" he asked incredulously. But again, she mistook him.

"No—why? Is my face disfigured too? If it is," she challenged, glaring at him now, "it's nothing I've done to it. It's always been this way. If you're offended, mercenary, I will put my veil back on. I'm used to it." The Assassin made as if to rummage around in the pile of garments near her makeshift bed, but to her chagrin, she was too weak even to stretch that far without pulling at her half-healed wound. She would have to ask for the mercenary's assistance even for this! Fresh humiliation blossomed in Isabeau's cheeks. Lying back, she avoided Jared's gaze once more, close to tears again. What was this weakness she seemed to have around the mercenary? She was on the verge of weeping all the time lately!

"Offended?" Jared was startled into laughter. "Sweet Jesu, woman. I've been to Jerusalem, looked upon the church of our Savior. I've woken at dawn to watch the desert sun rise above the Great Pyramids of Egypt. I've been entertained in the halls of the sultan himself, and attended by his most lovely odalisques. And yet, without a doubt, *you* are the most beautiful thing my eyes have seen in all my years of life!"

She kept waiting for the mercenary to smirk, to show some sign of mockery after this extravagant praise. But he didn't. And when she finally dared look in those amber eyes she read only warmth and compassion there—or was it pity? She couldn't bear this man's pity! Not when she was already in such a weakened state. "It matters not," Isabeau said shortly, choosing to ignore his hyperbole rather than challenging him on it. "In my profession, looks are not important. Only my strength matters—but of course, I have not even that much to rely on, at least temporarily."

It had been a humbling experience, allowing the mercenary to care for her; to feed and wash her and look after her wound these past few days. She hadn't been forced to rely on another human being like this since Jamal had brought her into Malik's harem as a child. But now she could not even dress herself without his help. Even acknowledging this patently obvious truth made Isabeau feel horribly vulnerable, and her next words showed it. "And since that is the case, I suppose the next move is up to you, mercenary. You've held out long enough without laying your ultimatum on me. So tell me, what is it you want?"

"Want?" he repeated cautiously. "I'm not sure what you mean, Isabeau."

She still couldn't get used to hearing that name coming from the mercenary's mouth. Childhood memories intermingled with the present disturbingly, until she was not sure who either of them was anymore—friend or foe, child or adult. But Jared was no little boy, she mused with a shiver that could not be ascribed to her now-broken fever. In his arms, holding her while she cried, he'd shown her he was every inch a virile male, and in his prime at that! And she, unfortunately, couldn't deny that as a woman, she'd noticed it.

"I mean, now that you know I'm female, what do you plan to do about it? When I've told you all, what will you do with the knowledge?" Isabeau was tired of people holding the secret of her femininity over her head, tired of having to make concessions to those men who thought a woman could not rule her own destiny. She'd had enough of men holding the power of life and death over her, just because she was female! Malik al-Fayed had wielded that power, forcing her to behave the way he thought a woman should; at least until she'd won free of the bastard. The Old Man of the Mountain *still* wielded that power, dangling the threat of exposure like a sword over her head every day until it should suit his whim to use it. Even Jamal ad-Din, her closest confidant and ally, could wield that power should he ever choose to betray her. And now Jared, too, held sway over her destiny. So how would *he* choose to use it?

The mercenary knew what he'd *like* to do. He'd like to resume where they'd left off the night she'd stepped naked into his embrace! But at the moment that didn't seem to be a very likely option. Jared sighed. "For now, I would ask nothing but that you be honest with me enough to trust me with your story. If you are up to talking, Isabeau, I suppose

I would simply like to know what *happened* that day in Lyon, and what has transpired in the long years we have been apart since."

Oh, was *that* all? He didn't ask much, did he?—just enough to tear apart the carefully constructed defenses that had kept the renegade alive for the last decade and a half, and to leave her utterly vulnerable without them. Yet she supposed that after all he had done for her—even his rescue when she'd fallen exhausted from her horse a week ago would have earned him that much—the mercenary deserved to know all she could tell him. And in truth, Isabeau was more than a little curious to learn his side of the story as well, though she feared that learning it could only burden her already guilty conscience further.

The renegade waved her right hand between them, as if it were as simple a task to wave away her years of slavery and oppression. "I suppose it's as reasonable to start with this injury as at any other place," she said, forcing herself to speak nonchalantly, as though the remembered events had no power to affect her. The Assassin studied the shortened digit dispassionately. "For it happened the very same day we parted, in the year twelve hundred and twelve." She sighed and dropped her hand back to her side. "The tip of my finger was bitten off by a boy in the crowd in Lyon," she said shortly. "He wanted that ring you wear around your neck for his own. It seems he didn't get to enjoy it long after all, eh?"

Isabeau ignored Jared's sympathetic wince—she'd almost say he'd blanched, though she couldn't imagine why he should care so. It hadn't been that debilitating a wound, she thought dismissively, ignoring the fact that, for the gently reared girl of but eight summers she had been, that event had been unbearably traumatic. It wasn't so bad, she told herself. Her hand might not look pretty, but she could still wield a weapon without difficulty, and that was the important part. The only real trouble had been with the fever and infection that had followed the untreated wound. "I passed out when it happened," she said, rolling her eyes at her own faintheartedness. "Soon after, I awoke to find myself on crusade, headed for Marseilles in the back of a hand-wagon." The renegade's wry smile looked more like a grimace.

How could she speak so callously of the terrible events she'd endured at such a tender age? Jared could only imagine what worse things had made these tragedies seem tame to Isabeau. Certainly, the devastating trail he'd seen strewn along the road to the coast did not disabuse him of the notion. Pursuing the Children's Crusade had been like walking in the path of a hurricane. "I know," he interrupted softly. "I followed you."

"Did you?" Isabeau asked offhandedly, as though it made no difference whether he'd chased after her or not, though in truth she found herself both writhing inwardly in remorse, and secretly gratified at the news. She'd wondered for so long whether Jared had been concerned for her, whether he'd bothered to search when she'd gone missing. It made her ache to think of him riding through the crowds with the impossible task of picking her out among the thousands of deluded children who'd followed twelve-year-old Stephen's oriflamme banner and gold-canopied chariot.

"Well, there was really no way you could have found me," she offered, wishing she could do better in terms of assuaging his obvious guilt. "The girl who cared for me when I took ill after the injury was touched in the head—thinking me her sister, she hid me in her cart for days under a pile of straw until we finally went aboard the ships in Marseilles."

Straw. It had always made his little Beau sneeze, Jared recalled. How wretched that she had been forced to breathe the stuff! His hands curled into fists of helplessness, even after so many years. But now he remembered something else—the image of the demented girl and the handbarrow she'd hauled triggered a previously forgotten recollection. "Was she fair-haired like you, Isabeau?" the mercenary asked tensely. "About fourteen or so?"

"Why, yes—Crazy Lucille, they called her . . ."

Jared hit his forehead with his palm, squeezing his eyes shut as though with unbearable pain. "We came so close! Blast it, I believe Sir Guy may even have questioned that girl. I remember a handcart overflowing with straw and filth. Your father's castle garrison had combed through the crowds for days at that point, searching, and I with them. We had just begun to interrogate a girl answering that description when we were called away by another false lead. Christ, to think we came so close, and never knew . . ."

It was amazing how much it could hurt to talk about this even now, Isabeau discovered. She wasn't sure she could get through her story if she had to hear how her own stupidity had forced so many men-at-arms to search futilely for her, to hear how much pain and trouble she had unwittingly caused those around her. "Well," she hastened on, "soon enough, when we'd reached Marseilles, and the seas naturally failed to part for us as the boy-preacher Stephen had promised, we were all herded aboard seven great ships donated by a pair of 'pious' local merchants." Isabeau shook her head regretfully. "We believed the merchants' promise that our safe passage to the Holy Land was being offered purely in exchange for the expunging of their sins. What fools we were.

"My memories of that time are very faint, Jared, and in truth I do not miss them," she confessed. "I believe I was really too ill to understand much of what was going on until we were well at sea and the sailors ordered that we all be put in chains. 'Twas only then that we learned of the merchants' duplicity."

"Hugh the Iron," Jared said flatly, "and William the Pig."

"Yes," she averred, surprised. "Those are the names I remember. I don't know what ever happened to them."

"They have been dealt with," Jared said shortly. "Be assured, they have paid for their crimes." Their interrogation had been the squire's last act before stowing away himself aboard a ship bound for the Holy Land. It had also been the first time he had killed, but he had no regrets.

What he had learned from the two unscrupulous traders before dispatching them had been enough to assure him they'd be roasting long and justly in hell. But Jared had no intention of burdening Isabeau with the details of that grim night.

The wounded renegade seemed prepared to accept his unrevealing assurance without comment. "My closest companion, the girl they called Crazy Lucille, took sick after a few weeks of storms aboard the ship, and could keep nothing down," Isabeau went on, determined to share the rest of her story as quickly as possible before the painful memories could swamp her. "I should have realized she was with child—the sailors had all taken turns raping her so many times."

Ah, this was harder than she'd thought! Her own guilty relief at having been spared that fate had gnawed at Isabeau for far too long. *Why her and not me?* she'd asked God a hundred times, though she knew the answer didn't take a deity to explain. She'd simply been worth more to her captors untouched, unlike the older girl whose innocence had already been despoiled before they'd ever embarked. It was all about profit, not justice.

"But then Lucille began to starve in earnest, and they did nothing to help her. I tried, but what could I do?" Isabeau's eyes begged the mercenary for understanding, and her trembling voice betrayed her anguish. "She would not accept the rations I saved for her; she just kept getting thinner and thinner, wasting away a little more each day." She paused, caught up in memories, then blurted, "God, Jared, they drowned her right before my eyes!"

The ragged urchin, her befuddled eyes still childishly trusting, had been unchained from the rest of the wretches shivering on the deck, kicked and shoved until she reached the side of the ship where they'd all watched so many of their fellows tossed overboard in recent days when fever or famine took them. Isabeau had fought to reach her, for despite the girl's insanity, Lucille had been a tender soul, and she'd cared for the duke's hitherto pampered daughter as

lovingly as if she'd truly been her own lost sister. But the
guards had held their eight-year-old prisoner back, cuffing
her soundly for her resistance as they dragged the other,
dying captive over to the railing. The older girl had only
seemed to realize what was happening to her at the last
minute. *"Fare thee well, dear heart,"* Lucille had said at
the last, calm and clear-eyed for the first time before Isabeau as she met her fate. *"I'm to join my Florie now, sweetness. No need to cry for old Lucille."* And then she had
been gone, slipping unprotesting beneath the waves forevermore.

"We lost two vessels to shipwreck off the island of San
Pietro in Sardinia," Isabeau continued resolutely, ignoring
the comforting hand Jared extended. If he touched her right
now, she thought she would shatter! Drawing in a deep
breath, she said, "Or so they told us when the Saracen fleet
met us just off Bougie, in North Africa. Many more still
had died of starvation and illness on shipboard. But those
were the lucky ones." She gulped hard, trying to swallow
down the bitter remembrances. The renegade hadn't allowed herself to think about this in so long—and now she
knew why. It was beyond her to cope with the memories!
Rather she would take a dozen scimitar blows than deal
with such remembered agony. But Jared deserved to know.

"What then, Isabeau?" Jared prodded gently. "What of
the rest?"

"You must know what happened to the balance of us, if
you followed our trail East," the Assassin said unwillingly.
The memories were just too degrading, too awful to revisit,
even for Jared's sake.

"I know that most were sold into slavery by the merchants' underlings."

"Aye—sold to the very Saracens we'd come to conquer.
Exchanged by our own countrymen for a few paltry ounces
of gold. The whole deal was arranged ahead of time, as it
turned out. Ironic, is it not?" Isabeau laughed mirthlessly,
not truly expecting the mercenary to comment.

"Most were sold right away, in North Africa. The rest

of us, about seven hundred or so, I believe, were deemed of greater worth for sale in Egypt, in the great slave markets of Alexandria. Eighteen were martyred there on the block, for refusing to accept Islam. But I was not so noble—I converted quickly enough when I saw what had been done to my fellows! So much for my crusading ideals, eh?" Isabeau looked at the man who'd been her betrothed, as if expecting him to smile along with her, but his face was dead serious. She went on. "Many went from Alexandria to the court of Baghdad for training in the art of translation and interpretation—and I heard that by the generosity of al-Kamil, then governor of Egypt but not yet sultan, those were not forced to convert. Being among the few who were literate, I would have been sent there too, had not the slave traders decided I had . . . other, more valuable merits."

Isabeau said no more, but she did not have to. Jared had lived in the East long enough to know that her youth, her fairness of features, and above all, her virginity would have been dearly prized in the slave markets. If she had not been raped by her captors . . . she would have been worth a fortune indeed. The mercenary squeezed his eyes shut once again, sickened by the thought, though he had trained himself to accept the possibility long ago. Now, looking at his fair betrothed, so beautiful and so wounded in spirit as well as body, he wished he had the culprits in his grasp again, so he could pummel the life out of them a second time and expend some of this anguished rage.

"And then . . ." he bit off tightly, hardly able to bear hearing her continue.

But Isabeau was prepared to go no further. Not today, and perhaps not ever. What had happened once she'd become a slave was too shameful a memory to share with the mercenary. "There is no 'and then,' de Navarre. I was sold into slavery with the rest. What did you think happened?"

"But you are not still a slave now," he pointed out.

"No," she agreed with a certain dark satisfaction. "I escaped."

"I can see that," he said with some humor returning to

his eyes. Jared allowed his admiration for her tenacity to
distract him from the horrors of her past. "You are certainly
no slave now! What I want to know is, how?"

"I've had enough of hearing about myself, mercenary,"
Isabeau protested. "Fair's fair. Will you not share your own
story with me now? Besides," she sighed, then yawned con-
vincingly. "I grow weary of talking. Tell me of yourself
instead."

Yes, she hoped to divert his attention with this change
of subject, but it was also true that she wanted to hear Jared
speak. It was strange to talk thus with the mercenary, to be
so frank and open. Despite the pain of her memories, Isabeau found it almost . . . enjoyable. The renegade told herself she was merely intrigued with the mystery and eager
to put together the pieces after so many years. And indeed,
she *was* curious. From what he'd said so far, she had developed a picture of the mercenary's last days in France,
the reasons for his journey East, but nothing more. The past
sixteen years of his life were a complete mystery! Well,
save for the legends she'd heard about the Black Lion, of
course. Those tales were enough to fill out sixteen lifetimes,
let alone sixteen years.

Jared began simply. "When you were lost, the duke's
castle guard searched diligently for over a fortnight under
the command of Sir Guy. At first, I joined the men-at-arms.
We questioned every villager, pilgrim, and merchant along
the road to the coast, rode through the great mass of children in the crusade calling your name and chasing everyone
bearing even the faintest resemblance to you. We stopped
dozens of children, handed out bribes and rewards for information, but it was as though you had disappeared into
thin air. At last, after remaining in Marseilles for several
days and sorting through the disappointed children who
were waiting for some miraculous event to help them cross
the seas, Sir Guy made the decision to call off the search
for you. He was concerned about leaving Lady Margery
undefended for so long in her husband's absence, I believe.

The men agreed with him—the search was hopeless. But I refused to accept it, and I stayed behind."

Indeed, Sir Guy had not exactly *permitted* the young squire to remain in the strange city. He had heard out Jared's impassioned insistence, smiled sympathetically, and, with the greatest of care, coshed him over the head when the boy absolutely refused to leave with the rest of the castle garrison. Jared had awoken with a throbbing ache in his head the next morning, strapped to his own horse's saddle as they rode north and west for Lyon. It had taken him hours to wriggle free of his bonds and escape back down the road toward the coast, and he had had to return afoot, without the handsome gelding that would have fetched him a good price in trade. By that time, however, the ships carrying the deluded young crusaders had already launched without him. It had taken days of making inquiries along the docks and alleys of the port city to discover the true destination of that doomed fleet, and to discover the infamy planned for the innocents aboard it. At the first chance, he had followed them.

"I had no real choice about my landing port when I set out for Palestine," Jared said, "and no useful information about where to start my search either. I suppose I must have thought of the Holy Land as a single city, the land of milk and honey," he smiled ruefully.

Isabeau found herself quite breathless in the face of that engaging, candid grin. She wanted to pass it back with a smile of her own, but forced herself to simply nod instead. "You were not the only one under that misapprehension, mercenary," she admitted. "Go on, what did you do when you arrived?"

"Well, I was quite surprised to learn that there were many, many territories and sovereignties, and that they tended to change hands with as much frequency as a dinar in a moneylender's stall. To make a long story short, I arrived in Antioch several weeks after setting sail—the crew had discovered me early on stealing from their stores at night, and thankfully all they did was force me to work

aboard the ship in exchange for my keep, which I was more
than willing to do. When I arrived, I was fortunate enough
to come to the attention of a man called John of Brienne.
Perhaps you have heard of him?"

Heard of him? Isabeau thought incredulously. That she
had. The king of Antioch was well known to be a fair man,
educated far beyond his kind, and a shrewd politician indeed. After having succeeded to the throne of Antioch
through marriage, the sixty-year-old knight had traveled to
the East at a time when most would have been content to
enjoy their twilight years sitting at home before the hearth,
and had gone on to secure for himself the whole of this
well-populated territory with relative ease and little loss of
life. Unlike most of his fellow conquerors, he had troubled
himself to learn some Arabic, and had cultivated the acquaintance of learned men in his demesne, both Muslim
and Christian alike. Still, like most Westerners, his goal had
been to take and hold as much profitable territory as he
could under the guise of holy war.

What Jared did not mention was that he hadn't immediately been taken under this powerful man's wing. He had
survived for several months on the streets before that lucky
break, living hand-to-mouth in a strange country with
stranger customs and a language he did not begin to comprehend. If it had not been for Big Pierre's intervention,
and then John's, he would surely have died within the first
year there. All he said was: "I joined with King John's
retinue out of necessity—what else was a half-trained
squire to do?—and at first my comrades among his entourage managed to convince me I would have little luck lo-
cating a single Christian slave in all the vast territories of
Syria and Persia. There'd been no word of the crusader
fleet's arrival, no mention of a sudden influx of white slaves
anywhere. It seemed hopeless that I would ever succeed in
finding you. Still, when the knights urged me to take the
cross as they had done, swearing myself to the cause of
holy crusade, I refused. I told them I had a prior vow to
fulfill before I could take on any other cause. But having

had no success, I still needed to keep body and soul together," Jared confessed, glancing at Isabeau and then quickly away as though he feared to read condemnation in her eyes. "It seemed easiest to throw my fortunes in with my countrymen, and so I followed John when he took his campaign throughout Syria and thence to Egypt."

Carefully, Jared avoided speaking of those doomed campaigns, of the horrors and outrages he had witnessed there, and the infuriating mismanagement of their slim resources caused by too many leaders sharing joint control but harboring very different motives.

He did not want to burden his betrothed in her fragile state, but he couldn't hide from Isabeau. She knew what had happened—all Syria knew of the bloody battles that had raged between the crusaders and the Muslim factions who had been—and still were—wrestling for primacy throughout the coastal states. Nothing was too brutal or heinous for these warmongers, from betraying one's own comrades for gain, to the rape and pillage of innocents by soldiers hell-bent on outdoing one another's atrocities. Such had been going on in these disputed territories long before the first crusaders ever arrived from over the seas, and would continue, she knew, for many years after the last one had left.

"So that is where you gained the name 'the Lion of Antioch' . . ." she hazarded. "Fighting in the campaigns along the coast?"

"Actually, I assumed my name and banner in deference to your family," the mercenary confessed. "I took the silver lion of Lyon, changing it to black to reflect my sorrow for what I had done—or failed to do—in losing you. But it was in Damietta, on the mud-slick plains of war, that I received my spurs from John of Brienne."

Modestly, Jared did not mention that it had been his suggestion that had given the crusaders access to the fortified city that was the gateway to all Egypt, after months of unsuccessful siege. Unable to break into this stronghold on the Nile delta by land, their only hope had been to breach it by the river gate, which had been protected by a great iron chain none could pass. It had been Jared's idea to float several tall barges up against the chain so they could cross—an idea that had finally gotten them all over the barrier and into the city. Still, they hadn't held it long, he recalled, due to political intriguing behind the scenes between the Egyptian governor al-Kamil, the pope's fanatical representative Pelagius, and his own master John.

"I was twenty-one then, and the pressure from my comrades to take the cross and confirm my loyalty was growing. Despite my gratitude to my adopted liege lord, I could not comply, and so at last I struck off on my own. By then, I had learned to speak Arabic, and had formed several friendships in the cities through which I'd traveled with those sympathetic to my quest. In Alexandria, I learned of a girl answering your description who'd been sold several years before for a great sum of money to someone in the court of Baghdad, although I could not discover the particular buyer's identity. It was a slim thread of hope, yet it was my best lead in years. It encouraged me to keep up hope, to keep searching.

"I became a mercenary in the end," Jared concluded. "It made sense—I could travel at a moment's notice, I made contact with slave buyers and merchants quite frequently, and it allowed me to earn enough money to send home and aid my brother's cause back in Navarre. Eventually, others joined me, and at length the Black Lion's Pride was formed. But until the Shadow Hunter's summons reached us, I had come no closer to finding you, Isabeau, than if I had stayed in France, or even returned home to Navarre." Jared shook his head in wonder. "I sense the hand of God in this chance meeting, Isabeau. This was meant to be."

What was meant to be? the renegade wondered. Their meeting, or something more further down the line? Just what might Jared be expecting to come out of this strange reunion of theirs? Surely, he knew it was too late for them to uphold their parents' intentions, so long deferred. Isabeau had not been speaking facetiously when she had urged the

Black Lion to forget her after she'd first woken. She was no longer the girl Jared had thought to wed when he was a lad. Indeed, should he ever learn the true depths of her disgrace, the debasements etched upon her soul, marriage would be the last thing on his mind. It was just as well that she couldn't have accepted his suit in any case.

Zahra's need still came before her own desires—even if she *had* wished to marry Jared after all this time, which of course was ridiculous! And that was even supposing the offer was still on the table, which the mercenary had by no means yet suggested. Isabeau had a duty to the girl who'd shared the bonds of her slavery, a duty that had not ended with her failure to rescue Zahra from Malik ten days ago. There could be nothing permanent between herself and the mercenary until she had redeemed herself at least that far, by paying the debt she owed her heart's sister. And even after, it would be best for the noble Black Lion if she were to disappear back into the Shadow Hunter's outlaw persona and never cross his path again.

Quite simply, he deserved better than her. Though at first Isabeau had believed Jared a money-hungry mercenary, whose morals and methods changed each time he accepted a new employer, she saw now that he was nothing of the sort. No. Instead, Jared was every good thing she had believed of him when she was a child, and more besides. He was chivalrous, honorable, true-hearted. He was constant, steadfast, and noble. He deserved a woman who could match his strength and nobility, a woman who could give him children and keep his house—not some freakish oddity of a female whose only skills were with sword and dagger! He deserved everything he'd been promised when he'd been bound to wed little Isabeau de Lyon—a good woman, a pure woman, and above all, an *innocent* woman.

The Assassin could offer him none of that now. All she *could* do, if she still had a stroke of honor in her, was give him release from his vows, send him home while he still had a future. But did she have the strength to do it, when sending him away was the last thing she wished? And how could she repay him in the meanwhile for all his dedicated service to her cause?

Isabeau was silent for a long time. At last, however, she spoke, and when she did there was a note of respect in her voice, of seriousness that had never been present before. "You have given me much to think upon, Black Lion. Your bravery and tenacity on my behalf have been . . . extraordinary. And I . . ." She could not think how to phrase the enormity of her gratitude, her shame at not living up to his ideal, and the remorse she felt at knowing he had sacrificed everything for her. "Appreciate it," she finished lamely.

By Allah, that was not what she'd meant to say at all! These feeble words expressed nothing of the Assassin's true deep feelings. Damn it! She just wasn't good at speaking her thoughts—for too many years she had made a habit of suppressing them, and now they simply would not come when she called. Still, she needed to convey her feelings somehow.

Perhaps, she thought spontaneously, actions could speak louder than words.

Frustrated, the renegade reached up, slid her hand into Jared's glossy auburn locks, and kissed him.

CHAPTER SEVENTEEN

Jared was stunned. And that was putting it mildly. Once again he felt his fiery betrothed's lips upon his own in a kiss she had initiated, and under the searing heat of her welcome onslaught his thoughts evaporated instantly.

Her full lips shaped his, clinging and consuming even as her tongue slipped daringly into his surprised but welcoming mouth. Isabeau arched up and put her whole effort into the kiss, her slender arms twining about his neck and her breath mingling sweetly with his own. Her lips and tongue worked expert magic upon his senses, taking his pleasure in with urgent licks and suckling, and offering of themselves generously in return. Blatantly sensual, even carnal, it was more shocking, stirring, and arousing than any other kiss he'd ever received.

Jared moaned, sweeping his cherished betrothed into his arms, still instinctively remaining careful of her wound. He didn't know why she was doing this so suddenly, but he was beyond asking as she wrapped him in her sensual magic. Isabeau was offering herself to him, something he had been beyond hoping for, and the joy of it was enough to make his blood sing in his veins. She came willingly, trembling but without protest, pressing her scarcely clad body up to his like an offering. Yet something was not quite right, Jared sensed, and after a moment, he was able to pinpoint the trouble despite his raging ardor.

It was a courtesan's kiss.

Isabeau was giving him this pleasure as a *reward,* as if in payment for some act he'd performed! She did not offer it freely, he realized, out of her own desire. The mercenary went cold. Tearing his lips free of her own, he looked down at Isabeau as if he had never seen her before. Her eyes were closed tight, however, keeping her secrets still from him. "What is this, Isabeau?" he asked shortly, still panting slightly.

Her eyes flew open, full of startled sapphire brilliance. "This?" she asked quizzically. Her slim hand rose to trace the line of his jaw lightly, invitingly, but her gaze slid away again from his own. The usually fierce Assassin seemed almost embarrassed now.

To Jared it was tantamount to an admission. He was at once infuriated and disgusted—infuriated that she should think to placate him in this manner, that she thought so little of him as to offer up sexual currency in lieu of thanks, and disgusted because she clearly knew no better than to barter herself in trade like some downtrodden army camp follower. What lessons had life taught Isabeau, to make her behave this way? he wondered bleakly. Yet though his anger was not directed at her, but rather at those who had enslaved and warped such a gentle and giving creature as his betrothed had been, that wasn't entirely clear from his tone. He was simply too upset to modulate his voice.

"This *kiss,* Isabeau. Do you think you're doing either of us a favor by offering yourself to me out of some misplaced sense of gratitude?"

Isabeau was stung to the quick by this too-insightful accusation. "I wasn't! I never . . ." But she had.

At first, hers had indeed been a practiced kiss, one of display rather than pure emotion, meant for the pleasure of the recipient rather than to gratify her own longings. She'd wanted to offer him something of herself when she'd surprised him with her rash caress; to make a sacrifice that, if perhaps it failed to match his own, at least came from her heart. The Assassin had had nothing save herself to offer up, and so she had made her impulsive move, though she knew it could never be enough to repay Jared's astonishingly determined quest to find her.

Isabeau had never thought of herself as alluring, the odalisques of the emir's harem having teased her too often for her pale European complexion and delicate features for the renegade to believe she was other than an ugly aberration among women. Yet still she'd sensed her advance would not be entirely unwelcome to Jared, since the mercenary appeared to share al-Fayed's predilection for fair women. He'd seemed to enjoy her odd looks, had even called her beautiful once before. And she was certainly well-trained enough in the art of love to please a man, she'd reasoned. She'd only wanted to make it good for him! But as she took in Jared's angry gaze, it seemed she'd failed to do even that much.

The mercenary was incensed. "Don't lie to me. I can tell when a woman wants me, and when she doesn't." Jared's hand slid down her hip, crudely slipped between her parted thighs and beneath her tunic to cup her most intimate flesh. "And this," he whispered angrily, simultaneously sliding an oddly gentle finger into her cleft, "tells me you don't want it." She was barely moist there, certainly not dripping with desire as her kiss would indicate.

Isabeau cried out. It was both shock and torment to feel his big hand invading her there, where she had never given permission for a man to come. And yet it was not distaste she felt at his intimate touch, but something else entirely. Heat blossomed in her cheeks, even as she went still in his arms. She was trembling, waiting to see what he would do next, afraid of his anger and yet warmed by his passion. But Jared did nothing, seeming riveted in place as well by the feel of her velvety flesh beneath his questing fingers as by his own daring foray into it.

God, had he really touched her there? *Here,* where his fingers lay in shocked delight, pressed up against her dampening petals? How had he dared? Yet Isabeau did not protest his presumptuous move, gazing up at him instead with some unfathomable emotion darkening her eyes. Dare he hope she was not merely surprised but aroused by this invasion? He knew he was. By Christ's blessed redemption, the urge to explore that silken flesh, to arouse her as he sensed he could with just a subtle motion of his hand . . . to fondle and explore every last perfect feminine inch of her until she was panting and wet and writhing for more,

and then to plunge his fingers deep inside and feel her core
convulse with need for him . . .

But he had not meant to show his betrothed such dis-
respect, and he was aware that even her overtly carnal kiss
had not invited such depth of intimacy on his part. Jared
knew he should remove his hand and apologize before they
both had something to regret. Yet his body was loath to
take such an action despite the urging of his mind, and he
waited instead without moving for Isabeau to make the next
move.

It was too late already for the renegade to stop him, even
if she'd had a thought of doing so. Liquid heat was flooding
Isabeau's whole being, and desire coursed fast and heavy
through her veins. He'd caught her playing her impulsive
game of seduction, and now the game was up! The mercenary said he didn't want her carefully choreographed
gratitude. Still, Isabeau instinctively sensed that didn't
mean he didn't want *her*. And she was discovering she very
much wanted *him* in return. She'd thought the gift of her
body might please the Black Lion, but she had never expected it to be a pleasure they could share. Now the renegade knew differently.

Sex was no stranger to Isabeau. She'd grown up around
its matter-of-fact expression, had even been taught to think
of it as an art. Yet she had never been taught to *like* it. At
first neutral toward the lessons in a concubine's duty she'd
received from youth, and later appalled and abhorring the
acts forced upon her and upon Zahra in her presence by
Malik al-Fayed, the harem slave called Gulbayez had never
thought to become caught up in the coils of desire herself.
But that was exactly what had just happened.

She was no ignorant maiden, and life had stripped her
too thoroughly of innocence for Isabeau to deny that what
she felt now was passion. But neither could she fight it.
And why should she? If Jared made her tremble in ways
no man had ever done before, if the very sight of him made
her body hunger like a ravening wolf, why should she not
avail herself of his willingness to bring them both untold

ecstasies inside the protective circle of his arms? Perhaps she could not afford to let her guard down in front of Jared as she wished. Perhaps she risked losing her soul to him in the process of exploring this novel desire. For the chance to experience passion in the arms of the one man who had never betrayed her, who had only her greater good in mind, it was a price she would willingly pay. Jared de Navarre had already saved her once from damnation, just by having faith enough to suffice for both of them.

Isabeau looked up solemnly at her savior's face in the firelight—so earnest, so faithful, so committed in his belief in her. He made her want to feel that faith too. And in a way she did—Isabeau might not believe she was worth all Jared had given up for her, but she knew *he* was worth everything she had to give. She stroked his cheek tenderly, thinking of all she would risk to keep him safe, and closed her eyes against the rush of weakness that flooded her when he turned his lips into her wrist and kissed her there. For Jared, Isabeau thought, she would take on the sultan himself!

She lay back upon the furs, keeping her arms locked loosely about his neck to play teasingly with his hair and leaving his deliciously invading hand exactly where it lay. She remembered his accusation that she did not desire this intimacy flowering so splendidly between them. How false it seemed now!

"*Make* me want it, mercenary," the renegade challenged softly. And her hips arched up against his hand just enough so there would be no mistaking her meaning.

"Ah, Isabeau!" he growled softly. His palm pressed involuntarily up against the mound of her pleasure, applying pressure just where he knew she needed it most. "Are you sure?" Jared couldn't bear it if she were not . . .

"More than sure," she gasped. Suddenly desperate, Isabeau arched up and pressed her longing lips to his again, imparting upon his surprised but eager mouth a kiss of such depth and ardor that Jared moaned and gathered her tight into his arms, letting his right hand slide up from her belly

to curve about her waist as he held her close to him in a
rush of fierce emotion. And even then, he was careful of
her wound, cushioning her against any sudden pressure or
harm. He would *never* let harm come to her, Isabeau
thought dizzily as she let her mouth become consumed with
his.

"Jared," she whispered between deep, drowning kisses.
"Jared—oh, my Lion. You never left my heart." Her strong
arms curled tight around his corded neck as she made this
spontaneous confession, pulling him close and yet closer
still. This was no kiss of gratitude. Nor was it necessary
for Jared to teach her how to enjoy it after all. Though
Isabeau had been innocent of passion's pleasures up until
this point, she learned them fast. Absorbed them through
her lover's skin as it pressed hot and sleek against her own.
Breathed it in the air they shared between devouring kisses.
Smelled it in the sweet musk of his flesh and soft hair
surrounding her. Tasted it upon his tongue as it mated with
her own in the dance of love.

This was at once both studied and artless in the extreme—Isabeau remembered none of her lessons in pleasure now, but learned them all anew under Jared's expert
tutelage. She sought her teacher's knowledge like a blind
woman, sliding her palms over his arms, back, and shoulders as if to learn him tactilely. And oh, how willing Jared
was to teach her!

"Isabeau, Isabeau," Jared murmured ecstatically. "Oh,
my sweet little Beau. What a woman you've grown into!"
He couldn't get enough of her, kissing her, touching her,
just reassuring himself she truly was real, here in his arms.
He knew he should stop—she wasn't ready, she wasn't
well—hell, she didn't even know if she really wanted this!
There was so much unresolved between them, but oh, how
her challenge had spurred him on! *Make me want it.* If he
could make her desire him half as much as he desired her,
she would never get enough of him. "Isabeau," he whispered again against her ivory neck. "How can I please you
best?"

"Be with me, Jared," she pleaded softly. "Just be with me and do not let me go."

"I never shall," he vowed breathlessly. Jared looked down upon his betrothed's flushed features, and her fair blond beauty nearly broke his heart. Isabeau was everything his dreams had ever hoped for, the fulfillment of a thousand whispered prayers over the years. "I have you, Isabeau; here so dear in my arms. I pledge my life to you, sweetheart; you'll never have to go without my presence again."

Ah, such a reckless promise when she was not free to make the same. So poignant, and yet so awful! "Just be with me now, my Lion," she begged hoarsely. "Now must be enough."

And yet in the end, it was too soon.

Her wound might be healed enough, but her heart was not ready for the full commitment of their lovemaking. Jared knew it, even as he traced the sweet outlines of her face with his thumbs, even as he caressed her flushed and fevered skin. His palms stroked her shoulders and tender breasts, fingers thrilling the nipples with perfectly gauged squeezes, outlining their sweet curves with delicate awe. He skimmed past her bandaged midsection and down again to stroke the virgin territory of her belly. The smoothness of her there, below the flat plane of her abdomen, excited him unbearably, yet his touch was light, requesting rather than demanding.

At last, when she bumped her hips urgently up to meet his hand, he again dipped into the crease of her womanhood, absorbing her ecstatic gasp upon his tongue as he stroked across her now soaked and heated petals and touched the very bud of her desire. With knowing fingers and eager encouragement whispered into the delicate shell of her ear, he raised the timbre of Isabeau's excitement higher and higher, stroking her heated core until she was sobbing and arching helplessly against his hand. Isabeau wanted him now, Jared knew; if not as much as he wanted her in return, then very nearly. He could possess her body, and she would not demur—no, she would relish the pos-

session! But he did not think the time was right—too much
still lay unspoken between them. For now, the mercenary
decided, he would content himself with the gift of his part-
ner's pleasure.

Generously, eagerly, he pressed back against her, ignoring his own raging erection and pushing her until at last it
was too much for the aroused Assassin. Crying and clutching his shoulders, she came against his hand with powerful
shudders that wracked her slender body more fiercely even
than the chills of her fever had done just days before. Hearing her impassioned cries against his ear, feeling her shuddering completion, Jared felt a sense of well-being wash
over him that was more powerful than any orgasm, more
ecstatic and more humbling.

His woman had found fulfillment, and the satisfaction
of it sat profoundly in Jared's mind.

His kisses gentled, slowed, and became comforting then,
rather than passionate. He knew he had made the right decision when Isabeau did not clamor for more, beg for a
deeper completion, but accepted his soothing caresses. Exhausted and emotionally overwrought, she allowed him at
length to stroke her into slumber once again, while he held
her securely in those arms he knew she had missed for too
many years.

The Black Lion breathed in her scent, buried his face in
the soft cloud of her tousled moonlight curls, and listened
to her breathing grow slower and steadier until Isabeau
slipped at last into dreams. Her head was pillowed trustingly on his arm and her back tucked into the sheltering
curve of his chest, his aching desire cushioned against her
softly rounded buttocks. For a moment the urge to guide it
inside her this way, from behind, almost overwhelmed him,
but Jared forced himself to lie still until it passed.

Sighing, he lay still and listened to the evening sounds
surrounding their cave sanctuary, hearing nothing to disturb
his heightened senses. The fire popped and sizzled, the logs
shifted and settled into the stone bed he'd hollowed for
them. The nocturnal denizens of the canyon began their

evening song, and the night wind echoed mournfully
through the steep walls of the canyon to complement it.
Jared's stallion whickered in his makeshift corral, and
Zephyr answered softly with a whinny of her own. All was
well. Eventually Jared, too, was able to drift into sleep,
content just to have Isabeau near.

It was time to talk.

Morning had come upon the canyon, and even this deep
within its steep sides, a shaft of late-autumn sunlight had
penetrated, creating a shining wall of light that rained down
like a waterfall of yellow heat. Isabeau stood in it, feeling
the indescribably wonderful sensation of pure sunshine on
her face. Such a simple feeling, and yet it had been years
since she'd experienced it. Years since she had dared to go
unveiled.

In the harem, it had been unthinkable to allow oneself
to be seen by a man without the proper coverings, and little
sunshine had ever penetrated the screened confines of the
enclosed courtyards, marble-domed hammams, and orna-
mental gardens of the walled prison where she *had* been
allowed to go bare-faced. Later, even after she'd escaped,
it had been a matter of life and death to be recognized going
abroad as a female, and so the veil had remained. But now
she was free, at least for a little while. Free to stand in the
sun. Free to face Jared de Navarre in her own true guise.

How would it be to live in a place where she would
never be forced to hide her face again? Isabeau wondered.
Where she would always be cared for and protected by this
man, however she chose to confront the future? For that
was what the mercenary had just forced her to consider, in
asking her to accompany him back to the West.

He had not mentioned the possibility of a wedding between them yet, probably guessing with his native tact that
it was still too soon to broach the matter, but she knew the
possibility still existed in Jared's mind. Even without marriage, Isabeau thought the chance to journey by his side to
the place where it had all begun sounded almost unbearably

appealing. To stay with him forever was more than the
Assassin could even begin to consider, though her heart
thrummed unsteadily with excitement at the prospect. Yet
as tempting as it was, she knew she could not accept. Not
even after the incredible sensations he had introduced her
to last night, and the yet more powerful emotions such near-
complete lovemaking had evoked in her heart.

Turning away from the light, the Shadow Hunter faced
the mercenary sadly.

"It can never be, Jared," she said softly.

He had just proposed that she return to the West with
him, yet his betrothed wore that strange, faraway look upon
her face again, as if he'd spoken in a foreign language
instead of her own native tongue. "Why can it not?" Jared
asked, trying to sound reasonable though he found himself
feeling unaccountably wounded. Silhouetted by the morning sunlight at her back, her hair alight with white-gold
flames and her fair skin beginning to take on the pink tones
of health once more, Isabeau looked like a fairy princess.
Yet Jared could not seem to capture this magical creature
long enough to make her grant his wish. The Assassin's
uncanny ability to dodge had not deserted her with the re-
moval of her male disguise.

"It . . . it simply *cannot*! Please," Isabeau cried, her fists
balled at her side. "Leave it be, Jared. You don't know what
you're asking. You don't even know who I am!"

"I know who you are, Isabeau," Jared reassured her, a
bit bemused. Why was she fighting him on this? he wondered. It wasn't as if he had offered to drag her back to a
family that hated her, after all. And it wasn't as though her
life here in the Persian badlands was so easy. Outlaw and
renegade, there were few places where his betrothed could
ever be safe, even in the male disguise of Sayyad al-Zul.
Especially now that she had made such a mortal enemy in
the emir Malik al-Fayed.

The renegade was running out of time—and she must
know it as well as he did.

So why was she so adamant about staying? He might

not know the whole history of his betrothed, but Jared knew enough to sense there had been much pain in her life in the East, and little pleasure indeed. What would she be giving up, and how could it compare to what he offered—home, hearth, a reunion with the family who loved her?

Perhaps he had not made his intentions clear enough, Jared thought slowly. Yet though he still had every hope of bringing Lady Isabeau before her parents in triumph, and, when the time was right, asking them to uphold the oath of betrothal they had made with his father, he felt it was still too early to bring that up with the skittish woman before him. She seemed ready to bolt already! "I know you, Isabeau," was what he settled for saying again. After last night, how could she doubt it? "I have *always* known you."

"No." She refuted him flatly. "You don't. And if you did, trust me, Jared, you wouldn't be so quick to offer me a return to the promises of our youth. Please," she entreated. "You must believe me when I tell you those doors have been closed to us both forever. That world you speak of means nothing to me now." The last was a lie, but the rest was true enough, Isabeau thought sadly. Too much had come between them to ever regain the simple innocence of their shared past.

"How can you say so?" Jared demanded. "Don't you even care to hear news of your family?" he asked incredulously. "I notice you've not mentioned them or asked after their welfare once in all this time. Don't you want to know all you've missed?"

Of course I do! Isabeau thought. "No," she said instead, as coldly as she could. "No, I don't want to hear any of it." She couldn't afford the knowledge when it was just one more glimpse at a life she could never have again! There was only so much the Assassin could bear, and her betrothed was sorely testing her limits. Had he no idea how painful this was for her?

Jared was suddenly furious. "Well, you're *going* to hear it, understand! You're going to sit right there—" he pointed to a boulder nearby—"and you're going to listen to it;

every last word I know about your family and mine. Then
you will tell me again how none of it matters to you, Isabeau."

"No . . . I don't want—" she began, but Jared had already begun.

"Did you know it was your mother who kept in touch
with me all these years?" He didn't wait for an answer,
glaring at Isabeau until she sank miserably onto the stone
seat he'd indicated. When she went to cover her ears
against the diatribe, however, he pulled her hands down
and held them firmly in his own.

It was a mark of her combined emotional disturbance
and physical exhaustion that the Assassin did nothing to
break the mercenary's presumptuous hold on her. Her
hands, cold and shaky, rested in his grasp like frightened
birds afraid to be crushed, and her breathing was shallow,
panicky. In contrast, his words flowed over her like hot
lava, burning through Isabeau's last defenses and leaving
her heart all cinders and ashes.

"She sent me tidings all these years, did Lady Margery,"
Jared said. "Always kind despite my failure to uphold her
faith, always begging me to return. Always forgiving my
grave sin as though I had not single-handedly been responsible for the loss of her beloved child. She never once
blamed me in her letters, Isabeau. Not once!" The mercenary shook his head, his hands unconsciously tightening
their grip upon her own. "I believe it was those reports,
infrequent and often delayed though they were, that kept
me alive when hopelessness threatened to overwhelm my
soul." He took a breath, wondering if the stony-faced renegade was taking in any of his words, or if she truly had
turned to granite before his eyes.

"She told me many things about my own family in her
letters, as well as yours. When my father happily wrote me
off for dead, she made contact with my brother on my behalf, so that I might at least keep that connection alive. If
not for the kindness of the duchess . . ." Jared shrugged his
shoulders. "I would know nothing of my father's demise,

or of my sibling's plight back in Navarre. And speaking of siblings, Isabeau, did you know you have a brother now?"

"No . . ." she whispered, trying to pull her hands away and cover her ears once more. Yet the Assassin was too enervated to put much force into the effort. She could not afford to think of her family now . . . didn't he understand how his words were tearing her apart? Isabeau ruthlessly strangled the sob that had caught in her throat.

"Aye, and a sister too. I'm told she looks much like you, with fair curling hair and winsome blue eyes."

Isabeau hid those blue eyes behind a curtain of her hair now, bowing her head. Her mind was whirling, picturing places and people she had not dared to think of in nearly two decades. "And my father?" she could not help asking in a whisper. Jared had not mentioned Duke William yet. "Is he . . . ?" She was afraid to know the answer.

"Very much alive," Jared confirmed, "and well, though I am told his hair and beard went gray the day he learned of your disappearance. The de Lyon family prosper still."

"Oh," she said softly. "Oh." Isabeau could not think of anything else to say. There seemed to be an enormous fist squeezing her heart dry, compressing her lungs until she couldn't breathe. "Enough, Jared!" she cried at last. The renegade mustered the strength to tear her hands free finally, though it jolted her bandaged side to do it. But she did not get up from the boulder that had become her seat, though she longed to run from Jared's revelations as fast and as far as her weakened limbs would take her.

"By God, it's *not* enough, woman, and it won't be until you realize your place is there, back with your family. Back with *me*," he finished tightly. "Don't you think your mother and father deserve to know you are alive—to see you once again after so many years without daring to hope?"

"Better they believe that I died, mercenary," she cried furiously, "than that they should learn the truth!"

"*What* truth?" he demanded. "What could possibly be so bad that you cannot forgive yourself? Isabeau." Jared's voice was suddenly gentle. "What troubles you so? If it is

your enslavement . . . if you think that somehow makes you
unworthy . . . Be assured, no one at home would ever hold
it against you." He wasn't quite sure how to broach the
subject tactfully. The touchy renegade had assiduously
avoided talking about it up till now, yet he knew her experience had had a profound effect on her psyche. "Please
tell me," he begged softly. Jared squatted down before her
so that he could look up into her anguished eyes instead of
towering above his distraught betrothed.

Isabeau felt her heart splinter as she saw him there, so
beautiful and so masculine crouching before her with his
big hands held loose before him on his knees and his amber
gaze so compassionate and concerned. She wanted to tell
Jared, but how could he ever understand? How could any
man?

"They called me Gulbayez," she said abruptly. Out of
nowhere. Isabeau's eyes focused determinedly on the rocky
walls before her, not on the mercenary at her side.

The White Rose. Jared translated the word in his mind.
The name suited her, he had to admit. She was as fair and
delicate of face and form as the freshest of rosebuds. But
Jared was thinking of something else. A deadly calling card
left by the Assassin Sayyad al-Zul.

"Yes," she confirmed, seeing the awareness grow in his
eyes when she at last dared to look. "I took the white rose
as my emblem after I escaped, as a symbol of the oppression I would no longer tolerate." The Assassin's voice was
shaking with suppressed passion, with outrage. "Right off
the slave block, you see, my master had taken away my
name, and given me a new one I did not even comprehend.
It was worth a whipping just to use the old one within the
hearing of the harem guards, and most girls brought into
that place soon learned to leave behind their birth names
as well as everything else about their pasts if they wanted
to survive.

"I never forgot *my* name, though. I never forgot who I
was," she rasped. "Never in all the days they tried to break
me with their tortures and temptations." Then Isabeau's

voice lost its edge of defiance, became almost apologetic. "Yet I did not fight them either, not for long. I kept silent, Jared," she confessed. "I bowed to them, for in the end I had no choice." Would he understand why, when she had told him all? Or would he fault her for her shameful capitulation? Isabeau didn't know, but she had come too far to turn back now. The mercenary had asked for the truth. Now he would get it!

"I learned their language and I followed their rules, Jared. I behaved as a proper Muslim female should in every respect. And when I grew old enough to be noticed, recognized as a woman, I did every last horrid, perverted thing my master ever asked of me . . ." Isabeau stopped speaking, her voice strangling in her throat.

After a deep breath, however, she went on, not looking at the mercenary for fear of what she might see in his eyes—dismay, disapproval, disappointment. "I swore once I had left that life I would never go back; not for anything. But there is one thing—one person—for whom I must make the exception. Because she took the punishment meant for me. She took all my punishments." Isabeau knew she probably wasn't making much sense to the mercenary, but she could do no better. All the words of explanation were jumbling together in her mind, the memories crowding in tightly and tearing at her heart. *Ah, Zahra!*

"I would have died rather than submit, Jared. I swear it." Her eyes begged him to believe it, for she could not bear her betrothed to think she had been so weak as to obey without some overriding cause. "I would have forced them to kill me with my rebellion, had it not been for that one sweet girl whose arrival in the harem changed everything."

Indeed, she had often supposed that Jamal had bought Zahra with that in mind. The cunning eunuch who was both harem master and secret Assassin, seeing his young protégée's unwillingness to assimilate, had taken extraordinary measures when it seemed he would have to write her off as unsuitable for the master he ostensibly served. His manipulations had worked perfectly, Isabeau had to admit, for she had loved gentle Zahra from the first moment she'd seen the frightened younger girl take her first steps into the dangerous world of the emir's harem. How could she explain to Jared what Zahra had meant to her? What she still meant to this day? Once again Isabeau flashed back to that recent day when she had so briefly felt the other girl at her back once more, only to lose her again. She would have to start from the beginning if Jared was to have a hope of comprehending that special bond.

"Younger still than I, and from a land far distant from my own, the girl could yet have been my twin, we looked so much alike," the renegade began. "She was of Greek origin, stolen from her family by corsairs from the Barbary Coast and sold so many times by the time Jamal, my new owner's harem master and chief slave buyer, got to her, she had no concept anymore of where her home might lie. Still, because she spoke the Hellenic tongue you and I were taught in childhood, we were able to communicate when she arrived in the harem just six months after I had. She and I became close, dear as sisters as we clung together in that friendless place."

Isabeau did not bother to describe how the other concubines and slaves had viewed them with suspicion and then jealousy as they grew to womanhood, how they had plotted and schemed against them almost constantly, nor how it had never been safe to turn one's back in that harem, despite Jamal ad-Din's powerful championship. Poisonings and suspicious "accidents" had been common, with rivals stopping at nothing to get each other out of the way.

"At first it was not so bad. We were too young then to attract our master's attention, and we had only to follow the harem chief's orders to avoid punishment. Even so, I had rebelled so hard against my captivity by the time my new friend arrived that they were nearly ready to send me into the fields as a common laborer, despite my enormous purchase price. But she . . ." Isabeau clenched a fist. "She gave me a new reason to live; someone to care for, to protect, when I no longer cared to fight for myself. And for the first time, a reason to obey my captors.

"I did not want us to be separated, and I could not afford to do anything that might cause it." Isabeau paused, not sure how to continue. "Then, when the master took note of our blossoming womanhood . . ." She choked on the words. "When he took interest in us, I thought briefly of rebelling again, but that option was taken from me. For when I refused at all costs to do as my master ordered, he learned that there was still one way to make me obey . . ." Isabeau growled out the words, impotent fury every bit as strong now as it had been during the days of her captivity.

"All he had to do, you see, was give Zahra whatever punishment he deemed I had earned." The renegade squeezed her eyes shut in remembered helplessness. "It was so simple, so diabolical, and so effective, that I dared not disobey a single command."

Indeed, had it not been for Jamal working his clever machinations again on her behalf, she would have suffered much, much worse, Isabeau knew. Yet if she had taken her proper punishments, then perhaps her self-adopted sister would not have suffered them in her stead . . . But the Assassin could not bring herself to divulge the sordid details of that twisted arrangement to the chivalrous knight whose quest for so many years had been her salvation. She knew he carried a heavy enough burden of guilt already. "And so I suffered his disgusting rituals for as long as I could, but at last it was too much for me. I ran, and I left al-Zahra behind."

Purposely, Isabeau shared the name of her heart's sister with the mercenary for the first time, knowing he would be quick to grasp its significance.

She wasn't disappointed. Isabeau heard Jared's sharp inhalation as he put it all together. The woman named Zahra; the sadistic master . . . and of course, the Shadow Hunter's reckless determination to seek a "jewel" from a certain emir at the risk of her own life . . . Now, she thought regretfully, he would begin to understand how little she'd deserved his devoted search all these years.

"Malik al-Fayed—" he croaked, shock evident.

"Was my master. Yes." Isabeau met the mercenary's gaze firmly now, nothing left in her to hide.

"I'll kill him!" Jared seethed. Enraged, he surged to his feet and turned his back on the woman whose revelations so pierced his heart, unwilling to let her see the full measure of his shock and the rage that accompanied it. His powerful fists clenched until the knuckles went dead white, and he shook all over with unaccustomed tremors of mingled denial and disgust. The monster known throughout all Arabia for his cruelty and depraved practices had . . . he forced himself to think it . . . had *owned* Isabeau.

The knowledge made the mercenary want to vomit, and he felt his eyes sting with bitter tears of rage. By the blessed wounds of Christ, this was worse even than any of the myriad wretched fates he'd ever imagined befalling little Isabeau! His heart ached with sympathy for the brave, proud girl who had been forced to submit to that depraved man, even as it swelled with pride at the way she had defended both herself and the other girl from the malevolent emir. Without Jared or any other protector to turn to in her time of need, she had still managed to survive and make some sort of life for herself, violent and dangerous though it was. Where any other woman would have given up and submitted to her captors, Isabeau had remained proudly defiant, escaping them and even seeking vengeance on her own terms in the aftermath of her captivity. Jared remembered how strong she had always been, how even her father had called the little girl his lioness . . .

She had never lost that quality of selfless courage, Jared realized. Not though a monster had tried to beat it out of her. She still protected those she loved with all the ferocity of a lioness guarding her cubs! Alone and unaided, she had managed not only to escape from a brutal and demeaning captivity, but also to mount a daring rescue attempt that, if she'd been captured, might well have doomed her to spend the rest of her days suffering her vengeful master's torments all over again. As it was, she'd very nearly died in the effort, though Isabeau made little of the injury. Admiration filled the mercenary, swelling in his breast until he could barely speak. What a woman Isabeau had become!

The renegade laughed bitterly. She'd seen the look of disgust cross Jared's face before he turned away, and had interpreted it in her own way. Jared knew enough of the rumors swirling around the sadistic emir to realize what it meant that she'd been his slave. "It's too late for killing him to do any good, much as I would love to see al-Fayed's entrails fed to a pack of wild dogs before his still-living eyes," she said with matter-of-fact bloodthirstiness. "He has already ruined me. But what he did to Zahra was worse," she assured Jared softly. "Any torment you can imagine that bastard dealing out to me, he inflicted upon Zahra tenfold. And for that, I *will* kill him, if I ever get the chance. Yet for now I will settle for stealing my dear jewel out of his filthy clutches. From what I know of Malik—and that is more than anyone should!—I believe that loss will shake him harder than a thousand incursions upon his wealth or reputation, perhaps even worse than an attack upon his person, for it is an attack on his o'erweening pride."

The mercenary was still several sentences behind, however. "*Ruined* you?" Jared echoed sharply, ignoring the rest of what she'd said for the moment as he focused on the renegade's startling choice of phrase. "Wait a moment— what did you mean by that, Isabeau?"

"For marriage, of course," she reluctantly explained. Wasn't it obvious from what she'd said? "And for anything else for which a proper woman is good, I suppose. Because of him I am unclean. And because of him, I know in my heart that I will never be able to obey any man again, as a woman is taught to do. I cannot bear to be a slave again to any master, Jared—I should rather die. Perhaps, in pursuit of my goal, I shall." Isabeau shrugged fatalistically. "For now, I hide beneath the guise of the renegade Assassin and strive to free my sister from oppression. Though I must deny my sex before all the world, at least this way I have some small chance to help my heart's sister. And if I fail, if I am killed beneath the veil of the Assassin Sayyad al-Zul, then so be it. At least I will die free!"

Were those the only options Isabeau could imagine? Jared wondered sorrowfully. Either submit and make some man her master, or deny her womanhood altogether? If that was how she felt, then Malik had ruined her indeed, warping his slave's beliefs and emotions until there was nothing left of the woman but hatred and despair—and a terrible feeling of responsibility for the actions of a madman she could never have hoped to control. None of this was Isabeau's fault! Could she not see that? "How can you blame yourself for what happened, Isabeau?" Jared asked urgently. "What choice did you have?"

"I could have *stayed*!" she cried. "I could have stabbed that son of a dog in his sleep, though it would have meant death upon the instant when the guards fell upon me. I could have," she searched wildly, flailing, "I *should* have done something—anything! But instead I ran, and left Zahra to that monster. For that alone I have forfeited all right to happiness, even had Malik not sullied my innocence and ensured no man would ever want me." Isabeau curled in upon herself, letting her long hair fall forward to shield her face and hugging herself tightly with folded arms.

How could he show this woman that there was nothing ruined, nothing spoiled about her? In Jared's eyes she was perfect, everything he had ever wanted and believed he could not have. Nothing she had told him, nothing she had done or suffered had changed that. "Isabeau, listen to me!" he demanded. "You have spent the last—what?—five years . . . ?"

"Seven," she admitted softly.

"Seven years striving to make it right. Whereas if you had stayed, taken his abuse yourself, you could have done nothing from within the harem to help either of you, am I right? Believe me, Isabeau, I know something of this matter of failure and restitution." Jared's lips twisted wryly. "If you want to blame someone for all this suffering, blame me! After all, it was I who caused all of this torment and sorrow by letting you out of my sight that day outside your father's castle walls."

"That's not the same!" Isabeau cried, swinging around to face him in surprise. Did his self-castigation truly go so far? Though she'd known the mercenary felt responsible for her plight, she'd had no idea his guilt ran so deep. Knowing only made her own that much worse. "Jared, you cannot still blame yourself for that—no one else faults you! Why, you said yourself, even my lady mother does not!" But Jared wouldn't face her now, turning his bleak countenance away to stare into the fading shaft of sunlight. A chill wind blew through the narrow canyon, raising gooseflesh on the Assassin's arms. Or was it her own thoughts freezing her blood? Urgently Isabeau stood and grasped the tormented warrior's tunic front in her hands, shaking him to relay her seriousness as she spoke.

"You were only a child then yourself, Jared. There was nothing you could have done to stop the hand of destiny that day." Isabeau was shouting now, earnestly imploring him to see her fault and forgive his own. "Nothing to stop *any* of it. If you must blame anyone, blame me for my willful self-indulgence. 'Twas I who ran from you on the practice field that afternoon. The fault lies with me."

"Isabeau," Jared whispered sorrowfully, sounding her name like a prayer. It was so like her to absolve him of his just responsibility in this matter—his fierce lioness would always try to protect others and take their burdens on herself. His hand lifted to stroke through her unbound mane of hair, absorbing the silken texture of it as he smoothed a lock from her face tenderly. "Ah, my sweet, sweet Beau. Do you think you could have known any better? A child of eight summers, taken so brutally . . . simply to have survived is miraculous . . . But to have kept faith the way you have with this girl Zahra, when it brings you so perilously close again to your own tormenter ... To have done all this ..." Jared shook his head.

"How can I convince you you are not ruined?"

"You don't know ..." she insisted weakly.

"I know," he countered. "And I believe you more pure and beautiful than any other woman in this world. You're too good for me, Isabeau," he whispered softly. "But I would have you if I might ..." And his lips descended even as he spoke to tell Isabeau more deeply than with words just how much he longed to make her his own.

CHAPTER EIGHTEEN

Isabeau was drowning, consumed with the mercenary's words as well as his firm, insistent lips. To hear how he wanted her—wanted her still!—even after learning the worst of all she had been and done made the Assassin's head swim. Yet it was her body that was full of sudden, liquid heat. Forgetting her injuries, forgetting all her pain, she surrendered to the pleasure of his touch, wanting so much to believe in all he'd promised. *I would have you if I might,* he'd said . . .

"Then have me!" she gasped. "Take me! Before it is I who must take you . . ." she warned rashly.

The mercenary's surprised laugh was smothered by the Assassin's tender assault as she returned his kiss with every ounce of willingness in her soul. Jared swept her carefully into his arms, whirling her around once in pure, joyful enthusiasm before he began backing them both toward the entrance of the cave hideaway they shared, wildly kissing every inch of her face with each step even as she kissed him back. Before he knew it, the light had shifted abruptly to shadow as they stepped under the overhanging lip of the cavern and into its cool shelter. A moment later they'd reached Isabeau's pallet, Jared sinking down with her in his arms so that she collapsed gracefully upon his chest and he absorbed her slight weight with eager arms.

"I have you," he promised softly, his hands coming up to cup her soft cheeks as he stared into her sapphire eyes. The mercenary hoped she understood the unspoken words that underlay the vow. He would always have her, always keep and protect her for as long as he lived.

He would always *love* her, Jared realized in a flash of humbling insight; if there'd ever been a doubt that the Black Lion should love the elusive lady he'd sought for half his life. Yet this love was so much more than the devotion that had spurred him on to champion her cause many years before. No. His duty might be owed to the child he remembered, but the Black Lion's *heart* belonged to the woman she'd become.

Isabeau was undone by the Black Lion's promises as well as by his kisses. Her heart swelled and her senses soared to dizzying heights as she lay secure within his arms, making her wonder if he had some sort of sorcerer's magic in his touch. This was beyond the simple pleasures of the body, she knew. Though her own experience with desire was but one day old, the renegade sensed that they had already transcended that today. This was something more; this was . . . commitment.

It made her fearful, for she longed to accept all that Jared offered, but knew she should not. Even knowing this solemn ecstasy couldn't be hers to keep, the renegade found herself willing to give the mercenary all she had at this moment, for her heart was his already. He had more than earned it, she knew that well; yet it was not Jared's actions, but the heart that beat behind them that had captured her own. Isabeau loved this man who saw only good in her despite the vile, despicable things she had done. Despite the coldness she'd been forced to adopt, and the unwomanly ways she had learned were her only hope of survival. She loved his devotion, his honesty, his fidelity. She loved his generosity of spirit, his forgiveness, and his slowness to judge. If Jared somehow still desired a scarred, defiled, castoff of a slave, she vowed he would have all she had to give. Isabeau melted into his kiss.

Jared swept his hands tenderly over her shoulders and back, feeling the sleek muscle and bone of her strong yet delicate physique beneath the simple tunic and trousers she wore today, feeling the band of linen that protected her half-healed wound, and carefully bypassing it. In an instant, he had swept off the tunic and slid down her trousers, yet she did not protest even as he shed his own attire, only gasping briefly against his mouth as their heated flesh met skin on skin for the first time. Her moan became one of eagerness when she felt his erect shaft pressing up against one thigh, and she instinctively spread her legs to cradle his hips and welcome it. His eager, pulsing manhood slid between them, finding her moist heated core with only the softest tuft of new-grown fuzz to guard it.

They both moaned this time, overcome by the sensation. Their mating would be swift and sure, Jared knew suddenly. No waiting. He didn't think either of them could handle prolonging this consummation of their desire. Even as he stroked his rough palms across the incredibly silky skin of her back and moved to grasp her firm buttocks in his hands, he felt her sweet honey dripping down to coat his surging member and the aching, sensitive sac beneath that carried his seed. Positioning himself at the tight, luscious entrance of her body, Jared paused, looking up into his lover's eyes for confirmation that she was ready.

Isabeau, straddling the Black Lion like a cat in heat, had never felt more ready in her life. It might be sudden, it might be hard and swift rather than sweet and tender, but then, she thought wryly, neither of them fit the mold of sensitive swain. *This* was how she wanted Jared; bold and fierce and hers! Her hair falling all about them in clouds of silver-gilt silk, the renegade nodded solemnly into his amber eyes. "Do it, my Lion . . . Do it now!"

The Assassin screamed hoarsely as his enormous phallus surged up and filled her tight, virgin channel, deflowering her in one incredible thrust that pushed him to the hilt and pressed hard up against her womb.

The sound echoed in the tiny limestone cave as they both went still in shock. Even Isabeau was not sure if her own cry had been one of pleasure or of pain—the sensation between her legs was so intense! She panted harshly, striving to accustom herself to the feel of him inside her, like a hot, satiny spear that throbbed in time with her own pulse. With all she knew, she should have been prepared . . . yet nothing could have prepared the Assassin for this, she thought—especially not her years as the twisted Malik's helpless plaything.

She was not helpless now, she knew, though Jared held her firmly impaled upon his lap. She felt anything but constrained. On the contrary, Isabeau felt wild, untamed, empowered as she rode astride her beloved. The heat of him, the sheer fullness, was beyond anything she'd ever experienced. It was even a little frightening, Isabeau had to admit.

Yet when Jared, wide-eyed and tense with concern, tried to withdraw from her, she snarled a soft denial and pushed him back to the furs. Now that she had her prey, she thought, she would not set him free just yet!

The Assassin attacked her mercenary lover with a sweet assault of lips, teeth, and tongue; kissing his lips, his throat, his shoulders, anything she could reach as she balanced above him with her elbows on either side of his head and her breasts brushing his hair-roughened chest until the rosy nipples stood out like tiny pebbles of desire. The pain had receded, leaving only excitement in its wake. She had to have more! Her hips pushed down upon his to make up for the inch or so he'd withdrawn, taking his shaft deeper even than before.

"Isabeau," Jared gasped, squeezing his eyes shut with the pleasure of it. "Wait! I didn't realize . . . I don't want to hurt—"

"And I don't want to hurt you either, sweet mercenary," she growled softly as she rode above him with natural, feline grace. "Don't make me beg," she threatened teasingly, even as her strong inner muscles clamped down upon him, milking him for his heated essence.

Even though she smiled, Jared could sense the element of seriousness in her tone. "I wouldn't dream of it," he replied, groaning at the feel of her hot, wet hold on him as he once again cupped her cheek in his hand. "I am at my lady's service."

And oh, did he revel in providing that service!

The shock of his betrothed's virginity began to wear off quickly for the mercenary. It was replaced with a heady rush of satisfaction and a resurgence of his raging desire as

Jared realized he was still somehow, miraculously, the first and only man to possess this incredible woman he loved. The mystery of her untouched state would have to be explained later, however. For now, it was all he could do to keep up with her fiery demands! Jared began to see about the renegade's satisfaction with a determination only equaled by the fervor of his long quest to find her.

Pushing up gently into her welcoming femininity, taking his cues from her facial expressions and the soft moans and gasps his movements elicited, Jared guided her sensual foray with infinite patience and breathless urgency. Isabeau seemed to know exactly what to do, how to pleasure herself and him both, however, and soon there was no leader and no one following, just two lovers conjoined in the escalating dance of passion. Jared watched her as she writhed above him, so lovely he could not believe she was real, so sensual and sexy he could hardly keep himself from spilling his seed into her instantly.

Every surge and ebb of their bodies brought him closer, every spasm of pleasure upon her face excited him more. Even the quivering of her full, upturned breasts, their pink nipples peeking impudently through the veil of her fair hair, made the mercenary feel like coming hard and fast. He tried to be gentle, yet the escalating rhythm she initiated was so infectious, he could not help following it eagerly. Could Isabeau, a virgin, truly take to lovemaking so fast? He must be sure this first experience was everything she had hoped for and more, Jared thought. His thumb found the hidden bud of her desire, and he massaged it firmly as Isabeau circled her hips upon him.

She'd never felt so powerful, and yet at the same time so completely helpless, the Assassin thought raggedly, almost screaming from the sudden assault of his knowing hand upon her sensitive clit. Her inner muscles clenched around him even harder in response, squeezing hard to give them both the maximum pleasure. Jared moaned an incoherent prayer, or was it an incantation to protect him from her charms? It was no use, Isabeau thought giddily. He was hers now. All hers, to do with as she wished. Not even in command of her band of loyal *fidai'in* did she hold so much control over another human being as she did over the mercenary right now. His desire for her, inexplicable as she found it, enslaved him to her every bit as much as she had ever been enslaved to Malik al-Fayed. She could see his surrender to the ecstasy that raged between them in the rugged planes of his face, read it in the fluid lines of his muscular body as he followed her demanding rhythm. She could sense his commitment to her own pleasure even before he began to stroke her shatteringly sensitive center, and Isabeau knew he was in thrall to the force that bound them every bit as much as she.

Because of it, though sexual acts had always been a matter of fear and disgust during her years of captivity, Isabeau found herself not afraid now. Even though he was so much bigger than she, though she was wounded and vulnerable and engaged in an activity with which she had no actual direct experience, she did not fear, because she knew Jared would never hurt her, never take advantage of her. And it was that which rendered her helpless to him, in the end. Not her virginity, or her relative frailty in the face of his strength and experience. It was his very generosity that made her his.

Spiraling out of control under the urging of his hand and the upward thrusting of his hips, Isabeau felt herself crying out harshly, over and over, realizing only hazily that what she chanted was his name. Meeting those fervid thrusts, her hips slammed downward again and again until she could not stop grinding herself against him, could not let him go even to surge once more inside her body. Her whole world was the mercenary, her whole heart his own as much as her body was.

"Isabeau," Jared murmured, his powerful body arching up against hers over and over, his thick shaft bathed in her sweet benediction, tormented to the edge of explosion by her needy grasp. "Isabeau!" he cried triumphantly. "You are mine!"

Or had he said that he was hers? The mercenary wasn't sure. All he knew was that they were together, and their reunion was better than he had ever imagined it could be. Consciousness splintering, he clamped his hands hard upon her hips, holding their bodies fused until they both melted rapturously into one another, in a blinding, earth-shattering culmination that sent them both spinning out of all control.

* * *

"When you said Malik had ruined you, I thought . . . I mean, I assumed . . ." Jared began hesitantly when he could breathe again, many minutes later. He stopped, not sure how to continue without bringing up a subject that was sure to be both painful and disturbing for both of them. His palm skated cautiously along the curve of her perspiration-dewed hip and thigh, a gesture that was half encouragement, half reassurance.

Isabeau, nestling close to Jared's warm body, understood what he meant to say. She buried her face in the mercenary's neck, breathing in the comfortingly masculine scent of him and trying to avoid the necessary explanations yet a little while longer. Spent and in awe, she was still having difficulty believing they'd just done what they had done, but she found she was not sorry. Nothing that felt that good could be wrong! And it was all the sweeter to the renegade that she had been able to come to him untouched, if not innocent.

Jared had always been the one to whom she was meant to surrender, the one and only man who could claim the right to possess her body, and he certainly had not betrayed her trust with their lovemaking today. She supposed he deserved to know how it had come about that she'd still possessed her maidenhead despite her years exposed to Malik's not-so-tender mercies. Still, it was like opening another wound as dire as the saber thrust that had cut her side just to talk about it. And added to her difficulty was the fact that the renegade must share yet another long-secret confidence to do so.

"I know," she sighed at last, cheek nuzzled against his

pectoral muscle both for comfort and so that she would not
have to look at him. "And had it not been for the manipulations of a very clever man named Jamal ad-Din, it would
have been so. But know this," she said urgently, turning
her face up to Jared's. "I am glad it was you, betrothed,
who received the gift of my virginity; yet the fact that I
still possessed the gift to give is due to little more than a
stroke of good fortune, compounded by the lies of a master
schemer."

When Jared merely squeezed her tighter in his arms in
response and urged her softly to go on, Isabeau launched
into her tale. "The eunuch Jamal ad-Din was both my closest jailer and my greatest liberator during the years of my
enslavement. Master of al-Fayed's harem as well as chief
slave procurer for the emir, Jamal has always served an
entirely different master in truth—the master of Alamut."
Isabeau smiled wryly when she saw the look of comprehension grow in Jared's eyes, then turn to confusion as he
tried to work out what Jamal's position in the harem had
had to do with Isabeau's own strange twists of fortune.

"Oh, he bought me innocently enough, make no mistake.
Jamal knew his so-called owner had a predilection for the
fair-haired women of Europe, and his only purpose the day
he snatched me off the slave blocks was to placate the emir.
He needed to win the man's favor in order to ingratiate
himself yet more deeply into his counsels than he had already done, so that he might spy upon him and report back
what he saw to his true lord. Yet Jamal saw something in
me that day—I know not if it began when I kicked my new
purchaser the instant he came to claim me off the block, or
later, when I cursed him in every language with which I
was conversant." Isabeau laughed halfheartedly, remembering that day with mixed feelings still. Jamal had certainly saved her many times, yet she could not ignore the
knowledge that if he'd never interfered in her life at all,
she might have had a vastly less turbulent fate.

"Perhaps he admired my spirit, or believed me to have
other attributes he could exploit at some later date. What-

ever it was, Jamal ad-Din, enigma that he was, decided to make of me a sort of protégée. I've often thought," the Assassin confessed, "that Jamal harbors a secret storehouse of sentimentality in his heart, and that I reminded him of the sort of child he would have liked to have, had his true master not deprived him of that ability long before with the cruel rite of castration.

"Though I'm sure you know it is a common practice and makes for extremely valuable slaves who are capable of rising to a uniquely high position with their masters," Isabeau continued, "I do not believe that Jamal has ever completely forgiven the Old Man for inflicting that fate upon him in his youth. Why he serves the master still, and what his true game may be, I will probably never learn. There is a well of darkness in Jamal, friend and ally though I name him, that I would never want to touch." Isabeau shuddered, glad to feel Jared's strong presence at her side while she remembered these long-ago events. The memories remained as fresh as ever. Somehow, though, with the mercenary so warm and solid next to her, they had lost their power to wound. *Strange,* the Assassin thought. *I've never felt this safe, and yet this is the first time I have ever allowed myself to become so vulnerable!*

"In any case, when he brought me to the harem of the emir, Jamal became a sort of champion for me, preventing the worst of my torments and ultimately shielding me from the depths of what my new master would have done to degrade me, body and soul. I must confess, I was ungrateful at the beginning. As a child, spoiled and unused to the strict laws that govern Muslim households, I did not see how much he truly did for me in that horrible place. But he did not give up on his little protégée." Isabeau smiled in remembrance. "It was Jamal who brought Zahra to me, when I remained defiant even through all of his coaxing and coaching, all of his teachings meant to ease the way into my new life." The Assassin laughed then, but there was little humor in it.

"Jamal read me well that day. He always did! Zahra and

I became fast friends, and grew to love one another dearly
as sisters over the years, just as Jamal had guessed we
would. But even he did not anticipate what the master
would do to test our affection once we came of age." Isabeau's voice went flat then, her rage suppressed and her
anguish contained behind a wall of sheer will.

"The eunuch knew me well enough to understand I
would refuse to serve Malik's evil perversions even though
it meant my death to disobey. I had been taught all the
ways of a proper concubine, as had the rest of the emir's
slaves, of course, studying everything from erotic dance to
the sacred texts depicting the ways and means of pleasuring
one's husband in the conjugal bed. I was forced to absorb
all of these lessons, from massage to musicianship, but I
swore from the start I would refuse to use them at the command of my master. Long before Malik first noticed me
and demanded I wait upon his needs, Jamal had foreseen
that the day would eventually come when I caught the
fancy of the master—after all, he had bought me with the
emir's taste in mind. Knowing I would rather die than submit, the harem master dreamed up a tale that convinced the
emir I was no good for . . . that sort of activity.

"You see," Isabeau explained, her admiration for the eunuch evident, "Jamal had a reputation with the emir as a
sort of mystic, an astrologer if you will, to whom had been
given the gift of prophecy. And so, not long after this cunning keeper of the harem had taken me under his auspices,
he arranged an audience with his master to read his astro-
logical charts and take the auguries. Plying the emir with
the forbidden spirits and opiates he loved so well, Jamal"—
the renegade snickered with relish at this part of the tale—
"*prophesied* to Malik that it would mean his downfall if he
ever dared to copulate with a certain fair 'White Rose' of
the West—a rose with a single imperfection. Even to lay a
hand on this flawed female, Jamal warned, would be to
invite instant damnation."

Isabeau held her right hand up against the firelight so
Jared would understand what she meant, showing him the

unusual outline of her shortened pinky in comparison with her other shapely fingers. She almost forgot what she'd been saying, however, when the mercenary clasped her hand and brought it to his lips, kissing each slender finger reverently to show her without words that he saw no "imperfections" there. Her breathing became unsteady, tender emotion swelling her heart even as her loins rekindled at the invocation of his kiss.

This was why she could not help loving Jared, the renegade thought with a tingle of bittersweet sadness. He took all of her most painful moments, her harshest degradations, and replaced them with purity and innocence reforged in the crucible of his noble heart. By Allah, he tempted her to forget all her anger, her sworn vows, and simply revel in his healing touch . . . She must finish the story before all thought fled beneath these bewitching ministrations!

"Malik, as superstitious as he was stupid, believed every word of Jamal's so-called divination. He became as frightened of the prophecy's fulfillment as he had been eager to pluck his 'white roses' in the first place. Immediately, he had all his slaves and concubines inspected for the 'imperfection' that had been foretold. But the eunuch saw to it that my defect was not found then, so that I might not lose my place under his protection in the harem just yet.

"Years later, when I had come of age, Malik ordered Jamal to have me brought before him for inspection. I went, perfumed and primped and burning with hatred for him every step of the way, for I had seen what my master had done to others brought before me into his so-called chamber of love. Jamal presented me with a great flourish, claiming to have inspected me for his master's pleasure. But even as he took my hand to draw me forward—and this we had rehearsed together ahead of time, you understand—he pretended to notice for the first time the disfigurement of my finger. Throwing up a great fuss—Jamal has ever been a master of theater—he flung himself to his knees before the emir and begged forgiveness for having so imperiled his master's life!" Isabeau chuckled in earnest at that. "He reminded Malik of the 'prophecy' he himself had invented, and warned him against making me his intimate slave.

"Well, Malik was all for having me anyway at first, but eventually Jamal managed to convince him that I was tainted goods, not fit for a man of substance such as the emir even if I had not been a dangerous temptation to his fate besides. Even to touch me, or, Allah forbid, to punish me in any way, would earn the emir a thousand misfortunes, Jamal claimed. The harem keeper was so formidable, so convincing that night," the Assassin declared, "that even *I* began to believe him!" Then memory dimmed the brightness of her tone as she went on. "I was spared the lecherous pawings of my master that evening, but the reprieve was short, and the consequences worse in the end than if I had meekly submitted."

Isabeau passed a shaking hand over her eyes, hoping to swipe away the moisture there before Jared could see it. Voice shaky, she continued. "The more frustrated he grew over having to leave me alone, the greater his desire for me became, and by extension, for Zahra as well. You see, it didn't take Malik long after that to notice Zahra's own budding ripeness of figure, and to covet her for his own. Watching us covertly from his many hidden vantages above the harem's hammam, bedchambers, and gardens, the emir observed both our friendship and our resemblance, and he hungered to sully the love between us just as he had soiled everything else he ever touched. Jamal, probably not expecting to care for this second fledgling he had taken under his wing as he had grown to care for me, had prepared no ready lies to cover this circumstance and protect Zahra. Even if he had, I doubt even the clever eunuch could have stopped al-Fayed for long, for our master was utterly determined to have us however he could. Though he tried, Jamal could not put the emir off forever. One night, Malik ordered that we both be brought before him . . ." Isabeau began to choke on her words. "Brought to entertain him."

She finished the rest of the distasteful tale in a rush, wanting to be done with it quickly, though the memories of those endless helpless nights could never be banished so easily. "Not able to touch me as he wished, he had me dance for him instead while he . . . played with Zahra. Everything he would have done to me," she whispered with remembered horror, "he did to her instead . . . while I was forced to watch. And to . . . divert him with the dance. If I dared to refuse, he took out his thwarted fury upon her instead of me, fearful to tempt fate with his revenge. Oh, how many nights she suffered for some fault of mine!" Isabeau anguished. "We both knew that what Malik did to Zahra was made the worse by his frustration and desire to have me as well, and my dancing only heightened his lust.

"I swore I would kill myself, cut up my own feet or burn them with hot coals, or even simply infuriate him with my refusal to obey his commands until he was forced to punish me instead of her, but Zahra begged me not to do anything so rash. I listened at first, for I knew I would only make things worse for her if I disobeyed. But I could not stand to watch him torment my heart's dearest the way he did, could not bear to stand by helpless for long. And so I begged Jamal to teach me what he knew of the Assassins' ways.

"At first he refused, of course. It was unheard of to teach such things to a woman, and even to admit he himself served the master of Alamut was a dangerous act of recklessness I could tell he much regretted. But Jamal, of all men, knew the foolishness of underestimating a woman's resolve when cornered. He had inhabited the world of the harem much too long to believe the fiction of us as soft, helpless creatures longing only for pretty jewels and other finery with which to bedeck our bodies. He knew eventually I would find a way to achieve my end, and he did not wish me or Zahra to be hurt in the act.

"Finally he consented to teach me the fundamentals of fighting—claiming it was purely to defend myself from any assailant sent to harm me by one of the other women who were beginning to resent my 'popularity' with our shared master. I was already adept at the dance, my body honed and used to acrobatic exercise. The martial drills he showed me were not so very different, though he tried to keep it to a mere diversion at first." Isabeau studied her fisted hand for a long moment before she let the fingers relax. "I believe Jamal thought my aggression would run its course if he simply created the illusion of giving me some effective means with which to challenge my fate. He must have hoped I would become resigned to my place in the harem, but instead of placating me, the exercises only enflamed my hunger to learn more. Soon I demanded to learn everything he knew, and mastered it all with a swiftness born of pure hatred.

"I would kill Malik when I learned enough, I vowed to Jamal, but he managed to convince me otherwise in the end. The eunuch told me I was not ready, that I must first seek out the Master of Alamut for further training if I did not wish to perish alongside my slain master. Surely, he admitted, I could kill him—any fool with a knife had a decent chance of that if he had the element of surprise on his side!—but Jamal reminded me I would not be likely to survive the encounter when the emir's guards fell upon me in revenge. In that case, Zahra would simply be sold to another, possibly equally cruel master. I would have accomplished absolutely nothing to aid my heart's sister except to deprive her of my company.

"Still, I could not long bear to play Malik's games, and Jamal knew it. Zahra was growing despondent, her slender frame and sweet nature never meant for the abuse the emir heaped upon it. As she grew more withdrawn and miserable with the passing days, the daggers of sorrow and guilt drove themselves ever deeper into my heart, and into Jamal's as well, I believe. We agreed that something must be done, and so the eunuch contacted his true master for assistance, telling the Old Man only that he wished to send him a talented and devoted protégée for training in the Assassins' arts. Jamal then arranged my 'death' in order to smuggle me outside the harem walls, and I was taken to Alamut, where I swore myself into the service of the Assassins' cult.

There, I vowed to learn all I could, hoping someday to be able to strike back on behalf of all women against the monster who had oppressed myself and my heart's sister. And meanwhile, Jamal and I hoped that once I was removed as a pawn from Malik's cruel games, he would lose the pleasure of tormenting Zahra simply to get at me as well. We thought he would ease up on her, perhaps choose another favorite to concentrate on once I was gone. Alas, that has not proven so," the renegade confessed. "Jamal tells me he holds her closer to him than ever since my loss."

Isabeau knew she was glossing over some very important details, but she thought it best not to explain the rest to Jared—how she had followed Jamal's teachings and slowed her breathing and heart rate down until it seemed she had expired; how the vicious Ullayah had believed her to have been the victim of her own paltry machinations; and how one of Jamal's most loyal slaves had journeyed with her subsequently to the far-off and frightening bastion of the Assassins' infamous stronghold in the mountains.

Nor did she choose to share how the Old Man had seen through her disguise immediately upon her arrival when he had interviewed her in his private chambers—the single most perilous few moments of Isabeau's life!—or why it had nonetheless pleased him to permit her to train alongside his elite army in the end, with himself the only man the wiser about her sex. That, she still could not fathom herself, and she had long since found it an uncomfortable exercise in futility to ponder that man's inscrutable intentions. Any speculations and explanations with Jared regarding that period of her life could come later—or never!—Isabeau decided, for her time at Alamut and directly afterward had been hard indeed, and she would prefer never to burden her betrothed with the details of it. Though he seemed to accept her now—even to desire her despite her past—Jared de Navarre did not need to know all the rigors with which expediency had tested her over the years.

"That is how we came to meet as Assassin and mercenary," she said in conclusion. As if it were all as simple as that. "How kismet has brought you and I back together in the fullness of time, and given you that to which you were always entitled, Black Lion; if not the true innocence you deserved. I am sorry it could not have been more."

Jared did not speak for so long that Isabeau feared he had fallen asleep and missed all of her long and painful explanations. But the mercenary was wide awake.

"I do not know if I was 'entitled' to anything, Isabeau," he said, turning her over carefully so that the renegade faced him squarely, their nude bodies flush against one another and their solemn eyes inches apart. "But I know that I am honored by this precious gift you have given me." The Assassin averted her gaze, clearly embarrassed, but the mercenary refused to let her look away. The renegade's revelations had given him a much clearer picture of the degradations to which she had been subjected, and of the true bravery it had taken to overcome them. That Isabeau thought the gift of herself might not be enough to satisfy him was absurd! He took her chin between two fingers and tenderly kissed her, hoping to infuse the caress with the full measure of his feelings.

Jared's admiration was boundless, but his gratitude, if possible, even outstripped it. Knowing nothing of love and far too much of lechery, Isabeau had yet trusted him to touch her, to love her, and to be intimate with her when all she had ever known of intimacy was revulsion. Her courage was simply enormous, the mercenary thought as his lips shaped hers with delicate ardor. She met the kiss fearlessly as always, and he knew that valiant heart of hers had saved his betrothed from true ruination far more so than even the clever eunuch who had championed her cause. Her heart had kept her pure and true when such a life would have taken all a lesser woman had to give, and left her but a shell of humanity. Hell, the mercenary thought, even now Isabeau's only thought was for others—for Zahra, whom she had tried so hard to save, and for himself, whom she believed she had cheated in some fashion. He could not have felt less cheated had she offered him a sultan's treasure!

Breaking the kiss reluctantly at last, Jared's hand stroked gently down her rose-flushed cheek as he stared into Isabeau's shimmering sapphire eyes. He repeated his last words in the hope that she would take in the truth of them and understand his deep respect. "I am *honored,* my sweet, and deeply moved. I would prove myself worthy of your gift, if only you will let me," he breathed.

"*Let* you?" she sighed softly, incredibly relieved by his ardent response. Hiding her grateful tears, she joked, "Jared, if you do not, I shall *make* you!"

The Black Lion was pretending to sleep—or perhaps he really had dozed off; Isabeau wasn't sure. He lay on his stomach with his face turned away from her, breathing soft and sure into the furs. She stared at the sun-bronzed expanse of his shoulders, almost a match with the rich color of the desert sand, due no doubt to his Basque ancestors in Navarre. Her hands felt the deep compulsion to touch that skin again. So did her body. But she did not want to wake him if he truly did sleep—he had more than exerted himself enough for one day, she thought, feeling a new sort of womanly smile cross her lips in remembrance. Though he'd sated her thoroughly not long before, Isabeau now needed to absorb her lover in a way she couldn't have explained if she'd tried. She wanted to *know* him as he'd known her, to understand the workings of his pleasure as he so instinctively had understood hers.

She shifted restlessly next to him on the soft bedding so redolent with the scent of their love, reaching out to stroke his sleek, muscular shoulders and back. But that wasn't enough to satisfy her for long. Soon Isabeau had worked up the nerve to shift her body atop his, her oversensitized breasts brushing against the hot smooth skin of his shoulders, her taut belly pressing into the small of his back, her downy mons against the tight, high curve of his buttocks. Slowly, with an Assassin's infinite patience, she let him take her weight a little at a time, not wanting to wake Jared yet if he still slept. But soon enough the urge to press her aching pelvis against the convenient rise of those lovely, hard buttocks proved too much and she ground softly against him, sighing with pleasure against his ear.

And soon after that, she found she had succumbed to her every fantasy of touching the beautiful mercenary. Stroking every inch of his flesh. Learning each angle and curve, each play of muscle on bone. Her mind became an organ of pure sensory reception, her hands the relay of each new experience in masculinity, her body the sponge that soaked up the Black Lion's extraordinary splendor.

Isabeau had forgotten to wonder if he was awake, so enraptured was she with her newfound exploration. In her mind, she tried halfheartedly to recall the lessons of her harem days, but this exploration was not so much about skill as it was about discovering every secret her betrothed had kept to himself, familiarizing herself with the planes and surfaces of his musculature as if she could somehow use them to erase the time they'd been apart. Still, there were *some* things she would have never thought to try if it had not been for those early lessons in the pleasuring of a man . . .

Lessons, she now discovered as she slipped a hand around beneath his belly to discover his rigid tumescence hard and waiting for her, that could please a woman as well as a man!

Jared, though an avid disciple of Eastern pleasures, had never had a sensation quite equal to the one he got when he felt his very adventurous new lover begin her hesitant explorations. As she ran her questing hands about his back and shoulders, his buttocks and thighs, the feeling was about equally divided between mellow relaxation and the new stirrings of passion for the mercenary, and as she slowly learned him, he drifted drowsily in the pleasure, almost lulled into a state of trance from her tender ministrations. But when her caresses grew bolder, his impatient excitement grew apace, and soon he had to grit his teeth and breathe shallowly to keep himself from spoiling her innocent explorations by tossing her over and ramming impatiently deep inside that hot, wet furnace between her legs.

When her questing fingers, so cool and light in their touch, slid hesitantly around his side and began to tease his cock, however, the mercenary lost control. "God, Isabeau!" he groaned, trapping her hand before he could explode. "If you want me again, all you have to do is ask!" Flipping over and carrying her with him, he caught her surprised expression with his laughing mouth in a kiss that started off being teasing, but soon turned to gasping ecstasy as he sank himself deep inside her body.

"Ah, Jared," she cried breathlessly, suffused in the sweetness of this moment. "I will want you *always* like this!" Isabeau wrapped her long, strong legs about his waist and urged him deeper still. "Always . . ."

"Then you shall have me always, little Beau," he promised, his face buried in the fragrant hollow of her throat. "Always, and never have to ask."

Jared awoke to the sight of the same nude siren who had graced his hashish-laced dreams the night before the battle outside Baghdad. This time, however, his glorious goddess stood in full sunlight just outside the cave he shared with the renegade, naked and poised in that fierce martial posture that had turned so sultry in the moonlight only days earlier. Her back was to him, gold and silver hair cascading down the length of her body to reveal teasing glimpses of her high, firm buttocks and the long, long legs that could kick out or curl around a man's waist with equal zeal—depending on her intent.

Isabeau, he gathered, was practicing.

The mercenary watched her with similar measures of lust and admiration, his arms folded behind his head and his erection pulsing pleasurably as he observed the fluid postures and lightning-fast reflexes of the woman he loved. She spun and kicked out hard, lashing the air above her head with one deadly accurate foot. Without a pause she turned that kick into a flip, then came up to punch and chop the air with chilling precision. A series of furious jabs later, Isabeau paused and drew that power inward with rigid control, containing what Jared sensed was a storm's worth of energy within her body and letting it settle upon her like a mantle of invulnerability, growing so intensely still he thought she might shatter. She seemed to be gathering energy rather than expending it with this practice, the mercenary noted, focusing herself into the purest form of warrior. Isabeau was regaining her strength quickly, he thought, continuing to watch her practice with pleasure. Even after a night as exhausting as the one they'd just shared, she still had the stamina to exercise her formidable skill in combat first thing in the morning!

He knew it ought to bother him, seeing his woman engaged in such a masculine activity. He knew it ought to turn him off, leave him cold. But just the opposite was true. Most men might long for a woman who was no more than a willing vessel for their seed, a soft, biddable wife to ease their needs and see to their comforts. Until Isabeau had reentered his life, Jared might have said the same, if he'd ever allowed himself to think of taking a wife other than the sworn betrothed he had believed lost to him. But now that he *did* have her back, wanting any other sort of woman was simply unthinkable . . . The Black Lion didn't desire some squeamish female who'd faint at the sight of his wounds instead of helping to bind them up after battle. He didn't want a girl who couldn't tell a mace from a flail, some swooning damsel who'd shriek in fear at the very notion of warfare. Such a woman could never understand the mercenary, never be a helpmeet or true mate to his scarred and battered soul.

Isabeau could. After all, had not their entire lives paralleled one another? Jared asked himself, feeling a deep satisfaction. Indeed, the Shadow Hunter was uniquely qualified to be his bride. His betrothed might be as powerful as a man, skilled enough in the arts of war to defeat even him when it came to her preferred form of hand-to-hand combat, but she was *also* all the woman he would ever want. Assassin she might be, and renegade too. Warrior she certainly was. If he could only convince her to be both lover and wife . . . He'd spend the rest of his life convincing her of that if he had to, the Black Lion decided. But for now, Jared thought as he watched her expend her explosive energy against the phantom enemy she battled, he had only one suggestion for his beautiful renegade. There were other ways to use that energy . . .

* * *

Isabeau was deeply absorbed in her Assassins' Ritual when the attack came.

Waking to find herself in her beloved's arms this morning, she had found herself the victim of an unfamiliar emotion. It took her some time to figure out its peculiar nature as she listened to the mercenary's contented breathing at her back and felt the rough solidity of his hard-muscled arm securely wrapped about her waist. But at last she had it.

What she felt was happiness.

No sooner had the renegade identified it than the emotion evaporated, however, to be replaced with a surge of guilt so powerful she felt literally breathless. *Zahra,* she thought remorsefully, *how could I enjoy myself so thoughtlessly while you still suffer for my sake?* The Assassin was horrified at her venality, even though she could not quite bring herself to regret the time she had enjoyed with Jared. *But it must be over now,* she told herself, leaving no room for argument in her mind. *You've had your pleasure, but now you owe it to Zahra and Jamal both to remember your mission.*

Though she knew it would be practically impossible now, with Zahra closely guarded behind the walls of Malik's new palace in Damascus, and his guards on the alert for anyone mad enough to attempt another rescue, she must still continue to try. She must somehow find a way to rescue her heart's sister from her sexual bondage, Isabeau determined guiltily—especially now that she knew how it was

supposed to be between a man and a woman. Now that
Jared had taught her.

Wracked with remorse, Isabeau had slipped away from
her lover to renew her commitment to her precious jewel's
release, knowing she should forsake all such pleasures now
and forevermore if she wished to attain her goal. Though
her love for Jared de Navarre was bright and sparkling with
newly deepening affection, though she wanted nothing
more than to be with him for the rest of her days, she had
an older promise to uphold. Jared would be better off in
the end if he could be convinced to forget her, Isabeau told
herself. He could find himself a proper woman, now that
he was released from his vow to locate his childhood love
after so many years. He could marry and raise a family as
he had been meant to do, the Assassin decided glumly—
just not with her. For all their sakes, she must tear herself
away from this selfish love and re-devote herself to Zahra,
no matter what the personal cost.

This time, when Isabeau moved through the patterns of
her combat rituals, her form was utterly perfect. No one
watching would ever guess her heart was breaking with
each step.

And eventually, her focus had become so total, so intense, that when she felt the arm snake about her naked
waist, she reacted with pure instinct. Before she could stop
herself, she flipped the man who'd been fool enough to grab
her as she sparred. Then she gasped with horror.

Isabeau cried out even as the mercenary flew past her
shoulder with a startled yell of his own, and she fell to her
knees beside him instantly, all apologies and concern as
she checked him for injury. But Jared, though winded, was
not angry. Indeed, he was laughing.

"I suppose that's no more than I deserve, sneaking up
on you that way," he said around a grin, clasping her hand
and kissing her palm as she reached out to touch him and
assure herself he was well. "Next time, I'll announce myself
ahead of time."

"It's no joke, Jared," she cried remorsefully. "I could

have killed you!" *I could have hurt yet another of those I love,* she thought to herself with sorrow piercing even the sweet effect of his smile upon her fragile mood.

"I'm not," he grunted as he tugged the surprised Assassin down upon his chest and rolled atop her to pin her to the grassy earth, "as defenseless as I look."

Neither of them wished to tussle quite at the moment, however. Jared had sensed Isabeau's somber frame of mind as well as her determination to exercise her way back to full strength, and he was not insensitive to her mood. "You're thinking about Zahra," he said. It wasn't a question.

Damn him for being so intuitive, Isabeau thought glumly, wishing for once that Jared was less in tune with her emotions. She didn't reply, not wishing to discuss her decision with the mercenary quite yet, for she knew he would balk when she told him they must soon part ways. "I wasn't thinking at all, mercenary," she demurred. "Assassins are taught to react, not to think."

Jared, blessedly, seemed content to move with the direction of the conversation for the moment, even as he leapt lithely to his feet and helped her do the same. Isabeau left her hand in his even after she rose, however, only letting it go as she moved past him inside the cave to don her renegade's robes and tame her hair once more into a long braid down her back. Even as he moved to stir up their fire and heat up last night's rations in the pot braced above it, she barely left his side, helping him at each step and fitting seamlessly against his side.

Jared didn't fail to notice how well they worked together, even as he joked with his lover. "And that is what you were doing just now, was it?" he teased. "Being an Assassin—in the nude? I see. Just as you were the night you so nearly seduced me upon the riverbank. And here I thought you were merely teasing me with a show of your prowess in order to have your wicked way with me," he grinned, ducking as Isabeau threw a wild onion at his head in mock pique. "I imagine you could stun any man into a stupor with the sight of all that voluptuous beauty revealed. Hell, even a single smile from those rosebud lips could strike an unwary man dead upon the spot!"

Isabeau couldn't help herself. She blushed. "It was not meant for show, and you know it—though you have shamelessly spied upon my private rites twice now!" she accused without heat. "The Old Man of the Mountain had many such strange rituals, but none were meant for exhibition."

"Tell me of them, Isabeau," Jared entreated. "Tell me of your time at Alamut, and of what made you break with the movement . . ."

"I . . . would rather not, Jared," the renegade said with uncustomary diffidence. She did not wish to alienate the mercenary, yet to speak of the lonely time she had spent, and the things she had done out of necessity to achieve her goals, would surely sicken even this hardened warrior. And though she wasn't sure how she'd earned it, she found she cared deeply to keep his good opinion. "It's not something I think about often, or easily."

"Yet it consumes your sleep at night, Isabeau," Jared argued gently. "I know you dream of that time often, for last night was not the first time I have heard you cry out in your slumber about 'the dead' . . ." He let his words trail off, seeing his betrothed's intense reaction. He guessed rightly that she'd hoped to keep that nightmare, whether real or imagined, from his knowledge.

Isabeau went white. "I had no idea I spoke aloud," she admitted softly. "I no longer experience the dreams often," she assured him, "and would not have burdened you with them. I am sorry if I disturbed you."

"It is no burden, Isabeau, to know the truth." Jared could hardly believe she was apologizing. Beneath her tough warrior's façade, he was learning, beat the heart of a very vulnerable woman. "I will always wish to hear the truth from you, no matter how bad you think it is. I can bear it, if you can," he promised.

"You may disagree when you hear, my brave lion," Isabeau warned, "but you have come this far without shying away, and so I will trust you to go the final step. Once you know this, you will know all." She took a deep breath.

"I dream about the dead at night because it was through death that I gained my reputation as the Shadow Hunter." Seeing the slight flinch cross Jared's otherwise expressionless face, she clarified. "I did not say through *killing*. I said through *death*. For it was a field reaped bare of life I came upon, during my first and final mission for the master of Alamut." Isabeau was drawn unwillingly back into her nightmares, into memories she could not erase with a thousand years of sleep.

Fresh from her training, Isabeau had been young and apprehensive, yet eager to test her worth when the Old Man had ordered her to collect a tribute owing from his neighbors in the Elburz Mountains. These were a tribe of fiercely independent bandits only nominally under the dominion of Alamut, and it seemed their proper tithe had fallen behind. Knowing his young protégée was ready to prove her mettle, eager to be away from the other deadly disciples who were so wary around the constantly vcilcd and silent apprentice he himself had dubbed the "Shadow Hunter," the Old Man had offered her the challenge of collecting the disputed tribute—by whatever means necessary. And Isabeau, not yet sure if she meant to obey her deadly new master or steal away with his training to seek her own revenge, had accepted the mission. Yet when she'd arrived at the nameless mountain fortress, all her schemes had fled in the face of what confronted her.

Everyone was dead.

"I came to hold that fortress where we met at about the same time I gained my renegade's reputation," Isabeau explained tersely. "The tenants of that isolated place had displeased the Old Man, and he wished me to remind them of their loyalty to him. I obeyed my master and set out alone, though I was not sure what I would do when I arrived. I was one against many, though trained to inspire fear in my enemies." Isabeau took a deep breath.

"For days I sat watch outside those walls to get the lay

of the land, hidden in the rocks of the ridges below with none but the desert creatures for companionship. And for days I saw nothing to indicate whether there were people inside that fastness or not, until I noticed the many scavenger birds circling the minarets above. It was then that I began to suspect something had gone wrong in that place."

The Black Lion recalled his own eerie feeling waiting on the Assassin with his Pride below the walls of that nameless stronghold in the desolate mountain range. He remembered thinking the inhabitants could all have died inside with no one the wiser . . . "And you left to gather reinforcements?" he hazarded. It was what the mercenary himself might have done, had he been as young and inexperienced as she.

"On the contrary," Isabeau corrected tonelessly. "I scaled the walls and went inside. I was afraid to face my master with such craven evidence of failure, you understand—I knew I must at least scout the interior before I left, for to return without explanation would have been grounds for execution. The Old Man tolerated no cowards among his disciples." But oh, the horror of that moment! The utter terror the Assassin had felt as she let herself down inside the fortifications with her rope and allowed her body to drop soundlessly to the ground. Then the wall of stench had hit her.

Every living creature in that place had been decimated.

"It seems a plague had come upon the bandits hiding inside the compound," the Assassin related dispassionately. "In the courtyards, along the walls, in each hallway and in every garden, cluttering the guardhouse, the bathhouse—*everywhere*—there were corpses. Even the animals had succumbed, either to that same pestilence or to starvation subsequently—it was . . . hard to tell, after so long. The bodies were . . . as you might imagine." Isabeau didn't bother to go on. She knew the mercenary, veteran of many battles and shocking sights of carnage, could picture the scene she described. "But I considered myself fortunate, since at least the danger of contagion had probably passed after so much time."

How did she have the fortitude to try to mitigate these traumatic events for his sake? Under such pressure himself, Jared didn't think he'd do as well. "How old were you then, Isabeau?" Jared asked then, taking her hand in his and absently tracing the lines of its delicate bones with his fingers.

Why should he ask that? the renegade wondered, but saw no harm in answering. "I could claim nineteen summers that year, I believe, and had two years at Alamut to my credit by then."

"Ah, sweet Beau," Jared whispered hoarsely, squeezing her palm and raising the back of her hand to his lips to kiss. "If I could have spared you that . . ."

"Well," she said, trying uncomfortably to shrug off the mercenary's sympathy. "I suppose it was better than if they'd all been alive and after my hide," she joked. But she could not maintain her light tone.

"What did you do then, Isabeau?" he asked.

"Well, I knew I had a choice to make," she said pragmatically. "I could return to my master and report back what I had seen, then wait to be assigned another mission. It would have been the safe thing to do, but it would have brought me no closer to my goal of rescuing Zahra and revenging myself upon her captor. No." Isabeau shook her head. "Though the Old Man seemed to have plans to effect the emir's downfall, or at least keep his power in check— thence the sending of his prized agent Jamal into Malik's household—I could not be sure of the date or the outcome of those plans, and could not hope to be made privy to my new master's counsels. The Old Man works in his own time, uses his own methods, and keeps his secrets well," Isabeau informed her lover darkly. "I knew I might never get the chance to strike at the emir myself if I returned as I had been ordered. So I decided to stay."

"But how . . ." Jared protested. "Were you not afraid to remain in that pestilent hall of death?"

"Of course. I feared the wrathful ghosts lingering in that place, especially as darkness fell, but more than that I feared my master's retribution when he realized I wasn't coming back." Isabeau tried to shut out the visions in her mind of corpses, bloated and stinking, flies buzzing everywhere, and the wind howling through the corridors and courtyards like the screams of tortured children . . . "I knew I must make the place secure, and so I took action." Isabeau could not continue, fearful of the mercenary's revulsion when he learned what she had done next.

"Go on, Isabeau," the Black Lion urged. His heart felt nigh to bursting thinking of his precious Isabeau left so alone and scared in such a terrible scene of devastation— no one to comfort her, no one to help her, no friend in all the world. No Jared of Navarre to ease the way as he had been born to do.

"I . . . made an example of them," the renegade began haltingly. Even now she felt the urge to retch as she recalled her gruesome but highly effective actions that day. "I set up wooden pikes along the walls and atop the gates, locking myself inside with what supplies were left. And then I gathered up the bodies, one after another, and I . . . impaled them upon the spikes." Despite herself, tears surged to her eyes, bile to her throat, and Isabeau could not continue.

But she did not have to. The brilliance of her simple plan was perfectly clear to the mercenary. And so was the cause of her nightmares. Isabeau must have worked for days at her unspeakable labors, hauling bodies, installing her grisly trophies upon their perches. No one would know they had died of natural causes after this much time, especially not after the way the bodies had so obviously been positioned as a warning to hopeful opportunists. Such a sight would, indeed, have been enough to fend off any interlopers thinking to usurp the fortress, and news of the haunted stronghold would have spread throughout the surrounding areas as a place of certain death and destruction. But what had the Old Man made of it? Before Jared knew it, he'd already asked the question.

The renegade was grateful to steer away from those haunting memories and onto safer ground. "For reasons of his own—still unknown to me unto this day—" Isabeau admitted, glad to be done with her tale, "the Old Man chose to spin the story to his own advantage, claiming that his minion had single-handedly slain the traitors who thought to deny him his just tribute, and laid their bodies out as a warning to anyone who thought to do the same in future." Isabeau smiled sardonically. "I hear his coffers were full, indeed, that year." She wasn't surprised when Jared didn't laugh. He was probably gagging in horror at the knowledge of what she had done. Yet, grim as it had been, the renegade herself did not regret her actions, only their necessity. She would do worse for Zahra's sake, if she must.

"The Assassins' master sent no word of criticism after my daring defection, nor messenger of vengeance to recall me, though I roosted fearfully in that mausoleum for months, watching for any sign one of my brethren had come to take my life. There was only one message from my master in all that time, however. A black veil was left at my doorstep several weeks after I had gone to ground there. It was the Old Man's way of reminding me he knew my secret," Isabeau admitted, grimacing. "His way of telling me he could unmask me any time he liked. But why he chose not to, I do not know, except that it must have coincided with his own plans." The renegade shrugged fatalistically.

"Sometime after, Alamut began to send me reinforcements as I sought to garrison my position. They arrived in ones and twos—mostly men unsuitable for the master's training but eager to follow his precepts—and eventually, others came to my banner individually as well, drawn by the success of the raids we engineered to secure ourselves food and supplies. Eventually, the Shadow Hunter's band of outlaws became a force with which to be reckoned, but I was feared before I ever took my first step into outlawry. I had earned my deadly reputation without harming a single soul," Isabeau finished ironically.

Except her own, the mercenary thought. That, she had wounded to the core. Sweet merciful Jesus, how *lonely* she must have been. He wanted to weep at these poignant and terrible revelations. Jared was silent for a long time while he processed this last and greatest of his betrothed's confessions, the final piece of the puzzle that was the Shadow Hunter, and the source of her legendary status in these parts. It was a lot to take in, added to all he already knew of her, and more than he'd ever thought to have to absorb about the duke and duchess of Lyon's lost daughter.

He imagined his Isabeau as he'd last seen her in their youth—a child, surely, and an innocent, but even then endowed with more spirit and determination than ten full-grown warriors. She'd always been a fighter. The endurance that must have served her well during the months and years of her captivity had helped the renegade even more so when she'd escaped slavery to strike off on her own, even daring to draw the wrath of the single deadliest man in all the Middle East. And not only had Isabeau survived all this, he marveled. She'd *won*. She had transcended her fate, refusing to ever submit despite the horrors she had seen and the abhorrent acts she'd had no choice but to commit. With no one to lean on, no friend in the strange Arab world she'd landed in, she'd gone from helpless slave girl to avenging fury.

And she'd done it without his help.

Jared hadn't been there to protect her all these years, as he'd sworn to do. He'd done *nothing* for her all this time, he knew, and the guilt rode the Black Lion hard. He'd searched, he'd suffered, yes; but still he'd been no use to the girl he yet remembered as eight years old, delightfully defying him on the road to Lyon. Jared had not been there for any of it, though if he had, he might have been able to spare her these nightmarish memories and the sad awareness of men's evil that never left her lucid blue eyes.

But now, at last, he had the chance to do something for Isabeau. To help her achieve the final victory; to save her heart's sister—and, he hoped, simultaneously to free the renegade from the bonds of self-excoriation with which she so obviously struggled. For too long he had failed her, but now the chance to make things right had come, and the mercenary knew right then and there that nothing was going to stop him.

Jared solemnly withdrew his massive broadsword from its sheath. Isabeau's eyes narrowed for a moment in a frown of incomprehension, then widened as she understood. The mercenary knelt before her where they stood just outside the cave and thrust the tip of the sword into the grass at her feet. They were alone in the canyon together, the silence palpable in the little space surrounded by the rocky walls. The mighty steel blade quivered in the stony earth until the Black Lion's large hands clasped themselves around its worn jeweled hilt, stilling it.

"My lady," he began, then had to stop and clear his throat. "My lady, I hereby pledge my sword, my life, and my fealty to you as I once did to your father. I understand your quest, and wish more than anything to make it my own. I do not know this Zahra you cherish so dearly, but I do know you—" *I do love you,* Jared wanted to say— "whether you call yourself Shadow Hunter, White Rose, or long-lost scion of Lyon. And if you say this woman deserves your aid, then she deserves mine as well. I could not help you in your hour of need, Isabeau," he acknowledged somberly, "but perhaps now, together, we two can help *her.* To that end, I vow my service and my heart unto your cause. I will go where you lead, Isabeau de Lyon; till death and beyond."

When his beloved seemed too stunned to speak, Jared went on determinedly. "Only promise me one thing," the Black Lion begged in conclusion. "Promise me, when this is over, that you will consider coming home with me— coming home as my bride. Swear you will think on it, at least."

Isabeau stared down into the extraordinary amber eyes of the man who was her lover, her once-betrothed, and so much more. Her heart ached and she longed to throw her arms around him and surrender to his warm embrace. How could he offer himself to her so generously, over and over, and always ask so little in return? She longed to accept all that lay unspoken in the depths of his gaze, all the promises resting there, but in the end she took only one thing.

Clasping her hands reverently around the jeweled hilt of the longsword atop Jared's, the Assassin said solemnly, "You do me honor, Black Lion, both by offering to ride by my side and by asking me to be your bride. I accept your service, Jared de Navarre, with all gratitude; and yes, I will swear further to consider your flattering request with all the seriousness it deserves." She paused then to swallow down the aching lump in her throat, one hand rising to rest trembling upon his uplifted cheek.

"We ride for Damascus at dawn."

CHAPTER NINETEEN

As it turned out, they headed first for the Assassin's secluded fortress in the mountains, and not for Damascus after all. Upon reflection, the Black Lion and the Shadow Hunter had agreed it would be best to regroup with their followers, find out where they stood, and then formulate a more concrete strategy for accomplishing their dangerous mission before setting out upon it.

Despite her impatience to attempt another rescue for Zahra, Isabeau had herself reluctantly suggested to Jared that this would make the most sense, especially since she knew it was vital to see what news Jamal's carrier pigeons might have brought before proceeding with any new plan they might devise. Yet she feared returning to the outside world as never before.

The renegade sighed heavily and shrugged her tight shoulders, trying to ease the tension gathering there as she and Jared carefully wound their way on horseback through the chilling autumn weather that had settled upon the Elburz foothills.

For herself, Isabeau wasn't worried. But for Jared, she was terrified! Too many people had already suffered for her impulsive acts—this man especially. Looking at him obliquely over her shoulder as they rode, her heart suffered a painful spasm. The Black Lion sat tall and straight upon his ebony stallion, his face set in harsh planes but his eyes warm as they gazed back at her. That face had become as dear to her in the past weeks as it ever had been in childhood; and far more so now, for the love she bore Jared was no child's affection, but that of a full-grown woman. She could not bear to lead him into further danger.

Yet he had sworn to aid her in rescuing Zahra, and craven though her need was, the renegade knew she would not refuse that help.

If she'd had her fondest wish granted, she would have
stayed with Jared de Navarre in their little canyon haven,
safe and unobserved and thus free to be their true selves
for the rest of their lives. She would have given up all the
power she'd wielded, all she'd scraped out of the bare earth
with her scarred hands over the years for the chance to stay
holed up with him in that modest little corner of heaven
they'd created. But it was impossible to enjoy paradise
when she knew another suffered perdition for her sake.

They'd both known her wound was healed sufficiently
for Isabeau to travel. Though sore and stiff, the scabs of
the cut on her side had already been replaced by an angry
red line of new scar tissue, and would eventually fade to a
thin white tracing following the natural curve of her waist
and hip. The more she exercised, the veteran warrior knew,
the more limber she remained, the faster it would heal completely. Beyond her own selfish wants, Isabeau could offer
no valid excuse for them to stay, and so this morning she
and Jared had reluctantly gathered their few belongings and
saddled their mounts in preparation for their return.

They'd worked side by side, saying little but growing
grimmer each moment until the Assassin had at last drawn
the hated veil up over her nose and fastened its trailing end
securely once again in her keffiyeh. She'd felt as though
she were shutting the door of her heart as she did so, and
had fancied she could almost hear the clang as it was locked
away once more behind a wall of expedience and deceit.

The mercenary's expression had been as veiled from her
view as her own from him in that moment though he wore
no disguise, only a stony mask of acceptance upon his face.
Still, she knew Jared had been every bit as sorry to go as
she was—their lovemaking last night, still so tender and
new, had contained an element of desperation and daring
that was all the more poignant because both knew it might
be the last time they would ever be so free to be together,
to explore each other's delights and the deep, solemn mysteries of their love. He, too, had known they could not hide
forever—they both had men depending on them, waiting

on them. If they did not return soon, she knew the *fidai'in* for certain would come looking for her no matter what assurances Jared had given them of her safety. And the Black Lion's Pride would surely do no less in defense of their own beloved commander, she was sure.

If, she thought grimly, remembering their unfriendly rivalry, *they haven't all killed each other by now.* Glancing worriedly at Jared's stark profile once more and catching the tight, sympathetic half-smile he flashed in return, the Assassin spurred her mare to a faster pace. Beside her, the dark stallion matched Zephyr's quickened stride as they headed higher into the mountains.

In the end, however, much of Isabeau's worry was for naught. As they rode inside her tall gates at last, four days after they'd set out from the secluded canyon where she'd recovered, the renegade was relieved to see that the mercenaries had not run into any trouble with her own *fidai'in,* as she'd half feared. In fact, both mercenaries and bandits lined the walls of the stone fortress side by side to welcome their two commanders with cheers, much banging of swords upon their dented shields, and unrestrained cries of joy.

In the interim while their leaders were absent, the two bands of warriors had apparently come to some sort of grudging understanding. It had turned their uneasy truce after the lost battle into a spirit of cooperation which was, if not friendly, at least moderately cordial. The *fidai'in,* after all, were Muslims, many of them descended of the proud Arabian tribes of the desert. That meant they took the job of hospitality with deadly seriousness. Once convinced to let their uneasy allies cross the gates, they'd opened the doors of their fortress home to the mercenaries with surprising graciousness, treating their wounded with as much care as their own brothers and making the mainly Frankish warriors of the Black Lion's Pride welcome to every scrap of food or gear for which they could think to ask.

The Shadow Hunter felt she had returned to an entirely

different world when she at last wearily passed within her own walls, the Black Lion a bare half-pace behind her. And it was a world where she no longer necessarily even belonged. Though it had been her own awful efforts that had secured the mountain retreat for them all those years before, it no longer seemed like home, if ever it had. The Assassin was a different person from the coldly determined renegade who'd originally claimed this place. No, Isabeau corrected herself. She was a different *woman*.

Everything had changed now that Jared knew the truth.

Now that they had made love—and *found* love together—with such devastating sweetness, continuing to seek it every night of their journey when the all-enveloping veil of darkness allowed them to wrap themselves together in feverish need after each day of careful, painful estrangement, everything was different in a way Isabeau did not want changed. She couldn't pretend anymore to be the emotionless, faceless Sayyad al-Zul whose reputation for ruthlessness was only overshadowed by the recklessness with which the Assassin was known to regard his own life. It would be hard, indeed, masquerading as a male in front of her men now that she felt womanly as never before. The bindings that masked her feminine physique could not alter the revolution that had gone on in Isabeau's mind. With the blossoming of her affection for Jared, the lessons in passionate forgiveness he had taught her with such masterful expertise, she felt, for the first time in years, as though she had something to live for besides Zahra's freedom. Something else worth fighting for—and that something was her new-forged love for the Black Lion of Navarre.

And so, just before they passed into the Great Hall in the middle of the nameless stronghold to greet their men formally, the renegade took a last, daring chance. A moment before their momentum carried them into the large, firelit room where the warriors were gathered, the renegade slipped her scarred hand fleetingly into the mercenary's larger grasp. And then the veiled Assassin broke her long silence. Expression inscrutable behind the gauzy black cloth that hid her face, she leaned close for a brief second and whispered the truth into his ear. One squeeze, and she flowed past him, letting go his hand and gliding on into the room.

The soft words were drowned out instantly when her men rose with a relieved clamor to greet the notorious Shadow Hunter's return, yet Jared's ears rang for long hours after with the power of that soft confession.

I love you, Isabeau had said.

She might as well have slipped her dagger into his heart.

* * *

"I wonder what they're talking about, up there," Pierre grumbled around the joint of roasted goat he was chewing. The men around him grunted or nodded agreement as the fullness of their mouths allowed. "I'll tell you this," he added. "Whatever they decide, I'm not letting that close-mouthed Assassin convince Jared to go off without us again. I don't care what that cursed sorcerer offers to persuade him." *Even,* he thought privately, *if Jared believes it's some kind of Holy Grail.* The mercenary's strange words that day at the oasis still perplexed him. *I haven't heard him talk like that since . . .*

Across the fire, several of the bandits stiffened even as the mercenaries indicated their approval of Pierre's declaration. Rashid, having grown into his place as their spokesman with grudging grace, scowled warningly at the dwarf. "Nor would we let your overgrown cat of a master persuade us to forget our duty to *our* sworn leader, little man. Should our master choose to pursue vengeance against Malik al-Fayed, with or without the Black Lion at his side, we would never allow the Shadow Hunter to ride out without our honor guard at his back! Sayyad al-Zul bears the favor of Alamut," he informed the diminutive lieutenant and the others ranged about him in the hall. "And we serve at the pleasure of its master. As long as that is so, we defend the Shadow Hunter. *To the death,*" he stressed direly.

But Big Pierre merely laughed disarmingly. "I think we are in agreement, pup," he said. As he looked out at each face, whether Frankish or pure desert Arab, he received only nods of affirmation. None of the men liked the way their two leaders had behaved with such stiff, guarded discomfort in their presence this night. Nor had that unease been relieved by the reluctance of both to discuss the time they'd shared while they'd been apart from their followers. If not celebrating a victory, the two at least should have been glad to have gotten away with such light casualties, for miraculously, as Pierre and Rashid had been happy to relate to them, none of the wounded had died on the retreat. But both Assassin and mercenary had sat on the peripheries of the gathering tonight and allowed their men to carry the majority of the conversation, staring broodingly at each other until both bandits and mercenaries had begun to wonder what had transpired between the two during their sojourn in the foothills to leave them so diffident toward each other now.

And then Sayyad had risen abruptly and announced his intention to retire to his tower-top retreat before the meal was even half completed. Yet what had raised eyebrows had not been the early leave-taking, but the quiet invitation the renegade had issued, all unprecedented, to the Black Lion to join him in this private refuge. To say the men were curious would have been a gross understatement. What could the Assassin have to say to the mercenary whose sword he had once bought, but to whom he now owed his life? What further engagement could they be plotting without the support of their most ardent followers?

"I think no one here has any intention of letting those two have all the fun without us," Pierre said, grinning through his beard.

Across the fire, Rashid nodded agreement. "Aye. We will follow where our masters lead, whether they ask it or not."

*   *   *

As soon as he reached the top of the narrow minaret, Jared impatiently thrust open the iron-bound trapdoor and climbed through it out onto a small, rounded rooftop balcony. The bright white light of a full moon flooded the black, surreal mountain vista confronting him, hanging there just above the mercenary so coldly brilliant that the stars themselves paled to insignificance beside it.

Not so the woman whose beauty the moonlight illuminated, however.

A mere ten feet from him, her back against the wire frame of what looked to be some sort of dovecote, Isabeau stood waiting for Jared. Slight and frail-looking in her dark renegade's robes, she looked as Sayyad al-Zul had always looked. Distant, and definitely dangerous. But to Jared, there was no woman in the world as alluring as she. With a single stride, the mercenary was upon her, gathering the Assassin up in his arms and impatiently tearing aside her veil to kiss her full, anxiety-bitten lips with a hunger that suggested a separation of a hundred nights, not merely several hours. Swallowing her gasp of joyous welcome, the Black Lion devoured her willing mouth hungrily for several long minutes.

At last, however, he set her free, cupping her cold cheeks in his callused hands. "And *I* love *you*, Isabeau de Lyon," Jared declared emphatically.

He stated this as though they'd merely paused momentarily in the midst of a private conversation, instead of keeping silent for agonizing hours while they greeted their men and regrouped, trying desperately all the while to protect a secret big enough to get them both killed should anyone discover the love they hid. "Never make me wait to tell you that again, you troublesome witch. Christ's wounds, I love you more than life itself!"

Isabeau was both laughing and crying at his adamant declaration, her forehead resting against his while her breathing hitched and she absorbed her lover's welcome presence. "Are you sure?" she asked breathlessly.

"Can you ever doubt it?" he returned teasingly. "I have sought you my whole life. And now that I have found you, I need nothing more."

Since his lips had again descended to capture her own,

the Assassin did not immediately reply. But at last she
broke free reluctantly, and her own strong but slender hands
cupped his stalwart jawline in return. "I will never doubt
you again, Jared of Navarre," she swore. "*Never,* my brave
Black Lion."

Even desire was blanketed then by the deeper need to
simply hold one another, tight, against the world. For a long
time they stood together thus, lovers and warriors both
comforting each other, but at last it was the fighter in each
that took precedence.

"Come, I would show you something, Jared," Isabeau
said, taking the mercenary's hand in hers and leading him
toward the cunningly worked birdcage that housed about a
dozen gray-banded doves.

"Carrier pigeons!" the mercenary said, smacking his
forehead lightly with one palm. "I wondered how you communicated without the tedium of sending messengers all
that distance. I should have guessed."

"Jamal ad-Din, the man I told you about in Malik's
harem, raises and trains them himself, and he taught me the
way of it," the Assassin said matter-of-factly. She reached
inside the cote and withdrew a cooing dove that looked
sleepy, but not alarmed by her gentle handling. "He has
many uses for these delightful little creatures, not least
among them communications with the true master he
serves. When I first came here, we set up this system as a
way to relay information without endangering Jamal's position in the harem. He sends me regular updates on Malik's
doings, as well as Zahra's welfare. There should be a message here now, if Jamal has not been caught in his treachery
to the emir." Isabeau put back the first dove and inspected
a second, then a third, until she found one with a small
silver-embossed tube tied on its leg. "Praise be to Allah,"
she breathed in relief as she opened the message and began
reading. "He has not been unmasked. They have reached
Damascus safely, and the Mamluks have been recalled to
their master, though the hunt for the 'bastard Assassin' and
his 'barbarous accomplices' goes on."

Jared sighed with relief as well, glad that the eunuch who had done so much for his betrothed was still alive and well, but also grateful to have his continued assistance at their disposal. Without it, the mercenary knew their task would be well-nigh impossible. "Does he say if your Zahra is well?" he asked solicitously.

"She is alive, though under suspicion because the nature of the raid made it all too apparent the goal was an attempt to steal her. Jamal could not relate much more in such small space, unfortunately." Isabeau crumpled the little note in her fist and clutched it to her tightly bound breast. "Ah, Jared, I fear for her so! What if I have endangered Zahra's life to no avail? What if, instead of helping her with my actions, I have doomed her myself?"

Jared didn't have to say that no fate could be much worse than what she had already endured under Malik's thumb. She knew it better than he, a fact he bitterly regretted as it was. "We *will* save her, Isabeau," he promised, his chin resting on the top of her head, keffiyeh and all. "We'll pry her loose of her captivity if it takes a thousand men."

She sighed, soaking up the comfort of his words for a moment as she simultaneously drew of the warrior's copious strength by leaning against his side. But at last she pushed away and stood on her own two feet. "Well, I've been thinking about that," the renegade ventured with soft-voiced resolution, "and I do not believe we should take *any* men with us, Jared. I do not think our forty, or even a hundred more like them, would avail us much in these circumstances. It would be impossible to bring such an army into Damascus unnoticed. And equally impossible to bring them back out unharmed, even if we were able to infiltrate the harem in search of Zahra. The city is, if anything, better guarded than Baghdad, and far harder to navigate, with its twisted, narrow streets and the huge garrison left there by the sultan."

"Agreed," the Black Lion said without hesitation. He had been a guest in Damascus too many times to disagree with the Assassin's assessment of the place. If anything, she understated the difficulties! "I, too, have been considering this rather thorny dilemma," he admitted, "and now that we have a means of communicating with your faithful eunuch, I believe I may have come up with a way to make the impossible possible—without engaging ourselves in some futile frontal assault sure to risk more lives than it saves. Don't worry, little Beau," he reassured her, taking the forgotten dove from her loosely cupped hands and returning it to its perch. "We *will* return your jewel to you safely. I have a plan."

It still amazed her that he cared so much for her concerns, though they were not his own. Isabeau was suffused with such a sense of gratitude for Jared, she had to blink away her tears. Veil blowing out behind her in the chilly evening breeze, she stepped up close to him again. Her jewellike eyes glistened as she looked up at the tall form of the warrior who was her beloved, her betrothed. "Tell it to me later," she whispered, her voice going low and sultry. "For tonight all I want is to be with you, here and now."

Because forever may not be an option, was the thought she did not speak.

The renegade stood on tiptoe and raised her lips to receive the Black Lion's kiss.

CHAPTER TWENTY

Jared did, indeed, have a plan, or at least the beginnings of one. But before he could put it into play, he and Isabeau were forced first to depend on the homing instincts of the gray-dappled doves she housed, and the discretion of their true keeper Jamal, now far away in Damascus.

It had been nearly a week now since the conversation he and the Assassin had had in Isabeau's minaret. That night, after giving the bird a few hours to rest, they had set aloft the same pigeon Jamal had originally sent them from Damascus, for it was the only one in Isabeau's cote that knew to fly there and not to the emir's palace in Baghdad. Attached to its leg, it had borne a carefully composed note informing the eunuch that Isabeau wished to meet him at an inn on the outskirts of the city she knew to be an Assassins' safe house, if Jamal was able to get away—and to tell him that she would be bringing the Black Lion with her to that meeting.

At the time she couldn't have written more to her ally even had the small surface of the missive allowed, for this had been all Jared had revealed of his scheme to Isabeau by then. He *still* hadn't told her the rest, wishing to wait until they were away from all prying eyes and listening ears before he divulged the remainder of it. Too many people's lives might be endangered if he chanced speaking out of turn, Jared felt—innocent people who would be risking their own lives and reputations by agreeing to play their parts in the plot he'd hatched, even if all went well. Yet surprisingly, Isabeau, usually so impatient for action, hadn't pressed him overmuch for details, he noted. In fact, she had been rather quiet, even after they'd finally received a response from her ally in Damascus late yesterday.

Last evening, thankfully, another of Jamal's pigeons had arrived in response to their missive, flapping exhaustedly to its perch in the dovecote under the guidance of one very anxious Assassin and her mercenary cohort. The reply pigeon had carried a message of mingled relief and worry from the much-burdened harem master, urging them to exercise extreme caution but not to abandon all hope of making a successful rescue just yet. And Jared, knowing how fragile, how tightly wound Isabeau was these days, had carefully reinforced that hopeful exhortation to his beloved, both then and in the short time since.

As he had promised, he did have a plan . . .

The first part of that plan had been to get them away from the well-meaning but intrusive scrutiny of the men who served both himself and the renegade he loved. Jared's mercenaries, though initially eager to collect their fee and move on, had fortunately accepted his decree that they stay among the outlaws a while longer. Even Pierre hadn't made as much of a fuss as the Black Lion had expected at the decision to linger among the renegades. But after all, why should he? It wasn't uncommon for their company to winter in some secluded spot between engagements, and the Assassin's fort, though uncomfortably lonely, was well supplied with everything they would need to weather the cold mountain winter until the passes cleared in spring.

No doubt the dwarf would be surprised to find the note Jared had left for him this morning, explaining that the mercenaries would be wintering without their leader this year. As would Rashid and the rest of Isabeau's *fidai'in* be to find hers, Jared knew. It hadn't been easy getting away from their zealous followers, the mercenary thought wryly. To elude someone as canny as Pierre particularly, one had to get up pretty damned early in the morning—so early it was practically still night. This was exactly what they'd done, less than an hour ago.

Now, steam misted the breath of both humans and animals as the two set out on horseback down the lonesome mountain trail. Dawn had not yet come, and the Assassin and her lover rode with their horses' hooves muffled and their packs securely strapped down against jangling in an effort not to alert any of the men sleeping in the fortress above. Soon enough, though, they were out of sight of it, riding around a sharp bend in the steep gorge that cut through the side of the mountain.

So far, so good, Jared thought cautiously. The rest of the trip, even accounting for the far greater distance from the Elburz Mountains to Damascus, should take them no more than nine days without the encumbrance of the caravan that had slowed them last time. It was almost *too* fast, the mercenary worried. Too soon before they must confront the demon that waited at the end of this long and painful road they'd traveled over half their lives. Was his beloved truly ready to finish the journey? Jared wondered, glancing over at her.

Isabeau was barely visible to him beneath the layer of furs it was now necessary to wear to combat the coming winter chill this high in the mountains. Swaddled in a warm fox-fur cloak atop the full leather and chain-link armor she wore, her steel helm wrapped about with both the dark blue silk of a turban (the ever-present veil attached to it, of course) and the fox-fur hood of her cape, his betrothed was little more than a blurry, vaguely human shape seated atop her high-stepping mare. Still, even hidden beneath all her shrouds and veils, she was beautiful to Jared. And more precious than a thousand jewels. He would ask no more of God than to allow him to ride beside her thus for the rest of their shared lives.

Jared looked around him, breathing deeply of the bitingly cold air. Transformed by winter's special sorcery, the familiar landscape of the Elburz Mountains had become a whole new world almost overnight, he thought. Or was it love that had given the mercenary new eyes to see?

The soaring, conical peak of Mount Damavand, rising far away up to his left, was completely snow-covered already, and the lesser mountains below it were beginning to develop a coat of white as well. Even in the pre-dawn dimness, the Black Lion could sense their magnificence, and when the first shaft of sunlight broke free of the rocky horizon, he was utterly awed by the transfigured landscape. Before he could turn again toward his betrothed to point out the way the light illuminated the peaks so dramatically, he felt her knee brush his as she urged Zephyr closer of her own accord. A minute later, just when he had begun to think the contact an accident, her mitten-wrapped hand fumbled clumsily for his, and Jared felt his face break out in a grin of pure, unadulterated happiness.

Gently removing her thick mitten and handing it back to Isabeau to hold in her other hand, the mercenary tucked her left hand into his own sheepskin mitten beside his larger one. Their palms rested together thus atop his thigh, their fingers entwined as they rode on, each silently drawing comfort and pleasure from the other. Neither spoke, knowing they would only be forced to break the ephemeral spell of happiness if they did. For the nonce, Jared was simply glad to be able to share this stunning natural beauty with the woman he loved, even as he feared for her safety in what was to come.

But eventually, knowing that Isabeau preferred to be aware of all that went on around her, Jared did confide the rest of his scheme to his beloved. After they'd made it past the topmost twists and turns of the Safid Pass, the mercenary gently squeezed the hand that rested so trustingly in his. "Little Beau," he began tentatively.

"Yes?" she sighed.

Then the daydreaming Assassin broke free of her reverie, drawing her hand back into her own lap as she focused her sapphire gaze on him, much to Jared's disappointment.

"You seemed as if you were a thousand miles away, just now," he ventured.

More than that, she thought with a twinge of sorrow. *Just how far* is *Navarre from here?*

Isabeau had been remembering what the mercenary had told her of his family's struggles, thinking of all he had left behind in his homeland to search for her. Once again she felt the terrible guilt encompass her at having diverted Jared's energies to deal with her own sorry affairs when he should have been focusing on the just and true commitments that required his competent management at home. If there was any way not to involve her betrothed in the endgame of this reckless mission upon which they had embarked, Isabeau was bound and determined to find it. At least he should be spared the dangerous final showdown, if the renegade could do that much for him. "I'm sorry, Jared. I was just thinking . . ." The Assassin shook her head disconsolately, as though trying to shake off her reflections as well. She missed his hand in hers already.

"About Zahra?" he asked.

Glad not to have to admit the real trend of her thoughts, the renegade readily agreed. "Yes, about Zahra. I didn't like the tone of Jamal's last missive, Jared," she said, speaking honestly enough. "I hope he is not concealing the true state of affairs with her to protect me," she said tightly.

"I am sure Jamal has enough respect for your formidable capacity of both mind and spirit not to do so, beloved. But we will find out for ourselves soon enough, if the plan I have conceived succeeds," Jared said, neatly segueing into the topic they both needed to discuss.

"I suppose it *is* time we talked of that," Isabeau agreed dully. She'd been thinking about this rescue mission for days now, and she'd been able to devise no suitable solution of her own that would not end with the death of one or both of them.

Assassins were trained to break into palaces and strongholds, yes—even enemy encampments in the midst of an army. But they were not similarly trained to get *out* again afterward. Most Assassinations were suicide missions, in fact, with the "blade" striking boldly, in public, on behalf of his master, and then waiting with perfect resolution for the vengeance of guards, friends, or kin to fall upon him. But though Isabeau might be willing to die to free Zahra— that was, after all, her sworn mission, and she had accepted the possibility of death in pursuit of it long before—she was not willing to sacrifice Jared so callously.

No, she thought, *he deserves better than that. Better than me*. She should let him go home and find himself a proper wife, fight for his castle and his lands before it was too late. He should not have to give up so much for her. Yet Isabeau was reluctant to let her betrothed go quite yet. Hell, reluctance didn't begin to describe the agony that tore at her innards like a thousand screaming djinn at the notion of allowing Jared de Navarre to pass out of her life once more! She told herself she could keep him by her side just a little bit longer—just until she'd figured out some alternative plan for rescuing Zahra that did not require exposing her beloved to danger. *Let me at least enjoy these last few days together with him, before I am forced to say goodbye to him forever,* Isabeau pleaded with a God she wasn't even sure she believed in.

Jared must have seen some of the conflict in her eyes, the only portion visible of her face—he'd grown only too skilled at seeing beneath the veils of her privacy. He cocked his head to study her soberly. "Are you sure you're ready for this, Isabeau?" he asked softly. "I am concerned for your state of mind, for you do seem a mite . . . troubled."

"Go on, beloved," she entreated, vowing to do a better job of keeping her thoughts to herself in future. "I'm sorry if I seemed distracted. I am ready to hear what you have to say now. Please, tell me of your design." If only this plan of his could change the hopeless feeling in her heart!

But perhaps it could . . . As Jared outlined the plot he had devised, Isabeau found her hopes rising in spite of herself.

"This is what I was thinking, little Beau. I know of a doctor in Damascus," Jared began. "A very learned Jewish physician, even reputed to be attendant to the sultan's own nephew, al-Adil. This man—his name is Abram—and I have a friendship of many years' standing, and I trust him completely. It occurred to me that we could use his help to gain access to the emir's harem on the pretext of a medical emergency, without arousing suspicion . . ."

As the mercenary continued, Isabeau's sudden flare of hope grew into a steady flame, brighter and brighter within her breast. It could work! "Yes, Jared," she cried. "I see it! But what then . . . ?" she encouraged.

"Well, if we can get word to Jamal, tell him to have Zahra feign an illness—some feminine complaint, say"— he grinned as if to say he knew how easily that excuse would work with most men—"we could see to it that the doctor who is summoned is our man. After all, the emir is new to the city, and a few convincing words from Jamal, along with Abram's golden reputation, should be enough to ensure he is the one who tends to Malik's most precious jewel. And if the doctor should happen to have two veiled assistants? Well." He grinned. "Abram is known to have two grown daughters—one nigh as tall as I, if you can believe it, and hunched a bit as well. No one would think to question their presence during the examination, as they often help him with his female patients.

"Should Zahra's mysterious ailment not improve right away during his visit, I'm sure we could see to it that the physician's daughters were allowed to remain overnight in the harem to, ah . . . 'observe' her condition. Meanwhile their father would return home for the night, or go to tend another case. Then, later, with Zahra disguised as one of the physician's daughters, yourself as the other, I myself would assume the role of Abram, and we would simply stroll out another gate with no one the wiser—that is, if Jamal can see to it that the guard at that portal is unaware of the doctor's earlier leave-taking. I swear, Isabeau, we could pull it off!"

"Yes. Yes, I think we could! Jared, you're brilliant," Isabeau crowed enthusiastically. *Why,* she thought, *if we do it this way, I wouldn't have to leave Jared behind while I* . . . Relief flooded her, as well as a resurgence of gratitude for the man who made things so incredibly much more bearable, just by being there. He brought her new hope, when for so many years the Assassin had lived without it. "And I know Jamal will agree, once we get in touch with him in Damascus."

Isabeau herself had not thought beyond their arrival and

her meeting with the eunuch. Having lived in a harem herself, she knew *exactly* how difficult it was to get into—or out of—one alive. She'd hoped Jamal might be able to show her an option she hadn't yet thought of for getting Zahra out; an alternative to the simple outright frontal assault she'd pictured that seemed so much like suicide. Now Jared had done it for her.

Pushing back the furs that hid her face, the renegade flashed the mercenary one of her rare smiles, so bright he could have seen it even through her wrappings. "I only hope that once inside, you are not so distracted by the unveiled beauties of the palace that you forget your mission," the renegade teased. Leaving off her joking then, Isabeau stripped off her mitten once more to tuck her hand back inside that of her betrothed. She held it securely as they rode side by side for Damascus.

As he squeezed back reprovingly, the mercenary's retort was nonetheless gallant. "*My* beauty wears a veil both indoors and out, and I love her more than all the lovely houris crowding the divans of Paradise."

CHAPTER TWENTY-ONE

The inn they had chosen for their rendezvous wasn't much to look at from the outside. In fact, "not much" might be giving it a great deal too much credit. Occupying the dead end of a run-down, trash-ridden alley in the poorest part of the ancient city, too close to the street of dyers and tanners to do anything but reek from their pungent chemical odors, the tiny Assassins' safe house looked more like a den of iniquity than a place to stay safe from those who would do them harm.

But inside, as the renegade had hoped, it was an entirely different story. As Isabeau and Jared ducked to pass inside the low, fire-blackened lintel, they were met by a rather surprising degree of luxury. Gold, copper, and silver silken draperies vied with gauzy strips of embroidered fabric to billow about the walls, while several low-burning lamps fended off the gloom that was otherwise alleviated only by a few windows cut high in the walls.

The center of the chamber was left open, but strewn with luxurious, dense-woven carpets Isabeau knew were produced locally by some of the finest rugmakers in the world. Low, intimate couches occupied most of the wall space in the vaguely circular chamber, the rest taken up by a door that the renegade decided probably led to the kitchens, judging from the delectable smells emanating from it, and the open staircase leading up to the second floor. In addition, there was the curtained-off alcove of a small private dining area at the far end of the room, perfect for discussing confidential business matters or arranging a quiet assassination. It was as though they'd entered the luxurious confines of a djinn's secret chamber at the bottom of a bottle, she thought whimsically, peeking sideways at Jared to see if he felt the same. His bemused return glance and raised eyebrow told her he did.

A man glided out from the shadows. "Greetings, effendis," he said unctuously. "Perhaps you have entered this humble abode in error? There are no vacancies to be had, alas . . ." He waved his hand to indicate how full his establishment was, though there was not a soul in the tavern at the moment, only a cat napping in a stray beam of sunlight upon one of the cushions. Then the man stopped abruptly as Isabeau made some swift, difficult-to-capture gesture with the fingers of one hand.

"Ah," said the middle-aged man, so plain of face and dress he could have been any innkeeper in any city or town under Sultan al-Kamil's dominion. His dark eyes sized his guests up swiftly once more. The unctuousness was gone, but now he seemed to have developed a real desire to serve them. "You are welcome here, my brother—yourself and your companion as well. How may I serve you?"

Isabeau sighed in relief. Her information about this place had been good. There was no feigning the look of recognition the innkeeper had shot her when she had passed him the sign identifying one Assassin to another. He might not be an active operative of Alamut anymore, but he obviously still served its leader in his own capacity. If the renegade knew her former master at all, she would guess this innkeeper probably owed the Old Man both for his establishment and for the right to run it. Especially if he was habitually turning away stray patrons in order to keep the place in readiness for any unexpected visit from one of his brethren.

"Just a room," she whispered in Sayyad's harsh voice. "And water to wash with, for now. We will have need of a swift-footed messenger later on, however, and a safe place to meet a . . . friend who does not want to be seen."

The man didn't even glance at Jared, beyond his first swift assessment of the mercenary when they'd come to the door. He focused solely on the one who'd been identified to him as one of his own. "It is yours, *ra'is*," he swore. "By the holy mandate of him we serve, you may be assured of your privacy here."

Relieved, Isabeau motioned for the innkeeper to lead them on through the dim, incense-perfumed main room and up the whitewashed mud-brick stairs to the lone guest chamber above. The man bowed and gestured for the two tired warriors to follow him, and inside, they found the bedchamber reflected the same muted splendor as the downstairs room had done. A cone of sandalwood incense smoldering in a brass dish upon the central table masked the inevitable scents seeping in from the outside, while an alabaster lantern illuminated several richly inlaid wooden chests and carved divans, as well as a deeply cushioned sleeping couch. It looked more like a love nest from one of the poet's fantastic tales than a fugitive killer's hideout.

Somewhat nervously, Isabeau turned to Jared when the door had shut behind them. Twirling the trailing end of her veil idly, she smiled at the mercenary as he shrugged his saddlebags off one broad shoulder and laid them on the nearest table. Now that they were so close to their final destination, it was nerve-wracking to be forced to wait a while longer, but that was exactly what she knew they must do. They should not send word to Jamal until after dark, when the messenger was less likely to be seen. But what were they to do until then? the Assassin asked herself nervously. It was hours yet until sundown, and she was full of anxious energy. "Wonder what he thinks of us sharing a chamber, eh?" she ventured. "Assassins rarely travel in pairs when they're on a mission."

"Oh, the innkeeper seemed like a sharp enough fellow to me. I'm pretty sure he guessed correctly what we intend to do in here," Jared said, crossing the cozy chamber to stroke one thumb down her velvet-soft cheek as he smiled whimsically down at the renegade. "He just doesn't know it isn't two men doing it."

Her startled laugh was smothered beneath the heat of the mercenary's smoky kiss. Ah, to have him this way forever! Isabeau thought for what must have been the hundredth time, as desire swept over her and drowned her earlier nervousness. To have him thus and *keep* him thus, until he

never, ever wanted to leave . . . Hungrily responding to the
challenge of his lips upon her own, the renegade set out to
make that happen.

A knock at the door interrupted her before she had much
of a chance.

Stepping away from the mercenary hastily, Isabeau
yanked her veil back over her face and drew back behind
the door even as Jared unsheathed the dagger at his waist
and went to answer it. Had they not been so focused on
the sudden possibility of danger, the pair might have noted
how seamlessly they worked together, how naturally they
made a team, guarding each other's backs as though born
to the task.

But the small person on the other side of that portal
turned out not to be so great of a foe. In fact, he could not
so much as speak, as he made clear with a series of exaggerated facial expressions and gestures, his eyes bugging at
the threat of the mercenary's dagger that was being leveled
at him. Their host was, indeed, a careful man, Isabeau
thought, coming out from behind the portal and resheathing
her own weapon. His servants, at least, were absolutely
guaranteed to be discreet. "Have you come to bring the
water for washing?" she hazarded when the boy had gotten
over the fright of finding the Black Lion's blade at his
jugular.

The boy nodded.

"Well, then," she asked, as patiently as possible. "Where
is it?" The youth's hands were patently empty.

The boy gestured excitedly over his shoulder, urging
them to follow and making washing motions with his
hands.

"I think he's trying to tell us there's a bathhouse," Jared
guessed.

The boy nodded eagerly.

The mercenary looked at the Assassin, raising a brow.

They nearly bowled the mute slave over in their eagerness to get to it.

Though nothing so grand as the multiroomed hammam

Isabeau had known in Malik's palace, or the great public bathhouses centrally located in all the great cities of the East, where Jared had gone over the years to cleanse himself and take part in the communal male ritual of bathing, this particular bathhouse had several things going for it.

First, it was built on the foundations of a Roman original, called a *thermae,* and thus had its lead heating pipes running beneath the marble floors so that they warmed the slabs meant for resting as well as the small central pool. Second, it was scrupulously clean, well-maintained, and thankfully not sulfurous as many bath springs were, so that the water which heated the pool was fresh and delightfully inviting. And third, it was private.

The other two features could have gone to hell for all the lovers cared. All that mattered was that they were alone—or would be, as soon as Jared gave the mute slave a dinar and instructions to stand watch outside.

The small circular pool steamed invitingly, and through the octagonal holes cut in the mud-brick dome of the roof, slats of sunlight let in patchy light and allowed the humid air to cool. Pigeons were nesting in some of the apertures, cooing gently to one another and flapping a bit as they resettled themselves again behind the shutting door that left the innkeeper's boy on one side and the two warriors on the other.

Isabeau dropped her cloak on a marble bench.

With a jangling clatter, her armored hauberk was next, then her turbaned helm with her braided hair unwinding to land in a heavy rope of gold and silver upon her left shoulder. Delighted to let her bound hair go loose for once, the renegade released the tresses from their confinement with nimble fingers, shaking the mass out in a flaxen cloud that settled gently about her head.

Seeing it, Jared gulped with a sudden jolt of desire, removing his own outer wrap and fumbling to unbuckle the leather-and-steel cuirass strapped round his manly chest, then swiftly yanking off the soft tunic beneath it to bare his magnificent torso.

In response, the Assassin began unwinding the linen strips that hid her curves, staring at him challengingly as she made a seductive, swaying twirl of it, as if inviting the mercenary to take hold of the end and spin her free of her bindings himself.

Quirking a brow, Jared simply pulled at the drawstring that held his trousers to his waist, letting free the cord.

Now it was Isabeau's turn to swallow a lump of desire.

In the next moment it became a free-for-all, a race to see who could shed their impeding garments the fastest and get into the bath before the other did. In the end, it was Jared who reached the pool first. He slid in and seated himself on the waist-deep ledge with a sigh of pleasure before she could get herself settled, though Isabeau was not far behind. But once they had both reached it, all haste was forgotten in their impromptu sensual game.

Isabeau lowered herself gingerly into the hot water, inch by inch, though her care wasn't due to the heat. It was a flame of a different kind that burned as she set one foot onto the ledge of the pool at Jared's hip, letting her long, shining hair drape her body as she turned to face the mercenary and deliberately put her other foot on the ledge at his other hip. Slowly, slowly, she bent, her eyes never leaving her lover's, until she was kneeling, straddling him. Her moonlight curls teased both of them, enclosing them in a silken curtain even more intimate than the confines of the bathhouse itself.

"Jared," she whispered.

The mercenary stroked a lock of her hair back behind her ear. "Yes, beloved?"

"Nothing," she sighed. "I just wanted to say your name."

His eyes crinkled as he smiled, his big hands scooping up handfuls of the steaming water to warm her and letting them flow down her back deliciously. "Say it as often as you like," he invited. "Say it or whisper it or scream it at the height of passion. I will always be there to answer." But would Isabeau be there to call? The mercenary wondered that with a pang, even as he gathered her close with

infinite tenderness and sampled the nectar of her lips for
the first time in far too many hours. Sometimes she still
seemed so far away—though thankfully now was not one
of those times.

The Assassin's whole body went up in flames as Jared
kissed her, his wonderfully sensitive lips damp from the
steam, and his bristly stubble, unshaven most days while
they were on the trail, abrading her soft skin in exciting
contrast. She could never get enough of Jared, Isabeau
thought wildly. Never though they sat fused together a
thousand years. Settling herself deliberately upon his naked
lap, his jutting erection pressing urgently against the bud
of her pleasure, they both gasped as she rolled forward and
pressed herself to him wholly from neck to knee. Yet when
the renegade rocked back, she surprised Jared by having a
sea sponge in one hand and a cake of soft, fragrant soap in
the other.

"Where did you get *that*?" Jared asked, laughing a little.
"I didn't see any bathing chest back there."

"One section of the floor tiles comes up to reveal a convenient little cavity," she informed him loftily, lathering the
sponge in a leisurely fashion. "Inside the compartment lie
all the oils and unguents one might ever want to accompany
one's bath."

Jared was momentarily distracted by the sight of the
soapy runnels of water dripping down the sponge to moisten the renegade's chest and belly. He only needed one
accompaniment to complete his bathing pleasure, the warrior thought heatedly, and Isabeau was it. Still . . . "How
did you know it would be there, if this is your first time at
this inn?"

"It may be my first time at this establishment, but it is
not, however, my first time in a bath built for love," she
began teasingly, but the memories that admission brought
to light were not happy ones, and Isabeau did not continue.
Malik had liked to watch his women at play in the ham
mam . . . A shadow crossed her delicate features.

Jared was quick to see it. Sliding his callused palm up

the taut rise of her belly and up the center of her chest, he
spread the soapy slickness over her torso, massaging the
tension out of it in a way that was both comforting and
intensely sensual. He rubbed his palm in reassuring circles
over her fast-beating heart, warming it in a way that had
nothing to do with friction, and everything to do with true
love. "Shh, love. Shh. We'll make it right together."

I will make it right for you, he vowed with silent resolution, *no matter what I must do to protect your life and
sanity.* Even if he had to lie or deceive her, Jared knew he
would do whatever it took to keep Isabeau safe . . . But then
he dismissed the subject from his mind for the moment,
knowing his plans could wait a short while longer. He still
had a little time yet to enjoy her innocent love. He drew
his beautiful blond temptress close again in an effort to
forget the uncertain future, his hands tangling in the hair at
her nape as he soothed her with his kiss, feeling the warm
water lap in soft waves against his waist, tickling Isabeau's
bottom and making the place where their bodies pressed
together invitingly slick. Jared mimicked the motion of the
water with his tongue, sweeping it inside her willing mouth
rhythmically, lapping at her own tongue in warm waves,
making her moan and press her body against his urgently.

The sponge was caught between them, and the rough-
soft rasp of it tickled Isabeau into drawing away momentarily. "Don't distract me, mercenary," she warned jokingly.
"I am determined to cleanse you of all your sins." The
Assassin waved the sponge at him in mock threat.

" 'Twould take more than that," the Black Lion scoffed,
eyeing the soft weapon askance. Then he sighed as she
applied it expertly to his chest and shoulders. "Ah . . . all
right, woman! Mayhap that *would* do the trick . . ."

The sponge moved lower. "Oh, that will definitely do
it!" he averred. Then a moment later its abrasive excitement
was replaced with the softness of a soap-slick hand, applied
where it would do the most good between their two bodies.
Jared gave up talking. He was gasping now, achingly erect
and eager, pulsing in her grip. But he worried that Isabeau

might not feel the same. Was she, drawing on unpleasant memories of similar places and positions, once again offering him a courtesan's caress? "You don't have to serve me, Isabeau," he said seriously, meeting her surprised sapphire gaze with the frank amber flame in his. "Do nothing that does not give you pleasure," he said.

"You think this does not?" she asked laughingly. Still, Isabeau's heart turned over despite her teasing tone. That was *so* like Jared—always concerned for her, always aware of any discomfort she might feel even before she herself could sense it. But in this case he worried needlessly. What might have been degrading or ugly in other circumstances was nothing of the sort with her betrothed. She could touch him for the rest of her life and never get used to the electricity that sparked between them and excited her so unbearably. Wiggling, she encouraged him to find out for himself. "Go on, my Lion. See how well it pleases this little houri to serve you so."

Her knowing fist milked him with deliberate, delightful pressure, and for a moment, Jared could not even comply, too busy holding back his raging need to succumb to her persuasions. "Ah, you witch," he groaned weakly, laying his head back on the rim of the tub. "Give me that soap." A moment later his slippery hands curved over her round, silky buttocks and slid down to explore the crease between.

The sponge slipped out of her reach altogether.

"Ah," he rumbled happily against her neck as his fingers found slickness of a different sort between her legs. "I see it pleases you well indeed."

Growling with mock ferocity, the renegade took matters into her own hands, though the sensation of his knowing fingers invading the soft, sleek flesh of her most intimate area was almost enough to make her forget her intentions. Only the promise of feeling that thick, throbbing column of manhood thrusting up within her body was enough to keep her to her purpose. Raising up and pressing her breast to his eager lips to suckle, Isabeau slid his velvety tip back and forth across her petals teasingly, positioning him properly at the entrance to her body. Then she let gravity do its work, sliding down upon his shaft until every last inch of it was imbedded within her pulsating passage.

Both groaned this time, and the pleasure was almost too much for Isabeau. "Help me, my Lion," she pleaded, nipping his ear encouragingly and grinding her hips against his.

In response, he surged up within her with such desire, hands at her hips to hold her in place, that brilliant sparks of ecstasy flashed behind her closed eyes, and Isabeau thought she might faint. Squeezing him, gasping, she held to his strong shoulders, burying her fists in his wet auburn hair and feeling him suckling her tender rosy nipples until everything was pleasure, her whole body a conduit for Jared's loving.

Help her? But he was helpless himself, the mercenary thought, cast adrift on a tide of thunderous ecstasy that surged and crashed upon him like waves upon a rocky shore, until although the still pool they inhabited had no current of its own, they had created one together to rival that of the sea.

But neither noticed the flooded floor of the bathhouse, or the birds they'd disturbed in the rafters above, each too wrapped up in the fervor of their love, the reaffirmation of the promises they had made to one another, to see beyond the other's pleasure. And at last, that affirmation came with a surge that washed over both of them simultaneously with such force that they could only hold each other tightly and ride out its waves, muffling their ecstatic cries against each other's necks as the climax transported them to heaven and beyond. Growing still at last, shuddering, the warriors clung together in awe as they let the aftershocks take them where they would.

It was a long time before they finally summoned the messenger to take their brief missive to Jamal.

The eunuch met them that night in the curtained alcove of the tavern, where the innkeeper himself stood prepared to serve them with his own hands. One moment they were alone, Isabeau seated as close to Jared as her male disguise made wise, the mercenary relaxed but alert as he accepted a cup of wine from the proprietor. The next, they had been joined by the cunning harem master so smoothly that it was almost as if he had simply materialized in his seat across the low table.

"Christ's wounds," Jared sputtered, letting go his instinctive grip on the dagger at his belt only when Isabeau put a restraining hand quietly on his wrist. Behind the veil, her eyes flashed a warning not to harm their sudden guest.

"Do they *teach* you people to do that?" He meant sneaking up and appearing so effortlessly wherever they went.

"Yes, they do," replied both Assassins, equally impassive. Jamal calmly reached for the water pitcher, eschewing the forbidden wine in favor of a more neutral libation, while the renegade cracked a walnut between her fingers and nonchalantly ate the meat. Neither one expressed any sign of affection or offered a welcome aloud, but the mercenary saw that there were other cues to watch for that showed him their deep and abiding bond.

Jared noticed Isabeau adopted the same studied posture of indolence as did her mentor; that indeed, many of her mannerisms mirrored those of the inscrutable, wasp-waisted older man who had joined them. If the innkeeper noticed this similarity, however, or thought anything of the suddenly increased gathering at his table, he gave no sign, merely offering the eunuch a plate of his own. Apparently, as an Assassin himself, it did not startle him to find others of his ilk popping up unannounced every now and then. The tavernkeeper left them with a murmured word of blessing and a reminder that he would be available at their call should they require anything. The three were finally alone at the table, and a good deal of curious scrutiny went back and forth between the Black Lion and the harem master who had devoted himself to the cause of the woman he loved.

The mercenary felt a surge of gratitude for this odd

stranger, who had taken on his task of protecting Isabeau
for so many of the years he should have been doing the
job himself. He offered the eunuch his hand. "Sir," he said,
feeling oddly as though he faced Isabeau's father. "It is an
honor to meet the man who has had the rearing of my . . ."
He stopped short, glancing askance at the innkeeper, who
had nearly reached the kitchen door across the way. "My
. . . friend Sayyad here."

Jamal had apparently already guessed Jared knew the
truth, for, despite her declared intention not to tell the mercenary her identity when last they'd met, the eunuch
showed no surprise at the hesitation that showed him Jared
was aware of Isabeau's femininity. Indeed, his keen eyes,
deep-set in the seamed and creased dark face, seemed to
know exactly what the situation was, down to the details
of what they had been doing all afternoon while they waited
for him to be able to slip away and meet them.

"At last I understand," he said with satisfaction, not appearing to respond to Jared's compliment. Rather, his eyes
had rested calculatingly upon the veiled Assassin, as if he
spoke to her, or perhaps he intended the remark rhetori-
cally.

Isabeau, knowing the eunuch never spoke idly, took up
the gauntlet. "Understand what, old friend?"

"What the Black Lion seeks. He has found it now, has
he not?" This time the query was unquestionably directed
at Jared.

"I have." The mercenary guessed the thrust of the other
man's meaning clearly.

"*We* have," Isabeau corrected. "Together, Jamal." Her
happiness could not be concealed, not even behind the thorough disguise of the Shadow Hunter.

Jamal's faced creased upward in a craggy smile. "Ah,
that is good news indeed; more than I dared hope for! This
is kismet at work, my children. Perhaps soon there will
even be new little ones for me to rear?" he asked teasingly.

Isabeau squirmed uncomfortably under that knowing
gaze, not saying anything.

Jamal seemed to find it all very amusing, directing those liquid black eyes of his back and forth between the lovers and reading their similar expressions of discomfort without doing anything to alleviate it. At last he sighed and folded his hands comfortably at his knees. "You have my blessing, mercenary, and there is no need for thanks. I have done this one here"—and he nodded to the veiled Assassin—"more harm than good with my interference over the years. I am just glad that fate has given you the chance to regain what you lost, and that my . . . charge here seems to find you suitable." He sized up the tall, handsome warrior for a moment longer, then nodded again. "I think the Shadow Hunter has made a fine choice in you, Black Lion," he said approvingly.

Said Shadow Hunter was beginning to feel annoyingly like a piece of furniture in this discussion. "Yes, well, if you two hovering mother hens are finished clucking with each other over me, we have serious matters to discuss."

Jamal glanced over at her in mild reproof. "I have not forgotten, O impatient one," he said. "Remember, it is I who have chanced the wrath of my master to meet you here tonight. Indeed, I cannot stay long this evening for fear of his spies, or Ullayah's, noticing my absence.

"Malik's first wife enjoys a position of more authority in the harem than ever, *ra'is*," he informed Isabeau, "since it was her cursed interference outside Baghdad that alerted the emir to the danger to his favorite odalisque." He paused to let that information sink in. "I am sure you remember in what high regard that woman holds me." The eunuch spoke now with elaborate irony. "When all this is done, I will be forced to flee the only home I have known these twenty years, and risk the displeasure of my true master as well by leaving the post he has assigned me. So be assured I know the seriousness of the affairs we discuss here."

Stung with remorse, Isabeau hastened to reassure her old mentor, even as she silently digested the unsurprising news that it had been her old enemy who'd betrayed her. The only wonder was how the vicious, scheming witch had

learned of her planned ambush, but the Assassin knew she
might never discover that much. "I know the danger I have
put you in, old friend, and believe me, were it not for this
man's flawless scheme"—she nodded to Jared—"I would
never ask you to risk yourself again for my sake—"

"Not for you alone, *ra'is,*" the eunuch reminded her gently. "But for the sake of our jewel as well. It is for you
both that I do this."

"Yes, for Zahra," she sighed, not needing the reminder
of the woman for whom they all risked their lives. "How
fares she, old friend?"

"Not well," the harem master admitted. "But she will
fare better if I bring her news of hope to lift her spirits."

"This news will indeed, Jamal!" Isabeau said enthusiastically. "Yet you must ask her to behave as though unwell
indeed . . ."

At the eunuch's uncomprehending glance and questioning expression, she explained. "The Black Lion has devised
a plan that calls for some acting from both of you, and
nerves of steel as well. Yet if you are up to the challenge,
it will prove far more likely to succeed than all the schemes
we have discussed and dismissed together over the years."
The renegade gestured toward the mercenary. "Tell him
what you told me, de Navarre," she said, slipping into the
more formal mode of address as they spoke of military
matters. Now the mercenary was more compatriot than
lover to her, though her heart remained his to hold no matter what guise he wore. "Tell him of the physician and his
daughters," she bade, and Jared did as she asked willingly,
explaining his concept to the eunuch exactly as he had to
his lover.

When he was done, he saw Jamal nod thoughtfully.

"I think it can be done," he said slowly. "Selim at the
west gate can be convinced to see what he is told to see,
for a price, so long as it is plausible enough not to cost him
his head with the lie. And for the rest of it, I believe I have
an 'illness' for Zahra to feign that is sure to gain her whatever attention she demands."

Isabeau drew in her breath, understanding the eunuch's meaning even before he had a chance to say it. "Of course, Jamal! It's absolutely ingenious. If al-Fayed believes his favorite concubine is pregnant, he will deny her nothing in her demands—he has wished for this so long now."

"Aye, and never gotten it, thanks to the herbs I provide, that son of a dog," the eunuch agreed. "Though Ullayah continues to pump them out like the bitch she is. Malik will want the world to know it if he has sired a son by his favorite concubine, and so he will want the finest physician in all Damascus. Abram ben-David is well-known here," Jamal concurred, "and I will have no trouble convincing the master he is the only doctor fit for his jewel. If you, Black Lion, can arrange it with the doctor himself . . . ?" he let the sentence trail off.

"I can. I am sure Abram and his family would be willing to do me a favor or two; even one of this magnitude. I will go directly from this meeting to find him tonight, when we are finished."

Isabeau had known he intended to find the doctor to-night, and so did not look surprised at the announcement that the mercenary would leave her side so soon. Yet there was much more to Jared's association with the Hebrew physician than he had shared with her. Though out of modesty he did not say so, the doctor owed the Black Lion this much assistance and more, for saving the life of his young grandson one day, when the boy had been set upon by a group of anti-Semitic youths in the square behind the Umayyid mosque. Returning the boy to his grateful family that day nearly a decade ago, Jared had been invited into the world of the close-knit Hebrew community in the city, and he had never regretted offering them his aid. In return, he had diligently protected the sanctity of his connection with their oft-persecuted community, only seeking their aid now for the sake of his beloved.

"Then I will go and start events in motion on my end as well." Jamal rose and brushed imaginary crumbs from his simple black robes, so like the renegade's own. "Black

Lion, if you will alert your friend to expect a summons by
tomorrow evening?"

"I will. But allow me to escort you to the end of the
street, ad-Din, before we part ways," the warrior offered
courteously, rising as well. "It is not as safe in this neigh-
borhood as one might wish."

The eunuch grinned humorlessly. "Oh?" he asked facetiously. "Perhaps this may come in handy then," he suggested.

When he drew his hand out of the inside pocket of his
long *abba,* where it had been resting casually, the mercenary saw that the eunuch was holding a long, deadly sharp
blade in his palm. "Perhaps it may." Jared laughed, clap-
ping the older man on the back and drawing him toward
the door.

Isabeau felt another burst of annoyance as the men ignored her for the second time that night, but she told herself
that the emotion was beneath her. All that mattered was the
end result of this all-important mission. Her ego had no
place in the coming conflagration. Still, it troubled her that
these two forceful, intelligent males had so neatly taken
over the rescue mission she had been planning herself for
nearly seven years. *My part will come soon,* she told herself
bracingly. *I only regret that our scheme does not involve
the taking of Malik's damnable head in the process.*

*   *   *

Outside in the alley, the mercenary let his arm drop from
around the harem master's shoulders, leaning one powerful
shoulder of his own against the rough, mud-brick wall of
the tavern as he turned to face the older man. Looking
around swiftly to assess the possible danger in the narrow
lane, Jared could see nothing to stop him from speaking
frankly with his companion, no spies or curious idlers
about. *Good,* thought the warrior. He sensed his false cheer,
maintained inside for Isabeau's benefit, would not wash
with the perceptive eunuch out here. And he was right.

"You have something further to say to me, Black Lion?"
Jamal asked politely. "Else I assume you would already be

about your mission to the Jewish quarter, not wishing to leave your betrothed's side for even the short time it takes to walk me down the street."

Jared surmised from this gently sardonic comment that the eunuch was telling him two things at once, both of which indicated he approved of Jared's relationship with Isabeau. "So, the renegade did tell you who I was before you left the fortress that day," he mused aloud. "And may I take it you are not opposed to my aiding her in her quest?" Still, he was not sure if he could trust the renegade's longtime ally to agree with what he would propose, and so he did not come directly to the point. After all, if she herself were to learn of his plan, Isabeau would undoubtedly count it as the ultimate betrayal.

"You are correct," Jamal allowed, relaxing back against the opposite wall and folding his arms across his hollow chest. "Yet I sense you are not merely intent on aiding her, but reclaiming her as well," he probed candidly.

"If she will have me," the mercenary admitted, once again feeling as though he were dealing with Isabeau's father. "She has agreed to consider my suit after all this is over. I would take her away with me if I may, back home where she will never have to hide again." His tone was passionate, grimly determined. "But I intend to make sure she is still safe and well enough to make the trip when the time comes, Jamal," Jared warned. "And that is what I would speak of tonight, if you are of the same mind."

"My mind is always open to any design that is for the benefit of my charge," the eunuch said. "She is as a daughter to me, dearer than anything to my heart, except perhaps her heart's sister Zahra, who needs her so badly now." Jamal leaned closer and spoke confidentially to the mercenary. "Zahra is not well indeed, de Navarre. I did not want to disturb the Shadow Hunter unduly with all that is on her mind presently, but since the thwarted rescue attempt outside of Baghdad, our jewel has gown quite gaunt with strain—almost haunted in her desperation to be free. I fear that Isabeau will not be able to contain her reaction—indeed, her wrath—when she sees her dear one's condition. This could prove dangerous for all of us.

"As a distraction to Zahra these last few months, I have tried to teach the girl some of the lessons I once gave Isabeau, but it is not enough. She still burns for vengeance, for surcease from her torments, yet fears to hope." Jamal shook his head sadly. "I have much to repent of in my dealings with these two brave girls," the harem master confessed. "I would give my life twice over to keep them from harm's way."

"That will not be necessary, Jamal ad-Din," Jared assured, "though I thank you for your willingness. Anyone who stands by my beloved's side is a friend to me, and so it is as a friend that I tell you the following." He paused to take a deep breath before confiding his secret to the eunuch. "Expect only one assistant to accompany the physician Abram when he answers your summons tomorrow eve." His voice began to shake with sincerity. "I will not have Isabeau brought anywhere near that hellish prison she so narrowly escaped, now that she is free of the twisted whoreson who enslaved her there once before!"

Jamal showed no evidence of surprise or disapproval, merely nodding to show he understood. "I agree, mercenary. Our . . . mutual friend . . . should not reenter that place again if it can be helped. He thinks her dead now, praise be to Allah for small blessings. But should he learn his White Rose still lives, the emir would hunt her down throughout the farthest reaches of the sultan's great empire, sparing no expense to get her back. Malik was utterly obsessed with the slave he called Gulbayez," the eunuch informed the sickened mercenary. "For her to walk back into his clutches this way is insanely risky. The consequences if al-Fayed should discover her true identity would be . . . indescribably bad. But it is her neck to risk, in the end, though you may wish to guard it for her. How will you prevent your woman from taking this chance?" he asked shrewdly. "The Shadow Hunter will not be easily convinced to stand idly by while her accomplices risk themselves for the sake of her heart's own sister."

"I don't intend to convince her," Jared confessed baldly. "I intend to take the decision from her hands. Tomorrow, when I contact Doctor ben-David, I will request a special decoction he has made on occasion before—mostly, I understand, for wives who would prefer to avoid their husbands' attentions," he admitted with a wry grin. "When placed in her wine or sherbet, it will make the Assassin sleep, heavily but harmlessly, for a period of no less than twelve hours. By the time she wakes, I hope to be able to present Zahra to her safely, with no risk to my beloved."

The eunuch laughed soundlessly. "So long as it is you who presents her to the Shadow Hunter, and not I. I would rather face Malik's wrath back at the palace than face the angry renegade when she wakes to find how you have deceived her."

"It is a risk I will gladly take, Jamal," Jared assured him. "For Isabeau's safety, I must chance the fury of her retribution. I know she will not like it, but *damn* it all, I am her protector! I cannot let her walk into danger when there remains aught I can do to prevent it."

"I do not disagree, Black Lion. And I will do nothing to stand in your way. That much I will pledge. However, you must realize that what you do may affect her decision to give herself to you in the end. Once burned by your deception, she may fear to trust you ever after."

"Better that my beloved live to curse my name than die believing me the best of men," the mercenary said stonily, not about to be swayed. "I have taken an oath to protect her welfare, and that is what I will do."

"Then there is no more to discuss," Jamal said, shrugging. "I will do my part to accomplish this rescue, and you will do yours, *insh'allah*. Tell the doctor to expect a summons by tomorrow night at the latest."

And with that the eunuch melded seamlessly back into the shadows from whence he had arrived.

Jared was left staring after him, wondering if what he had decided to do was right. *It has to be!* he decided

tensely, thinking again of the wrenching distress in his beloved's expression when she'd described the torments she
and Zahra had suffered at the hands of the brutal emir
who'd been their master. *I cannot allow Isabeau to expose
herself to such peril again . . .*

CHAPTER TWENTY-TWO

Jared shut the door gingerly behind himself when he arrived back, near dawn, at the comfortable little love nest he shared with Isabeau. He did not mean to wake her just yet, but of course, with an Assassin's instincts, she stirred the instant he set foot in the room. He supposed he should have known she would.

"Is it you?" the raspy, disembodied whisper came to him out of the darkness. Until he identified himself, the mercenary knew the Assassin would not assume it was he who had woken her, no matter how familiar the footfall that had alerted her to his presence in the chamber. Her conditioning had simply made her too wary not to take precautions. Yet Jared, having learned her ways well over the last several weeks, could still hear a hint of grogginess in the harsh tone Isabeau assumed, though he knew she strove to hide her recently wakened state. Her guard was not as good just now as she might like to think. Now was the time to do what he must.

"Yes. 'Tis I," Jared confirmed softly. *I, Judas,* he thought.

Abram had warned his friend that the potion he'd given him was highly potent, and would certainly keep its intended recipient in a drugged slumber far into the evening, even if he administered it now. By nightfall, when she was able to shake off the potion's grip, it would be too late for Isabeau to stop Jared's plan, though not to reap its rewards. Still, though this was exactly what he had intended, and the only way to keep her safe, the mercenary felt like the worst sort of betrayer for what he would do.

If he didn't get this unpleasantness over with quickly, Jared wasn't sure he'd be able to do it at all. Already, bitter gall burned the back of his throat at the thought of deceiving the woman he loved this way. Had the stakes not been so great, the possible consequences so dire, Jared would never have taken the choice to fight from Isabeau, for not only did he know her to be a deadly enemy, a matchless warrior in the cause of those she loved, he knew her to be a singularly proud, independent woman. But, as he had told Jamal last night, Malik's palace was the one place the mercenary simply could not bear seeing his beloved go; the struggle against the twisted emir the one fight he could not let her chance, even by his side. It was simply too much like dancing in the heart of a fire.

Unaware of Jared's struggle, Isabeau's voice was warm now as she answered from the generously sized sleeping couch they'd shared. "Then join me a while, beloved. It's still early yet," she invited, and as the Black Lion's eyes adjusted to the dimness that was slowly growing into light, he saw she held up the coverlet for him to slip under.

Jared drew closer, making a show of the goblets he held in his hands. "I cannot, until I have set these down."

"What have you brought?" she asked curiously, smelling a sweet scent rising from the cups as Jared placed them on the small table beside their bed.

"Just a gift to perfume the mouth from our friend the innkeeper. His boy was waiting for me when I arrived," the mercenary said, hating himself but speaking truly enough still. She hadn't asked what he'd *added* to the brew, after all.

The renegade reached out an arm and pulled aside the heavy drapery that covered the window by her left side. A fuzzy, gray sort of glow lightened the room through the intricate stonework of the lattice screening as she hitched herself up in the bed. Jared noticed to his mild disappointment that she had slept fully clothed, too much afraid of discovery to do else in this place so near her enemy's new seat of power, even though they were tucked away in an Assassins' safe house. Only the veil was missing from her disguise, but it was enough to let Jared see Isabeau's unsuspicious expression, the trust and love she bore him. Unbidden, her words to him that day in the minaret came back to ring in the Black Lion's ears. *"I will never doubt you again, Jared of Navarre,"* she'd sworn.

After this, would she ever *trust* him again? It was a chance he had to take. The mercenary told himself firmly that as her avowed champion, it was his whole purpose in life to fight battles like this one for Lady Isabeau de Lyon. It was just his bad luck that the lady herself could not be persuaded to see it that way. Frustrated, Jared sat down on the side of the bed, facing away from her in part to compose his expression, and in part to hide how he arranged the cups on the bedside table so that he could recall which one was which.

But the renegade did not like to be ignored, even when it was with the best of intent.

Isabeau snaked a hand up her lover's spine in a gesture that was at once both sensual and innocent—or would have been innocent, had she not negotiated it beneath the loose end of Jared's tunic so that her cool palm and fingers stroked the warm, solid mass of muscle that was his back. Her mind was slowly clearing of the cobwebs left there by sleep, and she was determined to enjoy this calm before the coming storm.

"It smells good, whatever is in there," she commented softly, rubbing circles on Jared's broad shoulders. She felt oddly shy all of a sudden, though she could not explain why. Perhaps it was how distant the Black Lion suddenly seemed, when all she wanted to do was get close to him. Funny, the renegade thought wryly, she was never this diffident in the heat of battle. It was only with her beloved that she became so girlishly tongue-tied.

" 'Tis palm wine, warmed and mixed with honey and spices," Jared answered softly. "I thought you might like to try it."

"You know such spirits are forbidden to all good Muslims," she reminded him without heat. The innkeeper must have brought the liquor for the obviously Frankish warrior, thinking it might please his foreign tastes, she decided.

"Just how 'good' do you plan to be this morning?" the

Black Lion queried archly, turning so that her questing hand slid round to his front, slithering down his muscular abdomen to rest on the stiff bulge below. Jared caught her surprised hand and pressed it there hard so there could be no misunderstanding his meaning. Now he was no longer keeping himself aloof from her.

"Not very," Isabeau admitted wryly. Still, she hesitated, never having tasted the spirit of alcohol before, though her abstinence had always been more a matter of lacking desire to feel its intoxicating powers than true devotion to religion. But Jared's own brand of intoxication was another matter. She allowed the handsome mercenary's teasing to sidetrack her from her worries, his seduction too powerful a tool of distraction to resist. Her hand, of its own accord, began a rather . . . lengthy exploration.

"Perhaps you would prefer hashish?" he teased breathlessly, allowing himself to enjoy her ministrations for a guilty moment. "I seem to recall the Shadow Hunter having quite the head for it, though I cannot say the same for myself. Methinks I saw a spirit that night under its influence—the spirit of seduction." Jared smiled in memory, and saw his beloved do the same. *Pray she takes the bait quickly,* he thought, *'fore I lose the nerve to deliver it!* The mercenary shifted away from her for a moment, reaching for his own cup as well as hers, and sipping deliberately from the one he had not doctored with the physician's brew.

Isabeau took the goblet he offered. "In all seriousness," she said, sipping cautiously of the unfamiliar substance, "there is something I would say to you before the day is over, Jared of Navarre." The sweet, burning tang of the wine covered her tongue in novel sensation, and, still not sure whether she liked it or not, she took another swallow of the mellow warmth for courage.

"What is it, love?" he asked, but before she could answer, Jared had captured her tingling lips with his own, administering a very thorough kiss.

Isabeau could hardly remember what it was she had meant to say when the mercenary was done proving again what a seductive force he could be. She placed a hand on his chest, feeling the rapid beating of his strong heart. "I wanted to thank you, beloved . . ." she said, then stopped and drank when he offered the goblet up to her lips again. The brew was heady indeed, she thought, or perhaps it was the intoxication of her lover's skillful lips she felt tingling in every limb.

Yet today those lips seemed to be conveying two messages to her—desire being the obvious one, but with a subtler suggestion underneath that she could not quite capture . . . She went to taste them again, trying to figure it out.

It was only her own passion she tasted, the Assassin convinced herself as she surfaced from yet another drugging kiss. Each time she went under, she came up with a little less consciousness. Before he seduced her entirely, she must remember her original intent, or he might never know her true feelings . . .

"Jared," she murmured, alternating between sips and kisses as he encouraged her to drink, sighing at the feeling of his clever tongue seducing the sensitive skin of her neck each time she swallowed. "I . . . just wanted you to know . . . ah." She sighed again, losing her train of thought. "Wanted you to know how . . . grateful I am," she forced herself to say. "Were it not for your aid and the plan you have devised, I . . ." She struggled for words, feeling strangely light-headed and excited simultaneously. "I do not think I could have—ah!" she cried again as this time the mercenary took her fully into his arms and crushed her to him in a flurry of passion.

"Don't thank me," he begged softly against her ear as the renegade succumbed softly to the drug he had administered. "Curse me, kiss me, *love* me, Isabeau, but never thank me, after this . . ."

Had the second sentiment in his kiss been sorrow? Isabeau wondered as drowsiness overcame her, subduing even passion in its wake. Or had it been remorse? But what could Jared possibly have to regret? Strange questions, she mused fuzzily.

The answers eluded the renegade as consciousness receded on a slow ebb tide and she slid pleasantly into slumber.

Jared left her sleeping there, deeply drugged and looking so serene, so heartbreakingly beautiful, that it almost stopped his heart to leave her there, even when he had drawn up the veil to hide her kiss-swollen lips and return her again to the renegade's guise.

Abram had better be as good a doctor as he was reputed to be, the mercenary thought grimly. If the dosage had not been exact . . . Giving Isabeau too much or too little of the potion could be equally disastrous, he knew. If she woke too soon and discovered his perfidy, there was no telling what trouble she might incur if she followed rashly after them to Malik's palace—or what vengeance the angry renegade might exact from the man who'd taken her freedom of choice away.

The mercenary could only hope the gift of the precious jewel she sought would be enough compensation to ameliorate Isabeau's righteous anger when she woke. If it was not . . . he might have lost his beloved forever in trying to save her life.

Jared strode out into the breaking dawn to find the physician. *Best get this wretched business over with as quickly as possible,* he brooded, *before my conscience catches up with me!*

*   *   *

But nothing moved quickly in a harem, the mercenary soon discovered. Hunched by the old Jew's side, wrapped and muffled in about eight layers of shapeless draperies and veils, the newly dubbed "Leah" allowed her "father" to cuff her reprovingly into doing his bidding several hours later. "She" shuffled awkwardly over to the bag the doctor had left on the table by his patient's bedside, all the while murmuring apologies softly in Hebrew and praying silently in at least four other languages not to be unmasked.

Now the Black Lion fully appreciated for the first time

the danger his betrothed had faced every day of these last seven years, for he knew that to have his sex discovered in today's dangerous masquerade would mean an instant death sentence for him. Yet the danger he faced only reaffirmed his decision not to bring Isabeau into this clandestine recovery mission, as if he'd needed that surety bolstered.

Thank the Hebrew God that Leah, Abram's oldest child, was known to be a woman of imposing height just like her father. She had also been burdened with a spinal affliction which, rumor had it, had caused her father to take up the study of medicine in the first place, though Jared could not bring himself to be glad of that! The crippling disease had affected her face, disfiguring it so that even among the women of her own kind, who did not go about veiled like Muslims normally, she kept her face covered modestly. Her humped silhouette and covered face had allowed the mercenary to assume her identity with relative ease, if not comfort.

His height could be disguised by her odd posture, but little else of his evident masculinity would be hidden if anyone were to look too closely. The mercenary just prayed the outline of his weapons would not be noticed! He glanced around cautiously under the trailing edge of the striped woolen veil that covered his forehead and face, hoping no one would notice any undue curiosity in the ungainly child of the famed physician. Luckily, that same veil hid the black scowl Jared wore at what he saw around him.

The slow pace of Zahra's medical exam might have had something to do with the number of curious onlookers and busybodies interfering with their progress every other second, he thought, getting in each other's way with annoying—and in the case of the nervous interlopers, alarming—regularity. As it turned out, a doctor's visit inside a powerful man's harem was an event of some magnitude, with as many excited female spectators at hand as there would have been eager bettors during any male game of chance. Jared's hurried conference with Abram earlier today had not prepared him adequately for the spectacle, though he

should not have been surprised to see that the inner workings of the flamboyant emir's household were as lavish and
disorganized as any theatrical production. Indeed, inside the
brightly lit receiving chamber in the harem of Malik al-
Fayed, there played out a farce of at least a dozen charac-
ters, major and minor.

First there was the physician, an older man of imposing
stature with a full, flowing white-striped red beard that
reached halfway down his chest (a crude replica of which
beard Jared carried in one of the pockets of Leah's robes,
for when he would, if all went well, later assume the physician's identity in the wee hours of the morning). Abram,
with not a dissimulating bone in his body, disguised his
nervousness at this unaccustomed playacting by behaving
with brusque impatience, snapping and swiping imperiously
at anyone in his way. Nervous women, including the man's
disguised "daughter," scattered in his wake like clucking
hens.

Abram's sterling reputation had earned him the right to
a little bad humor, the mercenary thought as he avoided the
old man's not-so-gentle cuff this time by ducking a bit
closer to their patient, though Jared knew him to be a very
even-tempered man on most occasions. Unfortunately for
both of their nerves, neither applying reason nor sheer bad
temper had been able to convince those in charge of this
fiasco to clear the room so that the crabby physician could
examine the emir's favorite concubine in peace.

The harem master Jamal, who had called upon Abram's
services earlier today, was standing dark-eyed and inscrutable as always, in his proper place in one corner of the
bustling room, supervising the humiliating public ordeal of
the examination as was his duty. To the anxious mercenary,
his role in this rapidly escalating farce seemed to be to
orchestrate the confusion, but not to assist in any way in
calming it. Still, Jared knew Jamal was only doing what
was necessary to preserve the illusion of normalcy.

Any time a noncastrated male must enter this exclusively
female province, even a doctor, the chief eunuch must be

present to make sure propriety was properly observed. In this case, when the patient was the master's current favorite, that meant a number of other slaves and attendants were also at hand at the eunuch's beck and call, though what use they served except to get in everyone's way and heighten the patient's inevitable tension was debatable to the mercenary. Which brought Jared's thoughts to the central character in this unfolding play.

Zahra lay like an invalid before Jared's eyes, pale and wan, her fully clothed body draped in a great embroidered bed sheet beneath which her slender form could only be guessed at, trembling as she waited on the divan to be examined in front of half the world, as harem custom demanded. The mercenary thought she looked far too small and frail to have the hopes and concerns of so many pinned upon those slight shoulders. Far too small, certainly, to carry that bastard Malik's child.

And he wasn't the only one who seemed to have reason to doubt Zahra's pregnancy. For there was Ullayah, who had demanded to be present as the only one of the emir's wives to have conceived and borne a son by him so far. Scarcely bothering to pretend concern for the younger girl, she had swept into the chamber much to everyone's dismay a few moments ago, bringing along her own retinue of slaves and eunuch bodyguards to be present while the renowned physician determined whether or not her rival was with child.

Her presence caused true chaos to descend on the already disordered gathering as she swept her unveiled gaze around the room. The mercenary could see how years of petty disappointments and vicious scheming had drawn sharp lines of dissatisfaction down her otherwise classically beautiful Persian face. The bloom had certainly worn off that rose, Jared mused to himself, not bothering to be kind in his thoughts. Perhaps the woman did indeed have cause to fear her rival. Yet if Jared had anything to say about it, he would actually be doing Ullayah a favor by removing the one woman who stood between her and her husband's affections. He counted it an unfortunate consequence to an otherwise satisfactory plan. The venomous witch was watching him closely—far too closely for Jared's comfort.

Not only his life was at stake in this perilous masquerade, Jared knew, but the physician's and Jamal's as well. And if Zahra were to be implicated . . . the punishment for an unfaithful concubine was worse still.

Thus it was that, beneath the heavy Hebrew robes, the false Leah had been sweating profusely, even before Ullayah had made her dramatic entrance. Jared was fairly counting the steps to the exterior gates in his head, his mind going over just how far it might be to the west exit, where the easily bribed Selim would be expecting to allow two hurrying Jews to pass through later tonight. If all went well, he and Isabeau's jewel would be strolling out that gate in a matter of mere hours. If it did not, however, they might need to cross that barrier much sooner . . .

Well. He would just have to make sure all went well, and no suspicions were raised, Jared told himself. But with the eagle-eyed Ullayah glaring at his every move, even the mercenary's steely nerves had begun to fray. How much worse must it be for Abram—and hell, for Zahra, who knew only that two strangers were working to help her escape, but not who they really were, or how they were to accomplish the rescue?

Thankfully, during his many visits over the years with Abram's family, Jared had learned something of their tongue, and so it was with fair verisimilitude that he was able to answer his "father's" questions as the man spat them out in rapid-fire Hebrew. That would help throw off suspicion, he hoped, for very few nonbelievers spoke the language. At the nervous physician's request, he reached for the medical bag Abram had brought with him, trying to ignore Zahra's visible flinch as he leaned across the distressed girl.

But just then there was a stir in the hallway, where yet more guards stood waiting to protect the chamber. Looking up to check what the interruption could be, Jared froze at what he saw.

Malik al-Fayed strode confidently into the room.

The final player had just joined their little farce, turning it into a very serious drama, indeed, with his unexpected entrance.

Events in the harem unraveled quickly after that.

CHAPTER TWENTY-THREE

Al-Fayed was not at all as Jared had expected.

"As you were, as you were, good women and almost-women," the emir said with a smirk, gliding into the room as if he owned it—which in fact he did. He grinned at his own lame joke, waving a hand to brush away the hovering eunuchs who accompanied him into the chamber. "Don't let me get in the way; I am only here to observe—and to make sure my precious jewel has all she needs, of course."

Coming over to the divan where Zahra huddled miserably, he ignored her obvious flinch and stroked her limp blond hair with cruel affection. "Tell me, good Jew," he ordered jovially. "Have I made this little whore the mother of my son?"

Jared saw red.

The girl was obviously terrified; humiliated and on the verge of tears. Yet under the emir's public taunting she managed to hold those tears off and wait stoically while her master made the humiliation worse with every word. The mercenary thought her courage in the face of such constant degradation was admirable, as was her fright understandable. Malik was quite good at intimidating helpless women, he acknowledged with slowly smoldering fury. But how great a foe would this preening, obnoxious coxcomb of a man prove to Jared himself? The mercenary looked him over from beneath the protection of Leah's striped woolen veil.

Somehow, he'd envisioned an ogre, some hideous, corpulent obscenity of a man, who would show every vice and perversion on his features like a banner advertising his sins. Malik al-Fayed, however, was nothing of the sort. In fact, he was quite handsome.

Oh, the signs were there for a discerning man to see. Despite his dark, true Arabic splendor of form, al-Fayed had become a trifle dissipated, the firm muscle tone of his youth running to pudginess as he aged, and his dark, limpid eyes glittering with the fever of too many late nights, powerful opiates, and flagons of potent palm wine. But Malik was still a man in his prime, a proud desert prince, confident in his stature and in command of all he surveyed. Of course, standing in his own harem, believing himself about to be proclaimed the father of a child he had gotten on his helpless slave through rape and degradation, any man might be forgiven for believing himself to be in control.

Jared wasn't about to forgive him, however.

This was the man who had dared to touch Isabeau! The cause of her nightmares and pain, the very center of her conditioned distrust and disillusionment. If his hands had not been so tightly clenched around the doctor's bag, Jared thought they would have crushed the life out of this twisted, puffed-up toad who stood so close by in total ignorance of his peril. Instead he compressed the leather handles of the bag so hard his knuckles turned bloodless around them. For Isabeau's sake, he wanted to kill the emir, but for Isabeau's sake, he could not—not if he wanted to abide by her wishes and carry out the mission she'd struggled so long to achieve on her own.

Jared saw Zahra's blue eyes, so like Isabeau's own, flicker toward the harem master for reassurance, then light upon him as well, knowing at least from the few things Jamal had been able to tell her that the veiled "assistant" was here to help, if not who that assistant was in truth. The Black Lion gave her an almost imperceptible nod of encouragement, and he saw the girl relax a tiny bit as she endured her master's boastful possessiveness.

Malik seemed immune to the tension he had caused, however, strutting and preening before his women like the only rooster in a henhouse, while the doctor made a show of washing his hands in the basin someone had provided in the meantime. Slowly, deliberately, the physician began rolling up his sleeves.

The Black Lion barely heard Abram's murmured plea to

the emir for a moment to examine the girl before he gave al-Fayed his answer, so caught up in his own dark musings was he.

"Leah!" The doctor's urgent voice jolted Jared out of his violent fantasies. Clearly this was not the first time he'd called his daughter's name. "My bag, girl! How many times do I have to ask you? I cannot give the emir his answer until you obey me!"

Jared, still roiling inwardly with rage, reached out across the divan with stiff arms and offered him the case mechanically. But Ullayah, peering over the nervous physician's shoulder suspiciously while her husband stood on the Jew's other side, suddenly lashed out like a cobra with one quick arm, gripping the mercenary's briefly bared wrist with surprising strength.

Gripping his too large, too *masculine* wrist, with its revealingly manly reddish-brown hair, and impertinently pushing back the sleeve of the voluminous shawl he had worn to cover it.

"Husband!" Ullayah shrilled at Malik, living up to her name and ululating the alarm on a rising wail of sound. Simultaneously, she pointed to the evidence she held in her grasp. "Look! You are betrayed!"

Everything went to hell very quickly after that.

Screams of alarm rent the chamber and fainting women were suddenly everywhere, unable to choose between covering their faces and fleeing the sudden presence of an unsanctioned male in their midst. The eunuch guards seemed not to know whether to protect the women first or attack him, so Jared took advantage of the momentary confusion to salvage what he could of the situation.

"Get Zahra out of here!" he growled, breaking free of the noxious woman's grip and whipping off the impeding robes he wore, since his disguise was ruined already. Thrusting the bundle of distinctly Hebrew cloth toward the stunned doctor, he shoved Zahra at him as well, rolling her toward the edge of the bed where Abram stood to get her moving. He used the sheet that had covered her to throw over the wailing Ullayah, still standing next to the physician, who himself remained stock-still in shock, his bag forgotten in his hand. Fortunately, Malik's jewel seemed to have snapped out of her own paralysis, and quickly grabbed the feminine robe from Abram as Jared drew the short-sword that had been concealed beneath it.

More shrieks, both female and falsetto male, followed at the sight of the gleaming steel blade, and Jared brandished it menacingly at the emir and the others in his way, wishing it were the longsword that was capable of doing so much more damage. All he could think of was clearing a path for the girl and her rescuers to flee the room, giving them some slim hope of getting away before they were all captured together. Catching Jamal's eye as he raised his guard defiantly, he knew from the other man's grim nod that the harem master had understood his intent.

Jamal would know the Black Lion himself had no chance of escape now, but he wouldn't be foolish enough to allow the mercenary's sacrifice to remain in vain. "Take her out of here, man, and do it fast!" he yelled to ad-Din as the first of Malik's guards began rushing in the doorway, and steel rang off steel with an earsplitting clang. More quickly even than he would have believed, Jared was surrounded.

He resolved to go down fighting, for he knew Isabeau would have wanted it that way.

Isabeau awoke that evening, feeling woozy, to find a dream come true.

Zahra was in her arms, weeping with what she could only assume must be tears of happiness, even as the last red rays of sunset filtered past the latticed window of the Assassins' inn to paint her bedchamber scarlet and rose. Yet she sensed something was terribly wrong with this vision of joy, though she saw Jamal's concerned visage standing just behind her dearest heart's sister in the cozy room. Why, the renegade wondered blearily, was Zahra here, crying, when they had not yet gone to rescue her? It was all very confusing.

She'd been dreaming of their mission, of that the Assassin was fairly sure. Had they already accomplished it then, so easily? Why, then, was she not deliriously happy? But though surrounded by those she loved, this otherwise perfect picture lacked a single element—a necessary element—without which the Assassin could never be content. The other half of her soul remained at large, she thought in panic, for Jared was missing! Her foggy memory held no explanations for his absence or the presence of her long-lost soul sister. Out of habit, she turned to Jamal ad-Din for help.

"What . . . what *is* this? What's occurred, Jamal?" she asked, stroking her dear one's hair and trying to comfort the crying girl despite her own bemusement. The Assassin saw that it was nearly nightfall, though her last memory had been of dawn breaking—and of Jared's kiss . . .

"Why have I been sleeping here so long?" Isabeau asked, her vision growing dark as suspicions began to form. It must have something to do with the unfamiliar spirits Jared had encouraged her to swallow. Was this the fabled hangover of which she had heard so many cautionary tales in poetry and song? the renegade wondered. Indeed, her head throbbed oddly, and gray mists of fading consciousness still came and went before her eyes. Her mouth was terribly, terribly dry . . . Yet just a cup of wine could not have done so much to incapacitate her, she thought incredulously. Something else must have been in that goblet!

Had Jared suffered a similar effect? she worried. But why then was he not still lying by her side? Hanging on to what was real and solid for dear life, Isabeau clung to the girl who'd returned to her embrace against all expectations, burying her face gratefully in Zahra's long, golden hair and breathing in the jasmine scent of her accustomed perfume. How could her beloved jewel be here, without the aid of herself and the Black Lion?

Jamal knew what she needed to understand, despite the renegade's garbled questions. "You have been drugged, *ra'is*," he informed her rapidly, "and the rescue has taken place without you. Only, it has not gone off without a hitch . . ." Jamal's dark face was ashen with concern.

Isabeau felt her belly grow cold, even as Zahra sobbed the rest of the story into her shoulder. "That man, the Frank—Jamal called him some sort of 'lion,' though I don't know why, unless it was because he fought so ferociously on our behalf—he took on the whole of Malik's personal guard to help us go free, Isabeau; and in return we left him there . . ." Zahra cried in anguish. "Oh, my sister, I cannot bear it if that brave warrior should suffer trying to free me! Who was he, anyway? Some soldier you hired?" she asked innocently, but even in her travail, Zahra was perceptive enough to see her friend's face go white with shock and sorrow.

"Not just some hired warrior then, but a man you cared about," she stated quietly. "And he gave his aid to save me because you asked it of him." Remorse was starkly writ upon her tear-stained porcelain features.

"It has been long indeed, sister, since we had leisure to talk of such things, but now is not yet the time for confidences," the Shadow Hunter told the girl with whom she had waited so long to reunite, her heart aching. Now they might never have that time, she thought heavily. "Tell me all of it, Jamal," she ordered.

The eunuch obeyed, swiftly relating all that had come to pass since the mercenary had left her sleeping, duped into complacent slumber. "We ran while the Black Lion fought off the harem guards, and were able to disguise our 'jewel' in the robes the mercenary had worn, so that she and ben-David passed through the gate as father and daughter, while I claimed to offer them escort to the Jewish quarter. Had we waited even another minute, our escape would have been cut off," Jamal said solemnly, his admiration for the man who had given them the crucial opening quite plain.

"The physician has gone into hiding with his true family, while we raced through the city ourselves, taking several twists and turns to ensure we were not followed here. Zahra is exhausted, for I dared not draw attention to our flight by hiring a sedan chair, and she is not used to running long distances after the enforced indolence of the harem. Yet though I saw no confirmation of pursuit with my own eyes, I think it will not be wise to linger in this house for long," Jamal warned. "We should be on our way while the night is yet young."

The Assassin ignored his recommendation for the moment. "And the mercenary?" she asked tightly. "What of Jared, man?" she demanded anxiously.

Jamal merely shook his head, having no comfort to offer. "We saw the last of him inside Malik's harem. Though I did not see him go down, there was no way he could have escaped and still managed to hold off our pursuers as long as he did." He paused delicately before dealing the death blow to her lingering hopes.

"As I came in, our friend the innkeeper told me he had heard worse tidings yet. Now brace yourself, my brave one," the eunuch cautioned.

"Just *tell* me, damn your eyes!" Isabeau cursed her old friend, ignoring Zahra's flinch as the girl cowered in her embrace. "Tell me the worst of it, Jamal." She begged more softly this time.

The harem master did as he was bid, though with a heavy heart. "A captured Frankish warrior is apparently to be the main attraction at a banquet held in honor of the sultan's nephew tonight," he confessed in his high, strained tenor. "A banquet at the palace of none other than our enemy. Malik plans to display the Black Lion before all, to show how he deals with those who would try to steal what is his.

"Of course," the eunuch finished in a voice marked by weary irony, "the emir has no plans to announce that the mercenary was successful in his quest to liberate his favorite possession—Zahra. He hunts privately for her, I am afraid. And now for me as well."

In her arms, Zahra shuddered with remembered disgust, burrowing deeper into her adopted sister's embrace. But the Assassin's mind was already ranging far ahead.

Isabeau did not ask if Jamal had known of Jared's intent to render her useless to their mission beforehand. She was not sure she could contain the rush of fury sure to come over her if the eunuch confirmed their conspiracy! Nor could she afford to feel anger toward the mercenary just now—not if she wanted to save him from the certain death that awaited. Afterward, if they both lived, there would be enough time for recriminations, time to deal with the consequences of his loving betrayal and unasked-for sacrifice. But Isabeau did not truly believe that time would come for them, even as she began to make her plans.

"What are we to do?" Zahra begged softly, once again looking to the older girl for counsel as she had done so many times in their youth.

Isabeau's heart tightened around a hopeless ache. "I'll take care of it," was all she said. "You and Jamal just concentrate on getting safely out of the city."

"But what can you do, against so many? Oh, Isabeau, I am afraid for you! I never meant to drag you into my troubles like this—"

"I'll take *care* of it, I said!" the Shadow Hunter repeated again, more sharply than she intended. She squeezed the girl tighter than ever then in remorse, clinging to her and kissing her repeatedly in gratitude for the gift of her freedom which Jared had given her. In returning Zahra to her arms at the risk of his own life, Jared had given her all she had ever asked for and more.

Now it was time for the Assassin to repay her beloved for his noble act. Struggling to rise from the couch after giving her adopted sister one final hug, she swayed and then stood up more steadily upon her own two feet. She must leave at once if she was to make her uninvited appearance at the banquet . . .

Had she turned back to see it as she strode toward the
door, Isabeau would have been shocked to see how Zahra's
expression mirrored the grim resolve on her own face. But
she never did look back. The Assassin was determined to
barter for her beloved with the only currency she had to
offer.

Her life.

CHAPTER TWENTY-FOUR

The octagonal pink marble banquet hall at Malik al-Fayed's new palace in Damascus was rich with the smell of fine perfumes, loud with laughter, and bright with smokeless torches that shed flickering light across the features of all who feasted there.

All except those of the infamous Shadow Hunter, of course.

Clad in the snow-white robes of an Assassin on a suicide mission, her face covered by the veil she had grown to hate, Isabeau's features remained concealed from view as she stood in the shadows from whence she had claimed her title, waiting and watching for the right moment to strike. Before she could claim vengeance upon the one who had dared to steal her beloved Black Lion from her, she must locate the mercenary first, for the Assassin's whole plan hinged upon her ability to clear a space long enough for Jared to walk out of these hellish festivities freely.

From her place in the recesses beneath the marble-cased arch of one of the eight airy entrances to the hall, an entrance used by servers from the kitchens too harried to notice one of their kind lingering idly by, she witnessed all that went on within with rising hatred and determination. Malik had obviously planned this celebration long ago—perhaps even before he'd arrived in Damascus. To go to such lengths to impress his guests, he must believe himself to be at the pinnacle of a long and ambitious career of political machinations and favor-currying.

Tonight, she decided, he would learn differently. He would not long enjoy this hedonistic affair.

Frankincense, aloe, camphor, and ambergris all competed to perfume the air for the guests' delight, while vessels of gold and silver containing rosewater for washing the hands and face glinted richly in the torchlight. In addition to the innocuous sherbets and ciders in some people's cups, the "daughters of the vine" were also in full attendance, Isabeau judged, to look at the obviously wine-flushed faces of the revelers.

Sanctimonious bastards, she thought in contempt. Many of these same patricians and potentates would wake up tomorrow with aching skulls to return to their places as judges, generals, and scholars of Islamic law, condemning the lower classes for this same sort of behavior they'd enjoyed the night before. Others, she knew, would exhort long-suffering wives to virtue when they returned home at the end of the night, after cavorting shamelessly themselves with the dancers, singers, and other, more dubious "entertainers" present at this gathering. There were certainly enough of them for the taking.

Dozens of barely veiled, scantily clad female singers and instrumentalists lined the walls behind the recumbent guests, playing listlessly upon lute, tambourine, and the kanun (a stringed instrument resembling a harp), as well as oboe and flute, while dancers whirled more energetically to the music and acrobats tumbled nearly naked for the pleasure of their audience. Some of the women danced about the graceful pillars that held up the domed ceiling, making a game of chasing one another round the fluted columns. One pillar in particular, the Assassin noted, was receiving particular attention, though she could not see through the cavorting bodies what object it was they clustered about.

Isabeau tore her attention away from the dancers for the moment, focusing upon the two powerful men at the center of this gathering instead. The sultan's nephew, al-Adil, she saw, reclined in the place of honor beside the emir, who hosted this party for him. His corpulent figure, lolling on the velvet couch provided, was not disguised by the rich fabrics he wore or the jewel-encrusted turban crowning his head. Sweat beaded his forehead as he reached out crudely to grab the trailing scarf of one of the dancers twirling by, pulling her off balance and onto his lap. He stuffed a fat fig into her open mouth and laughed uproariously as she gagged. At his side, Malik, resplendent himself in robes of raw silk and gold, looked on dispassionately, and Isabeau was surprised to see his attention was not glued as usual upon the female entertainers who graced his party, but on something else instead.

No, Isabeau corrected herself sickly, following the direction of his gaze. Some*one* else—the same someone who had been drawing all the attention of the entertainers. At first glance, catching sight of the gaudy costume only, she thought it was another of the emir's women, chained to the pillar at the center of the gathering in one of al-Fayed's perverse pleasure games. But as one of the acrobats flipped out of her way, baring the unfortunate prisoner to the Assassin's gaze, she saw the truth.

Isabeau flew into a rage.

In the midst of all the revelry, bound and beaten, her proud Black Lion had been displayed with deliberate mockery for the amusement of the emir's guests. *Displayed as a woman.* Decked out like some tawdry spectacle for an evening's delight, they had dressed him, Isabeau saw through the red haze of her fury, in the scanty costume of one of Malik's concubines. But even beneath the bloodstained veil and gauzy trousers, the beaded top and belled anklets shoved over his big feet above the iron shackles that held him to the pillar, her beloved remained all man. Jared de Navarre, she thought, was heart-stirringly handsome, possessed of an innate dignity no captor could steal though he tried a dozen derisive disguises.

She would have killed Malik for this affront alone, she vowed. But he deserved the death he would receive this night for far more than just this latest disgraceful deed. And as the Shadow Hunter watched a new phase of the festivities begin, she knew exactly how she would deliver it to him.

Servants were coming and going throughout the busy marble hall, ignored as slaves customarily were, except for the startlingly attired few who had now begun to approach the emir and his guest of honor, al-Adil. Each was carrying a covered dish. And each, she saw, wore a different-colored costume. This would give her the perfect opening to approach . . .

"Ah, about time!" cried al-Fayed in delight, gesturing grandly. At his shout and waving arms, the level of noise in the crowded chamber abruptly lessened, and all eyes focused on him. Those invited to attend the revelries began to sit up and take notice.

Just as he likes it, that son of a swine, Isabeau thought, ready to make her move.

"And now, dear guests, to thank the man who has so honored us with his presence here tonight," Malik al-Fayed said fawningly, "we have prepared a special series of delicacies to tempt his royal appetite—treats fit to tempt the tongue of a sultan!" he enthused, alluding to al-Adil's hopes to become the next ruler of the Abbasid Empire after his aging uncle passed away. "Each dish has been lovingly prepared by the hands of the bearer, who wears a costume designed to complement his cuisine. See if you can guess what they serve!" The emir chuckled at his own clever contrivance, and the guests laughed along as they followed the direction of his flourishing gesture and saw a series of slaves coming into the room in single file, each dressed in a different color.

There was a woman clad in scarlet and saffron, carrying a covered dish of delicately prepared rice steeped with the costly spice. There were murmurs of appreciation from the crowd for her colorful costume, and the dish that matched it perfectly.

There was a willowy boy, scantily dressed to resemble a tree with a costume built mainly of strategically placed leaves and almond flowers. He bore a dish of the candied nuts, which he revealed with a flourish before the amused al-Adil and the emir who sat beside him. Scattered chuckles and a few lewd invitations trailed the handsome youth as he sprinted back toward the kitchens.

There was a man dressed like a songbird in full-feathered regalia, bearing a dish of braised larks' tongues for the guest of honor's delectation. This got an even bigger laugh from the assembled throng.

There were young girls bearing lamb upon a platter, dressed in fluffy fleece with pinned-on tails that made the guests laugh and "baa" teasingly to entice the charming, barely nubile females to their sides.

And then, after a pause, there was one final server. The crowd hushed expectantly, trying to guess what this white-clad, silent figure in the veil represented. Perhaps he brought some frozen delight, a cone of flavored snow from the mountains to quench a parched reveler's thirst?

Even the emir did not seem sure. The musicians faltered to a stop, intrigued like all the rest, and the gamboling dancers and acrobats halted where they were as well, sensing some exciting surprise about to be revealed. Even their game of teasing the bound Frankish prisoner paled before this mystery, and the breathless women all turned their backs on their handsome captive's position to see what was going on across the hall, curiosity lighting their flushed faces. The anticipation in the banquet chamber was almost palpable; a fact which the emir seemed to relish, though his eyes flicked back and forth with patent incomprehension between the approaching slave and the door to the kitchens from whence he'd emerged.

The ghostly, white-shrouded figure glided up to the raised dais near the center of the room where the emir and the guest he meant to flatter reclined. This mysterious slave ignored the chained mercenary who had been placed a few yards away opposite the two men for them to mock as they ate, and focused instead only on the recipients of the offering. In the servant's hands was a silver dish like all the rest, covered with a chased-silver dome so that no one could see what lay inside. The figure came to a halt before the two men, and every breath in the hall was held. Then, in the silence, the server calmly lifted the dome off the dish.

Inside lay a single, perfect white rose.

Murmurs of confusion and consternation began to erupt

around the hall. Who was this strangely costumed man, and what was the meaning of his odd gift? Was this perhaps some new confection spun of sugar to tempt the jaded sultan's nephew? Many began to remark that the slave's clothes looked like the plain white shroud in which the dead were buried, and others commented that the flower he proffered was known to be the symbol of one very unpleasant renegade killer . . . Speculation turned to unease in the perfumed hall.

"Well, go on, man," the emir blustered to the slave when the veiled server made no move to present the rose to his guest of honor. "Give it to him."

"It is not intended for him, Malik al-Fayed," rasped a husky voice. "This gift is meant only for *you*."

Sudden comprehension widened the emir's eyes. The white robes, such as those worn by the notorious Assassins when they came to claim their victims . . . the white rose that was the special calling card of the one Assassin they all feared more than the rest . . . Everything came together at last in the emir's drink-addled brain. He felt his very loins recoil in reaction as the truth came home. "Sayyad al-Zul," he whispered in terror. What could the fiend want?

Behind him, still chained to the central pillar of the hall in disgraceful drag, the emir's prisoner was heard to smother a gasp of his own.

The stunned guests echoed the name throughout the hall, and fear spread among them like waves of sound, rippling through everything and everyone in the palace. The convivial mood of the soused and spoiled guests fled as if it had never been, for everyone here suddenly knew what the white rose meant as well as did its recipient. An Assassin was in their midst. And when an Assassin came to a gathering, he did not leave without taking the life of the one he had targeted.

Their host was a dead man.

The deadly "server" threw down the platter in contempt, letting the silver dish clatter and reverberate against the polished marble of the floor. The rose landed at the terrified emir's feet, one lone petal drifting more slowly down through the air after it. All eyes followed its progress, and so did not catch the blurry movement of the Assassin's hand as a dagger appeared as if by magic within it. It had leveled itself at al-Fayed's throat before the emir could so much as swallow. If he tried to call for his guards, he'd be dead before they could ever hope to reach his side.

"Close," rasped the killer into the shocked stillness. "But try another guess."

And Isabeau slowly pulled off the veiled headpiece that had hidden her identity. Blond curls spilled down her shapeless robes and caught the torchlight in skeins of silver and gold. Her blue eyes flashed with fury as she faced down her longtime enemy and one-time oppressor. A wave of gasps filled the hall.

"*Gulbayez!*" Malik choked in disbelief.

CHAPTER TWENTY-FIVE

The Shadow Hunter waited for the tumult to die down, ignoring with steely fortitude Jared's anguished cry of denial when she revealed her identity. She blotted out the other shouts and cries from those around her much more easily, not caring about anyone's feelings but her betrothed's, though she heard words like *sacrilege* and *blasphemy* floating through the aghast crowd. Let these people roil and froth at the mouth with outrage at a woman daring to defy male convention if they liked. There was only one man whose good opinion *she* longed for. The renegade focused all her energies on his captor, determined to set Jared free.

"Yes. 'Tis I, you filthy pig," Isabeau stated simply. "Though I no longer go by that slave's name, I was once the woman you kept. You have something I want, al-Fayed. I will leave with it, or I will leave with your life." Despite her flat tone, her eyes fairly crackled with ferocious intensity. Surprise would only help her so long, the Assassin knew, before someone in this hall came to their senses and realized she was only one against many. Of course, to succeed with the plan she'd hatched to free her lover, she didn't need an army, for Isabeau was grimly sure only one of them would be walking out of here alive tonight.

The Prophet knew she'd come in here under that assumption. But little as she wanted to die now, when for the first time she had so very much for which to live, the Assassin would never regret making the necessary sacrifice for Jared. And at least she would be taking her enemy with her into hell, no matter what else chanced to pass tonight. That was some consolation—for really, the death of one's nemesis was all an Assassin trained by the Old Man of the Mountain ever hoped to accomplish. Isabeau stared Malik evenly in the eye, willing him to see her determination, her absolute willingness—nay, eagerness!—to taste his hot blood upon her cold steel.

He seemed to get the idea, swallowing heavily so that her blade nicked his throat, then flinching as the blood rivulets ran down his neck. Still, she could tell he was having difficulty putting together the picture of the slave he had subjugated with the masterful renegade who threatened him now, his masculine ego revolting at the notion of being held at bay by a mere woman, even as Sayyad al-Zul's deadly reputation bade him be wary indeed.

Others in the hall seemed equally unsure what to do, milling about in confusion without seeming able to decide to run for help or stay and watch the spectacle. Isabeau was counting on that uncertainty to keep them paralyzed a little while longer.

"What . . . do you want?" Malik ventured cautiously.

Isabeau jerked her head toward the pillar behind her, where the Black Lion strained against his chains, his torn, ridiculous finery failing to humble the proud warrior. "Him," she said. "I want the mercenary freed at once, and allowed to walk out of here unmolested."

Behind her, Jared shouted his objection to this. "No, Isabeau! Don't do this—not for me. *Run,* beloved! Run while there's yet a chance!"

Cleverly, he had used their native *langue d'oc,* so that no one else in the vaulted chamber would understand their exchange.

The Assassin flinched visibly at the sound of her lover's urgent voice and his use of the language of their youth. Yet though she stiffened, understanding full well, she did not obey his harsh order. Nor did she turn to look at him. She addressed herself only to the emir. "You heard me, al-Fayed. Release him, or you die."

Fury took over in the perverted man who had been her master, winning out over caution. The emir laughed harshly, daring her knife point as he snapped, "Is he your lover then, Gulbayez? Do you spread your legs for him each night as Zahra did for me when you were too flawed to perform the duty of a true woman?"

The thin line of blood grew wider as the Assassin's razor-sharp blade dug deeper into his flesh, warning him not to push her. Isabeau dared a quick glance about the hall, seeing with relief the guests still frozen motionless on their couches, but noting with dismay the number of the emir's Mamluk guard who now crowded each of the eight entrances, just waiting for a chance to get her away from her hostage. She would never get out of here alive. But as long as there was a chance for Jared . . .

"Cease your prattle, swine, and order your men to let the mercenary go!" she demanded.

But the maddened emir was too enraged to heed caution now. "Think you I would *ever* allow your overgrown Frankish lover to walk free while I still have breath in this body?" He pounded his chest with one meaty fist for emphasis. "Not likely, you pale-skinned spawn of a she-demon. I will have you *both* killed!"

"Just me, Malik," Isabeau countered steadily. "You can have the pleasure of my death yourself, if you only let him go. I will surrender peaceably once the Black Lion is safely away." She knew how vulnerable this admission made her, but she saw no other choice.

"Jesus, *no*! Don't do this, little Beau," Jared begged. His voice was hoarse, as if clogged with unshed tears.

At last Isabeau spared him a glance. Her expression was rueful as she shrugged to make light of the sacrifice. "It is already done," she said simply, replying in their own tongue as he had. Her blue eyes begged his understanding for the brief second before they flicked back to settle on the dangerous emir.

But that small distraction had cost them. Malik was able to collect his wits just a bit during their interchange, and now he spat contemptuously at the renegade. "Filthy whore. Take your love talk someplace else before you sicken us all! In fact, why don't you both take it with you—to the grave?" he suggested. No one in the hall dared to laugh at this pale attempt at humor, however.

"I'll take you with me if you kill him," she warned. "Never doubt that, swine."

"I would *rather* die than live with the humiliation of letting your foreign-born lover shame me before all these witnesses, slut," he countered grandly. Malik was well aware of their audience, suspended in shock and disbelief as they were. If he did not prove himself a man before this feminine threat, he could kiss his coveted position as favored courtier to al-Adil farewell. Daring a glance at the sultan's nephew, who had edged away from the confrontation on the dais, he continued in the same vein. "Not even the taste of your heart's blood upon my blade would be enough to convince me to let the mercenary live, after this oh-so-touching display." Smirking, the emir then outlined his opponent's options.

"Leave me alive, Gulbayez, and I will make an example of you both such that lovers all across Arabia will vow chastity for a hundred years upon seeing it. Kill me, and my guard will still cut you both down before my corpse is cold. And believe me, slut, what they would do to you in revenge for slaying their master would make *my* vengeance look kind." Malik's smile was a hideous parody of humor. "Naturally, I would prefer you choose the former, not wanting to miss participating in your just demise; but I am not afraid to face the latter," he claimed. "The only way to live, my foolish White Rose, is to submit yourself to me, here and now, to grovel at my feet while you watch your lover die."

He wasn't bluffing. A wave of despair washed over Isabeau, followed by one of resignation. Malik al-Fayed was many things—a cruel, malicious sadist foremost among them, but he was not a coward. And she knew his pride would never stand for being bested by a woman. Still, she'd had no choice but to reveal herself as such, because she could not have hoped to get Jared out of the palace alive if she had simply killed al-Fayed in the guise of Sayyad al-

Zul. As Malik had so gleefully threatened, the Mamluks would have cut them both down before they'd so much as reached the doors. Isabeau's only hope of saving her beloved's life had been to bargain with the monster who had tormented her nightmares for so many years. Yet Malik seemed unwilling even to listen to her terms. This was what she had feared when she'd come here—that the emir would not accept her sacrifice, that he would instead demand both their lives in trade for his. Yet she had prepared for this eventuality as well. She still had one thing left with which to bargain. Determination stiffened the Assassin's spine. Lowering the blade deliberately, she sighed with weariness. "Stay your hand, al-Fayed. There is still another way."

"Oh?" he asked with exaggerated surprise. The emir was beginning to enjoy the theatrical aspects of their standoff now that he'd convinced himself he had the Assassin cornered. He made his next declaration for the benefit of their captive audience. "Do tell me, little slut, what could give me greater pleasure than your long, painfully protracted death?"

But the renegade upstaged him again.

In answer, Isabeau simply stepped out of her shapeless overrobe.

The collective inhalation of the crowd would have been comical in other circumstances. For beneath the white mantle, the Assassin wore a costume that seemed composed entirely of silver spangles, held together here and there with wisps of iridescent gauze. For a moment there was absolute silence in the hall. Then the emir's startled burst of laughter rang forth, echoing eerily among the marble pillars. It nearly drowned out the mercenary's howl of impotent rage as well, and the desperate stream of words that followed it.

"Don't do this, Isabeau! It isn't worth it, beloved," Jared pleaded hoarsely. "Better we die together than that I should live a day after this alone! Do you hear me, Isabeau? Don't sacrifice yourself this way. I cannot live without you anyway, so there is no sense in giving this madman what he wants. It will do no good, you hear?"

Yet though the Assassin heard her lover all too clearly, she could not obey him. *He will learn to live without me,* she told herself sadly. And after this humiliating affair, he would probably be glad to do so, once he came to his senses.

Both the former harem slave and the emir ignored the Black Lion's outburst. Gazes locked on one another now, Malik grinned hugely while he ran his black eyes over her nearly naked form. The renegade merely raised her chin proudly, not flinching from his regard. She knew her scanty costume ought to please him well enough—she had worn such outfits many times in the past, when he had required her to dance during his intimate little evenings with her and Zahra. This one ought to please his twisted tastes.

"Oh, you do know what I like, don't you, little whore?" he drawled. "Will you dance for me then, Gulbayez, as you once used to do?"

"Only for this man's life," the renegade qualified. Her expression was stony as a granite cliff, her eyes hard chips of sapphire ice. "Swear he shall live and I will give you what you want. Otherwise, resign yourself to die." She brandished the dagger once more close to his pulsing artery. "My soul is prepared to make the final journey, Malik al-Fayed. Can you say the same of yours?"

The emir shrugged off the Assassin's taunting question, his eyes refusing to meet hers with evident unease. Yet he was eager to exert control again over this upstart woman who had dared to threaten him in his moment of triumph. After the loss of his other fair-haired favorite this afternoon, he thought, it only seemed just and proper that the White Rose should fill his precious jewel's place. After all, Zahra had filled *hers* for many years, had she not? Filled it while he had burned impotently for the one he could not have. Now he again had his defiant, proud White Rose beneath his thumb, and there was no one to stop him from taking what he wanted this time! Not even the eunuch Jamal's mystical warnings of kismet and disaster could change his mind now—if they had not been just another ruse meant to keep him from this overly aggressive woman's bed in the first place, as he'd begun to suspect. The eunuch's treachery today had cast a pall on all his claims over the years. Now nothing would keep him from enjoying Gulbayez, right here in front of all these witnesses!

"It is agreed, my silver-haired slut," cried al-Fayed. "I will accept your little bargain. You will dance, and then you will die. Musicians!" he called. "Play something appropriate for the Dance of the Seven Veils." The emir ignored the warning look the sultan's nephew threw him then, brushing aside his quick whispering suggestion that perhaps this was not the most seemly time or place for such affairs. Al-Fayed was determined to see this challenge, begun publicly, ended the same way, with himself coming out on top. Once he'd subjugated the upstart woman and slain her lover, everyone would see his prowess, admire his firm action in the face of such blatant feminine waywardness. "Well? Go on," he shouted when no one made a move to touch their instruments. Foam flew from his mouth. "Play!"

"Free the mercenary first," the Assassin insisted, not moving as the first chords of the lute began tentatively in the deafening silence of the banquet hall. She thought despairingly that she could not stand it if Jared were to witness this ultimate humiliation, this submission to Malik al-Fayed that was more truly a repudiation of all the renegade Assassin had stood for these last seven years. The rest of the world could watch with eyes wide open for all she cared—but not her beloved Black Lion! After all they had fought through together, all they had meant to each other, it was unbearable to the renegade that he should see her reduced to this humbling position before her old master. But her triumphant foe would not allow her to keep even this small bit of dignity.

"Not a chance, slut," Malik denied her. "I want your lover to watch you prance and strut for me before he slinks off with your blood on his hands and the knowledge that your last act served the pleasure of another man. Only then will the Frank go free," he promised gleefully. "Now drop your blade and dance for me, Gulbayez!"

She must do as he bade, Isabeau knew. Surely, Malik would not go back on a promise made before all these witnesses! It was her only hope to save her betrothed. Yet if she did this, she would never be able to meet that honest amber gaze of Jared's again. It was as well that Malik intended to kill her when this ordeal was done, the renegade thought, for after this degradation, she could not imagine Jared ever being able to stand taking her in his arms again, and she could not live with the idea of his revulsion. This act must be her last farewell to the lover who had taught her everything she knew about tenderness between a man and a woman. Never after could she hold her head up and be the woman the Black Lion had wanted for his bride. Death, Isabeau thought in sorrow, was the only balm that could hope to dull that pain.

The Assassin's knife clattered to the cold stone at her feet, dropped from her nerveless hand as the emir demanded. But as Isabeau hung her head and composed her trembling limbs into some semblance of a dancer's pose, she knew she would not be dancing for Malik, no matter what he ordered. *No,* she resolved. *I will dance solely for Jared; the only man I have ever loved.*

The decision gave her the strength to lift her chin, stare directly into her lover's anguished amber eyes, and will him to see the love she bore him. "For you," she breathed on a mere wisp of sound. *Goodbye,* she thought silently.

Then she began to dance before the rapt audience.

CHAPTER TWENTY-SIX

By the time Isabeau finished, there remained not a dry eye in the hall.

When the renegade collapsed to her knees at the climax of the dance, her silver costume and her golden hair swirling to a halt about her body a moment later, the only sounds in the pink marble dome were those of her rapid, panting breath, and the crystals of her skirts clicking softly together in counterpoint.

No one whistled or clapped. No one leered at the nearly naked woman, vulnerable and exposed though she was. It was as if Isabeau had cast a spell upon her audience.

What she had done to the dance normally reserved for erotic seduction had elevated it to the level of pure, heartfelt lovemaking; so expressive it was awe-inspiring, so courageous it took the breath away. The graceful, twining gestures of her arms had told the story of a lover's longing, while the lithe, leaping steps of her feet had swept her into their hearts, even as they carried her effortlessly across the floor. Even the shimmy of her breasts, the slow undulations of her belly, and the sway of her slender hips had spoken of a love so chaste and true it shamed those who would have ogled her figure into a more respectful glance.

Every person in that room felt as if she had just taken their most intense fantasy and given it breath, as if she had lived their most passionate dream right along with them. Yet though each spectator took something of true love away from Isabeau's performance, there was no mistaking the one man for whom she felt this transcendent affection in return. Her every move had been made for him; each slightest gesture and glance, each supple twist and contortion of her lissome figure meant as a gift for that one man alone, though she'd performed them in a room packed full with strangers.

The Black Lion was weeping quietly by the time his beloved was done, unashamedly letting the tears run down his rugged features. He knew what she'd expressed to him with this bold display, and he only hoped he would somehow, someday, have the chance to say it back to her—unlikely as that seemed in their present circumstances. Yet how he could ever adequately express the depths of his love and admiration for Isabeau de Lyon, the mercenary couldn't imagine. It filled him past expression, suffusing him with such ineffable tenderness of spirit, such joy, he thought perhaps they'd died already, and despite the strange surroundings, that they had reached a Paradise of their own through the unique power of their singular bond.

The man who had tried so hard to humiliate his betrothed had failed, Jared thought proudly. She was more marvelous to his eyes than ever before.

Everyone here agreed with his assessment, he knew—except perhaps for the emir himself. The audience had made no mistake about Isabeau's actions in the dance, or the true meaning behind them. Through her courageous, soul-baring performance, Malik had been shamed in his moment of greatest triumph. In trying to degrade his former slave, he had only made himself look petty instead. The enraged emir, his face purple above his elaborately oiled beard and his black eyes bulging with wrath, knew it full well, Jared guessed, though he pretended otherwise.

Malik began to clap sardonically.

The woman at his feet, weaponless now and with her head bowed modestly, shuddered once at the sound but did not move. When the last echoes of his ridicule had faded from the vaulted hall, she spoke at last, her voice low but steady. "I have fulfilled my part of the bargain," she announced. "Now fulfill yours. Release the Black Lion, Malik!" she demanded.

The one-time Assassin spoke through the veil of her hair, still not raising her gaze to look about her. In truth, Isabeau was simply too ashamed to look up!

She had not seen herself as the others had seen her, did

not know what they thought, nor feel the admiration her audience bore her. She only knew she had abased herself utterly in order to save Jared, despite the fact that he had begged her not to do it. He must be burning with shame before all these witnesses, she thought, cringing mentally at the notion. One quick glance at his mortified face before she'd collapsed, one look at the tears of humiliation springing from his eyes, had been enough to convince her. He must be furious, absolutely abhorring her indecent behavior. For a female to put on such a display in public—surely not even the women of the West ever did such things!

She was nothing like he must have wished his little Lady Isabeau de Lyon would be—after all, had her betrothed not tried to keep her away from the fight today by means of the doctor's potion? That showed her, as if she'd needed further proof to make it clear, that Jared did not truly want a woman like her for his wife, despite the torrid bliss of their fierce lovemaking and the bond of their long-interrupted love. How *could* he want to marry a woman who knew no shame or propriety, no decency or dignity, only the necessity of fighting for the ones she loved? The Assassin wanted to die as this realization hit her. *Luckily,* she thought, *I soon will.*

Isabeau could not meet Jared's gaze again now that she had fulfilled Malik's wish, though she could feel his own eyes burning into her from behind the curtain of her hair. She was afraid she might see her true worth reflected in their amber depths after this degradation—a worth which was next to nothing.

For she was only a pleasure slave after all, it seemed. Whether they called her Shadow Hunter or White Rose, Isabeau was still valued most for her body, not the fiercely loyal heart that powered it. Nothing she had done in all this time had changed it, she thought bitterly, not all her struggles or her sacrifices. She would still die a slave, subject to a man she hated while the one that she loved was forced to witness her humiliation. Yet it would all be worth it if she could give Jared back his life, Isabeau thought achingly. Malik would be forced to honor his promise—given before all these witnesses—now that she had fulfilled her part of their distasteful agreement.

"Release the mercenary," she demanded again.

But al-Fayed was not in a mood to cooperate, it seemed; witnesses or no witnesses. And he was furious at how she had bested him yet again—just as she always had in the past. "I give the orders here, woman!" he roared. "Not you. And this is one command it gives me great pleasure to deliver." The emir was fairly licking his lips with relish as he prepared to deliver the final betrayal. He beckoned to the hulking guards still lingering uncertainly in the doorways. "Kill the infidel!"

Before the Assassin could do anything to prevent it, a blow to the back of the knees sent the Black Lion heavily to the floor as he was struck by one of the Mamluks. The man then growled, "Bow before your executioner, infidel dog!" and sent a mail-gauntleted fist crashing down hard on the side of the mercenary's head. She saw Jared grunt in obvious agony as he was laid out to the length of his chains upon the marble floor.

"No!" Isabeau shrieked her objection even as the remaining Mamluk guards began to move purposefully toward the captive mercenary. Her head came up and her eyes blazed at the deceitful emir, but it was from another quarter that the next denial came.

"No," said a different voice that came from behind the dais—a stony, determined voice that was nonetheless recognizably feminine.

And even as Isabeau dove for her knife where it had been kicked out of reach across the floor, she saw a blossoming fount of red erupting from the throat of the emir, the quick flash of a curving blade cutting across it with unhesitating precision. Shocked, Isabeau watched as Malik half rose, clutching his torn throat and attempting to speak through severed vocal cords, then fell to his knees heavily as the lifeblood began to drain rapidly from his body to rain upon his rich golden robes. Half lying herself upon the cold marble floor, the renegade looked on in incomprehension as a slight figure rose up behind the dying man, the wickedly curved knife blade clutched in her small fist.

"Only one man dies tonight," the lilting voice declared. Peeling back the flowing veil and pearl-beaded turban that had disguised her as one of the musicians, Zahra stood up proudly before her stunned sister, meeting her gaze fearlessly.

"It was *my* right to take his life, Isabeau," she claimed, a trifle defiantly. "I took the punishments meant for you all these years upon my own shoulders—and I was glad to do it, if it meant you were spared. But it is only fair, then, that I should also take your vengeance, sister. This I have done tonight." Her eyes swept the stunned congregation, their blue fire flashing wildly—almost madly.

"No woman should have to endure the terrors this man inflicted upon me and the other women in his keeping," she declared in a ringing voice. "No man should ever treat his chattel in the manner in which we were treated. A dog deserves better handling than we received! And just as a whipped dog will rise up to bite the master who torments him, I have risen to put an end to this man's twisted amusements for the sake of every woman who ever suffered at his hands." Zahra's voice resonated with satisfaction as she made her final pronouncement. "The reign of al-Fayed is *over*."

The Jewel of Malik's harem had claimed a long-awaited retribution.

To Jared, his head swimming from the tremendous clout the Mamluk soldier had just given him, the whole scene became like some surreal dream. One moment he was watching his beloved dance like the veriest angel, the next a woman who could have been her twin had cut down the man who held them all prisoner. *Zahra?* he thought wonderingly. That scared little creature he'd met this afternoon was the same magnificent amazon who'd just slain Malik al-Fayed? Jared tried to take in the knowledge that the emir was no longer a threat, but all he could hear was the man's last words. *Kill the infidel* . . .

The word *infidel* was still ringing in the Black Lion's head, in fact, even as an older, more deeply rooted memory flashed back at him. *Unfiddles,* he thought muzzily. His little Beau had called the nameless horde of Saracens that once, in ignorance. But now there were unfiddles everywhere, and other unexpected combatants as well . . .

Fighters were breaking into the hall from all sides, covering the exits and capturing the guards clustered there before they could even raise their weapons in self-defense. The mercenary recognized with disbelief his own men swarming into the room, wondering if he was seeing aright. Had they not been left behind in remotest Persia, in the mountains along with the Assassin's *fidai'in*? Yet here the bandits were as well, he marveled, shaking his head as if to clear it of the vision. All in white as their mistress had been, they streamed inside the hall and took it over effortlessly. The eunuch Jamal had arrived with them as well, Jared saw, striding confidently through the space the others had cleared in the crowd, as did his own second in command, the diminutive Big Pierre.

If it was possible to turn a cartwheel sarcastically, that was exactly what the dwarf who tumbled into the chamber did, mocking the chastened acrobats who now huddled in close groups about the room with the other entertainers, clinging to each other for comfort. As the grinning lieutenant swaggered up to Jared and began to work on his shackles, the mercenary recognized Rashid and a few of the other taciturn bandits as well, working in perfect concert with his own lion's Pride as they subdued every last bit of rebellion among the emir's guests and guards.

He looked about for Isabeau, saw her and Zahra hugging one another before the dais, seeming as confused and disbelieving as he was, but thankfully—thankfully!—still safe for the moment. Needing desperately to get to his beloved, Jared yanked at his chains.

"Come *on*, Pierre," he urged. "Get these blasted things off me before I tan your tiny hide for boot leather!"

The dwarf cursed his impatience. "Remain still then another minute, you great yowling lout, while I work on these tricky iron locks. I can see you're eager to get to your 'Holy Grail' over there," he said sarcastically, with a nod for the scantily clad Isabeau. This was his way of telling his commander he'd finally figured out the other man's cryptic comment, as he clearly expected the Black Lion to understand. "But I only brought along a few of my picks, so you'll have to hold your water another few seconds!" he growled irritably. "And by the way, you *could* show a little appreciation for the timely entrance we just made. It wasn't easy, you know, finding you and that lunatic Assassin you love!"

This the mercenary did with ill will. "Thank you," he said absently, staring anxiously over at his betrothed while he waited for the dwarf to free his bonds. She still hadn't looked back at him. What was wrong with Isabeau? After the passionate, albeit silent declaration she had just made of her love for him, why was she avoiding his gaze now? After her extraordinary dance to save his life just minutes ago, all the mercenary could think of was grabbing Isabeau up in his arms and holding her in his grateful embrace for at least a decade or two.

"Don't thank me, O snappish Black Lion," the little lieutenant corrected facetiously. "Thank *him*." Pierre pointed. "He's the one who found us freezing our asses off crossing the half-blocked passes of the Elburz Mountains near Alamut, and led us unerringly here to find you today. Found that eunuch your woman likes so much too, hiding at some strange little inn on the outskirts of town tonight, and brought us all here together."

The mercenary captain's eyes followed the direction of his lieutenant's stubby finger past his betrothed and her adopted sister, up to the platform where their slain enemy lay. And there, strangest of all, had appeared yet another figure clad in white. Jared stared in wonder at the man as his bonds fell free.

Out of nowhere, seemingly, the fellow had appeared in the center of the gathering, upon the dais where the dead emir lay and the sultan's fat nephew still cowered in fright upon his velvet divan. This new arrival seemed to be waiting for silence to fall over the crowd, which it did with alacrity once he swept his penetrating gaze about the hall.

Ancient beyond reckoning, his white beard flowing down his chest nearly to his waist, this stooped and fragile figure still commanded instant respect. At his glance, the renegade fell back to her knees from where she had risen to clasp Zahra to her breast, and made respectful obeisance. Jamal ad-Din, who had come to stand at her side, did the same. And so did Zahra, dropping her knife at last and touching her bloodstained hands repeatedly to her forehead as she quickly knelt before him.

The old man seemed to take it as his due. He kicked the dead man at his feet contemptuously, rolling him over to the floor below the raised platform with a thump. Then he looked around pleasantly at the assembled group.

"Greetings, honored guests," the master of Alamut said genially. "Do not be alarmed at what you have seen this evening. This is only justice being done. The little one over there"—and he nodded at the trembling Zahra—"is correct in what she says. A great wrong has been righted here to-night in the killing of this . . . abomination of an emir. As a humble student of the *Qur'an* all my life, I see no sin in what this young female has done," proclaimed the widely feared religious cult leader.

Though many might pronounce him a zealot, a rabid fundamentalist Shiite who interpreted the precepts of Islam with far greater strictness than the more populous Sunni Muslims did, no one would dispute that this dangerous man was indeed a great scholar of *Qur'anic* law. The Old Man of the Mountain was many things—a ruthless killer among them—but no one could claim he did not know his Scriptures.

"For after all," he went on in a tone of utmost reasonability, "does the *Qur'an* not say, 'But force not your young wives to prostitutions when they desire chastity'? Clearly the deceased emir disobeyed this holy injunction with his actions tonight. Yet that is just the beginning. For elsewhere, does our holy Prophet not exhort us, 'O you who believe! You are forbidden to inherit women against their will. Nor should you treat them with harshness . . . On the contrary live with them on a footing of kindness and equity . . . ' " The master of Alamut shook his head reprovingly. "Malik al-Fayed showed no kindness to those helpless females under his protection, no equity in all the days of his rule."

The ancient suras of the *Qur'an* flowed mellifluously from the Old Man's tongue as he continued to reproach his captive audience with these pointed reminders of how the Prophet had enjoined them to behave. The wine-soused guests grew shamed, those who were immodestly dressed moved to cover themselves, and the rest bowed their heads in repentance. Even al-Adil, a notorious hedonist, seemed to shrink before this strange yet magnetic teacher.

"Again, Muhammad reveals to us his wisdom in the following exhortation: 'O mankind! Reverence your Guardian-Lord, who created you from a single person; created, of like nature, his mate, and from this pair scattered like seeds countless men and women. Reverence Allah . . . and reverence the wombs that bore you; for Allah ever watches over you.' " The deadly old Assassin smiled beatifically, as if unaware of the irony of invoking his God's name when he had sent so many people to meet their creator in Paradise himself.

"And did he not *also* say, 'Among my followers, the best of you are they who behave best to their wives'?" the mysterious master of Alamut continued. "By these writings, it is clear our holy Prophet intended that we should respect women as the bearers of life, the vessels for our seed.

Though woman was made to serve man, even a slave deserves to serve with dignity.

"This . . . dog . . . at my feet blasphemed against the sacred Scriptures in these and many other ways," the Shiite religious leader claimed, "and it was my will that he should pay for his crimes. As he liked to persecute women for his pleasure, so I saw it fitting that a woman should be the instrument of Allah's sacred will, that she might more justly prosecute and execute him on behalf of her sisters in Islam. Thus did I set my Shadow Hunter upon him—though it seems this little one has beaten her to the prize," he said, nodding at Zahra with the tiniest of smiles glinting through his beard.

"Perhaps, with the proper training, this exquisite jewel would have made a fine Assassin in her own right. However," he said then, sweeping his gaze across the crowd to enforce his next words. "Let it not be said that I would condone a woman trying to usurp the place of a man in just any circumstance. On the contrary," the Old Man denied. "The time for my Shadow Hunter and her fierce sister to roam free has ended with the termination of their enemy's benighted existence. It would be an affront to all men of good faith were these women to keep up their warlike occupations beyond the point of necessity. Therefore," he proclaimed, turning to Isabeau, "you are an Assassin no longer.

"No more will you fight with the backing of Alamut—and I think you know just how long you would last on your own, should you stand against me in this and seek to continue your renegade ways," the Old Man warned. "But you will not be punished for what you have done today," he proclaimed, once again making sure with his ringing pronouncement that everyone in the hall could hear his tacit approval of the renegade, and confident enough of his power to be sure that no one—not even the sultan's nephew—would dare to countermand his decision.

"Take your sister and the eunuch Jamal and be gone from here, Shadow Hunter. You both have the thanks of

Alamut for your years of service—as does little Zahra, for
her last-minute intervention. Take the Frankish mercenary
with you also if it pleases you," he offered generously,
"though I must say his men have been most anxious to
retrieve him themselves.

"My thanks for your assistance as well this night," he
said graciously to the men of the Black Lion's Pride, where
they clustered at one end of the hall, binding the now helpless Mamluk soldiers securely together. "Though you be
nonbelievers, you fight like Muhammad's true warriors,"
he complimented. Turning away from the renegade and her
associates now that he was so plainly finished with them,
the Master of Alamut faced the waiting *fidai'in*. "Come,
my sons. 'Tis time we were away from this sinful and luxurious place."

Isabeau had barely heard the balance of what her old master
had to say. Overwhelmed by these wildly unforeseen turns
of events, yet anxious to assure herself her beloved was
well now that the danger was over, she turned to face the
Black Lion at last. He was standing not twenty paces away,
and her heart squeezed painfully at the sight of him. Big
Pierre must have found Jared appropriate masculine attire
while they listened to the master speak, she guessed, the
rich tunic and trousers he wore now taken no doubt from
one of the cowed party guests. In his borrowed finery, even
bruised and bleeding from a cut at the corner of his eye
and still rubbing the rawness from his wrists, Isabeau
thought he had never looked finer in her sight.

Amazingly, he seemed to be looking at her now with
every bit of the love he'd ever held in his heart for her
written unashamedly on his face. And oh, how she loved
every inch of that rugged countenance, with its slashing
brows and sensual lips. How she longed to plant kisses of
thanksgiving all over it, and to dig her scarred hands deep
into the rich depths of that glossy auburn hair while she
did so . . . Yet she knew she must never touch Jared de
Navarre again.

Better that she'd died at Malik's hand tonight than that she should be forced to live apart from her beloved ever after this moment, Isabeau thought sorrowfully. Still, that was exactly what she planned to do for the rest of her miserable existence. Her heart ached to spend every minute of the rest of her life never farther from her betrothed than they were from each other right now, but the renegade knew such to be the ultimate in selfishness. After tonight, the former Assassin had no right to claim this faithful, noble warrior for her own. Now that he'd fulfilled his part of the pledge they had made that day in their little canyon haven, Isabeau knew it was time that she fulfilled hers as well.

She'd agreed to think on his gallant proposal, and she'd done little else, waking or sleeping, Isabeau admitted to herself, since the day he had made it. She owed him an answer now. But though it broke her heart to acknowledge it, the renegade knew there could be only one proper response—one honorable response.

No.

If she wanted to thank him in some manner for his years of service, Isabeau knew that the best thing she could do would be to part ways with her lover, to tell him goodbye now. But how could she say her final farewell to the man she loved? And would he even let her? Jared was so determined to do right by her, he might not even take into account his own best interests. If she loved him, the renegade knew, she might have to do that *for* him. "Jared—" she began haltingly.

"Go, Isabeau," he urged. "I'll be right behind you."

She opened her mouth to speak further, then closed it again without a word, the way becoming clear. Her resolve was sure to weaken, she knew, if she was faced with that beloved gaze staring beseechingly into her own much longer. Best make this quick and clean.

Jared might follow, the former Assassin decided, but he would not find her again.

She grabbed Zahra's hand and ran.

CHAPTER TWENTY-SEVEN

Jamal ad-Din was right beside them as the two women fled, his sandals flapping against the tiled floors of the torchlit corridors alongside their smaller shoes. Knowing the palace better than they, he pointed out the way as they went, and they trusted his sure instinct to keep them away from any remaining guards.

A moment later, from behind her, the renegade heard a loud clap, as if of thunder, and saw a flash of brilliant light like lightning striking within the hall. She smelled sulfur and heard gasps from those remaining inside, even as she and her heart's sister ran down the long, labyrinthine hall-ways with their mentor, searching for a way out of the palace. Despite her pounding heart and the exhausting whirl of emotion she'd endured during this long evening, Isabeau felt a faint smile curve her trembling lips.

She could just imagine the shock on the faces of the banquet guests as they peered through the cloud of smoke that had filled the hall to find the Old Man had vanished from their midst without a trace. "Wish he had taught me that trick with the sulfur," she panted to Jamal as they turned a corner and found themselves at a small postern gate. It would have been much easier to disappear behind such a convenient smokescreen than to melt away the way she'd learned to do it!

There was no one to be seen at the gate, the guard apparently having deserted his post to investigate the uproar in the great hall, and so they were able to step out into the street without hindrance. The air felt cool on Isabeau's inexplicably wet cheeks.

"Isabeau—your face! I . . . I've never seen you like this," Zahra blurted in alarm as the three pulled up outside the door to catch their breath and get their bearings. The younger girl stared in amazement. "Are you all right?"

It was at that point that Isabeau realized she was crying. She must have been doing so for some minutes now, it appeared, for her face was quite drenched with tears.

"I . . . don't think so, actually," she stuttered, though she had meant to claim she was fine. Her voice came out strangely polite, remote to her own ears. Her hands and feet were cold as ice. Her body must be in shock from all the tumult she'd gone through tonight, she realized, from waking from her drugged slumber to finding that Jared had traded his life for Zahra's; from confronting her old master to watching him die at the hands of the gentle soul she had always considered too fragile to stand up for herself. And the worst of it was how Jared had been forced to witness her humiliation before all those witnesses—forced to see her true pathetic worth as a woman.

No, she amended then as the tears flowed harder. *The worst of it was how I was forced to leave him behind, without so much as a word of farewell.* Yet, if she didn't keep running now, she would just have to go through the pain of tearing herself away all over again!

The Assassin tried to get moving. All she could think was that Jared must not find her—not here, not like this. Isabeau didn't think she could bear to deal with confronting him, disheveled as she was in her stolen dancer's costume and with the stink of Malik's evil still on her. Yet though she told herself to run, she could not seem to make her limbs obey her. The renegade sat down hard on the cobbled street instead, her legs simply giving out beneath her. She was at the end of her strength, it seemed. She had finally reached the bottom of the well.

The tears began streaking down her cheeks in earnest then, and her slight shoulders shook like leaves in a strong wind. For long moments she could do nothing but heave and sob helplessly in reaction.

The younger girl tried to comfort her. "That man, the Black Lion—Jamal told me he was your betrothed back in France, the boy you used to tell me stories about when we were children in the harem." She looked over to the eunuch,

who nodded confirmation. "He will make this right when
he comes," Zahra said confidently, her experience standing
up to her tormentor obviously having given her new
strength. "He's just on his way, Isabeau, behind us. I can
hear footfalls now."

But the renegade had no intention of waiting for him to
catch up.

"Oh, great Allah, then we must run again!" Isabeau
cried, not noticing the startled expressions of her companions. Though exhausted, the renegade struggled to rise to
her feet once more. But it was already too late.

Jared skidded to a halt at the gate, Big Pierre and the
rest of his troop just paces behind. He leaned one strong
shoulder against the lintel as he looked down at the little
threesome crouching just outside it. He did not notice the
tension among Isabeau and her companions immediately
and a wide smile creased his sculpted features and crinkled
the corners of his eyes attractively when he saw her striving
to regain her feet. "Were you just going to leave like that,
without saying goodbye?" he asked teasingly.

The renegade replied with utter seriousness, however,
her one-word answer falling from her lips like a stone.
"Yes." She stood up and faced him wearily, swiping the
remnants of wetness from her cheeks and squaring her
shoulders bravely against the pain. It seemed she would
have to go through this awful confrontation after all.

Pierre looked from one warrior to the other and then
gestured to the men behind him. "Let's go, mates." He
beckoned, and the curious mercenaries crowded in the postern gate's shadow began grumbling and shouldering past
him into the street beyond, leaving the frozen tableau of
four alone just outside it. "We'll be waiting outside the west
gate of the city, Commander," said the small lieutenant.
"That's where we left the balance of our gear and supplies,
as well as our horses, back with Cedric and Ali. Catch up
when you can, eh?" He let the words trail off discreetly as
he and the other warriors made to leave.

Jared nodded, not removing his narrowed gaze from his

betrothed once. "My thanks, Pierre. And to all you men as
well for your welcome assistance in what took place tonight," he said. "Never have I been happier to have my
commands disobeyed," the mercenary admitted, allowing a
tight smile for the departing warriors.

A chorus of embarrassed male voices told him not to
give it another thought, then faded into the background.

"I believe we will take our leave as well," Jamal murmured tactfully, helping his younger protégée back to her
feet from where she had crouched beside Isabeau in concern. "Zahra is exhausted, and I could do with some rest
as well after tonight's singular events. *Ra'is,*" the eunuch
announced, "we will be waiting at the Assassins' inn for
you when you are ready. That is, if you are sure you can
make it there all right on your own?"

Isabeau shot him a look rich with sardonic disbelief,
distraught though she was. "I think I can hold my own
against any footpads that might approach."

"In *that* outfit, you'll have more than footpads to worry
about," the eunuch pointed out. He then removed his own
outer mantle and tossed it to her. She caught the cloak and
whirled it about to cover her body with automatic nimble-
ness, Jamal saw, which told the concerned former harem
master that his protégée still had her quick reflexes to rely
on. "Farewell, Black Lion," he concluded. His expression
remained as inscrutable as always. "Until we meet again."

With that, the eunuch took his younger charge's slim
arm in his and they melted back down the dark streets of
Damascus. The lovers were alone now in the alley outside
the palace.

When all were gone, Jared spoke softly to his betrothed.
"Why?" he asked simply. "After all we've been through,
why run away from me now?"

Isabeau tried to make her face look hard. "The mission
is complete," she returned just as simply. "Therefore, our
association can end. I have what I wanted with Zahra's safe
return, and you and your men have already been paid your
reward in gold. You can be on your way," she said dis-

missively, "unless you require further remuneration for your aid tonight?" The ex-Assassin made it a question, though she knew her words were an insult to the warrior who had done so much for her benefit, without ever asking a thing in return—except that she consider his suit! Yet for his sake, that was the one thing she must not do. "I would be happy to provide your men an additional bonus in gold," she choked off in conclusion, "now that my jewel is secure."

Isabeau folded her arms in an effort to look businesslike, though she felt more like she was holding her very guts in place. Someone must surely have slipped a dagger under her ribs, she thought, to make it hurt so deep inside her belly.

Jared flinched at the renegade's cold words. "Don't do this, Isabeau."

She shrugged. "If you are content with your payment, that is fine with—"

"No!" he growled harshly. "I meant, don't do this to *us*. Don't cheapen what we share with rubbish like this, not now, after all we've been through. I know you too well to believe this is all you truly feel, Isabeau. I won't believe that Assassins' attitude coming from you anymore. You're not Sayyad al-Zul now, and I'm not some faceless mercenary you've hired. It's far too late for such feeble pretenses, my love. I saw what you did for me in there."

He jerked his head back in the direction of the palace, still only steps away. "I saw what you sacrificed for my sake," he continued. "If you were so cold, so damned *mercenary* as you would have me believe now, woman, you wouldn't have bothered to come back for me after Zahra was freed—and don't tell me it was merely a matter of honor either," he cut her off when she opened her mouth to protest just that. "I saw the way you danced in there."

It only reinforced her decision. She winced.

"Aye, and it is *because* of that, that I do this now, Jared," Isabeau insisted, hating the tearful catch that trembled in her voice. Her unladylike ways had rendered the renegade unsuitable to be the Black Lion's bride, she knew. She'd simply strayed too far from the sweet little scion of Lyon she'd once been to ever walk that path again. If he did not see it now, sooner or later, she knew, the mercenary would wake to the truth. There was no place for her at his side back in Navarre, trying to fit in among the gently reared ladies of the French and Spanish courts. How could she make him understand?

"Look you," Isabeau said earnestly, wanting to put a hand to his arm but not daring to allow herself the contact. "Our families committed us to one another when we were far too young to agree of our own accord," she began. "Because of that promise, made before we could even understand the ramifications, we have been through a great deal they could never have imagined or intended for us. Or more accurately, I should say it is *you* who have been through all of this, Jared. I have *put* you through it, with my headstrong ways."

She hung her head, and tears sprang once again to her sapphire eyes. "For nearly twenty years, you have labored beneath the weight of an oath made before you could have had any hope of understanding the full repercussions of abiding by it. You have upheld our ancient contract with more than due diligence. But I release you from it now, Jared de Navarre. I cannot be the woman you were promised—the woman you deserve after all your years of selfless loyalty," she choked. "Therefore I must free you from your vow, and refuse the suit you have so gallantly continued to offer."

Jared laughed incredulously, for despite the pain of her rejection, he could see the deluded sense of nobility that fueled it. "Do you think my asking you to marry me was all to uphold some benighted *contract*?" His voice cracked on the last word. "Yes," he admitted, "once you were revealed to me as Isabeau de Lyon, I would have wed you as our betrothal required, even had you not been the extraordinary woman I have been so fortunate as to find again. But it *is* you I want, Isabeau de Lyon—you as you've become," the mercenary argued, reaching out to cup her cheek in his palm.

She drew away, silent tears streaking her pale face. "Isabeau de Lyon died a long time ago, Jared. The woman before you now has no name anymore, nor country of allegiance." She took a deep breath. By Allah's great angels, this was difficult! She wanted to believe the mercenary's words, but it was his very nobility that made her doubt them. He was willing to take her on, flawed as she was, and for that she was deeply moved. But she wanted the best for her lover, and Isabeau did not believe that was what she was. Tonight had proven it beyond doubt to this once-proud warrior.

"I promised you I would consider your suit once all this was over," she declared, swiping forlornly at her wet cheek. "Well, I have considered it. The answer is *no*, beloved. Though you are dearer to me than the sun that shines down upon the desert sands, closer to me than the heart that beats in this foolish woman's breast, I cannot be your wife, or return with you to the West."

"What?" he sputtered. "No, I will not accept this, Isabeau! Don't deny us both—" Jared began stubbornly, but Isabeau interrupted.

"Please," she choked. "Respect my decision. I know you to be a man of honor, Jared. Please uphold my wishes in this." Isabeau was crying so hard now as she turned her back on the man she loved, she couldn't even see the street before her faltering steps. She must fool his own vision now just as thoroughly . . .

Summoning all that was left of her training among the *hashishin*, the renegade managed to vanish then from Jared's sight down the dark twisting streets of the ancient city, albeit in a much less dramatic fashion than the Old Man of the Mountain had done earlier in the banquet hall.

Even if she'd looked back as she fled, the one-time Assassin would not have been able to see the hand the heartbroken mercenary stretched after her for the coursing tears that blinded her eyes.

Jared was left staring after his beloved, his mind and heart reeling with sorrow.

Never once, in all the years he'd pictured finding Isabeau de Lyon again, had he thought his long quest could end in such a way.

PART IV

Ah, my Beloved, fill the Cup that clears
To-day of past Regrets and future Fears—
To-morrow?—Why, To-morrow I may be
Myself with Yesterday's Sev'n Thousand Years.

—*THE RUBAIYAT OF OMAR KAYYAM,* VERSE 20

CHAPTER TWENTY-EIGHT

Isabeau busied herself with dismantling the dovecote atop her private minaret. Now that it was spring, and the passes were beginning to clear, she knew she could safely free the birds without fear they would freeze to death in these harsh mountain climes. That was exactly what she was doing now, for she had no further need for their services, and it seemed cruel to hold them hostage needlessly. Taking the pigeons out one by one, she stroked their soft feathers and cooing breasts with a gentle finger, thanking them for their aid, then raised them up above her head to fly free.

"This humble birdkeeper is not the warrior I recognize," said Jamal, coming up behind her in the windswept tower.

She smiled humorlessly at her old friend's comment, unsurprised that he had followed her here. Lately, the eunuch seemed to think she deserved no privacy at all. "The Old Man forbade me from all that, remember?" Isabeau said wryly.

"I have never known fear of any man's wrath to stop you from fighting for what you wanted in the past," Jamal pointed out.

"True," she admitted. "But that was different. That was before—" Isabeau broke off without finishing her sentence. Even now, after months had passed, the pain of talking about the past still caught her off guard. She lived with it each day, went to sleep with it each night, and still, even a hint of a suggestion spoken out loud was enough to make her grit her teeth against a fresh wave of breathtaking agony. Yet though she knew the perceptive eunuch was well aware of the events that had shaped her recent misery, she was unwilling to admit out loud that it had been her heartbreaking reunion and subsequent parting with Jared de Navarre that had so changed her from the spirited woman Jamal had known.

No, she thought more honestly, that time together had not just changed her; it had *defeated* her. Though her enemy was the one buried in cold uncaring earth, it was she who had lost a more precious gift than life. Without it, nothing seemed to matter.

But the former harem master wasn't quite ready to give up on his protégée, despite her own dull despair. "It is *no* different, *ra'is*," the eunuch disagreed. "You have simply grown a coward's heart since you met the Frankish warrior," he said bluntly.

Isabeau was startled out of her apathy for a moment. *"What?"* She laughed a little, sure she had not heard her friend aright.

"You heard me. I called you a coward."

"How *dare* you?" she flashed back, temper flaring for the first time in all the months since she and Jared had said goodbye in that fetid alleyway in Damascus—or more accurately, since she had said goodbye for both of them. Jamal knew just how hard it had been to make that sacrifice! Had *that* been the act of a weak-willed woman? It had nearly killed her to walk away from her beloved, sending him back to face a future that could only be brighter without her. And now to throw that agonizing decision in her face as if she'd had a choice? It was pure cruelty. "I have never been a coward in my life, Jamal!"

"Except when you refused the Black Lion's challenge," the eunuch disagreed, unfazed by her wrath. He folded his arms and leaned back against one tower wall.

"I did not refuse his challenge; I refused his *suit,* Jamal. And I did that *for* him; you know it as well as I do! I could not be a proper wife as Jared deserves, could not be the woman he needs to act as his rightful chatelaine. I had no hope of being those things to my beloved in Navarre. That is why I gave him up," she explained again, tired of having this conversation with her old mentor. This was by no means the first time they'd discussed her decision to leave the mercenary—though it was the first time she could re-member him being so unfeeling in his observations!—and the pain of it each time they did was enough to drive Isa-beau to distraction.

"You cannot be a proper woman or a wife here either," said Zahra, coming up the tower stairs to put in her opinion. "You cannot even show your face, most places," the former slave pointed out. Moving to stand beside the middle-aged eunuch, she took up a posture much like his, leaning hip-shot against the low retaining wall with folded arms. She gestured to their similar costumes, men's kaftans and *abbas* with sashes like those Isabeau had worn during her days as Sayyad al-Zul. The only difference now was that they wore no veils to hide their femininity. There was no need to, here in this isolated, almost haunted-feeling fastness in the mountains. But elsewhere?

Anywhere in the sultan's domain they would be perse-cuted even for this small offense in dress, if not for every-thing else they had done to flout convention. All three of them knew it. And so for the past few months while winter howled outside the walls of their little stronghold, they had lived like hermits alone in the mountains, acting as they chose at the expense of all human contact. It was no life for someone like Zahra, Isabeau thought now. No life for a young woman with all her youth and beauty still ready to blossom before her.

She was unfairly locking her heart's sister away by keeping her here, she knew. For herself, it did not matter so much, for she had already won and lost the only man she would ever want in her life. For herself, there was no more to look forward to, aside from others' happiness. But for Zahra? There was so much more the renegade hoped to see happen for her dear sister.

"I know this is no life for us," Isabeau apologized. "But what else can I do?"

"You can stop being so faint of heart," Zahra said bluntly.

Isabeau sucked in her breath at this unexpected blow.

She was beginning to think these two conspirators had orchestrated this little confrontation atop her tower ahead of time. She narrowed her eyes. "You too, little jewel?" the ex-Assassin asked, wounded despite her growing suspicions. "You would also accuse me of this weakness? After all we have been through together to be free?"

"Only of late, Isabeau," the former concubine said stubbornly, "but aye, I would. You have not been acting like the woman I grew up admiring; the fearless fighter I wanted to emulate from my first days in the harem. Instead, all I have seen of late is the maudlin mopings of a woman no better than old Ullayah was. You might as well go back to the harem if all you plan to do is sigh and grumble over the past."

Isabeau caught her breath again at this fresh accusation. "Zahra!" she breathed, shocked that her adopted sister could ever associate her with the woman they'd both so despised in Malik's harem.

"Well, it's true," Zahra said stubbornly, looking to the eunuch for backup. He nodded confirmation. "Since you let that magnificent mercenary slip through your fingers months ago, you have been no better than a ghost of your former self, wandering about this blasted fortress as though haunting your own grave. If you keep sitting on your dissatisfaction like this, moaning about the past, you'll soon be every bit as bitter as that awful woman ever was."

"Well, what would you have me do about it?" Isabeau snarled back, furious and hurt at the same time by this characterization.

"Do what you always did, sister mine. *Fight* for what you want!"

"But I cannot when it comes to Jared. He deserves better . . ." she protested, parroting her old line about her unworthiness again.

Zahra was sick of it. "Jared de Navarre is old enough to know what he wants, you stubborn fool. And has he *ever* said he wants anything other than you?" she demanded.

"Well, no, but—"

"But *nothing,* Isabeau! It's about time you showed the man some respect," the once demure concubine declared in a huff, "and about time you showed yourself some as well." She put on a fierce expression, but it was marred by the obvious love in her eyes for her big sister. "You are the most extraordinary woman I know—am I not right, Jamal?" Zahra demanded with a hitching laugh. She seemed caught between tears and a smile, beaming at her dear friend through moist eyes.

"You are most correct, O Pearl of Wisdom," the eunuch declared with false solemnity. Delight danced in his dark eyes as he watched this long-overdue confrontation between the two women he considered the daughters of his heart.

"Thank you," said Zahra. "And is Jared de Navarre not a man of surpassing nobility—not to mention a passing handsome visage?"

"He is," the eunuch allowed.

"Then what could make more sense than that these two should be wed?" she crowed triumphantly.

"The White Rose and the Black Lion belong together," Jamal pronounced, affirming Zahra's statement with a beaming smile of his own.

Staring back and forth between the two conspirators with damp eyes and the first stirrings of hope growing in her aching chest, Isabeau protested once more. "But he deserves—"

Once again Zahra cut her off. "That man deserves your *love*—the most precious gift I, for one, have ever received. Give him the chance to show that's all he wants, Isabeau! I know you will not be disappointed."

But if she was . . . oh, how could she bear the pain? Isabeau wanted desperately to do as her companions were urging, to go to Jared, surely home in Navarre by now, and throw herself at his feet, begging for the chance to be his bride.

Wait a moment, the renegade thought with sudden strength. *No.* That wasn't what she wanted to do at all! The words of her friends bolstered her, and the former Assassin felt a surge of indignation at her own weak impulse. She would never beg for anything. She was a warrior! If no longer the Shadow Hunter who had so terrorized the world with the very sound of her name seven years before, she was still a formidable fighter even now. She had not lost the strength of her body since the Old Man's declaration of her decommission, nor the skills she had struggled so hard to obtain. *I am still a woman of worth, damn it!* Isabeau thought.

She was tired of believing what Malik al-Fayed had wanted her to believe, tired of feeling the shame he had heaped upon her head. Who was the man, to so determine her worth before the world? Naught but a ghost dispatched to hell by the grace of yet another strong woman, the ex-Assassin thought with relish. And now that he was gone, she could dispense with his opinions as well. If she wanted something in the future, she would not beg. She would fight for it instead!

She would not go to her knees in front of anyone, Isabeau decided now, not even the warrior she adored. Once she had bowed herself down in humility for his life, but she would not do it for his love. Instead, like the fighter she had always been, she would challenge him for it!

The unaccustomed meekness of the last few months began to drop away from Isabeau as she looked about the sunlit tower with new eyes and felt a wondrous return to herself begin deep in her heart. For the first time in months, she smiled freely. "Yes . . ." she mused softly. "*Fight* for him."

Somehow, she doubted her beloved would put up much of a struggle if she went to him now. Jared had always known her true worth, Isabeau realized suddenly, trying with his steadfast loyalty and his exquisite loving to prove it to her. It was only she herself who had had trouble believing in it! Now, Isabeau began to see the truth. She was not the worst woman in the world for Jared. She was the *only* woman for him!

Who else could guard his back or rescue his hide if the mercenary got himself in trouble? Who else could stop a sword, ride at his side across a barren desert all day, and then make marvelous love to the Black Lion all night long until he purred like a kitten? Only *she* could. *He* hadn't ever wanted some conventional woman, Isabeau realized; it had been *she* who was presumptuous enough to decide that was what he needed.

But now, because of that faulty assumption, it might be too late to claim her warrior husband. She should have been helping her beloved regain his lands and castle all this while, fighting at his side to make reparations for all he had lost. Instead, she had been pining away out here like some maudlin mooncalf, stuck in the past when the future was calling! Her friends were right. She needed to get to Jared as fast as she could!

But what *of* her two dear friends? Isabeau could not leave them behind here, even had she been willing to part with her dearest sister and the man who had fostered them both throughout their youth. Jamal might have a fortune stashed away in gold that he'd gleaned from siphoning off wealth from the coffers of his former master, but he and Zahra were still not free to live just anywhere in the Muslim East—not after earning such notoriety in the fight against the influential emir! "But we would be parted if I choose to take up this quest across the sea . . ." the renegade protested. She trailed off, wondering why her companions were smiling so broadly.

It seemed her friends had got this part all worked out as well. Grinning, Zahra went to the top of the stairs, reaching down inside for a bundle she had apparently left in the stairwell. From within the sack, she pulled a battered steel helm forged in the crusader style, with a long, flat nosepiece and a rounded crown. She plunked the rusty thing down on her bright curls, while the eunuch rummaged inside the bulky satchel himself. The grinning former harem master withdrew a long tabard of white cloth, emblazoned with the red crusader cross. Dropping it over his head, he turned to his stunned protégée.

"We intend to help you in your quest," he announced.

Under the helmet, Zahra nodded vigorously.

Isabeau didn't know whether to laugh or cry at their ridiculous clowning. "Zahra?" she asked. "Jamal? You are truly prepared to make this pilgrimage to foreign shores?"

Plucking off the helm and tucking it beneath one arm, Zahra smiled tremulously, looking over to the eunuch, who had continued to teach her the Assassins' arts these last few months. She had grown into a very courageous woman in the time since her release, and she was ready to challenge a wider world. "Jamal and I have discussed it, Isabeau. We have developed quite a longing to see this land of Outremer."

"Well, then," smiled the Assassin, grateful beyond words for the support of her two dear friends. "Let us prepare for battle!"

CHAPTER TWENTY-NINE

Today seemed like a fine day to die.

Of course, without Isabeau, death looked preferable to living most any day, Jared thought with the sort of gallows humor he'd developed in the last few months. Today it just seemed more likely to *happen*.

As he caught the warning flash of sun on steel reflecting from off the inside of his shield, time slowed down and the Black Lion spun about to see a man he'd thought dead rising to his feet from the bloodied battlefield behind him, the other's gore-crusted sword swinging down to sweep at his head. Jared could hear the roar of his enraged enemy only as a thin wail compressed through the intervening space between them, only see him through a narrow channel of vision. He'd never be able to block the blow in time, Jared knew with eerie clarity, even as his gaze swept the field to make sure his brother was still standing and all else was well. Catching sight of Joscelin engaged with two of the last enemies left standing, the sturdy, wheaten-haired young man getting the better of both of them with the aid of some of Jared's own imported mercenaries, the Black Lion found he had few regrets if this was, indeed, to be his final moment on earth.

Here in the shadow of the Pyreneese Mountains where he'd been born, just a few miles from the beautiful city of Pamplona which was the little country's capital, sheep grazed in the hilly pastures off the Ebro River while grapes ripened in the ancient vineyards and birds called in the shady forests where his Basque ancestors had done their hunting for centuries. It seemed appropriate that he should lay down his life in such a worthy cause, defending that

ancestral home. And seeing that he and his young brother
were about to win their battle, the Black Lion believed he
had done as much as he could, even if he himself were not
to outlive the afternoon to celebrate the victory.

Jos would inherit the keep they'd won back today, God
willing, and the steadfast young lord would make a fine
castellan for Navarre, no matter how he liked to protest his
elder brother deserved the right. Jared, on the other hand,
would take this thrust that now threatened to cleave his
body, and sink down in death with only one wish—to see
the face of his beloved once more before he died.

But the sword would have to do its work without that
miracle, the mercenary-turned-home-defender thought, for
Isabeau had made her decision months before, and there
was no reason to believe his stubborn betrothed would ever
change her mind. And without her, there was no real reason
to live. No other woman could take her place, or heal the
wound she had left bleeding inside his breast. He might as
well let go. Jared shut his eyes to meet his fate, even as his
traitorous body instinctively tried to lift his longsword in a
futile gesture of defense.

For a moment the Black Lion believed he'd actually
raised the blade in time to block the strike. A tremendous
clang of steel on steel rang through the summer-scented air.
Yet though he felt no reverberations in his sword arm, neither did the warrior feel the white-hot searing of the enemy's sword cutting into his flesh. Was this what the
death-blow felt like? he wondered crazily. Was the last
stroke truly painless? Yet if that were true, why would he
still feel the other aches and pains of his exhausted body?
Jared opened his eyes in wonder.

What he saw convinced the tired warrior that he had
probably lost his wits somewhere on the battlefield, if not
his life. For there, between his blade and that of the burly
Basque invader who had so nearly been his doom, another
sort of sword had interposed itself.

Who the hell can be wielding a scimitar *around here?*
the Black Lion thought, recognizing the wickedly curved
Middle Eastern weapon. Then he followed the line of the

intervening blade up to the body that held it. And that was when Jared realized that he *had* actually landed in Paradise, whether or not he was dead.

The unknown savior swept off the concealing helm, and a cascade of moonlight curls fell down around his rescuer's grinning face.

Not seeming terribly concerned about the invader who still strove to break away from her binding blade, Isabeau de Lyon spun about lightning-fast, kicking the Basque free of the scimitar and smiting him handily with force of the backswing. She glanced about for a moment to be sure there were no further threats and saw that the battle around them had ended, leaving only the defenders standing to mop up the field while the would-be usurpers fled for the cover of the woods. Out of the corner of one eye, she glimpsed Big Pierre chasing avidly after one of the retreating men on his stout pony, and she was hard-pressed not to smile at his miniature ferocity. The renegade wiped off the curving blade she held and sheathed it smoothly.

Then her sapphire eyes met those of the Black Lion, and both of their breaths caught in their throats as it sank in that the renegade was truly here before her betrothed.

"Thought you could use a hand," Isabeau said cheekily. She dusted off her hands, smiling at her beloved with a strange sort of diffidence despite her confident words.

Behind her, dressed alike in crusaders' clothes, Jared recognized with incredulity the harem master who had been the Assassin's ally, and the young jewel of a woman they'd both fought to free. The two saluted the confused Black Lion jauntily when he caught their gaze, then strode off across the trampled field to offer their aid to the castle defenders. Joscelin, the onetime mercenary noticed with a touch of hysterical humor, seemed quite smitten with the blond warrior-maid who approached—and she with him, if the blush on her lovely features was any indicator. But there was only one exquisite fighter Jared truly cared about just now.

"H-how . . . ? Why . . . ?" he stuttered intelligently at Isabeau.

"I've always fought for what I want," his betrothed explained calmly. "And I am fighting for it now. Fighting for *you*, Jared de Navarre. You are what I desire, and I intend to have you," she proclaimed. "If you don't like it—tough! That's too damn bad for you. You must learn to accept me as I stand, Black Lion. I am who I am, and I will not change to meet some foolish ideal—"

But Jared broke in on his beloved with a laugh of pure happiness. "Ah, my love. What you are is all I could ever want!" He grabbed her about the waist, armor and all, and swung her about joyously until they were both dizzy. "Who else can guard my back as well as you, my fearsome warrior?" he demanded breathlessly, setting her down lightly on her feet. "Who else will love me until my very knees grow weak? Who else—"

He would have continued, but Isabeau put a stop to that, a grin of her own lighting up her jubilant features. "Shut *up*, you wonderful, spectacular lion of a man, before I do just that!" she ordered. Then she dragged him into her arms to kiss him soundly, laughing and crying all at once.

The two stood thus in each other's arms for a long time, oblivious to the rest of the world. But at last Jared broke free to stare down at the woman he loved, yet had not ever hoped to hold again.

"You may be fair as the whitest rose, milady, but you have a lion's heart—and that is why I love you so," Jared informed her softly. He reached inside his tunic front and retrieved the slender golden chain that had held her tiny ring close to his heart all this time. Kissing the ring softly in reverence, he removed it from around his neck and draped the chain about hers, then smoothed his hand down her chest after it to rest his palm upon her fast-beating heart. "You have always had the heart of a lion."

"The heart of the *Black* Lion, I hope," she replied, teasing and tender all at once.

"Forever," he promised. "Forever, Isabeau."

The Moving Finger writes; and, having writ,
Moves on: nor all thy Piety nor Wit
Shall lure it back to cancel half a Line,
Nor all thy Tears wash out a Word of it.

—*THE RUBAIYAT OF OMAR KAYYAM*, VERSE 51

MARRYING JEZEBEL

HILLARY FIELDS

AUTHOR OF *THE MAIDEN'S REVENGE*

Rafe Sunderland, the handsome, rakish duke of Ravenhurst, has it all—power, position, and all the pleasures of proper Society. But just as he's beginning to think it's too easy, things get a lot more complicated . . . he's just inherited a ward. To preserve the life he's always known, there's only one thing he can do: marry the chit off as fast as possible. A famed Egyptologist's niece, the beautiful, outrageous Jezebel Montclair has her future all planned out—and those plans *don't* include letting her arrogant, sinfully handsome new guardian boss her around. Determined to remain free, she refuses to leave Egypt and submit to the life of a staid, proper English lady. So when Rafe tracks her down in Cairo, despite her nearly uncontrollable attraction to him, she knows she must escape, or risk the madness she's always feared. From the sun-baked deserts of an ancient land to the ballrooms and bedrooms of Regency London, a battle of wits, wills, and glorious passion ensues . . .

"Hillary Fields takes us on a grand adventure."
—Kat Martin on *The Maiden's Revenge*

"Hillary Fields is a fresh new voice that brings a heap of fire and sensuality to sizzle your senses."
—*The Belles and Beaux of Romance*

MJ 8/01

THE
MAIDEN'S
REVENGE

HILLARY FIELDS

One of the fiercest pirates on the Main, the legendary Captain Thorne could raid a ship and wield a cutlass with the best. Woe betide any man who desired to get past the tempered steel to the woman holding it. Lynette Blackthorne—a.k.a. Captain Thorne—sails the high seas with only one goal: vengeance against the man who murdered her sister. Nothing will stand in her way—especially not a silver-eyed rogue with the power to make her tremble and lose her wits to the madness of passion. Now, the duel of wits and desire that began the moment they first laid blazing eyes on each other is about to play out in a collision course of passionate adventure . . . as two formidable opponents discover the ecstasy of surrendering to the only force stronger than themselves: love.

AVAILABLE WHEREVER BOOKS ARE SOLD
FROM ST. MARTIN'S PAPERBACKS

MR 8/01